Evan's War

Evan's War

Malcolm Stevens

Copyright © 2009 by Malcolm Stevens.

Library of Congress Control Number: 2009900399
ISBN: Hardcover   978-1-4415-0344-2
                Softcover   978-1-4415-0343-5

All rights reserved. No part of this book may be reproduced or transmitted in any form or by any means, electronic or mechanical, including photocopying, recording, or by any information storage and retrieval system, without permission in writing from the copyright owner.

This is a work of fiction. Names, characters, places and incidents either are the product of the author's imagination or are used fictitiously, and any resemblance to any actual persons, living or dead, events, or locales is entirely coincidental.

This book was printed in the United States of America.

To order additional copies of this book, contact:
Xlibris Corporation
1-888-795-4274
www.Xlibris.com
Orders@Xlibris.com

Contents

Part I

The Rhondda   1

Part II

Gallipoli   55

Part III

The Bosphorus   93

Part IV

Home From The Dead   199

Part V

Rhondda Station   239

Dedication

To the memory of Blodwyn and Evan John Evans, late of Ystrad Rhondda, South Wales, who sheltered two young evacuees from London in a time of war and treated them as their own.

And to the memory of my maternal grandfather, Charles Beresford, late of the South Wales Borderers, killed at Suvla Bay, Gallipoli, August 21, 1915.

Acknowledgements

A resource for this story was *A Rhondda Anthology* (Meic Stephens, Editor, Seren Books, 1993), in particular essayists Lewis Jones (*First Day in the Pit*) and Mary Davies Parnell (*The Lewis Merthyr*) for their vivid portrayals of life in the Rhondda coalmines. I have also quoted lines from two poems that were included in the Anthology: *In Gardens in the Rhondda* by Idris Davis and *Rhondda Grey* by Max Boyce; and from a poem by Siegfried Sassoon: *Suicide in the Trenches*. In addition, from the book *Poems Here at Home* by James Whitcomb Riley (The Century Company, 1883), I have quoted lines from four poems: *To a Skull, When She Comes Home, What a Dead Man Said,* and *Bereaved*. The following books provided historical and geographical insights: *Gallipoli* by Alan Moorehead (Harper, 1956); *Gallipoli* by John Masefield (Macmillan, 1916); *Men of Gallipoli* by Peter Liddle (David and Charles, 1988); *Constantinople* by F. Marion Crawford (Charles Scribner's Sons, 1895); and *The Bosphorus* by John Freely (Redhouse Press, 1993). Lines from Professor Freely's book are quoted with his permission. The image of the young woman on the cover is reproduced by kind permission of This England magazine.

My thanks to fellow writers Jeanne Bonaca, Laura Corning, Pat Eckhoff, Art Fern, Franklin Marshall, and my wife and coauthor in many writing projects, Marcia Reed Stevens. They all helped steer me in the right direction.

Author's Note

In the time frame of this story, Istanbul was known as Constantinople and the district of Üsküdar as Scutari, hence my use of these archaic names. Also, I have on occasion introduced Turkish words written in Latin script, even though Arabic script was used until the introduction of the modern alphabet in 1928. I took this liberty to give a sense of pronunciation.

Some Turkish letters and their equivalent English sounds are as follows: *c* like j; *ç* like ch; *ş* like sh; *ı* (undotted i) like the u barium; *j* like the s in leisure; *ğ* (silent g) lengthens a preceding vowel; *ö* and *ü* are pronounced as they are in German (or as *eu* in the French *deux* and *u* in the French *tu,* respectively.) Other letters are for the most part pronounced as they are in English.

While some of the locales for the story are factual or based on real places, and some individuals mentioned did exist in the historical context, other places, events and persons are products of the author's imagination. Any resemblance to actual persons, living or dead, is purely coincidental.

Part I

The Rhondda

The daffodils dance in gardens
Behind the grim brown row
Built among the slagheaps
In a hurry long ago.
                    Idris Davies, *In Gardens*
                                in the Rhondda

Chapter 1

When I was far from home I dreamt of slagheaps. Ugly gray-black piles of pit waste that debase the green hills of the Rhondda Valley, the valley of my birth.

Slagheaps are such an enduring symbol of the South Wales coalfields, it's no wonder they would intrude on my dreams. Now, after three short years away—years that seem like a lifetime—I find myself standing at the foot of the monstrous pile that rises no more than a fifteen-minute walk from home. I had no preset plan to be here; I simply went for a walk, but this is where my feet propelled me.

Most people call them tips, not slagheaps. "Stay away from the tip!" Aunt Beryl admonished me when, as a young lad, I arrived home black with coal dust from an afternoon of sliding down the steep slope on a piece of cardboard. "You're filthy!"

"You'll get yourself in trouble," Uncle Mervyn chimed in. "That tip's dangerous. You're lucky an inspector from the colliery didn't catch you."

"Off with your clothes!" my aunt said as she carried the tin tub in from the scullery and set it on the floor in front of the kitchen stove. Without ceremony she gave me such a thorough scrubbing with cold water, pumice and lye soap that I never ventured near the tip again.

The nation's insatiable appetite for coal was a boon to the Rhondda Valley. Coalmines sprang up wherever a decent seam was found; and when the good anthracite was shipped out, the waste from the earth's bowels was dumped in ugly heaps wherever the mine owners saw fit. Coal became the lifeblood of the valley. Row after row, terrace after terrace, of seedy brick houses were thrown up to accommodate the miners and their families.

I was born in one of those houses just three years before the Boer War sent thousands of young men to South Africa on ships powered by Rhondda coal. That conflict brought the nineteenth century to a bloody close. And now a far bloodier one has brought civilization to its knees, a war so terrible I don't see how the world could suffer such agony; a war I saw firsthand and have the scars to show for it.

I look up, half expecting to hear slag trams clatter along the track at the summit, positioning to dump more slag down toward me. The distant rumble of machinery at the colliery mingles with the gurgling of the nearby River Rhondda and the chattering of crows in trees along the riverbank. As a boy I often wondered what lay on the other side of the tip. Was there something magical there? Some new world to conquer? I smile at the memory of childhood innocence.

I look around to see if anyone is watching, but not a soul is in sight, not even the usual bicyclist pedaling along the macadam road above the river. Impulsively I begin to climb the steep bituminous slope, made wet and shiny by moisture carried inland from the Irish Sea. I pause now and again to catch my breath and stare back over the town. From half way up, the houses have shrunk to the size of dollhouses. Across the valley Leonard's farm lies hidden by rising mist, although some of his sheep still stand out as white dots on the deep green tapestry of grazing fields. I expect Mr. Leonard still delivers milk in those big cast iron churns, rattling away on the back of his horse-drawn cart.

That side of the valley remains beautiful with its woods and patchwork fields and windswept moorland. Perhaps this side is lovely too in a grotesque sort of way—but not even the damp mist can suppress the smell of coal dust. The valley of my birth; now that I've cheated the Grim Reaper, will the Rhondda be the valley of my death? Yea, though I walk through the valley . . . Ashes to ashes, coal dust to coal dust.

I turn away from dark thoughts and continue upward, sliding back when my feet encounter loose till, until at last the tip levels off. Buttoning my jacket against the cold, I step over the tram track and walk to where the summit drops off on the other side. Nothing magical there, just more hills fading into mist. To escape the biting wind I turn back and descend to a more sheltered spot where a handful of hardy dandelions have taken root. The whole town lies before me, row on row of slate-roofed houses covering the contour of the valley floor, where coalmining families eke out their austere existence.

That's what I was before I went off to war, an ordinary coalminer with not much money to my name. Before circumstances changed my life in ways I could not have imagined.

Across the tip-blackened river, perpendicular to the main road that runs up and down the valley, Victoria Street stretches uphill to woodland. Counting down from the end, I find the house in which my aunt and uncle raised me, guided me from infancy to manhood. Farther down on the other side of the street sits the Old Lamb Inn where my uncle bought me my first glass of beer. And on the hill above the pub towers the imposing granite-gray edifice of Bodringallt School, where a young beauty named Gwyn first caught my eye.

I should be heading down, but I can't tear my eyes from these scenes of childhood and youth. Voices from the past echo in my consciousness—Hugh Griffith, Dai Wilkins, Rhys Jones and a host of others. But above all, Gwyn.

The mist is turning to a light rain, but I barely feel it. Hands in pockets, I remain rooted to the spot as the past comes flooding back like ripples from a distant tide, carrying me to a more innocent time, when the universe was young and every day a new beginning . . .

* * *

I must have been nine or ten when I first noticed Gwyn—I mean, *really* noticed her. A rosy-cheeked girl a year behind me in school, with short brown hair and matching brown eyes, she would skip more than walk home at the end of the school day. Her plaid dress was drabber than those of her friends, most of them anyway, with tiny rips along the seams, and her black button-down shoes looked in bad need of fixing. Of course, I didn't see all those details at first; I was just taken with that pretty face and upturned nose bathed in freckles. I couldn't take my eyes off her, but I always kept a safe distance because I wouldn't want the lads to think I might be interested in a girl.

Once when she looked toward me I quickly turned my head away, and when I looked back she was skipping away down the hill. After that I noticed her in chapel on Sundays, always sitting on the other side of the aisle from us between two stern-faced women wearing broad-rimmed black hats. Every Sunday thereafter, while paying scant attention to Welsh hymns or Reverend Lewis's sermons, I stole glances in her direction; but she never seemed aware of my presence or the torture she was inflicting on me.

One fateful Friday afternoon Mr. Powell, my classroom teacher, held me back for a stern lecture on the merits of paying more attention to my lessons and less to daydreaming. Chastened, I descended the narrow stone steps from the school playground when I saw her below on Bodringallt Terrace. She was by herself, throwing stones toward a puddle left over from the morning drizzle. I slowed my pace, my heart racing at the prospect of meeting her face to face, and nervous enough that I almost wished she would continue on her way home. But she kept at her stone throwing until she turned as I approached.

"Bet you can't hit that puddle," she challenged me. The puddle lay several yards away, but she sent up a splash every time she let loose with a stone. She pushed hair away from her eyes and left a muddy mark on her forehead.

"Scared you'll miss?" she said when I didn't respond. Reluctantly I picked up a couple of small stones. Over her shoulder I spied a man, trousers down around his ankles, sitting in an outdoor brick lavatory behind one of the houses below the terrace. He was reading a newspaper, the blue-painted wooden door open for light. My cheeks reddened. The lads and I would laugh at a sight like that, maybe even toss down a few insults for good measure, but I didn't want her to see it. I turned away and threw a stone, missing the puddle by a couple of feet.

"Told you!" she laughed. My second stone found the target.

"What's your name then?" she asked.

"Evan Morgan. What's yours?" I began walking away to draw her attention from the embarrassing scene below.

"Gwynneth Williams," she replied, following me. "Everyone calls me Gwyn. Where do you live then?" she persisted.

"Victoria Street, just around the corner." I nodded in the direction we were walking.

"I live by the chapel, down on the main road." She stooped to pick up another stone.

"I've seen you in chapel," I said.

"I've seen you, too, with your mum and dad." My heart fluttered at the realization that she had actually noticed me.

"They're not my mum and dad. They're my auntie and uncle."

She stopped and looked at me quizzically. "Why don't your mum and dad take you?"

"Don't have a mum, she died when I was born."

"Well what about your dad?"

I hesitated, embarrassed at the truth about my father. "Don't have a dad either," I admitted at last, looking away from her. "He left when my mum died. My Auntie Beryl thinks he's somewhere in England."

"I'm sorry." A look of concern clouded her face. "My dad's dead," she said as if to take the sting out of my confession. "Died down in the pit. Swinging his pick, he was, then just fell over and died. My mum said it was his heart."

"Is that your mum you're with in chapel then?"

"Aye, my mum and my Auntie Gladys."

We had reached the corner of Victoria Street. "Here, catch!" she laughed, tossing her stone to me before skipping down the hill toward the main road. A short distance along she stopped and called back: "Did you see that man sitting on his lav? I was going to throw a stone at him, but I was afraid he'd chase me!"

§

After that first encounter, Gwyn and I slowly cemented our friendship. She often waited for me at the bottom of the steps and I would hang back until the lads went on ahead. In Sunday chapel she'd wave, which inevitably brought a rebuke from her mother. Wynnifred Williams did not take kindly to her daughter's flirting. Struggling to make ends meet on a pitiful pension from the mining company, she had turned bitter and argumentative after her husband's death. But Gwyn was feisty enough to ignore her mother's disapproving tongue.

One day after school, on an impulse, I asked Gwyn if she'd like to take a walk up the hill at the end of Victoria Street. We followed the unpaved track onto bracken-covered slopes and groves of oak, beech, chestnut and hawthorn. I led the way to a stately chestnut tree that I considered my private domain. A charitable configuration of branches challenged adventurous young boys to aspire to its upper reaches. Lower branches circled the tree's thick trunk like a tent, the foliage blocking out the sky, apart from a gap that gave a fine view across the valley. My best pal, Hugh Griffith, and I spent hours at this spot acting out our fantasy adventures.

Now I wanted to share my secret with Gwyn. To my delight she was captivated; but it took some persuading to get her to climb with me because her long skirt was not very practical for such an escapade. But once at the top she laughed with joy at the gentle swaying of branches caressed by the afternoon breeze.

The next time we ventured to my woodland sanctuary, we sat exhilarated after our climb, backs against the gnarled trunk, when suddenly she leaned over and kissed me quickly on my cheek.

"What did you do that for?" I stammered, while savoring the touch of her hair against my lips.

"Afraid the lads might see me?" she laughed, noticing my blushing. "I bet they'd be jealous."

"No they wouldn't! They'd think I was daft!"

She stared across the valley at a line of slag trams moving slowly down from the pithead to the tip. "Don't be so sure," she said softly, detaching a hand from her folded knees and placing it in mine. I closed my hand over hers and was suddenly happy in a way I'd never been before.

"Come on Evan," she broke the spell. "We have to get back before my mum goes on the warpath."

§

Once the lads realized there was something between Gwyn and me they had all kinds of fun at my expense, but as time passed they came to accept the fact, and soon began developing their own friendships with the girls. Hugh teamed up with Mary Thomas, whose parents were not at all pleased at their daughter's friendship with the son of a coalminer. Compared with most families in town, the Thomases were toffs, living in a large house above the school on Sandybank Road. Bevan Thomas worked for the town council, which must have paid him a lot more than the miners earned because Edith wore the latest fashions and Mary always dressed a lot smarter than Gwyn and the other girls.

I was actually relieved when Hugh latched onto Mary. Even though we were the best of friends, I was always a tiny bit jealous of Hugh. Besides living not too far from Gwyn, he was a strapping lad, fair-haired, broad shouldered and a good inch taller than I, a first-rate chap to have on your rugby team. But he never intruded on my relationship with Gwyn, and she paid no more attention to him than to any other of her friends. Mary was more Hugh's cup of tea, taller and more slender than Gwyn with long auburn hair that she learned early on to swing provocatively about her perfectly-proportioned face. No one ever made fun of Hugh and Mary.

To tell the truth, there were times when I had to convince myself that Gwyn really did like me. I wasn't the finest specimen of boyhood compared with most of my school pals; at least I didn't think so. I was shorter than most and my ears stuck out more than I liked, especially after Aunt Beryl went at my unruly mop with her scissors and clippers. Then there were some embarrassing pimples on my forehead, and a few more across my chest and shoulders. But Gwyn never seemed to notice my shortcomings.

As we grew older the kisses became more frequent and more intimate. And with the passage of time Hugh, Mary, Gwyn and I became a foursome, spending our leisure hours together and forging bonds of friendship not easily broken. We moved on from Bodringallt School to Tonypandy Secondary, until the time came when we began thinking of the future. For Hugh and me that future lay in the colliery.

Gwyn did her best to dissuade me. "Why would you want to do that?" she kept insisting. "There are more things in this world than coalmining. Do you want to come home filthy every night and end up like my dad, dead at the coalface?"

It never really occurred to me that I'd do anything else; that's where almost all the lads ended up, the poor ones anyway. "Coal is the lifeblood of the valley," our history teacher, Mr. Davies, thundered, his lesson reinforced by the relentless drone of mining machinery, regular coal trains heading down the valley to the docks at Cardiff or Barry, and coal-blackened workers returning from their shifts.

Truth be told, I admired that fraternity of tough, stoic men who commanded the streets between colliery shifts. To join them at the coalface would mark the beginning of manhood.

"Why not at least try for a scholarship?" Gwyn said in exasperation as the day drew nearer. "The teachers think well of you, Evan."

"Aye, Mr. Edwards said I should try out for Aberystwyth University. But only toffs go to university, Gwyn. Uncle Mervyn doesn't have that kind of money. He thinks I should start earning my keep."

"You've got to think big, Evan." She shook her head and raised her eyes, a gesture of acceptance. "Well, if you must end up in the mine, maybe you'll earn enough to try for something better."

By the time I passed my fifteenth birthday, my uncle, with some resistance from Aunt Beryl, had run out of patience. He made it plain that I didn't need any more useless schooling, as he put it, and it was time to apply to the colliery. Many of the other lads, Hugh included, were ready, and some of our friends had left for the mine the year before. On a school holiday in April, we put in our applications at Upper Pentre Mine and were told to show up when the school year ended. I felt very proud of myself after that, all grown up so to speak.

On the last day of the term, Aled Edwards, our gruff, brilliant headmaster, shook his head sadly as he bade me farewell; and for the first time I experienced misgivings at the prospect of a life working underground. But my course was set. I shook the headmaster's hand, put on a brave face and left my boyhood behind at the school gate.

Chapter 2

Uncle Mervyn had never set foot in a coalmine, which led me to wonder why he was so keen to place both of mine in one. One evening, when he was in one of his more pensive moods, he recounted to me how he began working at age fourteen in the huge slate mine in Blaenau Ffestiniog up in the north of Wales, just as his father and grandfather had before him. He didn't work underground; his job was to load railway freight cars with slabs of slate for transport to the docks at Porthmadog. It was strenuous, muscle-aching work and it didn't suit his temperament one bit, nor did he possess the build and physical strength of his fellow workers.

Before regular rail lines were extended to the town, slate was shipped along a thirteen-mile narrow-gauge railway to the docks, but now that line was used only for tourists or townspeople on excursions. On Sunday afternoons Uncle Mervyn liked to set out on foot along the narrow-gauge track, following the mountain ridge above the bucolic Vale of Ffestiniog, until he looked down at the stately mansion and manicured gardens where the mine owner and his family lived, imperiously overlooking the meandering River Dwyryd and village of Maentwrog. He didn't resent the family their good fortune or the contrast with the tiny cottage he shared with his mother, father and two brothers, with its outside toilet and puny weed-filled garden; he simply recognized the owners as his betters, and that was the natural order of things.

As we sipped hot cocoa in the worn, comfortable leather chairs near the coal stove while Aunt Beryl worked at her sewing, he told of how the railway, with its clattering trains and gaily waving passengers, came to symbolize an avenue of escape from the poverty of Blaenau Ffestiniog, the backbreaking labor and daily taunts from more burly workers. About the time he turned twenty, Uncle Mervyn had become enough enamored of the thought that he began looking around for a railway job. He had no success in the north, but after a couple of years he landed one down here in the Rhondda, just up the valley a bit in Cwmparc.

It was at a chapel social that he met my mother's sister, and soon thereafter they were married and living in our tiny row house on Victoria

Street. What attracted her to him I have no idea. He was a good inch shorter and thin as a rail. Early on his hair began to thin noticeably above his forehead, and perhaps to compensate he cultivated a moustache that accentuated his generous jowls, affording him a superficial resemblance to the red squirrels that spent their days scrambling for acorns and hazel nuts in the woods at the end of the street.

In her younger days Aunt Beryl was straight-backed and slender with a regal caste to her features, her chestnut-colored hair tied tastefully in a bun at the back of her head. She had small ears which, on special days, she accentuated with clip-on earrings with dangling onyx settings, a bequest from her maternal grandmother. She looked a lot like my mother, her younger sister, whose photograph sat among other framed photographs atop the sideboard in the front room. My own features mirrored theirs. Absent from the sideboard was a photograph of my father. That he was a handsome man and a gifted mechanic was all my aunt told me about him, and I didn't press her for more details.

Perhaps it was Uncle Mervyn's agreeable disposition that attracted my aunt. He didn't object when she brought me home from my mother's deathbed. She and Uncle Mervyn had no children of their own, whether by choice or circumstance I never knew, so I was the only baby of the family and the apple of Aunt Beryl's eye. After hearing nothing from my father for several months, my aunt and uncle were named my guardians. I was given the name Evan because my father's last name was Evans, and they didn't much like his first name—which suited me fine because I wouldn't want to have been stuck with the name Cecil.

Uncle Mervyn never realized his dream to be an engine driver; instead he spent his days coupling and uncoupling freight cars and pulling trackside levers to move shunting trains from one line to another. By the time I entered Tonypandy Secondary, he had worked his way up to signalman, in charge of a signal box that controlled several siding connections and a level crossing. It was said that the flowerbeds he maintained around his workplace were the best signal box displays this side of Pontypridd.

Besides the extra pay, being signalman afforded Uncle Mervyn some status with our neighbors. Every morning except Sundays, rain or shine, he set off for work on his rickety bicycle, tweed cap protecting his balding head, pipe sticking out of his jacket pocket. And like clockwork he was back, walking his bicycle up the hill in time for tea at five o'clock.

On a couple of occasions, from my refuge in the upstairs bedroom, I overheard Uncle Mervyn and Aunt Beryl discussing my future. "I'd love to see him working with you at the railway," my aunt remarked. "I don't want him down in the mine. It's such a dangerous job."

"It's not that easy," my uncle countered. "My own job is by no means certain these days. Lots of chaps I know have been let go. Maybe in a year or two things will get better, but right now the mines offer the only secure employment in the valley, especially now that France relies on us for coal."

"Oh, I suppose you're right," she said. "Maybe for a year or two then. But you will keep an eye out for him at the railway, Mervyn."

"Aye, I'll do that, love."

My uncle sought to reassure me that going into the mine was the right move. "The mines are where the jobs are," he said one evening. "There'll always be a need for coal. If you work hard, you could even become a supervisor, like Mr. Surtees." I never argued the point. Roger Surtees, who lived four houses down from us and well respected in the community, had retired early from the mine because of poor health.

Before the end of the school year, Hugh's father, a miner since well before Hugh was born, reminded the mine managers that Hugh and I would soon be joining the pit crew; and one week after our final day at Tonypandy, on a rainy Monday in July, I was ready to begin work.

§

Aunt Beryl woke me early while it was still dark outside. "Come on Evan, get yourself dressed. Your breakfast's ready."

I stumbled out of bed and pulled on my pit clothes before hurrying through the rain to the backyard lavatory. Usually miners wore their old clothes for work, but I'd outgrown all of mine and Uncle Mervyn's cast-offs were too small; so Aunt Beryl found some for me at a second-hand shop in Porth along with a pair of miners' boots. Even after trying them on a few times during the last week, the pit clothes felt stiff and unfamiliar. Inside the kitchen, in the light of the flickering oil lamp, I splashed cold water on my face at the sink and sat down to a larger than usual portion of my aunt's lumpy porridge. Uncle Mervyn, who didn't have to be at work so early and ate his breakfast later, stood shaving in front of the small oval mirror in the corner of the kitchen.

"Are you excited?" Aunt Beryl asked.

"Aye, but I'm a bit scared too," I admitted. "Being that far underground . . ."

"You'll be used to it in no time," Uncle Mervyn interjected as he deftly ran the razor over the stubble below his chin.

With a sinking feeling in my stomach, I spooned the porridge into my mouth, pondering what life would be like from this day forward. Six days a week in the mine and chapel on Sundays didn't leave much time for climbing trees or rugby matches with the lads. Aunt Beryl took my empty bowl and handed me a thick slice of bread smeared with marmalade. "You might want a bit of extra in your stomach today," she said.

"Thanks Auntie," I said, biting into the bread, but I had little appetite for it.

"I've made you a nice lunch," she said, indicating the lunch tin on the counter by the stove.

"Thanks Auntie," I said again, draining the last drop of hot, strong tea and placing the chipped mug in the sink. Uncle Mervyn, having finished shaving, made way for me, not that I had much on my chin to make the effort worthwhile. But on my fifteenth birthday my uncle had presented me with a brand new razor, a fine piece of Sheffield steel with a blade that folded into its bone handle, and I felt an obligation to use it. He had shown me how to sharpen the blade on his strop and had looked on critically as I tried it out for the first time, drawing blood from my upper lip and close by my left ear.

This morning, as I lathered my face, I realized for the first time that it was no longer a boy but a young man staring back at me from the mirror, thin faced with thick dark eyebrows and hair parted on the left, the way it had been ever since Gwyn tamed my unruly mane with her turtle shell comb. The pimples had disappeared but my body was still slender and sinewy, much as it had been five years ago when my aunt was doing her best to fatten me up. Instead Aunt Beryl had put on weight while I gained in height, now standing about five foot nine; and Gwyn, who used to match me in height, had to stand on tiptoe to kiss me. Gwyn once told me I looked too serious and ought to smile more. "It's all those heavy books you're reading," she said, referring to the weekly volume I checked out of Tonypandy library. It was, for sure, a serious expression I saw in the mirror. I was in no mood for smiling.

Gwyn's probably still warm in bed, I thought longingly, and wouldn't be up before I'm deep underground. Already I was regretting not being able to spend the day with her. I did a perfunctory job on my face and was wiping off the last vestiges of soap when the mournful wail of the colliery siren echoed through the valley.

"Five-thirty hooter, Evan," Uncle Mervyn said. "You'd better be going, lad. You don't want to be late on your first day."

Her eyes moist, Aunt Beryl handed me my lunch tin, water jack and work cap. "You'll do fine, Evan," she said, kissing my cheek. "Now don't keep Hugh and his dad waiting."

"That was a nice breakfast, Auntie," I said with as much conviction as I could muster. "See you tonight." Then I was out the door into the early light, lunch tin under my arm and water jack slung over my shoulder, striding down rain-slickened Victoria Street where groups of miners, hobnailed boots clicking rhythmically along the pavement, led the way.

By prior arrangement I was to meet Hugh and his father at the corner of Ivor Street, and as I turned onto the main road I saw them waiting. Hugh waved and I broke into a run to catch up.

"Bore da!" Good morning, Dylan Griffith greeted me in Welsh. "Are you ready, Evan, for a good day's work?"

"Aye, Mr. Griffith," I replied, doing my best to sound cheerful while stealing a glance across the street at Gwyn's house. I was hoping she might be at her window waving, but all the curtains were drawn. Hugh's father, stocky and close to six feet tall, set a fast pace, his bushy moustache glistening with raindrops that found their way under the brim of his cap. Ever since Hugh and I had become close friends, I was in and out of his house almost as much as my own, and Dylan and Maude Griffith treated me like a second son. Today Hugh's father was to be our guide and guardian as we received our initiation into the filthy, dangerous world of coalmining.

Once up the hill and inside the colliery gate, the rumbling of machinery growing louder with each step, we entered a small wooden cabin where two middle-aged men sat behind antiquated oaken desks. *"Bore da,* Dylan," one of the men addressed Hugh's father. Outside, the six o'clock hooter sounded so loudly that I jumped, for this was the first time I'd heard it up close.

"Not such a good day outside, Jim," Dylan responded once the din ended. "Well, here are the two new lads, my boy Hugh and this one is Evan Morgan."

"Aye, I have their names down," Jim replied, running his finger down the open ledger in front of him. "Welcome to the mine, boys. You're in good hands with Dylan." He opened a desk drawer and withdrew two metal disks inscribed with numbers. "Look after these, lads, they're your lamp checks." He pointed to shelves stacked with equipment on the opposite wall. "Go over there and help yourselves to knee guards and helmets. They'll cost you four shillings and it'll be taken out of your pay one bob a week."

"Thanks, Jim," Dylan said. "We'll be on our way then. Put those on here lads so you don't have so much to carry." He demonstrated how to strap the knee guards about our legs before leading us across a muddy yard, over several sets of tram tracks, and into a long wooden shed capped with a corrugated iron roof where dozens of miners stood in line. After a short wait we left the shed carrying our heavy brass Davy lamps and entered a separate cabin where an elderly man smoking a pipe took each lamp in turn, unscrewed the top, blew down inside and gave it a thorough going over before screwing it back together.

As we exited the cabin and approached the pithead, the clamor intensified—incessant, piercing, assaulting the eardrums. In the overhead gantry the iron wheel rotated noisily, raising the miners' cage from the depths of the earth by its stout steel cable, before screeching to a stop with a racket of gates opening and giant air circulation fans roaring. About thirty miners crowded into the cage ahead of us, the gate clanged shut and, with renewed rumbling overhead, the cage dropped out of sight with a loud bang as heavy wooden droppers slammed down over the mine shaft.

"We'll be on next!" Dylan shouted. "It'll take a few minutes!" He coughed hoarsely at the effort and spat on the ground in front of him. Most of the miners seemed to cough a lot, I noticed. After a brief halt to allow the miners out below ground, the cage returned to the surface, forcing the droppers up as it emerged. As soon as the gate was opened, we surged forward to take our turn. The gate slammed shut and I felt the floor give way as we plunged into the mineshaft and daylight disappeared.

Panic gripped me as we dropped deeper and deeper into the earth, but in a short space of time the floor pressed against my feet as we slowed to a halt and the gate was thrown open. Hugh's father led the way into an expansive well-lit cavern where coal trams, some full of shiny anthracite, others empty, took up a great deal of the floor space. Side shafts led out in several directions. "This way, lads," he said, guiding Hugh and me around the trams and into one of the tunnels.

We walked a short distance to where the shaft widened and a small wooden cabin sat against one wall. A stoop-shouldered man standing at the cabin door greeted Dylan before taking our lamps for a second safety inspection. "You be hewing today, Dylan," the man said, nodding down the shaft. "The lads can give you a hand, but there's some timber work needs to be done as well."

"Aye, I know the face," Dylan replied. "Come on boys, we've a good walk ahead of us."

We set off at a steady pace down the narrow tunnel, the only illumination coming from our Davy lamps. In places the ceiling sloped down and we had to bend over awkwardly to avoid scraping our helmets along the rough surface. "Watch out for the ropes," Dylan said, indicating two heavy cords between steel rails on the tunnel floor. "If they start moving, get out of the way."

"How far down are we, Dad," Hugh asked.

"About fifteen hundred feet, give or take a few," his father replied. A loud creaking sound echoed along the shaft, followed by a distant ghostly crackling. "Pay no heed," Dylan said, noticing alarmed looks on our faces. "It's just the earth settling a bit. Happens all the time."

"Is it safe, Dad?" Hugh asked uncertainly.

"Aye, safe enough. Don't you worry lad."

After about the length of two rugby fields the ceiling sloped up again and we were able to walk upright. Unnerved by the strange noises of shifting earth, I sweated profusely in spite of my still-damp clothes, and the air felt oppressive and claustrophobic. All I could think of was that mountain of earth above me, and how I wished to be back on the surface, bathed in sunlight with fresh breezes blowing through my hair. Oh Gwyn, why didn't I listen to you?

A whistle sounded in the distance. "Watch out lads," Dylan yelled as the ropes began slithering along the ground. He crowded us quickly into a one of the many shallow indentations I had noted along the right side of the tunnel.

"What is it, Dad?" Hugh shouted as banging and rattling echoed down the shaft from the direction we had come. With a deafening racket a line of six trams hurtled past, inches from where we were held back by Dylan's strong arms, before disappearing into the darkness ahead.

"They're the empties," Dylan said, releasing us from his grip. "We'll be filling them soon enough. Now step out boys, we've not so far to go now."

"How far in are we, Mr. Griffith?" I asked.

"About two miles, I'd say, or nearly so," he replied matter-of-factly. I had a vision of the tunnel collapsing behind us, and claustrophobia lay over me like a heavy shroud. About ten minutes later we arrived at our destination, a rectangular enlargement of the tunnel where the trams sat quietly awaiting our attention. To the left a low-cut excavation led into the coalface, and against the far wall a variety of tools lay atop a heavy wooden bench. To the right a thickset man stacked heavy timbers at the entrance of another freshly dug tunnel. Following Dylan's lead we placed our lunch tins and water jacks next to the tool bench.

"Hello there, Dennis!" Dylan greeted the man. "We've got some help this morning. This here's my boy Hugh, and this is Evan Morgan."

"Aye, I've been waiting long enough," the man replied grouchily. "Let's get going with the hewing then." Simultaneously Dylan and Dennis stripped off their sweat-dampened shirts and vests and moved over to the bench to select their tools. Hugh and I followed suit and stripped to the waist. A cool breath of circulating air felt comforting against my naked skin.

"Now here's what we'll be doing this morning," Dylan said, leading us to the coalface. Dennis and I are going under this cut and we'll be hewing out the coal. Hugh, you come in behind us and throw the coal back to Evan, and you, Evan, shovel the coal in that first tram. When I give the word, you change places." The two men lowered themselves to their knees and dragged picks, crowbars and Davy lamps under the cut, which could not have been more than four feet high and about ten feet deep. With practiced hands they attacked the roof, dislodging coal at a rapid pace, while Hugh, kneeling awkwardly behind them, shoveled the chunks back to me. As fast as the coal landed at my feet, I shoveled it into the tram, the labor taking my mind off the unpleasantness of my subterranean prison. Before long my back began to protest against the repetitious bending over and standing upright, and my arms ached from lifting the heavier pieces.

"You boys change over now!" Dylan's voice called out from the cut. I crawled under to take Hugh's place and quickly found this job to be much the worse because there was so little room to maneuver, and coal dust stirred up by the digging gathered in my throat and nose, causing me to cough and spit. Sweat ran down my forehead, carrying more coal dust into my eyes. Thus the morning passed, slowly, laboriously, muscles screaming in protest, but neither Hugh nor I daring to complain lest we be thought of as slackers. After what seemed an interminable amount of time, Dylan dropped his pick.

"Time for some grub, boys," he said, crawling out from under the cut. The four of us sat down, backs against the wall next to the bench, and started in on our lunches. I took a long drink of water before opening my tin to find two thick slices of bread, a layer of salted lard in between, and a large ripe plum. I ate hungrily, ignoring the coal dust covering my hands and arms. Once finished I set my hands down next to my outstretched legs and had no sooner rested my head back against the wall than I felt a sharp pain on my right thumb. Reflexively I pulled my arm away, and upended a large, orange-brown beetle, its legs beating in a futile effort to right itself.

"What's that?" I cried.

"Just a roach, lad," Dylan said, squishing the insect to a repugnant sticky mass with his boot. "They like to bite, but you'll get used to them. There's a lot more of them down here than there are of us, isn't that so, Dennis?" The other man grunted in reply. God, can it get any worse? I thought.

"Okay, boys, back to work!" Dylan said, slapping his son on the shoulder. "I want you two to give Dennis here a hand with those timbers while I get back to hewing." We followed Dennis into the tunnel where he pointed up.

"We need to shore this up before there's any more excavating in this shaft," Dennis said, his first words after hearing practically nothing from him all morning. A moody, middle-aged man with sunken eyes and hollow cheeks, he showed us how to line up the roofing planks and attach thick upright posts with iron brackets to keep them firm against the ceiling.

Using no more words than necessary, he kept us at it for a couple of hours until all the timbers were in place. Had Hugh's father not been more than a few yards away, I've no doubt we would have received a tongue-lashing at every misstep.

We returned to the coalface and spent the remainder of our time clearing out under the cut and filling trams, but Hugh and I were so weary we found ourselves stopping frequently, bent over, hands on knees, trying to summon up the energy to keep going. If Dylan noticed our exhaustion, he said nothing. At last, with all the trams full and a good two feet more of working space under the cut, we gathered up our empty lunch tins and water jacks, put on our shirts, and plodded wearily back along the two-mile tunnel.

At the entry cabin Hugh's father stopped to record our progress and to signal for the filled trams to be winched back to the terminal. "We're finished for the day, lads," Dylan Griffith said. "The next shift will bring the trams to the surface for screening and removing slag."

"Evan!" I heard my name called as we waited near the tram depot. It was Dai Wilkins, an old pal of ours from Bodringallt School who had entered the mine two years earlier, having failed the secondary school entrance examination. A short, stocky lad, barely five foot three, but a good rugby player despite his size, Dai was holding two mournful-looking pit ponies by their halters, a narrow length of board in his hand. We walked over slowly, almost too spent to return the greeting. "I heard you were starting today," Dai said. "I've been looking everywhere for you."

"We were down at the coalface," I replied, nodding in the direction of the shaft we had just exited. "What do they have you doing then?"

"I'm in charge of the ponies. Have been for a couple of months now," he said with the air of a seasoned veteran. "We use them for hauling trams in the shorter tunnels." He turned and whacked the nearer one hard on its flank, drawing a whinny of protest.

"What did you do that for?" Hugh demanded. "He didn't do anything!"

"It's good for them," Dai said defensively. "Let's them know whose boss."

"Suppose your boss slammed you with a bloody piece of wood a few times a day, just so you'd know he was the bloody boss," Hugh retorted, turning away in disgust.

"He's right, Dai," I said. "It's bad enough they have to spend their lives down here. Why make things worse for them?" Dai Wilkins looked sullen and didn't respond. I slapped him on the arm. "It's good to see you, Dai," I said. "Let's get a rugby match going one of these days."

"Aye, good to see you too, Evan. I miss the lads, being down here day in and day out." He turned and led the ponies over to their stalls at the back of the cavern.

"Bloody idiot!" Hugh exclaimed when I rejoined him. "Dai never was too bright."

Once the trams, filled with our day's labor, arrived back at the terminal and were checked off, we crowded into the cage and were lifted back to the surface, blinking into bright sunlight that had chased away the morning rain. We exchanged our lamps for the brass checks and set off down the hill in the company of several other miners, knee guards and helmets still in place and black from head to toe except for our pink lips and the whites of our eyes. To people we passed on the street we must hardly have been recognizable.

"You did well, lads," Hugh's father said as we approached Ivor Street. "In a few days those muscles will be used to it. I remember what my first day was like."

I didn't respond, being much too tired to acknowledge the compliment. Yet I felt some satisfaction, even pride, for having completed my first day in the mine. But I kept my eyes down when I passed Gwyn's house because I didn't want her to see me looking like this.

Chapter 3

I couldn't escape Gwyn's gaze for long. On the Thursday after I started work I spied her on the main road as I was heading home from the mine. Wearing a white cotton blouse and tartan skirt, she was approaching on the opposite side of the street, and once she recognized who was behind the coal-black facade she crossed over. "Well look at you!" she said, her welcoming smile belying any aversion she might have felt at my appearance. "You do look a sight."

"Aye, I feel a sight."

"What's that thing?" she said, pointing at the water jack hanging from my shoulder.

"Tin water bottle. Glass bottles aren't allowed in the mine. More poetry?" I asked, nodding towards the book she was cradling in her arm.

"Byron."

"Romantic," I said.

"Well you don't look very romantic," she smiled. "Why haven't you been around to see me all week?"

"Christ, Gwyn, I'm . . ."

"Watch your language with me, Evan Morgan!" she snapped, her face reddening. "I'm not one of your mates from the pit." A group of passing miners laughed at her scolding.

"Sorry, Gwyn. It's just that I'm so bloody . . . I mean I've been so weary every night, I just collapse."

"I'm not surprised," she said, her expression softening. "Why don't you take me to the Workmen's Hall Saturday night. The men's choir from Treorchy is having a concert."

"I'd love to, Gwyn. Look, I'll come over later this evening and we could go for a walk."

"No, you get your rest." She started across the street to her home. "I'll see you Saturday."

My footsteps felt lighter the rest of the way home. I wanted so much to put my arms around her, pit grime or not. From the playful chrysalis who used to skip her way home from school had emerged a sprightly and graceful young butterfly who walked with a brisk step that mirrored her energetic childhood. Still a pupil at Tonypandy, Gwyn had grown into a real beauty, a wholesome, confident girl with a figure I couldn't keep my eyes from. Her hair was longer now, tied in back with a checkered ribbon, but the freckles, although faded a bit, were still there. Her engaging smile and happy disposition had long ago won over my aunt and uncle. "Such a nice girl!" my aunt would say almost every time she saw her.

Uncle Mervyn had really taken a shine to Gwyn when he found out she liked poetry because he loved reading the stuff himself, especially Welsh poetry, and Gwyn was comfortable enough with the language that she could appreciate the poetry books he loaned her. Unlike Aunt Beryl and me, my uncle was completely at home in Welsh, fluency being more common in his part of Wales. Ellis Evans, who wrote under the name Hedd Wyn, was his favorite poet.

"We knew the family," he told me one evening, looking up from his slim volume of Hedd Wyn poetry. "They lived in Trawsfynydd, not far from us. Lots of children, ten or eleven, I think. Ellis is the oldest. Only twenty when he won his first poetry chair at the Eisteddfod."

For my part, I had made progress with Gwyn's mother who had grudgingly come to accept me as a fixture in her daughter's life. Last Christmas she'd even surprised me with a jar of her homemade damson jam.

§

Gwyn was still in my thoughts as I entered the narrow, arched passageway that led to our back yard. We seldom used the front entrance as this opened into what we called the best room, a part of the house used only on special occasions such as Christmas, when my aunt and uncle would sip sherry while seated on the chintz-covered settee, surrounded by rose-patterned wallpaper, their feet resting on the faded oriental rug that had been in my aunt's family for generations. Family photographs stared at them from atop a walnut cabinet displaying my aunt's seldom-used Staffordshire Blue china.

We spent almost all our waking hours in the back room, separated from the front by a small hallway and pantry under the stairs. The back room served as kitchen and parlor. Against the right wall as we entered through the back door sat the lead-blacked coal stove, almost always topped with a kettle of hot water, and next to it a porcelain sink with attached draining board. Overhead hung a wooden clothes rack, raised and lowered by rope and pulley, for drying laundry when it rained, which was more often than not on Monday washdays. A square oaken table with four chairs dominated the center of the room, and two comfortable padded armchairs faced the stove. A sideboard next to the stairs leading to the two upstairs bedrooms completed the furniture.

Out back our small, paved yard, sloping gradually down to a central drain, lay secluded between high brick walls, but not so high that we couldn't chat with our neighbors over the top. A scullery containing a large sink for laundry and storage space for the wash copper, mangle, and Uncle Mervyn's tools and bicycle occupied one wall; and next to the scullery was the lavatory with its overhead tank and chain for flushing. A wooden coal bin sat against the back wall. A clothesline, raised with a long pole, stretched across the yard from posts set against the boundary walls. Judging from the homes I'd been in, ours wasn't much different from most row houses in town.

I had to hand it to my Aunt Beryl. From my first day in the mine she'd been ready when I arrived home from work. "Don't be bashful, get out of those clothes and into the tub with you," she'd said. Before entering the kitchen I removed my boots and outer clothes and tossed them in the scullery. My aunt already had buckets of water heating on the stove. She poured the steaming liquid into the tub in front of the sink. I stripped down and sank into the water, knees drawn up to my chest, while my aunt refilled the buckets and set them on the stove.

"Are you tired, son?" she asked.

"Aye, I am." I welcomed the hot water against my skin, but wished the tub were large enough to immerse my aching muscles completely. I sponged water over my body and rubbed a heavy bar of lye soap and pumice stone over my face, arms and chest where coal dust clung the thickest. I kneaded soapy water through my hair while Aunt Beryl scoured my back.

"Close your eyes!" my aunt said, and she upended a bucket of warm water over my head. She handed me a thick towel as I raised myself, muscles protesting, from the tub. "Your clean clothes are on the table," she said. As I pulled on my clothes, my aunt grabbed the tub by one of its handles and began dragging it out through the back door.

"Wait, I'll do that," I said when I saw she was having difficulty maneuvering over the step. "That's too heavy for you."

"Oh, it's not so bad," she replied, but then stopped with the tub halfway outside. "It does give me a pain down here though," she said, clutching her stomach.

I moved past her and pulled the tub the rest of the way out and over to the center of the yard where I upended it to pour the hot water, as black now as the River Rhondda, down into the drain. I hung the empty tub on its designated hook in the scullery. Back in the house, Aunt Beryl was down on her knees wiping up spilled water with a piece of cloth.

I dropped into one of the easy chairs facing the stove and put my head back. "Where's Uncle Mervyn?" I asked.

"He'll be here shortly. I asked him to pick up a few groceries on the way home. And I expect he'll want to stop at Mr. Walker's to buy some tobacco." She wrung the cloth out into the sink and took it outside to the scullery. When she returned she busied herself laying the table and setting out dishes of black pudding, beets, tomatoes and sliced bread, while I sat with closed eyes, reliving my day in the mine. I had about dozed off when I was awakened by the sound of Uncle Mervyn's footsteps in the passageway. I heard the scullery door open, then close after he had stowed his bicycle. He entered carrying a string bag bulging with cabbage, parsnips, turnips, and leeks.

"So, Evan, how did the day go in the mine?" he asked as he hung his tweed cap on the hook next to the back door.

"Not too bad, Uncle," I lied. "But my muscles are a bit sore."

He carried the bag of groceries through to the pantry, then returned and sat in the other armchair. "I remember how sore I was when I started at the slate mine up north," he said. "But in a week or two I got used to it."

"Don't get yourselves too comfortable," my aunt interjected. "As soon as the kettle boils we'll be having our supper. You can talk about the mine while we're eating."

"Auntie has a pain in her tummy," I said, my eyes still closed.

"A spoonful of cod liver oil, that'll fix it," Uncle Mervyn replied, setting his pipe down on the arm of the chair. My uncle believed that cod liver oil could cure just about any ailment known to man.

§

With little variation, this ritual of bathing followed by supper occupied every evening of my working days, and sure enough, as the days passed my muscles ached less and less. Before long I could put in a full day at the coalface and still have energy left when I headed back to the surface. I worked in a variety of mineshafts, mostly at the coalface with pick and shovel, or digging and shoring up new tunnels with heavy timbers. Sometimes, when extra hands were needed on the surface, I separated slag from the coal, or sorted new coal by size in steam-driven screens that rattled back and forth with a tremendous racket. Working above ground afforded a welcome break from the gloomy world below, even though I was no longer bothered by claustrophobia when deep in the mineshafts.

Besides Dai Wilkins and Hugh, there were a number of familiar faces in the mine, friends from Bodringallt and Tonypandy. We formed a fellowship of shared misery that made life in the pit more bearable. But there was no question at the end of the day, in my moments of reflection, I found coalmining demeaning as well as exhausting. I often wondered why the older miners never complained about their lot, and how most of the time they exhibited such a cheerful disposition you'd think they were the most fortunate of Welshmen. The answer of course was that coalmining was a job, a livelihood that brought food to the table and money to pay the rent, or a pint of bitter at the pub on a Saturday night and a pack of Woodbines from Mr. Walker, the tobacconist. They may not have liked the work, but there were precious few alternatives.

"Why don't they have baths at the pit?" I asked one Sunday as we sat around the dinner table.

"I'd watch who you say that to," Uncle Mervyn said as he carved slices of lamb from the roast. "You could lose your job for talking that way if it got back to the management."

"It's just not right that Auntie has to get me cleaned up every night after work," I persisted. "The owners make plenty of money from our labor. They could easily afford it."

"Oh, I don't mind doing it, Evan," my aunt said as she spooned mint sauce over her lamb.

But it wasn't just getting me clean; the pit clothes had to be washed, a drudgery of pouring pails of hot water into the copper kettle in the scullery, immersing the filthy clothing and pounding it with the wooden dolly, rinsing in the sink and squeezing out the water with the mangle. Then, depending on the weather, the clean work clothes were hung out to dry on the outside clothesline or the inside drying rack. My aunt's hands often became raw and chapped, especially in winter.

"I'm not spending the rest of my life in the mine, Uncle," I said between mouthfuls. "It's an awful way to make a living."

Uncle Mervyn, reaching for the bowl of roast potatoes, didn't reply at once. At last he said: "Aye, I see your point, lad. But at least it's a living. Steady work, not like some parts of Wales where thousands are on the dole."

"True enough," I replied, looking him directly in the eye. "But if you hear of a job with the railway, I'd like you to put in a word for me."

"I'll do that, Evan. Aye, I'll do that."

§

Payday was Friday, the banknotes and coins handed out as we filed through the paymaster's shed near the main colliery gate. A number of wives waited for their husbands outside the gate to make sure they didn't spend their meager wages in the pub on the way home. My own pay, with the exception of a few shillings for spending, I handed over to my aunt.

"We don't need your money," she said, the first time I proudly handed her my wages. "Let's just save it for a rainy day." Unspoken was her hopeful expectation that the day would come when Gwyn and I would be starting out as a married couple and would need a nest egg. Not that I was thinking about marriage at that young age.

I really didn't need much in the way of spending money. Unlike a lot of the lads, I didn't smoke. On a couple of occasions after school I'd puffed on cigarettes that one or another of my pals had sneaked from his father's pack, but I'd done nothing but cough, and afterwards felt sick. I couldn't, for the life of me, understand why so many men took up the habit. Then Gwyn told me one day that she could always tell a man who smoked because he smelled so bad, and the last thing I wanted was to smell bad when I was around her.

Most of what I spent was on Gwyn. I bought her a couple of poetry books, Tennyson and Shelley, at Ferguson's bookshop in Tonypandy, and two inexpensive broaches from a shop in Porth. For entertainment we enjoyed going to the Workmen's Hall in Pentre. Built originally as a place for miners and other working men to congregate, the building housed a good-sized theater, nothing fancy, but on most Saturday nights there was something going on—plays, vaudeville, choir groups, or an occasional moving picture, with a stout middle-aged lady wearing a feathered hat playing an organ below the screen for accompaniment. Best of all, the shows didn't cost much, usually sixpence or less. Afterwards we often stopped for fish and chips, which we ate out of their grease-soaked newspaper wrapping as we walked home. Saturday night outings and walks in the hills on Sunday afternoons, or sheep dog trials and rugby matches at the local playing fields were a pleasant counterpoint to the coal-black, pick-and-shovel working world.

§

I'd been at the mine a couple of years when Hugh sprung a surprise on me. He was unusually quiet all day, from the moment I met him on the way to work. His face wore a troubled look, not the usual friendly grin and cheerful greeting to pals he ran into in the mine.

"You're looking awfully serious today, Hugh," I remarked as we sat eating our lunch after a morning at the coalface.

"I've got a lot on my mind," he replied without looking up from the sandwich he was unwrapping.

I didn't press him on the matter, just ate my lunch in silence while keeping an eye out for cockroaches. On the way home he kept to himself and I didn't attempt to force the conversation. But as he was about to turn up Ivor Street, he stopped.

"Evan, I need to talk to you," he said abruptly. "How about we go to the Old Lamb for a pint later on?"

"Sure, Hugh," I said. "I'll meet you at half past eight."

Hugh continued on his way up Ivor Street and I went my own way home, wondering what on earth was up with Hugh. Perhaps he's mad at me about something, I thought. Or, more likely, he's decided to leave the mine and he's in hot water with his dad about it.

After supper, I told my aunt and uncle I was meeting Hugh at the Old Lamb and wouldn't be late getting home. When I arrived at the cozy wood-paneled establishment that served as the local pub, Hugh was already at a table by himself, a pint of bitter in front of him, a Woodbine dangling from his mouth. I waved and crossed the smoke-filled room to the bar to pick up a pint of my own before joining him.

"Well, Hugh, you've been a bit preoccupied lately," I said, sipping foam from my glass. "What's on your mind?"

Hugh took the cigarette from his mouth and, with fingers already stained the yellow-brown of a regular smoker, crushed it in the ashtray. "Mary and I are getting married," he said without looking up, his voice low enough that it wouldn't carry over to the nearby tables. His face had turned a deep red, even up to his ears.

His words rendered me speechless for several seconds. "Well, that is good news," I said at last. "I didn't know you and Mary were even thinking along those lines."

"We weren't," he said. "Mary's in a family way."

I stared at him. "But how?" I stammered, realizing immediately I had asked a stupid question.

"We got carried away and . . . well, it just happened. My mum and dad are furious. And Mary's parents . . ." He shook his head and pulled another cigarette from his pack.

"But how? I mean . . . *where?*"

"Mary's mum and dad were away for the day, and I went over to see her. It just happened." He lit his cigarette and the match illuminated an expression that would have done justice to a Shakespearean tragedy.

"Well, I don't know what to say," I said, which was the truth; I was flabbergasted.

"Haven't you and Gwyn . . . you know . . . ?" He looked up at me.

"Well, I suppose we've been a bit passionate at times, but nothing like that!" Images of Gwyn and me lying among the ferns above town flashed before me. We'd been carried away at times, but never went that far; both of us were scared to death of the consequences.

"Have you set a date for getting married?" I asked.

"My mum talked to Mr. Lewis about having a chapel wedding, but he wasn't keen on the idea under the circumstances. So we're going to have it at the town hall. I'm only eighteen," he said, his voice trembling. "How can I be a father? All that responsibility . . ."

"Lots of chaps marry at eighteen," I said, although I didn't know of any.

"When we tie the knot, I'd like you to be best man, Evan. Will you do that?"

"Of course I will," I said, slapping him on the arm and dislodging a length of ash from his cigarette. "I'd be honored."

I didn't say anything to my aunt and uncle about Hugh's predicament—they would hear about it soon enough—but I did tell Gwyn the next day.

"I know," she said. "Mary told me she was in a family way a couple of weeks ago."

"And you didn't tell me?"

"Why should I have, then? She told me in confidence, not something to spread around the neighborhood. And don't you start getting ideas. I've no intention of having babies for a good long time!"

"You're not the only one," I said.

§

Hugh and Mary were married on Saturday, September 6, 1913, a day when a bitter wind blew in from the Irish Sea. Gray-black clouds blotted out the sun and unloaded occasional hard showers that turned the slate roofs and road surfaces wet and shiny and street gutters into rivulets.

With umbrellas folded in the stand near the entryway, we assembled in the atrium of the town hall before the mayor, a portly man dressed in a dark blue, pin-striped suit, his medal of office hanging by a heavy chain around his neck. Hugh wore his father's hand-me-down suit with a shirt that was buttoned so tightly around his neck that I wondered how he could breathe. He looked decidedly uncomfortable, nothing like the old Hugh who favored woolen pullovers and baggy trousers. Next to him, Mary cradled a bouquet of red roses. She look as radiant as always, her shiny hair down to her shoulders, cheeks tinted with rouge, and decked out in a brand new chiffon dress the color of fresh spring leaves that gave no hint of the life that was developing inside her body. In my Sunday best, I stood next to Hugh; and Gwyn, clad in a pale yellow cotton dress with a sprig of lily of the valley pinned to her left shoulder and holding a small bouquet of white carnations, stood alongside Mary. Behind us stood

Dylan and Maude Griffith, resigned looks on their faces, and Bevan and Edith Thomas, making no attempt to hide their displeasure at the fate that had befallen their daughter.

When the ceremony was over, we hurried under a still-threatening sky to Mary's parents' home on Sandybank Road where a local woman who ran a bakery had prepared refreshments. We sat around the dining room table making polite, but constrained conversation, while outside the rain began with renewed fury, driven by vicious wind gusts against windows, while torrents of water could be heard gurgling through gutters and downspouts.

When a break occurred in the weather, Gwyn and I took our leave. I shook hands with Dylan Griffith and Bevan Thomas and we planted kisses on Mary's cheek. The newlyweds were to leave shortly for a two-day seaside honeymoon in Porthcawl.

"Lets hope they have better weather than this," I said as Gwyn and I walked down the hill to her home. Rain began falling again and I opened my umbrella. It was not the most auspicious of days for what was supposed to be a happy occasion; but then the circumstances of the wedding were not exactly auspicious either. Perhaps it was a portent of things to come, because it was not long after that other events cast a shadow on all of us.

Chapter 4

*Christmas is coming, the goose is getting fat.
Please put a penny in the old man's hat!*

Hugh and I had chanted those words of beggary and celebration when we were youngsters. Now some neighborhood children were knocking at the door, carrying on the tradition.

*If you haven't got a penny, a ha'penny will do.
If you haven't got a ha'penny, then God bless you!*

Most people ignored them, but Uncle Mervyn always kept a few shiny new pennies on hand to brighten the children's holiday season, perhaps reliving memories of his own childhood.

That Christmas in 1913 was among the best I remember. The weather had been unsettled several days before, with dark skies and intermittent rain and sleet. And then, as if on cue, the precipitation changed to snow on Christmas Eve, falling in large wet flakes that muffled footsteps on the pavement outside the house, coated slate roofs, and painted white stripes on fence tops, clotheslines and leafless branches of trees and shrubs. Glistening tuffets of snow perched precariously atop stones protruding from the little brook that gurgled in front of the Old Lamb Inn.

That morning Uncle Mervyn picked up the long-ordered goose from Mr. Fairweather, the butcher, and Aunt Beryl spent the day plucking feathers, removing giblets and preparing sage stuffing and gravy. The day before she had cooked two good-sized plum puddings, each with a sixpence inside for good luck, as well as the traditional spicy fruitcake topped with marzipan and icing. My uncle and I ran colorful streamers across the ceiling, hung paper bells and sprigs of mistletoe, and set out red-berried holly atop the sideboard. At about five o'clock in the evening, Mr. Andrews, the music teacher at Bodringallt School, led a group of twenty of his young charges up Victoria Street singing carols they had been rehearsing for weeks. People up and down the street opened their doors and stood outside and, at Mr. Andrews' invitation, joined in, while the gasman lit street lamps with his long pole.

The caroling finished, I left with my aunt and uncle for Christmas Eve service, looking forward to hymns that are forever inspirational in a chapel decorated with holly and aromatic pine cuttings. We slid into a pew next to Gwyn and her mother, and throughout the service Gwyn and I held hands in rapturous contentment. No one can sing hymns like the Welsh; the rafters echoed with those sweet voices that I would always remember with nostalgia when far removed from my native soil.

Christmas morning Gwyn and her mother arrived by invitation for dinner. Mouth-watering aromas of spices and roast goose, still warm in the oven, greeted them as they stepped into the parlor bearing gifts wrapped in brightly colored tissue paper. With cries of "Merry Christmas!" all around, Uncle Mervyn ushered everyone into the front room for sherry.

"Perfect fit," I said as I slipped into the brown cardigan Gwyn had knitted for me.

"You must has been knitting all year!" my uncle exclaimed as Gwyn presented him with a blue and green-striped muffler, and my aunt with two multicolored woolen holders to protect her hands when she lifted the iron from its trivet on the stove. Gwyn's mother had brought her usual jars of homemade damson jam, one for each of us. I gave Mrs. Williams a scarf that my aunt had picked out; and to Gwyn, who had taken to writing poems of her own, a handsome fountain pen, a bottle of blue ink and a notepad.

Dinner was a gala affair with much merriment fueled by my uncle's generous portions of sherry. We popped open Christmas crackers and donned colorful paper hats. Uncle Mervyn, putting on an exaggerated air of pomposity that brought laughter around the table, carved the goose with a deftness of a surgeon, while Aunt Beryl loaded each plate with ample portions of stuffing, roast potatoes and parsnips.

Once the plates and dishes were removed to the sideboard, my aunt produced a plum pudding from the oven, topped it with a sprig of holly, poured on a little brandy and lit it with a match. Uncle Mervyn allowed the pale blue flame to flicker away before serving the pudding drenched with warm yellow custard. Gwyn's mother could hardly conceal her delight when her portion revealed the lucky sixpence.

The meal over, we sat back, our stomachs full, enjoying one another's company. Gwyn smiled as her eyes met mine across the table. No longer the schoolgirl, but a sweet, poetic beauty, Gwyn had taken a secretarial course and was now working at a bank in Tonypandy. I answered her smile with my own, convinced at that moment that there was no lovelier girl in all of Wales. What a lucky man I am, I thought.

Around five o'clock Hugh and Mary, followed by our immediate neighbors, joined us with holiday greetings. Aunt Beryl served tea and Christmas cake. Chairs were removed to the perimeter of the room and the table folded and put away. My uncle produced bottles of beer and cider, and the next two hours were taken up with singing and dancing, joined in by everyone but the arthritic Mrs. Williams who, even so, was moved to clap along.

At last the hour was late and our guests said their goodbyes. Gwyn and I walked her mother home at a slow pace in deference to her painful knees, her arms linked in ours. I kissed Gwyn goodnight and returned home to find the dishes mostly cleaned up, with Uncle Mervyn uncharacteristically pitching in. It was around midnight when we filled our hot water bottles and went upstairs to bed. Because Christmas Day fell on Thursday and Boxing Day Friday, the colliery had closed for the long weekend, thus we had plenty of time to recover from the partying. But it was back to reality and the coalmine Monday morning.

§

The magical snows of Christmas gave way to coal dust-blackened slush and cold drizzle as the year drew to a close and the new year unfolded, with only an occasional appearance by the sun, and even then on days when much of the sky was obscured by iron-gray clouds. So raw was the biting damp wind throughout January that the miners actually looked forward to entering the cage for their descent to the warmer temperatures underground.

Hugh and Mary had moved into a spare room with Mary's parents, a temporary arrangement until the baby was born and Hugh could find a place of their own. That Mary had a bun in the oven, as Dai Wilkins indelicately put it, was old news now and we all accepted that Hugh was a married man, which set him apart from our regular clique, at least when we were out of the mine. I missed his companionship and our dart games at the Old Lamb, and found myself spending more time with Dai Wilkins and Rhys Jones, a friend from my days at Tonypandy Secondary who had started at the mine a year after Hugh and me.

The morning of Shrove Tuesday I headed up the hill to the mine with Hugh and his father, anticipating a mouth-watering feast of pancakes that evening. Aunt Beryl always cooked pancakes for Shrove Tuesday supper, thin and crisp and sprinkled with lemon juice and sugar. At the mine entrance, Dennis Bertram pulled Dylan Griffith aside. "They want to see you in management," Dennis said, pointing with his thumb toward the plain brick building that housed offices for the owners and their staff.

"Well, what have I done now?" Hugh's father said. "I'd better be getting along, then. You lads go ahead with Dennis."

Hugh and I followed Dennis into the mine. I didn't much fancy working with Dennis Bertram, ever since I'd met him on my first day at work. He wore a persistent scowl and his temperament, even on good days, did not invite fellowship. But Hugh's father seemed to get along with him well enough. Dennis had lost his wife to tuberculosis several years ago, Dylan Griffith told me one day when I complained about the man's attitude; her death had soured Dennis on life in general.

For the past few days I'd been working with a team of miners, including Hugh, his father and Dennis, in a new shaft, the deepest yet, enlarging the working space, removing rubble and shoring up the roof. Deep in the tunnel we had uncovered a rich seam of coal, and today some of the men began exposing more of the anthracite, while Dennis, Hugh and I worked on a section of roof that still needed stabilizing. Water seeping through the ceiling and walls left muddy puddles along the tunnel floor and dripped steadily onto our helmets and upturned faces as we attached iron brackets to the timbers. Dennis was clearly concerned. "Too much water," he'd growled the day before. "The earth's soggy."

After about half an hour Hugh's father arrived with a pleased look on his face. "What was that all about, Dad?" Hugh asked, as we paused in our work.

"They've made me a supervisor," Dylan announced. "Beginning the first of March."

To my surprise Dennis came over and gripped Dylan's hand. "That is good news, Dylan," he said. "There's none more deserving."

"Don't be daft, Dennis. You're just as ready for the job as I am," Dylan replied.

"Does this mean I'll have to start calling you Boss instead of Dad?" Hugh laughed.

"Aye, it does—but only when you're not doing your job properly." Dylan put his hands on Hugh's shoulders. "You know, son, your mum's going to welcome a bit of extra pay. Now she'll be able to visit her sister in Brighton more often."

"Congratulations, Mr. Griffith," I said, shaking his hand.

"Enough of this nonsense, then," Dylan said. "You lads get back to work before I start acting like a supervisor now instead of waiting 'til next month." Then he was off down the tunnel to join the other miners at the coalface.

§

The first bits of dirt and stone began falling from the roof as we were finishing up for the day. Dennis and I were gathering our tools for the long walk back through the tunnel, while Hugh pounded nails into the last of the support beams. More debris, dislodged by the hammering, began falling all around us, small pieces at first, and then suddenly, with an unearthly roar, the roof of the tunnel gave way and I was slammed into the wall by a sledgehammer blow to the head. Dazed, and with a sharp pain in my left arm, I lay on the muddy ground while more stones and dirt fell around me and on top of me until, at last, there was only the steady drip, drip of water into muddy puddles.

The weight of earth kept me pinned to the ground, unable to move. I raised my head and in the dim light saw Dennis, still standing, pull a tin whistle from his shirt pocket and blow three shrill, piercing notes. He paused, and blew three more. Faintly, in the distance I heard three answering whistles. Then he was by my side, pulling rocks and dirt from my legs and back and hauling me to my feet.

"Can you walk, Evan?' he shouted.

I nodded, though my legs felt like jelly and my shoulder and arm throbbed with pain and were sticky with blood. The helmet that had saved me from worse damage was buried somewhere under the rubble along with my lamp. From behind came a deep, agonizing groan. "It's Hugh," I said weakly.

"Go, Evan, before more of the roof caves in," Dennis shouted, grabbing my arm and propelling me in the direction of the tunnel entrance. "I'll take care of Hugh!"

"I can't leave him!" I cried, wrenching free. I looked back and saw earth and broken timbers piled halfway up to the ceiling. I walked stiffly to the pile and began attacking the debris, joined immediately by Dennis who had barely been touched by the cave-in. Water drained down on us from above as we worked frantically in the dim light of Dennis's lamp, spurred on by the Hugh's tortured cries. A short distance back we found him, face pressed down into the mud by broken timbers, a massive slab of granite covering the lower part of his body. With difficulty I pulled off the wooden beams and lifted Hugh's head out of the mud.

"Oh, God," he whimpered. "Help me, Evan. Please help me." He was shivering and in a state of shock.

"Don't you worry, Hugh," I said. "Dennis and I will get you out."

Dennis worked his way around to where Hugh's boots protruded and, without success, tried to maneuver the piece of stone from his body. He moved around to the side and with a display of strength I could never have mustered, he slowly lifted the huge slab from the side and tilted it away, revealing a bloody mess around Hugh's legs and a shattered shin bone sticking out through the skin. Then, gently, Dennis cradled Hugh in his arms, lifted him away from the pile of rubble and laid him down on a dry stretch of tunnel floor. He pulled off his shirt and tied one of the sleeves tightly around Hugh's thigh to stanch the bleeding while I held Hugh's head in my lap.

"Get out of here!" Dennis barked at me.

"What about the others?" I asked. "We can't just leave them!"

"Can't you see the tunnel's completely blocked back there?" Dennis shouted. "There'll be a team down here shortly to dig them out." He stood up, grabbed Hugh by one of his arms and lifted him effortlessly over his shoulder, and without another word began trotting back along the tunnel, Hugh crying out in agony with each step. A short way back a group of miners carrying stretchers relieved Dennis of his burden. As Dennis and I made our way back along the tunnel, carrying Hugh on a stretcher so the other men could go forward to the cave-in, I regarded the surly man in front of me in a new light.

On the surface, in the evening darkness, the pit siren's blaring, intermittent blasts alerted the community and brought family members and medical teams converging on the colliery gate. I stayed with Hugh, sedated now by an injection of morphine, until he was placed in back of the ambulance for transport to the hospital in Pontypridd. I was turning back to the pithead when I spotted Aunt Beryl and Gwyn among several other women hurrying up the hill. As soon as she saw me Gwyn rushed forward and threw her arms around my waist, hugging me so tightly I could scarcely breathe and causing pain up and down my bruised body.

"Thank God," she mumbled into my shoulder. "I was so afraid it might be you."

"Evan, you're soaked to the skin!" my aunt cried. "And you've got blood all over you!"

Gwyn pulled away, her cheek and cotton dress stained with blood, coal dust and mud. "Most of it's Hugh's," I said, motioning towards the ambulance, now chugging out through the colliery gate. "But he's going to be all right. I just got knocked about a bit."

"Well get on home with you," my aunt said. "I'll clean you up."

"I can't, Auntie. Hugh's dad's trapped down there. They'll be needing everyone for the rescue."

"You can't go back down!" Gwyn cried, clutching my arm. "I won't let you!"

"Don't worry, Gwyn, I'll be fine" I said, gently detaching her grip. "You go down and call on Mary and Mrs. Griffith. Tell them Hugh's getting good care at the hospital. I'll stop by on my way home to let you know how things turn out." I turned away, still a bit unsteady on my feet, and walked back to the pithead where teams of rescuers awaited their turn to descend into the depths of the mine. At first they wouldn't let me go down, but I protested loudly enough that I was finally given permission, but only after my cuts and abrasions had been cleaned and bandaged.

We toiled through the night in shifts, two to three hours at a time, hauling out rubble and putting up new timbers to avert a further cave-in. It was slow, tedious work, but everyone kept at it with a grim sense of purpose. It wasn't until around mid morning the following day that the rescuers came upon the lifeless bodies, completely buried under mud and rock, a short distance from the coalface.

I was back at the staging area near the lift when the dead were brought out on stretchers. Once I recognized Hugh's father's battered face, I sat against the tunnel wall and buried my face in my hands, crying uncontrollably. Dennis came over, placed his hand on my shoulder, and without saying a word sat down beside me.

§

Looking back on that period following the cave-in, I think I must have been in a dazed, disembodied state because it all seems such a blur now. There had been other mine accidents and other deaths during my boyhood, but this was the first time I'd been touched by such a tragedy; and for the first time my steady, predictable day-to-day existence had been cruelly interrupted.

Exhausted, I stopped at Gwyn's house on he way home from the mine, but she was off at work. I walked up Ivor Street to see Mrs. Griffith, only to learn she was at the hospital with Hugh. Finally I went home and sat numbly in the tub while my aunt cleaned me off—gently because I was covered with abrasions and ugly purple bruises—and changed my filthy bandages. She kept her thoughts to herself, realizing perhaps that I was in no mood for conversation.

Scores of miners and their families crowded into Saint Dyfodwg Methodist Church for Dylan Griffith's funeral, for he was well thought of in the mine and in the neighborhood. Maude Griffith, clad in black, her face ashen, sat in front sobbing silently while her sister held a comforting arm around her shoulders. Hugh wasn't there because his injuries kept him in the hospital, but Mary and her parents shared the front pew with Maude and her sister. I sat farther back with Gwyn and my aunt and uncle, a choking feeling in my throat as I fought back tears. Afterwards Gwyn and I rode the train to Pontypridd to visit Hugh who was distraught and inconsolable.

Two days later I returned to work, but such a heavy cloud hung over the mine that the men just went about their business without saying much. Dennis was called in and offered the supervisor's job, but he turned them down, saying he couldn't take a job that was rightfully Dylan's. Give it to a man with a family, he told them; they need the money more than he did.

In mid March Hugh, walking awkwardly on crutches, left the hospital and immediately moved back in with his mother. Mary, now well along in her pregnancy, had already taken their belongings down from her parents' home. Hugh spent a couple of weeks moping around the house and smoking his Woodbines until, with encouragement from me and some of the other lads, we had him up and about to get strength back into his damaged leg.

With the onset of spring and the welcome appearance of bluebells and daffodils in the fields above town, Hugh gave up his crutches for a stout rosewood walking stick which he used to limp around the town with a renewed sense of purpose, and even up into the hills. "No more rugby matches for me," he said bitterly one sunny Saturday as I strolled with him along the river. Rugby was Hugh's passion, and I could only imagine how he must have felt when the doctors told him he would have a bad limp for the rest of his life.

By the beginning of June when fragrant purple lilac blossoms peeped over neighborhood walls, and fruit trees in the garden behind the Old Lamb showed off their early summer finery, Hugh tossed aside his walking stick and, with a determined limping gait, trudged up the hill to the mine to demand his job back. Once the owners were convinced that Hugh's leg would not get in the way of a good day's work, they agreed to put him back on the payroll. The mine couldn't keep up with the demand for coal and they needed every man they could get. "My mum can't pay the rent unless I have a job." Hugh told me when I expressed reservations. "Besides, it's all I know how to do. And I've got a family to support."

On the twentieth of June, in the stuffy upstairs bedroom of the Griffith home, a healthy seven-pound boy emerged to breathe his first breath and cry his first cry under the watchful eye of David Llewellyn, the local doctor. One month later the Methodist minister who had presided at Hugh's father's funeral christened the infant Dylan Griffith. Gwyn and I were named godparents.

Hugh embraced his new son with such affection and enthusiasm, dispelling any apprehension he might have felt at the prospect of family responsibilities, that he was transformed from the bitter, cheerless misanthrope he had become following the mine tragedy into something resembling his old self. Her new grandson also helped Maude Griffith emerge from the fog of mourning. Even Mary's parents were delighted in their new role as grandparents and began treating their son-in-law with some degree of cordiality, if not, at times, affection.

Yet even as these welcome changes transpired, happenings far removed from the Rhondda Valley cast a new shadow of uncertainty that would change my life in ways I could never have imagined.

Chapter 5

"The Serbs and Austrians are at each other's throats," Uncle Mervyn muttered as he read the newspaper while eating his Sunday breakfast of sausage and eggs.

"The Austrians are still mad about their archduke being killed," I responded. "Let them fight it out and be done with it."

"It's more complicated than that, lad. The Russians won't stand by and let the Serbs get slaughtered. And the Germans won't stand by if Russia steps in to help the Serbs."

"Well there's no need for us to get involved," Aunt Beryl said as she began removing dishes from the table. "The Boer War was bad enough."

"Aye, that's the truth," my uncle said. "Let's hope it never comes to that."

Of course, it did come to that. No sooner had the Austrians attacked Belgrade, Russia began mobilizing; and on the first of August, Germany declared war on Russia. From there events spun out of control, with no politicians having the will or statesmanship to stop the madness. Germany next declared war on France and sent its armies through Belgium's Ardennes Forest; and Great Britain, which had treaty obligations with Belgium, declared war on Germany. The strange thing was that nobody seemed overly worried; on the contrary, war fever gripped the country and newspapers spouted patriotic fervor and talked of the noble crusade against the evil Huns.

Most people thought the war would be over by Christmas, and I had no reason to think otherwise. I just kept working away at the mine as the conflict in Europe sank into a stalemate of trench warfare. By year's end the army was looking for new conscripts to replace the appalling losses.

"The Borderers are looking for volunteers," Dai Wilkins told me as I met him going in to work. "They've set up a recruitment center in Pontypool."

The South Wales Borderers—one of the Empire's illustrious regiments, with battle colors earned over centuries of conflict. "Are you thinking of joining up?" I asked.

"Aye, thinking about it. I'm fed up with this job. I want to see some of the world before I get killed in another cave-in."

Killed in another cave-in. Was that to be the fate of Hugh and me, or would we just grow older, coughing up coal dust until we were too ill to work, like our neighbor, Mr. Surtees? Would Gwyn want to spend the rest of her life with a man working at a job she hated? Dai's words hung over me like a cloud throughout the day.

"Dai said the Borderers are recruiting," I said to Hugh as we walked home that evening.

"Aye, I saw it in the paper yesterday," Hugh replied. "If it weren't for this leg, I'd be down there signing up today."

"What about Mary and Dylan?" I said. "You couldn't just go off and leave them."

"It would only be a short time, and if I liked the army life, I might have made a career of it. Get out and see some of the world outside of the Rhondda."

"That's what Dai said. See the world."

"What about you, Evan? Will you join up? They'd never take me with this limp."

"I don't know, I'll have to give it some thought. I don't like the idea of being away from Gwyn, but she's always wanted me out of the mine, even more so since . . ." I couldn't bring the words out.

"Since my Dad was killed," Hugh finished my thought. "Mary feels the same way. But I don't know what else I could do besides mining. It's what our family's always done. If I were in your shoes, Evan, I'd jump at the chance."

All week I pondered my future. For sure I was sick and tired of working underground, only seeing daylight on weekends during the long months of winter. Should I seize this opportunity to escape the mine, serve my country, and then seek new opportunities once the war was over? Apart from seaside outings to Porthcawl or Aberavon and occasional trips to Cardiff, I'd spent my entire life in the Rhondda Valley. Those distant places I'd learned about in geography class all at once seemed very enticing. Besides, I didn't want people to think I was shirking my duty when thousands of young men were volunteering every day. I didn't let on to Gwyn or my aunt and uncle what was on my mind; I wanted the decision to be mine and mine alone. Gwyn wanted me out of the mine badly enough that I was sure she'd be supportive if I enlisted. I wasn't at all sure about my aunt and uncle.

After talking the matter over with Dai and Rhys Jones, our excitement and enthusiasm at the prospect multiplied, especially in the evenings when we had a pint or two of beer under our belts. On Friday we stopped debating the issue and made our decision; next day we would take the train to Pontypool and sign up. On our way out of the mine we stopped at the management office to let them know of our plans, and were told our jobs would be waiting for us when we got back. The colliery manager shook hands and wished us good luck. I told my aunt and uncle I was taking Saturday off and going to Cardiff with Dai and Rhys.

The next morning the three of us met at the station and caught the early train to Cardiff, where we changed for Pontypool. Recruitment posters on the walls of the Pontypool station told us where to go, and by eleven o'clock, after waiting our turn with dozens of other eager volunteers, we signed up. Report to the Borderers' barracks in Brecon two weeks hence, we were told. Excited and filled with anticipation of what new adventures lay before us, we stopped at a nearby pub and celebrated with a lunch of crusty bread, slabs of Stilton cheese and pickled onions, washed down with a couple of pints of best bitter.

Still feeling the effects of the beer and basking in our patriotic commitment, we were in a downright cocky mood when the train pulled into Pentre station. Anxious to give Gwyn the good news, I walked quickly to her house, but there was no answer when I knocked on the door. I continued on home, feeling a bit nervous now about breaking the news to my aunt and uncle. When I walked in the back door, Uncle Mervyn was sitting at the table reading the newspaper, a cup of tea on the table in front of him, his pipe stuck in his mouth. Aunt Beryl, mixing up a batch of dumplings in a bowl for the evening meal, smiled broadly when she saw me. My uncle lowered his paper, an equally pleased expression on his face.

"Good news, Evan," my aunt said. "Tell him, Mervyn."

"Well," my uncle began, removing his pipe from his mouth. "I was down at the ironmonger's this morning, and I bumped into Ned Byford. He's the chap I told you about who runs the engine sheds in Cwmparc. He told me he has a job for you," he said, shaking his fist for emphasis. "Said in two or three years you could be an engine driver!"

Stunned I sank into a chair opposite my uncle. Their faces fell when I didn't immediately respond the way they were anticipating. "That is good news," I said, picking my words carefully. "Can he hold the job for me for a few months?"

"What on earth for?" my uncle demanded, his expression now turned to anger.

"I signed on with the Borderers this morning."

My aunt's expression changed to one of disbelief as she sank heavily into a chair next to my uncle, putting the bowl on the table with a loud thump. "Oh no, Evan, no," she said clutching her stomach. My uncle was speechless.

"It will only be for a short while," I said. "They told us—Dai Wilkins and Rhys Jones and me—that the war would be over in a few months. I'll be back before you know it." My aunt pulled out a handkerchief from her apron pocket and dabbed her eyes.

"Now don't fret, Beryl," my uncle said at last, his anger subsiding. "I can't say I blame the lad. I'd have signed up myself if I were a bit younger. It's this bloody war," he continued, uncharacteristically swearing in front of my aunt. "Tell you what, I'll talk to Ned on Monday about holding the job. He can't hold it against the lad for wanting to serve his country"

My aunt was not persuaded. "Why didn't you tell us you were going?" she said. "I don't want you going off to war, not after my cousin Andrew was killed in the last one."

"The Boer War went on for three years, Auntie. This one's different. It will probably be over before I even finish my training." My aunt continued wiping her eyes. "I just wouldn't feel right, Auntie, staying here when all the lads are signing up."

"What does Gwyn think about it?" she asked.

"I haven't told her yet, but she'll be happy to hear it. She's been after me to get out of the mine ever since I started. Right after supper I'm going down to tell her."

Conversation was only sporadic when we sat down to our meal, the reality and uncertainties of war weighing heavily on the three of us. My aunt was very upset, and Uncle Mervyn, despite his reassuring words, did not seem completely reconciled either. I could hardly blame him, given that he'd at last been successful in finding me a railway job. I left for Gwyn's house without waiting for my cup of tea.

§

"Evan Morgan, have you gone completely out of your mind?" Gwyn screamed at me as I stood facing her in her mother's kitchen. Mrs. Williams, sitting by the kitchen stove said nothing, just stared at me over her spectacles as she paused from her sewing.

"What are you talking about?" I retorted. "You've been nagging me about my job for years!"

"Of course I want you out of the mine! But not so you'll go off somewhere and get yourself killed!" She sat down and held her face in her hands.

I sat next to Gwyn and put my arm across her shoulders. "I won't be gone long. They told us at the recruitment center the war would be over in a few months. There's not much chance I'll end up at the front."

"And what did you expect them to tell you?" she said, angrily shrugging off my arm. "That the war will go on for years and you're likely to get shot or blown up? They don't get men to sign up that way."

"It'll be good for him," Gwyn's mother growled. "Make a man of him."

"Don't you think he's man enough after three years in the mine?" Gwyn glared at her mother.

"Look Gwyn. Lots of the lads are signing up. Dai and Rhys were with me today. I wouldn't feel right if I weren't doing my bit. I'll be back in no time."

"Aye, back to the mine," she said bitterly.

"No, I've had it with mining. I'll never go back there. My uncle said there's a good job for me with the railway. He's sure they'll hold it for me 'til I get back."

Her expression softened. "Let's go for a walk. I fancy a shandy." I helped Gwyn on with her coat and wrapped my scarf around my neck to guard against the January cold. "We won't be gone long, Mum," she said as we headed out the door. "I'll bring you back a cider." Her mother went back to her sewing without saying anything.

"She'd rather I brought her a whiskey," Gwyn remarked as we headed down the main road, her arm linked in mine. "I don't feel like talking in front of her."

"I think she's happy I'm going off," I said. "She never did take much of a shine to me."

"Don't be daft, Evan. She's very fond of you. But why, I'll never know."

A welcoming coal fire greeted us as we entered the Old Lamb Inn, crowded as usual on a Saturday night, the air thick with smoke. A noisy darts game was in progress to the left of the fireplace. We sat at the only empty table, a small one, stained with spilled beer and cigarette burns, and close enough to the entrance that we caught cold draughts every time someone entered or left the room. I picked up a pint of bitter and a shandy, and a bottle of cider for Gwyn's mother, and brought them to the table.

"Do you really think the war will be over soon?" Gwyn asked, sipping her drink.

"It's what everyone's saying, not just the recruiters."

"Well, I hope you're right. I don't like the idea of not seeing you for months on end. But what's done is done."

"I won't be far away, just up in Brecon. And if I get sent somewhere after my training, I'll write to you every chance I get. Then when the war's over and I'm demobbed, well . . . maybe we should think about . . ."

"About what?"

I reached over and took her hand. "Look, Hugh and Mary seem really happy together, married and with young Dylan and all. Why can't we . . . ?"

Her eyebrows raised. "Why, Evan Morgan! Are you making some kind of proposal?"

"Aye, I think I am." I blushed.

"Well, if it's marriage you're thinking of, couldn't you at least get down on your knee and do it properly?"

"Now that would be a bit out of character for an ordinary coalmining chap like me," I said, seeing the delight in her eyes.

"If you were ordinary, Evan, I wouldn't be sitting at this table with you." She reached out and touched my cheek. "You're the best thing that ever happened to me. Even if you are a bit daft at times."

I took her hand in mine. "And you're the best thing that happened to me. Ever since I first saw you at Bodringallt."

She laughed. "Remember that chap sitting on his lav? I'll never forget that day." She took another sip of her shandy.

"I'd noticed you well before that," I said. "I was just too shy to say anything."

"I'd noticed you too. At chapel, before I saw you in school. That was a long time ago."

The pub door opened and Mr. Surtees and his wife Doris brought in a gust of cold air. "Evening, Evan," he said, patting my shoulder and winking at Gwyn. His rasping voice advertised lungs ravaged by decades of coal dust and cigarette smoke.

"Evening, Mr. Surtees," I said as the couple crossed the room to join friends at a table near the fireplace. I drained my glass. "So it's settled then. We'll get married once the war's over?"

"I might consider the proposition," she said with a mischievous smile. "Ask me again when you're demobbed and I'll give the matter serious consideration."

§

I worked one more week at the mine, and then took a week off before I had to report to the barracks in Brecon. On Monday I helped my aunt with the washing, pounding the clothes in the copper, rinsing them in cold water and turning the handle of the mangle while she fed the sodden clothes through the wooden rollers. After lunch I walked to Cwmparc and sought out Ned Byford at the engine sheds to thank him for the job offer.

Two panier locomotives, powerful and ghostlike in the gloom of the engine shed, sat idle, while outside, switching engines belched steam as they shunted coal cars from one track to another before making their runs to the valley collieries. "Come see me again when the war's over," Byford said, shaking my hand. "I'm sure we'll find something for you. A lot of the men are joining up and we're getting a bit shorthanded." As I turned to leave he added, "The Borderers will show those murdering Huns a thing or two." I nodded, and headed back to Ystrad with the nagging thought that there seemed to be a lot of murdering going on all around over in Europe. Just as long as it was over before I had to get involved.

I spent the rest of the week relaxing and reading and helping around the house. Twice I went to Tonypandy to meet Gwyn for lunch at a tea house near her bank. One day after lunch we had separate photographs taken at a studio near the bank, photographs to carry with us when we were separated. I also bought a small suitcase and linen kitbag to hold my toilet articles. All too quickly the week was over, and with an increasing feeling of nervousness I prepared my mind for army life.

Gwyn and her mother came over for a goodbye Sunday dinner, a nice pork roast with Brussels sprouts and roast potatoes. To everyone's surprise, and with more than his usual bluntness, my uncle asked: "So when are you two lovebirds getting married?"

"Oh. Mervyn, what a thing to say!" my aunt rejoined.

"As a matter of fact I asked Gwyn to marry me after I'm demobbed," I said through a mouthful of potatoes. "But she told me where to get off."

"I did not!" Gwyn said, blushing. "I said I'd consider his offer. For all I know, he'll be bringing a mademoiselle back with him from Paris."

"If I get there, which is highly unlikely," I said. "Then I may bring a couple back, one for you, Uncle."

Gwyn punched me on the arm. "Get on with you!"

"As long as she does my washing and ironing," my aunt said as she brought out a quivering pink blancmange she had made in her rabbit-shaped mold. "Gwyn's such a nice girl," she said, placing her hand on Gwyn's mother's arm. Gwyn blushed anew and Wynnifred Williams actually smiled.

I said goodbye to Gwyn on her doorstep that evening because she had to leave for her job in Tonypandy early the next morning. Next day I bade my uncle farewell as he left on his bicycle for work, and I hugged my aunt who had cried on and off throughout breakfast. At last, with my suitcase packed with a change of clothing, toilet kit and some books to read, and with a lot less bravado than I'd felt the day before, I set out for Brecon with Dai and Rhys to begin my education in the art of war.

Chapter 6

"Louder!" the drill sergeant shouted as I lunged with my bayonet.

Now there's nothing that makes a chap feel more like a bloody idiot than screaming like a banshee while charging a straw dummy with a bayonet. I suppose soldiers the world over are taught the same way, but that didn't make me feel any less a fool. Yelling with all the force of your lungs scares the daylights out of the enemy, we were told. I had this vision of a field full of soldiers, all screaming their heads off, and charging at one another with bayonets. War seemed pretty ridiculous at times. Staying home with your family and earning a living in a civilized job made a lot more sense; although I wasn't sure coalmining was all that civilized.

Soldiering, I was quick to learn, was a lot tougher than I'd anticipated. It had taken us, Dai, Rhys and me, less than two hours to reach Brecon and the sprawling barracks that was home to the South Wales Borderers. In short order we were sworn in, issued kit bags, uniforms and blankets and assigned canvas cots in an expansive stone building, one of several lining the parade ground. From then on, when we weren't in classrooms learning battle tactics, weaponry and first aid, we were either marching or running.

Drill sergeants marched us from one end of the parade ground to the other until keeping in step and swinging arms to shoulder height became routine. They ran us over the rugged hills of Brecon Beacons with heavy packs on our backs and rifles at the ready until we were ready to drop from exhaustion. Range officers kept us at the firing range from sunrise to sunset until our aim was true and we were half deaf from the din of rifle fire. We disassembled our Lee Enfield rifles every evening so that cleaning and oiling became second nature. The company commander threatened us with every punishment in the military code, even death, if we did not obey orders unquestioningly. And when they were through with us, we were ready for any eventuality that the demands of war might thrust upon us—or so we thought. It was frighteningly efficient.

Instilled with the pride that goes with being part of an elite regiment, we ended our training with a full dress parade, brass buttons and buckles gleaming, marching to the regimental band's spirited rendition of *Men of*

Harlech. But there was one thing we hadn't counted on: the war was still being fought with the same ferocity as when we had joined up.

Still in our uniforms and a lot fitter than when we had first reported for duty, Dai, Rhys and I—now comrades in arms—took the train back to Ystrad. Ahead lay a week's leave before we had to report back to Brecon for deployment abroad. We weren't told where, but everyone assumed it would be France or Belgium.

I went straight to Gwyn's house where she greeted me with a bear hug, holding me tightly for a good minute or more. When she finally let go her eyes were moist. "Well, you do look handsome in your uniform," she said. "How long will you be home?"

"Just a week," I replied. "Then it's back to Brecon."

"Will you be staying in Brecon then? That's nice and close."

"No, Gwyn. We're shipping out. I have no idea where we'll be going."

Her expression changed and I could see fear, even panic, in her eyes. "You're going to the front, aren't you?" she said, her voice almost a whisper.

"I don't know . . ."

"Bloody hell!" she exploded. "What about the war being over before you finished training? God almighty!"

I'd never heard Gwyn swear before and I was taken aback at the desperation behind her words. I pulled her towards me, her face wet with tears.

"Gwyn, I don't know where I'll be going. I figure it will be somewhere in Europe. But I don't want you worrying about me. I can take care of myself, and I promise you I'll be back as soon as the war ends."

She didn't reply for some time, just held on to me. She took a handkerchief from her sleeve and wiped her eyes. At last she said, "All right, Evan. I'm going to hold you to that promise. Now, let's make the most of the time we have left."

§

The week passed quickly and none too happily, what with Gwyn and Aunt Beryl being so upset. I was pretty naïve about the realities of war when I'd enlisted. I knew well enough now that I could be killed at the front. Or I might come home missing a limb or two, or disfigured, even blinded. Would I be able to earn a living then? Would Gwyn still want me?

I walked into Tonypandy one afternoon to meet Gwyn on her way home from work. I went a little early to pick up a piece of haddock for Aunt Beryl from the fishmonger on the main road. From the fish shop I crossed the street, skirting dollops of horse manure and bicyclists heading home from work, to admire a shiny, yellow Morris Oxford with black mudguards parked outside the town hall. Motorcars were a rare sight this far up the valley, although I'd seen quite a few in Cardiff. I turned my eyes away from the car and saw Gwyn, her head covered with a scarf, leaving her bank. She spotted me immediately.

"Bought yourself a new motorcar, have you?" she laughed as she joined me.

"Aye, but you'll have to walk because I can't afford the petrol. What's that you're carrying?"

She handed me a newspaper-wrapped package. "Here's something for you to take with you when you go. A couple of American books I bought on my lunch break." I unwrapped the package and looked at the titles, one a novel, *The Last of the Mohicans,* by James Fenimore Cooper, the other a small volume, *Poems Here at Home,* by James Whitcomb Riley.

"I know poetry isn't your cup of tea, Evan, but this one's different. Americans have a funny way of talking, judging from some of the poems."

"I'll treasure these," I said. "I'll save them for when I go away, so whenever I'm reading them I'll be thinking of you."

"I want you to think of me all the time, not just when you're reading these books."

"Aye, Gwyn, I know I will. I'm going to miss you so much . . ."

"Don't talk like that or you'll get me crying again."

I lay in bed that night fingering the books Gwyn had given me before putting them aside and picking up my copy of *Bleak House.* I was almost at the end and I wanted to finish the book and get it back to the library before I returned to Brecon, but the candle on my bed stand was flickering and I had to strain my eyes to read the fine print. I rested the book on my chest and put an arm behind my head, not ready yet for sleep. I'd read most of what Dickens had written, just this one and a couple more to go.

I thought back, as I often did, to when I'd taken up reading as a serious pastime, when I'd begun my love affair with Charles Dickens. It began with an incident in Miss Pinchen's second-year geography class at Tonypandy. Aeroplanes were all the rage then, with most of us still in a state of disbelief that something that heavy could actually defy gravity. Rhys Jones, sitting at the back of the class, had constructed a paper aeroplane, which he sent soaring forwards to land next to my desk. I picked it up and dispatched it back in his direction just as Miss Pinchen, with exquisite timing, arrived at the classroom door.

She glared at me as she placed a stack of papers on the table at the front of the room. "Morgan, pick that thing up immediately and take it directly to the headmaster," she said, her eyes skewering me. "And tell the headmaster exactly why I've sent you."

Sheepishly I retrieved the paper plane. Rhys kept his head down, but I could see the grin on his face. Snickers from the other pupils accompanied me as, red-faced, I left the classroom and walked slowly down the long corridor to the headmaster's office. Aled Edwards had a reputation as one who brooked no improper behavior, so it was with much trepidation that I knocked on his door.

"Enter!" the headmaster's voice boomed.

I entered his office, a dark-paneled chamber lined with bookshelves and a single curtained window facing the playing field. Gray haired, dressed in a tweed suit and black academic gown, the headmaster sat behind his heavy oaken desk reading from a book propped up on his knee. He barely glanced at me. After what seemed like a full minute he flipped to the beginning of his book and began reading. "It was the best of times, it was the worst of times. It was the age of wisdom, it was the age of foolishness." He raised his head and looked at me through wire-rimmed spectacles, his bushy eyebrows accentuating his penetrating gaze. "Do those words mean anything to you, Morgan?"

"Aye, Sir," I said, astonished that he knew my name. "Charles Dickens, Sir, *A Tale of Two Cities.*"

"Hmm," Edwards said. "So you've read the book."

"Aye, Sir. It was a Christmas present from my aunt and uncle."

"And what else of Dickens have you read?"

"We read *A Christmas Carol* at Bodringallt, Sir."

"Is that all?"

"Just those two, Sir."

The headmaster turned his gaze to the paper aeroplane. "Is there some good reason why you are holding that piece of paper?" he asked.

I lowered my eyes. "Miss Pinchen told me to bring it to you, Sir. She caught me throwing it in the classroom."

"Look at me, boy!" the headmaster shouted. "You don't look down when you're holding a conversation with someone. You look them in the eye." He reached out his hand. "Give that to me." He took the paper aeroplane, studied it for a second or two, then sailed it across his office to a landing under a table near the window.

"The age of wisdom or the age of foolishness? Which is it to be with you, Morgan? Your marks here are commendable enough that I expect better from you. I expect wisdom, Morgan, not *foolishness,*" he said, emphasis on the last word.

Reaching for the bookshelf behind him, the headmaster pulled a volume from the middle of a matching leather-bound set and handed it to me. "As punishment for your *foolishness*"—again the emphasis—"you are to read this book, and one week hence, at the end of the school day, you will present yourself at this office, at which time you will tell me about what you have read. We will discuss the book, Morgan. Is that understood?"

"Aye, Sir," I said, relieved that the headmaster hadn't resorted to the cane.

"Now get out of here and apologize to Miss Pinchen for your foolishness," he thundered. "The next time you get sent to this office, for whatever infraction, you will regret the day you were born. Do I make myself clear?"

"Aye, Sir. I'm sorry, Sir." I turned to leave the office.

"Take that thing with you," he said, nodding towards the table. "And next time you choose to play with paper aeroplanes, fold the wings down. They'll fly better."

I hurried back to the classroom to offer my apology, dropping the object of my humiliation in a waste paper basket in the hallway. I glanced at the book title, *Great Expectations*. When Miss Pinchen saw the book in my hand, a light smile creased her lips. "Apology accepted," she said. "Now, before you return to your desk I want you to stand here and tell the class everything you know about our two outposts of empire, Uganda and Tanganyika."

Once I began reading *Great Expectations* I was captivated, even found myself neglecting my homework, so reluctant was I to turn away from the trials and tribulations of Pip. My discussion with Aled Edwards the following week lasted a full hour, interrupted only when his secretary served us tea. The headmaster raised such insights into plot and character that I wanted to go back and start at the beginning, and to devour whatever else Dickens had to offer. From that day forward I was seldom without a book to keep me company—and my remaining time at Tonypandy had more to do with wisdom than foolishness.

I snuffed out the candle and rolled over on my side. Tomorrow, I decided, I would look in on Aled Edwards.

§

After breakfast I sat by the stove and finished reading *Bleak House*, so much grimmer than Dickens's earlier novels that I was not in the best of moods when I walked to Tonypandy to return the book; but I brightened considerably after meeting Gwyn for lunch at the tea house. She seemed much happier to see me out of uniform. I walked her back to the bank and continued on to the school.

"Enter!" boomed the familiar voice as I knocked on the headmaster's door. I was surprised to find boxes scattered around the floor and Aled

Edwards, still in the familiar academic gown, pulling books from his shelves. He placed an armful of books on his desk and stared at me. "A familiar face," he said. "Evan Morgan, I believe."

"Aye, Sir. I didn't think you'd remember me."

"Sometimes I don't," he replied. "Now what are you up to, Evan? Come sit here by the fireplace."

I was struck by the fact that he called me by my first name, no longer the formality of school days. We sank into the same worn leather chairs I remembered from our book discussion years earlier.

"Are you moving, Sir?"

"I'm retiring at the end of the term," the headmaster replied as he kicked an empty cardboard carton out of the way. "I'm doing some advanced packing."

"I can't picture the school without you."

"At my age one gets tired easily." He picked up a pipe and tobacco pouch from the table next to his chair. "It's time for a more relaxed lifestyle. They've hired a good man to replace me. What about you? Still at the coalmine are you?" He tamped a wad of tobacco into the bowl.

"I've joined the Borderers," I said. "Second Battalion. We're shipping out in a couple of days."

His expression clouded. "Why, Evan? You didn't have to go, not with your mining job."

"I know, Sir. To be honest, I thought the war would be over by now. I was looking for a way out of the mine, and this seemed like a good opportunity."

"And what will you do when the war ends?" He lit a match and drew on his pipe.

"I should have a job waiting for me with the railway."

Aled Edwards pushed the pipe to the side of his mouth. "Have you given any more thought to continuing your education? I always wanted you to go to Aberystwyth."

"An impossible dream, Sir. I'd never have enough money."

"I could help you get a scholarship," he said, staring intently at me. "I have friends at the university. A word in the right ear can open doors."

"They'd never take on a coalminer."

"There's no good reason why they would not take on a coalminer if he has brains enough. You be sure to come and see me once this stupid war is over."

"So you think it's stupid too," I said.

The headmaster removed his glasses, breathed on the lenses and wiped them on a handkerchief. "No one with any common sense sees any good in this war, Evan. All wars are stupid when you come down to it. Frankly,

I thought you'd have more sense than to sign up, but I understand your motives."

"Well, Sir," I said. "I won't take any more of your time. I just wanted to say goodbye—and to tell you I've read almost all of Dickens."

His face broke into a broad smile. "And I've read them all at least twice. I'm glad you came in, Evan. I'd like you to stay longer but I have a meeting with some pupils in a few minutes, pupils who need a bit of straightening out. Just like you did once when you were their age," he said, his eyes twinkling.

"Aye, I'll not forget that day," I said. "*Great Expectations* was your punishment."

"I have great expectations for all my pupils." He stood and offered his hand. "Now don't forget. I'll expect to see you once the war is over. The new headmaster's secretary will know my address."

§

Sunday, my last day at home before returning to Brecon, everyone tried their best to be cheerful, but with the war news not getting any brighter, the tension among my aunt and uncle and Gwyn was played out in strained conversation and abortive attempts at humor. Myself, I was conflicted by a sense of dread of impending battle and excitement at the prospect of new adventures far from the confines of my Rhondda home.

For dinner Aunt Beryl prepared a nice rabbit stew, one of my favorites, and afterwards Gwyn and I strolled arm in arm up the hill above Victoria Street to the towering chestnut tree where we had sealed our childhood infatuation. We sat against its thick trunk looking out over the sunlit valley, our arms around each other. A stiff breeze disturbed the branches and propelled brown leaves down into the bracken.

After a prolonged silence Gwyn, her head resting on my shoulder, said, "I want you to take me with you."

"I can't . . ."

"I know," she said, squeezing my hand. "What I mean is . . . Just think of me being with you, wherever you go. If you're in the trenches, I'll be there holding your hand. When you go to one of those French cafés, imagine me sitting across the table from you. And when you lie down at night, feel my head on the pillow next to you. I want you to keep me with you always."

"That I will, Gwyn," I said, my voice choking. "That I will."

"I wish my mum would go away tonight so you could spend it with me."

I tightened my grip about her. "Fat chance of that," I said. "Or for my aunt and uncle to disappear for the night. But I'll be home soon enough and we'll have a lifetime ahead of us."

Next morning Gwyn, who had arranged to be at work late, walked me to the station. She held my hands in hers as we awaited the train, while Dai and Rhys stood away from us smoking cigarettes. When the train arrived amidst clouds of steam and the squealing of brakes, Gwyn's resolve failed her and her eyes misted. I held her closely for our final kiss goodbye, then detached myself and entered the train. I leaned out of the carriage window and held her hand.

"I will marry you, Evan," she said. "Come back to me."

Gwyn's face ran with tears as the train pulled slowly away from the platform. I watched her waving her handkerchief, getting smaller and smaller until she was just a tiny figure in the distance, and then the track curved and she disappeared from view. I brought my head back inside where Dai and Rhys sat silently without their usual cheerful banter.

§

Dearest Gwyn,

I'm writing this on the deck of a troopship somewhere in the Mediterranean. I would have written sooner, but ever since we left Pembroke Dock the sea has been so rough, especially in the Bay of Biscay, that it was impossible to put anything on paper and have it legible. Most of the lads on board were seasick, and I didn't feel very good myself for the first couple of days, but then my stomach got used to it. This morning we passed through the Strait of Gibraltar and suddenly the sea became nice and calm and the sun came out and it's very warm.

We had a nice send-off from Brecon, crowds lining the streets, cheering, when we marched from the barracks to the station. They'd let the children out of school and they were there too, waving little flags. The regimental band led the way. It made us very proud to be South Wales Borderers.

By the time you get this letter you will have read in the papers that we've started a new front in Turkey. I don't know if I'm supposed to write about this, but since it will be old news, I don't see why they would censor it. We are going first to Alexandria for a bit of shore leave and some extra training before we head for the Dardanelles for a landing on the Gallipoli Peninsula. This will be nothing like France or Belgium. No one expects the Turks to put up much of a fight, and we should be in Constantinople by June. Then there will be a supply route to Russia, and the generals expect the war to be over by the end of the year.

I'm excited about seeing The Dardanelles. Remember when you told me about Byron swimming the Hellespont? Well, that's right where we'll be. I wish you could share it with me. I heard that that Cambridge chap

Rupert Brooke, another of your favorite poets, is on one of the troopships. I once joked that you liked him because he's so handsome, not because of his poetry. (Remember? You said he's a lot more handsome than me and I'd better watch out!) I wish I could meet Brooke so I could tell him how you used to recite his poems to me, but he's an officer so there's not much chance of that.

Speaking of poetry, I've read all of Riley's poems, and I like them a lot more than I expected. I'm going to start memorizing them in my spare time so that when I get home I can impress you by reciting them when we go on our walks. Then you won't be able to resist me! I've also started reading Last of the Mohicans. It's a wonderful story and I'm sure I'll be reading it more than once.

I'm looking forward to Alexandria. Our letters will be collected for posting once we get there. I remember learning at school about the lighthouse at Alexandria, one of the Seven Wonders of the World, but I don't think anything is left of it. Still, it will be grand to see such an exotic place, not at all like the Rhondda.

Gwyn, I think of you constantly, and I can't wait to hold you in my arms again. I'm not homesick for Wales, just homesick for you. Keep me in your thoughts always. I'll write again soon.

With all my love,
Evan

Alexandria offered a welcome respite from the crowded conditions of the troopship, and it felt good to have solid ground under our feet. But training under that blistering Egyptian sun was as tough as anything we had endured at Brecon. Worst of all was practicing climbing up and down rope ladders on the side of the ship—Jacob's ladders we called them. We had time to ourselves on occasion to explore the city, swim at the beach, even to ride a camel, thanks to an enterprising local who brought two moth-eaten beasts along for our entertainment. One evening, against the admonition of our company commander, Dai, Rhys and I followed several other soldiers to a brothel in the Baquth district of the city. There I was introduced to the mysteries of womanhood by a voluptuous, dark-skinned beauty not much older than myself, who recognized immediately my inexperience and who guided me with humor and understanding. All too soon we were back on board and heading north for Gallipoli.

I was standing at the ship's rail with Dai when Rhys joined us.

"Did you hear Rupert Brooke is dead?" Rhys said. I felt a wrenching in my stomach.

"Who's he?" Dai asked.

"A poet," I said. "A bloody good one."

"Was he killed then?" Dai asked. "Have we already invaded?"

"I heard he died of some illness," Rhys said. "Blood poisoning, or something like that. They buried him on a Greek island."

Poor, dear Gwyn. She so much loved his poetry. How anguished she would be when she learned that such a gifted young man would no longer fill pages with his dazzling verse.

"I have to write to Gwyn," I said.

§

We arrived off the Gallipoli coast, joining a vast armada of warships, late on a Friday afternoon. The beauty and serenity of the scene captivated me, turquoise water leading to a landscape of gently sloping hills, rising to the high point called Achi Baba which, we were told, was to be our first objective. The green hills, fading to purple in the receding daylight, breathed the scent of spring, perfumed with the nectar of wildflower and birdsong. I was, I thought, looking at an earthly paradise. I was soon to learn I was seeing the gates to Hell.

Part II

Gallipoli

You smug-faced crowds with kindling eye
Who cheer when soldier lads march by,
Sneak home and pray you'll never know
The hell where youth and laughter go.
                    Siegfried Sassoon,
                    Suicide in the Trenches

Chapter 7

It was Saturday morning. We had crowded onto the deck of the battleship *Cornwallis* to listen to Major Geoffrey Alburton outline the strategy for the next day's landings. A large crudely drawn map of the southern end of the Gallipoli Peninsula served as a backdrop. Around us the sea lay calm, just a few ripples brought to life by the morning breeze. To the east a gradually brightening sky outlined the heights of Achi Baba in silhouette, but the still-dark landing zones ashore seemed lifeless and eerily quiet.

The major rapped his baton on the table and scanned our faces to make certain he had our attention. Tall and broad-shouldered, dapper in his crisp uniform and trim moustache, Alburton was every inch the professional soldier. He pointed with his baton at the eastern tip of a crescent-shaped bay. "We will be landing here at S Beach below Eski Hisarlik. We will transfer to lighters before dawn tomorrow and launches will tow us in as soon as it's light enough to see our objective. There will be a bit of a cliff to climb, but we don't expect much opposition because the Turks have concentrated their forces at more accessible landing sites." He paused to light a cigarette.

"The main landing by the Dublin and Munster Fusiliers and the Hampshire Regiment will be here at V beach at the western end of Morto Bay near Cape Helles," the major continued in his clipped Oxford accent as he moved his baton across the bay. "That's about four miles from where we'll be going ashore. Once we land we'll move west and cut the Turks off from the rear."

In rapid succession he moved his baton around the western end of the peninsula—Lancashire fusiliers at W Beach, Royal Fusiliers at X Beach, Anzacs at Gaba Tepe further north. A diversionary French force would be landing across the strait at Kum Kaleh on the Asiatic shore.

"Any questions?" the major barked.

One soldier raised his hand. "What about Turkish defenses, Sir?"

"We expect some opposition, obviously. They know we're coming. But there will be a heavy bombardment by the ships' guns prior to the landing to soften them up. I don't anticipate any difficulties. I expect you men—we expect all our forces—to be resolute and not deterred by a few heathen Turks. Understood?" His eyes ranged over the sea of faces before him.

"No more questions?" He nodded towards one of our company officers, Lieutenant Harry Whittaker, who stood to the major's right, hands behind his back. The lieutenant, who looked about my age, stepped forward.

"Major Alburton has asked me to liaison with the Fusiliers at V Beach. I will be leaving for their landing ship, the S.S. *River Clyde*, at noon. I need a volunteer to accompany me as runner." Runner was a job nobody wanted because it meant carrying messages between officers all over the place, and the poor sap had to go at a gallop to keep in his officer's good graces.

Whittaker looked around the sea of faces, but no hands were raised. I had the misfortune to be in the front row. "You!" he pointed at me. "Name?"

Accepting the inevitable, I said, "Private Morgan, Sir,"

"Thank you, Private Morgan, for volunteering. Meet me here on deck at five minutes before noon with your rifle and pack."

"Lucky you," Dai whispered in my ear. "No bloody cliff to climb."

A biplane from an aerodrome on the island of Tenedos flew overhead on a reconnaissance. We looked up with wonder, for this was the first time most of us had seen a real aeroplane. With its thin fuselage and wings linked together with struts, it seemed to me almost too fragile to stay in the air. The pilot's head, clad in a leather helmet and goggles, was clearly visible, as was the machine gun pointing out in front of him.

Once the noise of the plane's engine faded, Major Alburton spoke again. "You men will assemble here on deck at 0400 hours tomorrow with full gear. Biscuits and coffee will be served before we transfer to the lighters. The naval bombardment will begin once it becomes light enough for the gunners to see their targets. I wish you luck. I know you will acquit yourselves in the finest tradition of the South Wales Borderers." He turned abruptly and strode off towards the bridge.

§

"I'd rather go with our own lads," I said to Lieutenant Whittaker as we waited for the picket boat.

"So would I," Whittaker replied. "But I have my orders, and so do you. We'll be back with them soon enough."

We clambered down the Jacob's ladder to the gently rocking picket boat piloted by a sailor who couldn't have been more than seventeen or eighteen years old. Our destination, the *River Clyde*, was about as unimposing a bucket of a tramp steamer as one could imagine, in stark contrast to the massive battleships and cruisers that lay in wait for the coming onslaught.

"Where did you find a tub like that?" I shouted to the sailor as we approached, making myself heard above the throbbing of the boat's powerful motor.

"She's an old collier," he said, holding on to his hat as the wind picked up.

"Well that's all I need," I said. "I join up to get away from the coalmines, and where do I end up? On a bloody coal ship!"

The sailor laughed. "You should feel right at home then. This one's fitted out for invasion." He pointed. "See those ports cut in the side and those gangways? They're to give the troops a fast way onto the beach."

"You mean the ship's going all the way in?"

"That's right. She'll be grounded, but most of the chaps will go in on lighters first. They're the landing craft you can see tied up aft. We've more than two thousand men on board."

Whittaker followed our conversation with bemused silence. "What part of Wales are you from, Morgan?" he asked as we pulled alongside the *River Clyde* and the picket boat's motor quieted to a low rumble.

"The Rhondda, Sir. Ystrad. What about you, Sir?"

"Merthyr Tydfil," he replied.

"I'd bet you weren't a miner, Sir."

"No, I was studying economics at Aberystwyth University."

"That's where my headmaster wanted me to go. Not much hope of that though."

"This war will probably change things," the lieutenant said. "When it's over, maybe I'll see you there. Now, let's get a move on."

What did he mean, I wondered as I followed him up the gangway, about the war changing things? It was the barriers of wealth and class that kept ordinary lads like me out of universities and stuck us in coalmines and other menial jobs. Would a grateful nation reward its returning soldiers by lowering those barriers? I had my doubts. Or perhaps he'd meant that the world would be in such a mess that wealth and class would no longer have meaning.

§

For the rest of the day I stayed close to Lieutenant Whittaker as he conferred with officers on board the *River Clyde,* but I received no further instructions. I spent time chatting with some Irish troops who seemed remarkably nonchalant about the next day's mission. I looked out at the landing site, a gravelly beach under the shadow of a ruined fort. A small village of stone houses lay beyond, and above that the green hills sloping up to distant Achi Baba. Scattered groups of Turkish soldiers, some with binoculars, stared out at the formidable array of warships.

"You'd think the buggers would get away while they have the chance," a fusilier standing alongside me said in a rich Irish brogue.

I shrugged. "It's their homeland. Maybe they want to keep it that way."

Space was too cramped for writing letters, so I settled down on the deck, pulled out my copy of Riley's poems and began reading from the beginning. Since there was no bunk for me below, I spent an uncomfortable night lying on the hard deck, trying to catch a little sleep before the action.

At half past three in the morning, Sunday April 25, sergeants roused the men from their bunks, and while they crowded onto the deck, jostling one another with heavy packs and rifles, I sought out Lieutenant Whittaker and stayed by his side as sailors served rolls and bitter-tasting hot coffee. At four-thirty, in silence, the men began shuffling down the gangways into the five lighters now lined up alongside. A single picket boat manned by two white-uniformed sailors lay in wait a short distance away, its motor throbbing. I recognized one of the sailors as the one who'd brought the lieutenant and me from the *Cornwallis*. We followed the fusiliers into the last lighter and found ourselves crowded shoulder to shoulder near the back.

"Now we wait," Whittaker said, looking at his watch. "The bombardment should begin soon."

The men chatted quietly, making light of the job ahead. Conversation ended with the deafening roar of large-bore naval guns, and the tranquil beauty of Gallipoli gave way under an assault of cordite and shrapnel. Massive battleships shifted sideways from the recoil of their cannons, and the concussion jarred my body like an electric shock and set my limbs and back tingling. The picket boat's motor increased its tempo and the lighters began moving slowly towards the distant beach, eerily desolate in the early morning light. Standing on tiptoe we could see masses of earth and smoke erupt in the hills above the beach under the relentless rain of artillery shells. Nothing, surely, could survive such a barrage.

Abruptly the naval guns fell silent and only the chatter of the picket's motor disturbed the silence. No words were spoken as, with increasing momentum, we approached the shore. Soldiers checked belts and packs, inserted bullets into chambers, attached bayonets and waited for the unknown. After a tantalizingly long period which gave any surviving Turks ample time to return to their defensive positions, the lighters grounded onto gravel and sand, and we had to steady ourselves to remain upright.

Even before the lighter gates were thrown open, rifle and machine gun fire sent bullets clanging against metal and whipped surf into foam. Then the staccato of small arms blended with the screams of the wounded and dying as men poured from the lighters into withering gunfire. The first off our landing craft were cut down immediately, their riddled bodies careening into the sea, and those still at the front absorbed the full brunt of machine gun fire. Blood and brain mixed with bone fragments flew back in my face. I turned away and wiped my eyes clear with my sleeve, certain I was about to die. Then the machine gun sought a different target.

"Christ Almighty, move!" I screamed as the men ahead of me stood immobile. With horrifying clarity I realized that everyone in front of me was dead, a collection of corpses packed too closely together to fall. I pushed hard against them and one by one, like dominoes, the lifeless bodies pitched forward. Crouching and holding my rifle close to my chest, I stepped on legs and backs to reach the front of the lighter and into the restless surf, now red with blood. Those behind me followed, some losing their footing on the blood-slick deck as the lighter drifted away under the pull of the strong Dardanelles current. I stumbled up the beach and threw myself under the cover of a low sandbar where dozens of other soldiers had sought refuge.

The remaining men from our lighter, some on hands and knees in the surf, struggled ashore as the machine gun arced back to pick them off. Lieutenant Whittaker fell, half in and half out of the water, and tried to drag himself forward. "Bloody Hell!" I muttered. I laid my rifle across a piece of driftwood and ran back to grab Whittaker by the straps of his pack and pull him behind the sandbar.

Whittaker lay alongside me, grimacing with pain from a wound in his right shoulder. "Well, Morgan, we are in a pickle," he said.

I looked back at the carnage. Soldiers poured from sally ports in the side of the now-grounded collier, and snipers picked them off one by one as they made their way down the gangplanks. The launch that had towed us to shore was now drifting away, the bodies of the two sailors sprawled over the gunwales. For a good fifty yards out the sea ran red. Bodies floated in the water like buoys and covered the lower part of the beach with a deadly blanket. Some who made it ashore tried to breach the barbed wire and were almost immediately killed. It was a bloodbath, pure and simple.

Along with scores of other survivors, many bleeding from wounds, we lay under the protection of the sandbar for well over an hour. Turkish snipers fired intermittently from hiding places in the ruined fort and village. I poked my head up cautiously during a lull in the firing and spotted a lifeless soldier a short distance away lying like a stepping stone atop the barbed wire entanglement. Higher up sat the sandbagged machine gun emplacement that had taken such a toll, and to the right a shallow gully crowned with scrub brush. I ducked back down, waited a few seconds, and then cautiously took another look.

A stepping stone. Could I use the dead soldier to cross the wire? Filled with rage and despair at the hopelessness of our situation, I lay still for several minutes contemplating my next move. We were trapped, and who knew how long it would take the Borderers to reach us. Eventually the Turkish howitzers would find our position. I looked up again and saw the machine gun pointing away from us.

Common sense gave way to desperation. In the face of only occasional sniper fire, I gripped my rifle tightly, climbed over the sandbar and ran headlong at the barbed wire. With a single bound I set my boot squarely on the dead soldier's back and launched myself over the wire, stumbled momentarily, then continued running until I threw myself into the gully under the cover of yellow-flowering gorse.

I lay motionless, waiting for bullets to seek me out, but none came. After several minutes I raised my head and peered through the tangle of brush towards the machine gun emplacement. The gun was still pointing away from me, and I could see part of the gunner's helmet jutting from behind the protective sandbags. Sometimes he moved his head back into full view, then leaned forward again out of sight. I ducked down and checked to make sure no sand had found its way into my rifle barrel. I detached the bayonet and slid it into its sheath on my belt. Avoiding sudden movements I leaned up on my elbows, nudged my helmet back and positioned the rifle atop the lip of the gully under cover of the brush. I sighted on the location where the machine gunner's head had appeared and waited, finger gently squeezing the trigger. Sweat trickled down my back.

The gunner's head appeared momentarily and moved quickly forward again out of sight before I had time to react. I increased tension on the trigger. Seconds later the head appeared in full view as the gunner appeared to be reaching behind him. I squeezed the trigger. The rifle recoiled into my shoulder as the man's head exploded under the impact of the bullet. Another Turk, one I hadn't seen before, came into view, leaning towards his dead comrade. I pulled back the bolt and slammed another round into the chamber, sighted on the man's back and squeezed the trigger. His body swiveled and fell from view.

I ducked down and lay still, panting as if from strenuous exertion, but relieved that I'd accomplished what I'd set out to do. At the same time the reality that I'd probably killed someone revolted me, all that military training notwithstanding.

I became aware of movement behind me—soldiers moving in increasing numbers away from the beach. Some cleared the barbed wire as I had done, while others ran through breaches cut by sappers. They sprinted past with bayonets fixed, and ahead of them Turkish soldiers abandoned their positions and retreated into the hills above the village.

Slowly I pulled myself to my feet and walked over to the gun emplacement. Two bodies, both face up, lay in the hollow, one with a gaping bayonet wound in the stomach. My bullet, apparently, had not finished him off. The other there was no question; what had once been a face was now a grisly mass of tissue and bone. I began shaking.

"What's your name, soldier?" The voice came from behind me. I turned and saw a brawny officer with major's pips on his shoulder and a revolver in his right hand, his uniform wet and smeared with blood.

"Morgan" I said. "Private Evan Morgan."

'Regiment?"

"South Wales Borderers, Sir. Second Division."

"Well done, Private Morgan."

I didn't reply. I couldn't get my mind off the dead soldier's face.

"Well don't just stand there with your finger up your arse," the major said. He gestured with his revolver in the direction of the advancing fusiliers. "There are a lot more Turks to kill."

"I'm Lieutenant Whittaker's runner, Sir," I said. "I have to get back to him."

The major nodded and set off up the hill. After a few paces he turned and said, "I'm putting your name in for a regimental citation." With broad strides he continued on his way. I looked back at the bodies. There were hundreds of dead below me on the beach and in the water, but I was inextricably linked to these two.

Well done? I'd killed a man, smashed his head to pieces so there was no way of knowing if he was old or young, handsome or plain. I wondered if he had a wife and children waiting at home. Or perhaps a girlfriend—someone like Gwyn. I turned away and walked back to the beach.

§

Lieutenant Whittaker sat with his back against the sandbar, his shoulder bandaged and arm in a sling. I sat next to him. Medical corpsmen were all about, tending to the wounded.

"It seems I made a good choice when I picked you, Evan." I was surprised he addressed me by my first name. "That took a lot of grit."

"Grit?"

"Courage. Whatever you want to call it." Whittaker grimaced with pain.

"Grit had nothing to do with it," I said. "I just didn't see the point of sitting here while the Turks used me for target practice."

"If you say so, Private." He removed his helmet and wiped his sleeve across his forehead. "I don't suppose you have a cigarette on you, Evan? Mine are a bit blood soaked."

"I don't smoke, Sir."

Along the beach a detail of soldiers and sailors collected the dead and laid them in rows. It was going to take them a long time; bodies were everywhere, on land and in the water.

"Taking out that machine gun nest was a nice piece of work," Whittaker said. "But pulling me off the beach was bloody stupid. You're lucky you weren't killed."

"I was bloody stupid when I enlisted," I said.

"So was I," he replied. We sat in silence for several minutes staring out to sea, shivering in our wet uniforms.

"I'm being shipped out to the hospital on Imbros," Whittaker said. "There's nothing more you can do for me here. Stay with the Irish troops until our lads make it down."

"Very well, Sir."

He held out his good left hand and I took it. "Good luck, Evan," he said. "I'll not forget what you did."

"Good luck to you, too, Sir," I said. "If you're really lucky, they'll send you home."

I stood up and began back up the slope. Whittaker called after me. "If we meet up in Aberystwyth, the beer's on me."

"Fair enough, Sir"

As I made my way up the hill I replaced the bayonet on my rifle and inserted a fresh round in the chamber. *A lot more Turks to kill.* Even in the confusion of battle I knew I'd crossed a threshold of horror and would never be the same again.

Chapter 8

I never saw Lieutenant Harry Whittaker again. Some time after the landing I heard he had returned to combat after a brief confinement on Imbros, joining a company positioned on our right flank. On the second day back he led a charge against the Turkish lines and was almost immediately cut down by machine gun fire. So much for free beer in Aberystwyth.

For the rest of us the war settled into a routine of trench digging, probing actions and reconnaissance patrols to seek out the enemy's weak points before mounting full-scale attacks; but we made little progress towards our objective to take the heights of Achi Baba. During times when the battlefield was quiet, Dai Wilkins, Rhys Jones and I sought out one another's company, drawn together by our common ties to the Rhondda Valley, school and the coalmine.

Rhys and I had been good friends ever since his family had moved from Caerphilly to Tonypandy, where his father took over the local coal delivery business. Rhys was easily the skinniest boy in our class, with a sunken chest that some of the lads made fun of when our shirts were off for gym lessons. His less than robust stature and his occasional bouts with asthma kept him from rough and tumble sports like rugby; he was content to cheer us on from the sidelines and chase the ball when it was kicked out of bounds. Even now he was still thin as a beanpole. Dai liked to joke that if Rhys turned sideways he'd disappear.

Rhys and I both did well in school. We loved to read and we performed equally well on school exams, so a kind of friendly rivalry developed between us. He liked to remind me of how he got me into trouble with the paper aeroplane in Miss Pinchen's geography class.

"My dad said that when the war's over he's going to buy me a horse and cart so we can expand the coal business," he told me one day.

I tried to imagine Rhys cloaked in protective leather lifting hundredweight sacks of coal on his back and lugging them out to customers' coal bins. It took muscle to do that day in and day out. "That's great, Rhys," I said. "Beats working in the mine."

Dai and Rhys couldn't have been more different. Dai was the despair of his teachers. He had difficulty grasping some of the simplest concepts, and he failed the entrance exam to secondary school. Short and stocky, he compensated for his height by being an aggressive and skillful rugby player. We often reminisced about good times on the playing fields in Ystrad, and I found his cheerful disposition a counterpoint to the grim business of war. Like Rhys and me, he had no desire to go back to the mine when the war was over. "I'm saving my pay so I can learn a trade," he remarked once. "Maybe bricklaying. Something where I can work outdoors."

Back home Hugh Griffith had always been my closest friend. But Dai and Rhys were here and now, and friendship rooted in the bitter conflict bound us together. These days I seldom thought of Hugh. Every working day he limped to his job at the mine to toil in squalor deep underground, hardly ever feeling the sun on his face. Which of us was better off? I asked myself. Yet while I longed for Gwyn's presence, at least Hugh had Mary to come home to at the end of the day,

§

Dearest Gwyn,

It was wonderful to receive your letter and to learn all the news from home. I was sorry to hear your mum's arthritis is worse, but that was grand news about Hugh and Mary. I expect young Dylan will be excited about having a baby brother or sister.

Everything is fine with me and I'm keeping my head down, staying out of trouble, so you don't have to worry. From where I'm sitting I have a lovely view looking out to sea with the island of Imbros off on the horizon. Our commander-in-chief, General Hamilton, has his headquarters there. The water is wonderfully blue, not like the sea at Porthcawl. The hills surrounding me are green and filled with wildflowers, so you can see that life over here is not so bad.

I didn't want to tell her that the scarlet poppies, cornflowers, tulips, thyme and heather had all but disappeared under artillery barrages that turned these once-beautiful hills into a barren landscape of dust and shell craters; that the birds had fled—not a single one left to sweeten the air with its singing. Nor did I want to tell of bodies littering the ground and the awful stench of rotting flesh. And the flies that made life so miserable, swarming over our food, invading our eyes and mouths; and the oppressive heat that kept our bodies in a constant state of perspiration during the day so that we shivered in damp uniforms in the chill of night.

It does get a bit warm here in the middle of the day, but now and again they let us cool off with a swim in the sea. Other than that, when we are not working, I spend my days sitting around reading or chatting

with the lads and waiting for the Turks to decide they've had enough. I actually met a Turkish soldier a few days ago. He seemed like a nice enough fellow, with a family back home, even spoke a little English. They may speak a different language and worship a different way, but when it comes right down to it, they are pretty much like us.

There was no point in going into detail about my encounter with the Turk, the circumstances were too ghastly to recount. It happened during one of the periodic truces to bury the dead. Once the stench became unbearable, an officer, either British or Turkish, waved a white flag and climbed out of his trench to walk tentatively towards the enemy line. An opposing officer, with his own flag, met him halfway. The ritual never changed. One offers the other a cigarette, they chat for a few minutes, pointing this way or that, then shake hands and return to their own trenches. Then at an appointed time the guns fall silent and soldiers from both sides pour out into the wasteland to retrieve their dead. It was an appalling task. With mouths and noses covered with handkerchiefs or scarves, we dragged rotting, fly-infested corpses by their boots to some designated place behind the lines where they were quickly buried.

Toward the end of one recovery detail, a short, mustachioed Turkish soldier approached me. He pulled out a pack of cigarettes, shook one up and offered it.

"Thank you, but I don't smoke," I said.

The Turk nodded and pulled the cigarette out with his lips, cupped his hands against the sea breeze and lit it with a match. "Where you from?" he asked.

"Wales."

"England, Scotland, Wales, Ireland. I learn about Great Britain in school."

"You speak English."

"A little. Not very good. School lessons."

"Good enough," I said. "Where are you from?"

"Alanya. Beautiful town on south coast. Good fish." He reached into his tunic pocket, pulled out a thin wallet and extracted a creased sepia photograph of a young woman with attractive features. She sat in a straight-backed chair, her head covered with a scarf; a girl, perhaps three or four years old, stood at her knee and an older boy stood in back with his hand on his mother's shoulder. "My family," he said, pride in his voice.

"Very nice," I said.

"You have family in Wales?"

I have a girlfriend." I showed him my small photograph of Gwyn.

"*Çok güzel!* Beautiful," he said.

Whistles sounded the time to return to our own trenches. I offered my hand and he took it. "Good luck," I said.

"And to you," he replied. We parted reluctantly to return to the insanity of trying to kill one another.

> *I still enjoy reading Riley's poems and I've memorized a few of them. Dai Wilkins is reading Last of the Mohicans. And as soon as he's finished, I'm going to read it again. Rhys has already read it. We don't have that much time for reading because the officers always find something for us to do.*
>
> *When we first landed I was separated from our lads because one of the officers picked me to be his runner. Just my luck! We went in with some Irish regiments and I was stuck with them for a couple of days before the Borderers joined up with us.*

No point either in telling of the slaughter that took place that day, or that the officer was now dead and the Borderers had made a mess of things. They met almost no opposition when they went ashore and could have relieved us much sooner and saved a lot of lives. But whoever was in charge just sat there drinking bloody tea once they took the heights instead of advancing to encircle the Turks. Same with the Lancashires on our other side. If the generals weren't so bloody timid we could have secured the peninsula by now. Then again, the Turks were putting up one hell of a fight, and their generals knew what they were doing. And they commanded the high ground.

> *I miss you terribly and think of you every day we're apart. I don't know how long we are going to be here because the Turks are not running away like we were told they would. There are times when I feel like digging a hole and crawling in until the war is over. When Reverend Lewis at Chapel talks about a just and loving God, I don't think he knows what he's talking about. I don't think a loving God would allow such senseless killing. The utter stupidity of it all gets to me at times.*
>
> *Please don't pay attention to my complaining or worry about me. As I said, I keep myself out of trouble. I just wish those who get us into wars like this would come to their senses and put a stop to it.*
>
> *They're picking up letters in a few minutes so I have to finish up. Give your mum my best and tell her I hope her arthritis gets better. And be sure to extend my congratulations to Hugh and Mary. I don't get to write to my aunt and uncle as often as I should, so please stop by and read my letters to them. I think of you constantly. Must hurry!*
>
> *With all my love,
Evan*

Afterwards I regretted sending that letter. I wanted to put a cheerful face on what I wrote home, but I had allowed dark thoughts to get the better of me. I must write back quickly, I told myself, to tell Gwyn to disregard my melancholy, that I was just caught in a bad mood. I had slept fitfully the night before, as I usually did, and the straw dummy from Brecon Barracks had mocked me in my dreams.

What the generals had created at Gallipoli was much the same as the trench-lined wasteland the warring armies had inflicted on France and Belgium, and with the passage of weeks with little or no headway, there was no longer any talk of a triumphal march on Constantinople. In our spare time we played cards, held miniature war games pitting scorpions against lizards or cockroaches, and waited for the next order to advance on the Turks. I often wondered how the men managed to keep a sense of humor in the face of such adversity. If it wasn't the heat and flies, it was rain that dripped off our helmets and turned earth to mud. Keeping clean was impossible; we just existed, our faces masked with indifference and fatigue. No doubt our Turkish adversaries shared in the misery.

And then some mindless general in pursuit of personal glory would decide it was time to make another futile charge against the entrenched machine guns as if human life held no value as long as he could report that we were still carrying on the fight.

§

On a gray late-June morning punctuated by intermittent drizzle, Captain Ian Vaughn strode along the trenches, stopping every few yards to voice words of encouragement. We knew the routine. Line up at the ladders, fix bayonets, tighten packs, wait and pray, terrified.

"Once we get through their lines, there'll be no stopping us," the captain said cheerfully, hands clasped behind his back. "The sooner we get it done, the sooner we go home."

As he spoke the naval guns offshore began to rumble and shells screamed overhead to explode in a deafening crescendo along the Turkish lines. Instinctively we crouched down as if the act itself might offer protection against a misdirected shell. Sixty-pound guns from behind the lines joined in the barrage.

"All right, lads!" Vaughn shouted over the din. "Not much longer now 'til we go over the top. Wait for the whistle."

The bombardment continued for a good half hour. The captain returned to his command position, removed a whistle from his tunic pocket, and stared at his watch. Lieutenants down the line stood and raised their own whistles to their lips. The guns fell silent. In the unbearable tension Vaughn continued to stare at his watch as the second hand counted down to the designated battle time.

Vaughn's whistle pierced the air. Revolvers in hand, lieutenants answered in kind and led the way up the ladders. Dai, Rhys and I went up, one after the other, and began our run towards the enemy lines. We did our best to stay close, an unspoken agreement to look out for one another. Almost immediately Turkish mortars opened up and shells exploded, blowing men off their feet, severing limbs, shrapnel tearing into skin and muscle. I kept my eyes on the Turkish trenches ahead and tried not to think of what was happening around me. The uphill slog took a toll on my leg muscles. Jagged chunks of hot shrapnel sharp enough to cut into boots littered the ground. I skirted shell holes and burning shrub, stepped over a headless body and stumbled, almost falling, over a severed arm. As we neared the Turkish lines, rifle and machine gun fire became more deadly and men fell in increasing numbers. Smoke from shell fire and smoldering brush obscured the battlefield. Screams of the wounded combined with the chattering of machine guns and the thunderous clap of exploding mortars created a maelstrom of horror and absurdity.

I didn't hear the shell burst that hurled me backwards and drained the breath from my lungs. I lay on my back, semiconscious, for I don't know how long. The battlefield seemed suddenly quiet, my eardrums deafened by the blast. I rolled over and got to my knees, spitting dirt and saliva from my mouth. Terror gripped me as I opened my eyes to blackness. I wiped a sleeve across my face and the blood that had poured into my eyes was drawn away, and the surrealism of the battlefield returned. I tried to stand, but dizziness brought me back to my knees. I cleared my eyes again and felt around for my rifle, but it was nowhere near.

A nearby shell crater offered some shelter. Half blind, I crawled to the rim and slithered down the side. Again I ran my sleeve across my eyes and found myself face to face with Dai. He lay on his back, a tortured look on his face, one hand holding his stomach where entrails oozed out between his fingers from a gaping wound. The front of his uniform was drenched with blood. When he saw me he smiled and held out his other hand. As I reached towards him he shuddered and lay still, eyes open but seeing nothing. I remained on my knees holding the lifeless hand. Oh God, no! Not you, Dai.

Faintly I heard whistles blowing and voices shouting, "Back! Back!" Soldiers ran past above me, but I ignored them, thinking I might just lie here next to Dai and let the war go on without me. An exploding mortar shell showered me with mud and I choked on smoke and the stink of cordite. I let go Dai's hand and tried to get up, but my legs buckled. A strong grip under my shoulder pulled me to my feet and up out of the shell hole. Holding my arm firmly across his shoulders, my rescuer dragged me, half walking, half stumbling, back to the trenches from where we had set out on our futile charge. He dropped me to the ground, sidled into the trench, and pulled me in after him.

We sat side by side against the wall of the trench for several minutes before he dragged me to my feet again and led me through a gap in the trench to a sandbagged first aid station farther down the hill. He removed my pack and lowered me to the ground. Somewhere he found a towel and gently cleared the blood from my eyes. I recognized the man; he was one of the older soldiers in our company, one I hadn't met before. "These chaps will take care of you, lad," he said, and turned back toward the trenches. For the first time I felt pain.

With so many wounded, many in much worse shape than I, it was some time before one of the medical officers approached me. A tall, bespectacled man, his face lined with fatigue and white coat smeared with blood, he bent over and dabbed away at my forehead. "Not too bad," he said. "You were lucky. Looks like a glancing blow from shrapnel. These head wounds cause a lot of bleeding, but a few stitches will take care of it."

With scissors he cut away my uniform. "Some small puncture wounds here on your abdomen and your arm. A couple more on your right thigh. We'll get you into a cot and I'll go in and see if there's shrapnel in there. Then we'll get you cleaned up and back with your men in no time. You'll have a few scars for souvenirs."

"I'd rather you sent me home," I said.

He ignored my remark. Two orderlies were summoned to carry me into a tent where the doctor injected morphine into my arm and worked over my wounds. An orderly measured me and left for the quartermaster's tent, returning later with a clean uniform and rifle. Before the day was over I was back in the trenches, head stitched and bandaged, ears still ringing, but mostly in one piece. Still disoriented from the shell blast, I walked unsteadily, my back aching, head pounding, and a sick feeling in my stomach. Sharp pains radiated from the puncture wounds in my abdomen.

I found my rescuer in a section of the trench that had taken a direct hit from a Turkish shell. He sat with his back against the earthen debris reading a book, a pipe stuck between his teeth. Above him an ankle and foot protruded from a pile of dirt, the rest of the body completely buried.

I sat next to him and stuck out my hand. "It's time I thanked you for saving my life."

He shook hands with me and smiled. "Saved you for what? So we can do it all again? Anyway, you'd probably have made it back by yourself eventually."

"I'm not sure about that," I said. I judged him to be close to forty, a slender, wiry man with a dark moustache. His sleeves were rolled up and his jacket unbuttoned. "I'm Evan Morgan," I said. "You don't sound Welsh to me, more like the Midlands I'd guess."

"Charlie Beresford. And you're right, Birmingham born and bred." He took the pipe out of his mouth, reached up and tapped ashes from the bowl on the heel of the dead man's boot.

"So how did you end up in the Borderers?"

"The foundry where I worked in Birmingham closed," he said, pushing fresh tobacco into his pipe. "I was out of work for quite a while. Then I heard they were taking on miners in Newport, so I moved the family down there."

"But why the Borderers?"

"Coalmining wasn't my cup of tea, lad. I thought army service might lead to something better."

"So did I."

"Not too smart, eh?" he said as he put a match to his pipe. "I've got a wife and four little ones to support. When this lot's over I'm hoping for something that pays better."

I was becoming so inured to slaughter that a dead man just inches away did not seem out of the ordinary. "What about him?" I said, gesturing towards the protruding foot.

"Buried when the shell landed. We'll dig him out after dark and repair the trench. The snipers are too active to do anything now."

"Well, Charlie," I said, "thanks again for pulling me in. I've got to find a pal of mine."

I walked slowly back along the familiar trench, past leaking sandbags and strategically placed periscopes, past ladders every few yards that pointed the way to oblivion. To my relief, I found Rhys squatting down cleaning his rifle, looking none the worse for wear. He stopped when he saw me and looked up at the bandage. "I heard you were back being fixed up," he said. "How do you feel?"

"I was feeling a lot better before the morphine wore off. I've one hell of a headache."

"I overheard some officers saying we're pulling out of here," Rhys said, as he ran a brush down the barrel.

"We're leaving Gallipoli?"

"No such luck. We're being redeployed and a lot of fresh troops are coming in."

"Redeployed where?"

"Some place called Suvla Bay. North of here."

"It can't be any worse than this," I said. "Then again, who thought things would be this bad?"

"I suppose you heard about Dai," Rhys said, looking down.

"Aye, I saw him die." I sat down and rested my head against the trench wall. Neither of us spoke much after that. Poor Dai. He was a bit dimwitted at times, but a decent chap nevertheless. He must have been carrying *The Last of the Mohicans* in his pack because I never saw the book again.

Chapter 9

Suvla Bay marked the beginning of the end of my brief military career.

The landing on the night of August 6th went off better than anyone expected. Motor-driven launches equipped with landing ramps at the bow—beetles, the men called them—ferried us ashore. These were much more efficient than the old lighter we'd used at Cape Helles that had to be towed ashore; and they could land many more troops in a shorter period of time.

The Turks must have been taken by surprise because we met little opposition, no barbed wire and just a few snipers who quickly surrendered. It was a relief to be ashore for we had spent many long hours in the cramped beetles since we'd left Cape Helles. Together with thousands of fresh troops from England and other veterans of the earlier landings, we went ashore and moved forward over rocky terrain to the edge of a dry salt lake about a mile and a half wide. Ahead of us, visible in the brightening daylight, rose three low hills beyond the lakebed, two of them joined closely at their peaks. The bay was half-moon shaped with an inviting sandy beach broken by occasional dry creek beds. If it weren't for the war, Suvla Bay would have been a nice place for a seaside picnic.

The plan, we were told, was to take the low hills and then move on to the higher ground of Sari Bair to link up with the Australians and New Zealanders just a short distance south. Once the heights of Sari Bair were in allied hands, we would advance across the peninsula and gain control of the Dardanelles. Then it would be on to Constantinople.

As soon as we were organized on shore, we set off under a blazing sun across the white, salt-encrusted lakebed. Occasionally we heard the crack of a Turkish howitzer, followed by a shell exploding a good distance away. We moved quickly because it was just a matter of time before the Turks brought up more guns and found their range. At the other side of the lake we were ordered to dig in.

"What are we waiting for?" Rhys said. "Why don't we take those hills now before the Turks bring up reinforcements?"

A lieutenant standing nearby overheard him. "When we get our orders to move, we'll take them," he said. "Right now we dig in. Tomorrow a lot more men will be coming ashore." Rhys shook his head in disgust and began shoveling while I unloaded ammunition boxes from pack mules that had followed us inland. To the south we could hear the sounds of battle along the Anzac front.

It didn't take long for the Turks to bring up more men and artillery, so once we began our offensive to take the hills, we found ourselves in the same kind of fighting we had endured over the past four months. We took the low hills on a few occasions before being driven off again by ferocious Turkish counterattacks. Once again we had failed to take advantage of our superior numbers when we had the chance.

When we weren't fighting, digging new trenches or hauling supplies across the lakebed, I wrote letters to Gwyn and, less frequently, to my aunt and uncle. I also wrote a short letter to Dai's parents, telling them what a fine lad he was, a good friend and a good soldier. You would have been proud of him, I told them. It was a bit overblown, knowing Dai, but I thought it the right thing to do. I didn't know Dai's address, so I enclosed the letter with one to Gwyn and asked her to deliver it.

Ever since my meeting with the Turkish soldier in the field of corpses that was no man's land, I found myself looking more often at Gwyn's photo. It had never occurred to me before the war that Gwyn and I would ever go our separate ways. I saw her almost every day and we were perfectly comfortable with one another. As youth gave way to manhood, I had taken it for granted that one day Gwyn would be my wife. Now I wasn't so sure. I hadn't seen her for months. Perhaps I was taking her too much for granted. Would she still want me when—or if—I made it back to Ystrad? Could she live with someone who had willfully taken men's lives? Would my scars repel her? The one above my eye was not pleasant to look at.

At night, trying to catch a few hours of sleep, I longed for Gwyn's presence, her cheerful disposition, her smile, her touch. And I often thought of the Turkish soldier I'd met. My job was to kill Turks, but I desperately wanted that soldier to live and to return to his wife and children and the good fish of Alanya.

I was tempted at times to walk away from it all, to turn my back on the killing. But that would label me a deserter, and the penalty for desertion was the firing squad. Even disobeying orders could lead to that, a fact brought home to us a few weeks earlier when we'd been ordered to witness the execution of a platoon sergeant who had refused to take his men on night patrol. The men had been fighting all day, suffering heavy casualties, and were completely done in. Give me some fresh men, the sergeant told the captain, and I'll lead them on patrol, but these lads have done more than enough for one day. His men insisted that they would go with him, but that didn't stop some general authorizing the sergeant's immediate execution without so much as a trial for willfully disobeying an order.

The sergeant, a career soldier in his forties with graying hair and thick moustache, was made to stand with his back against the wall of a dilapidated mud-brick farm building. His uniform was bedraggled and smeared with mud; his expression a fusion of fatigue and disbelief. He refused a blindfold. Ten soldiers from a different regiment comprised the firing squad, five crouched at the front, the rest standing behind. The volley, delivered on command, staggered even those of us inured to the shock of gunfire. The impact hurled the sergeant against the wall and tore the front of his uniform to bloody shreds, before his lifeless body crumpled face down into the dirt. The faces of the men under his command, who had been forced to watch the spectacle, were gaunt with grief and anger. Judging from the pattern of bullet holes in the wall, some of the rifles had been aimed away from their target.

What utter stupidity! Killing Turks was one thing; killing our own men for no good reason was beyond the bounds of common sense. So, like the rest of the men, I followed orders, charged the Turkish lines, and prayed that somehow I would come out of this war alive and with my limbs intact.

§

It wasn't difficult to get lost on the Suvla front. We were fighting over a much larger area than before and the troops were scattered all over the place. Communication was poor and runners often ended up in the wrong place. I got lost during an assault on Scimitar Hill—and that led to my encounter with Jack Gammage.

It was a disaster from the beginning. The terrain was terrible to navigate, crisscrossed with ravines and crevasses and carpeted with impenetrable thorn brush. Ahead of us rose Scimitar Hill, or Hill 70, depending on which officer was describing it, not too high and not too steep. From a distance it looked like an easy target. Up close every step was a struggle, making us sitting ducks for Turkish snipers. How I didn't get hit is beyond me. To make matters worse, the brush lay tinder dry under the blazing August sun, and as soon as the Turkish mortars opened up, fires broke out all across the front.

I saw Charlie Beresford go down just as he reached the summit. The bullet must have caught him head on because he fell backwards into the brush where flames quickly engulfed him. There was no point in trying to get him out. Screams of the wounded caught in the flames pierced the air, and dense smoke turned the battleground into a confused muddle.

Against heavy fire from the Turkish lines I just reached the summit when whistles sounded retreat. Why the hell are we retreating? I thought. Were our casualties that bad? I turned back and almost immediately encountered flames shooting several feet into the air. I backed away, eyes running, gagging from the smoke. Most of the shooting was coming from the north side, so I turned and followed the burning brush in the opposite direction, hoping to flank the flames and then head downhill to our trenches. The smoke was so disorienting that I soon realized I had no idea where I was going.

Once I passed beyond the burning scrub I tried making my way directly through the underbrush, but movement was difficult and thorns penetrated my uniform and tore at my legs. At last I stumbled upon a narrow track trodden down by sheep or goats or whatever other denizens inhabited the peninsula. I followed the track downhill, reasoning I would reach the shore eventually. But at that point I had no idea in which direction our trenches lay.

To my left, in the distance, a small village nestled at the foot of a steep tree-covered hill, but there was no sign of life. To my right, where I kept hoping to see the Aegean, the sky had turned dark and menacing with billowing black clouds blotting out what just a short time ago had been brilliant blue sky. A vivid lightning fork illuminated the clouds and a rumble of distant thunder presaged the approach of violent weather, a fitting complement to the violence below. After about half an hour in the pathway the sounds of battle behind me faded, only to be replaced with more persistent claps of thunder. Large, sporadic drops of rain dampened my shoulders and arms.

Suddenly a shot rang out directly ahead of me. I hesitated, unsure what to do. Tightening the grip on my rifle, I moved forward cautiously. Then I heard voices shouting in English and two more rifle shots in rapid succession. I dropped to the ground and inched forward, propelled by feet and elbows, towards a bend in the track. As I rounded the bend I came upon a clearing where an allied soldier was leaning over another who lay prostrate. Another shot rang out and the soldier went down, blood erupting from his leg. Two Turks with bayonets fixed to their rifles burst into the clearing from behind a stand of fir trees and moved quickly towards the two downed men.

In times of war events often unfold with startling suddenness and move rapidly to a violent conclusion. I didn't act from any plan or heroics, it was just instinct and training that commanded my reflexes. From my prone position I sighted on the leading Turk and squeezed off a round. The bullet caught him full in the chest and stopped his forward motion, his knees buckled, and almost in slow motion he pitched to the side. The other man dropped to a crouch. He hadn't seen me. He waited a second or two, looking around, then rose and moved cautiously forwards, his rifle at his shoulder. Now the rain was falling in sheets, driven by a gusty wind. Lightning flashed almost continually and thunder reverberated from the surrounding hills.

I blinked to clear my eyes, aimed and squeezed the trigger. Missed! The Turk stopped, looked around nervously, trying to locate the source of the gunfire. With no more rounds in my clip, I sprang to my feet and ran at him as fast as my legs could carry me. He just stood and stared at me, a panicked look on his face, as I charged forward and rammed the bayonet into his belly. A guttural sound escaped his lips and he dropped to his knees. I shoved my boot against his chest to release the bayonet and swung the rifle butt against the side of his head, the motion causing flecks of blood to spatter my face. He fell backwards, his helmet careening off to the edge of the clearing, blood running from his mouth and stomach. He looked about sixteen years old.

Other voices, Turkish voices, shouted from nearby. I had to act quickly. One of the two allied soldiers was almost certainly dead, so I turned my attention to the other who was writhing in agony on the ground, his left leg shattered and bloody.

There was no time to lift him. I slung the rifle over my shoulder, grabbed his shoulder straps and dragged him to where the narrow track continued on the other side of the clearing. I went on down the pathway as fast as the encroaching brush allowed, leaving a trail of blood. After a short distance the voices seemed even closer. I stopped, unsure from which direction they were coming. Was I heading towards or away from them? In desperation I shoved the wounded man under the soaking brush lining the path and dragged myself in after him. He groaned as I pushed him further into a shallow gully.

The Turks were almost upon us. I placed my hand firmly over the wounded man's mouth and touched a finger of my other hand to my lips to signal silence. He stared at me and nodded slightly in understanding. What about the blood? I wondered. Would it betray our hiding place? I peered through the brush and saw that the continuing heavy downpour had washed most of the blood into the soil.

Now there was movement on the track and the boots of Turkish soldiers passed just inches from where we lay. Voices spoke words I didn't understand. The Turks stopped, no more than a few feet away, talking softly among themselves. The rain continued with less intensity and thunder rumbled more distantly inland. A voice called from farther away and one of the nearby Turks shouted a response. Then the soldiers, three of them I counted, retraced their steps towards the clearing. Soon only the sound of falling rain disturbed the stillness as daylight faded to dusk. I released my hand from the man's mouth and his face contorted with pain. I unwrapped the puttee from my right leg and in the confined awkwardness of our position, used it to bind a soggy tourniquet around his thigh. His face was ashen, his breathing shallow. He had lost so much blood I thought he might die at any moment.

Darkness descended swiftly as the rain abated. There were no longer sounds of talking, but I had no idea if the Turks were still close. I saw no point in moving; with the overcast sky it was too dark to see anything. I remember little of that night, other than the cold and damp. I dozed on and off and shivered in my wet uniform while water dripped on us from the sodden brush.

Dawn broke slowly. Somewhere off in the distance a cockerel crowed, other than that, silence. My body lay stiff and a nasty cramp gripped my right leg. I rolled over and peered at my companion. From the look of his uniform he was an Anzac soldier. I thought at first he was dead, but I felt a pulse and found he was breathing almost imperceptibly. I raised my head to look around and was immediately transfixed. No more than two feet from my head a human skull lay partially obscured by brush,

> *Grinning in that jolly guise*
> *Of bare bones and empty eyes!*

Almost reflexively the words from a James Whitcomb Riley poem came to mind. Tattered bits of uniform, Turkish by the look of it, clung to the rest of the skeleton that had been picked clean by insects or other predators. I reached out and placed a finger on the crown of the skull.

> *Was this hollow dome,*
> *Where I tap my finger,*
> *Once the spirit's narrow home—*
> *Where you loved to linger,*
> *Hiding, as today are we,*
> *From the self-same destiny?*

I stared, fascinated, for several minutes before tearing my eyes away and rolling onto my back. Our uniforms were still damp and I shivered in the early morning chill. I leaned over and pushed my head out from under the brush. The only sign of life on the narrow pathway was a prickly hedgehog three or four feet away that stared at me before scurrying off into the brush. After hearing no human sounds for several minutes, I inched myself out, barely feeling the thorns that tore into clothing and skin. I pulled the wounded soldier out after me and placed the rifle, barrel end down, across my shoulder.

The grassy, trampled-down path was still damp and sweet smelling from the previous night's rain, but not so sweet as to mask the stink of cordite that permeated every square yard of the Gallipoli peninsula. I looked up and down the track to convince myself we were indeed alone, before hoisting the soldier up over my shoulder the way we had been taught at Brecon—the same way Dennis Bertram had carried the injured Hugh from the cave-in at Upper Pentre mine. High above, wisps of clouds glowed orange-red against a deepening blue sky. An iridescent green dragonfly flitted in front of me and settled on a thorny gorse. I set off at a fast walk downhill.

A short distance along I turned onto a perpendicular track that ran more steeply downhill to the right. At times I had to stop to gather my breath. My shoulders and back ached under the heavy burden, but I didn't dare put him down because I wasn't sure I'd be able to lift him again. In places the track fell so steeply that I had to make sure of my footing before taking each step. Seemingly quite close, the welcome sight of the Aegean Sea sparkled under the morning sun, blue and calm. At last the track began to level off.

"Halt!" The voice rang out with such suddenness that I almost fell over in shock. Ahead I saw two soldiers, each crouched on one knee, their rifles pointed at me.

"Wounded soldier!" I shouted.

Warily the two men stood up and approached. "Blimey, it's Jack!" one of them said, shouldering his rifle.

"Follow us," the other said. "You can put him down up ahead. We'll get a stretcher."

The last time I'd heard that accent was the day Hugh and I watched the Australian and Welsh rugby teams play an exhibition match in Cardiff.

§

Medical corpsmen worked on the wounded soldier's leg while I was taken to a staging area where I received several slaps on the back and shouts of "Good show, mate!" and other assorted greetings. They took me to a mess tent and fed me a lavish breakfast of fried eggs, toast and piping hot tea. I wondered where the eggs came from, until later that morning I spotted a wire enclosure imprisoning at least twenty chickens and a rooster, perhaps the one I'd heard at daybreak. My clothes, reeking of soot and sweat and covered with mud and blood, were taken from me and laundered, and someone even stitched up all the rips caused by thorn brush. When I received a summons to report to the commanding officer, my spanking clean clothes hung from a clothesline, drying under the morning sun and brisk sea breeze.

"Sit down," the officer said, indicating a weathered wooden bench in front of his tent. "I'm Captain Elliston. And you are?"

"Private Morgan, Sir. Evan Morgan."

The captain sat in a chair fashioned skillfully from dead tree branches. His rumpled uniform, rolled-up sleeves and ruddy brown complexion bespoke of long months under the Gallipoli sun. His eyes scrutinized me. "All right, Private Morgan, would you mind explaining why a South Wales Borderer ends up on the Anzac front?"

"You tell me, Sir. Fact of the matter is, I got lost during yesterday's assault."

"Assault? I thought your lot was sitting on your arses up at Suvla while we did all the fighting."

I explained the circumstances to him, the failed attack on Scimitar Hill, the fire and smoke, the confusion. When I was finished, he said, "I heard you knocked off a couple of Turks when you got our man out. Nice piece of work."

"No offense, Sir," I said, "but I see nothing nice in killing. It was more a matter of kill or be killed."

"Look, I don't like killing either," the captain spoke sharply. "Sometimes we have no choice." He looked me up and down. "I can't say you look much like a soldier, Morgan." I was wearing nothing more than someone's borrowed undershorts and unlaced boots with no socks. "Are our boys taking good care of you?"

"Aye, Sir. Best breakfast since I landed on this bloody peninsula."

"Your C.O. might think you ran away rather than getting lost," Elliston said as he picked up a stick and used it to scratch his back.

"Right now they probably think I'm dead. I've got to find a way back up there."

"It's all arranged," the captain said. "We'll take you up in a launch this afternoon. Meanwhile I'm going to write a full report for your C.O. with a copy to Division headquarters. When they read it they'll think you're a bloody hero."

"I don't feel much like a hero. I'd rather go home."

"You're not the only one. But my report will come in handy when you show up looking like you spent the night at the Ritz. By the way, Corporal Gammage wants to see you."

"Corporal Gammage?"

"He's the bloke you brought in this morning. You'd better hurry, he's about to be shipped to Imbros. Go easy on him, he's in bad shape."

"Where will I find him, Sir?"

"Go straight back to the beach. He's in the Red Cross tent." Elliston stood up and I followed suit. He stuck out his hand and I took it. "Thanks, Morgan, for bringing our man in. Now go find Gammage. And if you salute me in that get-up, you'll have to swim back to Suvla."

§

There were about a dozen soldiers in the Red Cross tent, some lying down, others sitting up chatting or reading. All sported bandages of one type or another. A medical orderly led me to a cot at the far end of the tent. The man I'd spent the night with, who looked to be about twenty-five to thirty years old lay on his back, his eyes closed, his right leg heavily bandaged and propped up on two pillows.

"Jack!" the orderly said in a loud voice. "You have a visitor."

Gammage's eyes flickered open and he turned his head towards me. The orderly brought over a stool and I sat next to his cot.

"Funny uniform you're wearing," Gammage said.

I laughed. "Your mates took mine. They wanted to make me more presentable."

He smiled and held out his hand. "Jack Gammage," he said.

I took his hand in mine. "Evan Morgan." He released my hand and put his arm behind his head. "How are you feeling?" I asked.

"I've felt better," he said, still looking directly at me.

Gammage's face, handsome and angular under straw-colored hair, was pale, but his arms were deeply tanned and muscular. "The doc here says I may lose my leg." There was no hint of bitterness in his voice. "He said he didn't want to make that decision, that there's a good hospital on Imbros and they'll know what to do with it. Then it's home to Australia."

I didn't reply. I'd seen what a mess the bullet made of his leg, a lot worse than the cave-in did to Hugh's.

"Evan," he said, then paused as if trying to extract some meaning from my name. "I remember you sticking that Turk with your bayonet. I don't remember much after that, except your dragging me under some bushes. Then I sort of woke up and you were carrying me." He looked up at the ceiling of the tent while I fidgeted on the stool, wishing there was a back I could lean against. "Fact of the matter is I wouldn't be here if it weren't for you." He turned his head and looked back at me.

"All in a day's work," I said. "Truth be told, I was lost. Had no idea where I was when I came across you and your pal."

"Poor bugger," he replied. "Doug Carpenter. A good friend of mine." His eyes betrayed the sadness he felt. "He's not the first mate of mine to cop it," he said bitterly.

"I've lost a few myself," I said, for want of anything better to say.

"Where's your home, Evan?" Gammage asked.

"South Wales."

He laughed. "And I'm from New South Wales. I suppose there's something prophetic about that." He shifted his body and grimaced with pain as his leg moved. "So what did you do in old South Wales?"

"I was a coalminer."

"We could have used you when we tunneled under the Turkish trenches," he said. "You should've seen the explosion we set off. I think it rattled the Turks for a while. Not long enough though." He pointed towards my forehead. "Did you get that in the coal mine?"

"No, I got in the way of a piece of shrapnel. What about you, Jack?" I asked. "What did you do before the war?"

"Sheep farmer. My dad has a beautiful spread, five thousand acres of God's country. And the climate . . ." His voice trailed off, a wistful expression crossing his face.

"Wrap it up, Jack!" the orderly called from the entrance to the tent. "Your boat's arriving."

"Hey, Eric!" Gammage called. "Bring me some paper and a pencil."

The orderly left and returned almost immediately with a small writing pad and pencil.

"Here, Evan," Gammage said. "Write down your address at home. I'd like to stay in touch. It's not every day someone saves my life."

I did as he asked, ripped off the page and handed it to him.

"While you're at it, write down mine. We won't be seeing each other again, but maybe we can be pen pals, or something like that. Once the war's over."

I opened the pad and wrote as he dictated: *Jack Gammage, Canterbury Station, Mulltown, NSW, Australia.*

"My mum and dad lived just outside Canterbury before they went out to Australia in '88," he said. "I was two years old. They named the farm Canterbury to remind them of home."

Eric and another orderly entered the tent with a stretcher. "Time to go, mate," Gammage said to me. "I'm glad you stopped by, Evan. I didn't want to leave here without thanking you."

"No need to thank me," I replied. "Good luck with the leg."

"Good luck with the war," he said, shaking my hand.

The orderlies lifted Gammage onto the stretcher and carried him out. He didn't look back at me; he looked like he might pass out from the pain. I followed them from the tent and watched as they carried him down to the boat and lifted him aboard. Within minutes the launch was chugging its way across the blue Aegean towards Imbros, carrying Jack Gammage away from the war. Carrying him home.

Chapter 10

I didn't get back to Suvla Bay until late in the afternoon. After saying goodbye to Jack Gammage, I spent much of the day waiting for the launch to return from Imbros, passing the time walking on the beach and looking up at the precipitous terrain above Anzac Cove. How the Australians and New Zealanders had been able to advance up those steep, overgrown gullies against stiff opposition caused me to wonder at their fighting skill and bravery.

I also spent time looking out to sea, reflecting on the previous day's events. That I had killed, or at least severely injured, two Turkish soldiers did not infuse me with guilt or revulsion the way the killings at Cape Helles had. Instead, I felt almost detached from the deadly encounter, as if shooting one man and sticking a bayonet into another who looked too young to be out of school had all been a bad dream, a nightmare that would disappear once I woke up. But I knew it would never disappear; what happened above Anzac Cove would stay with me forever.

I thought too of the false promises of a short campaign and an early end to the war. Of how the Turks would never withstand the might of the British Empire. Yet the Turkish soldiers proved equally as adept at warfare, and their generals, it seemed, were the better strategists. This was their homeland and they were tenacious in its defense, while we were interlopers trying to take what was rightfully theirs. I'd learned from my meeting with the Turk from Alanya that the ordinary Turkish soldier shared our humanity. Like us they had families at home and wanted nothing more than to live their lives in peace and tranquility among those they loved. The more I thought about it, the more I hated war, the senseless slaughter. That I was beyond any perverse feelings at what I'd done the day before was proof enough of the dehumanizing effect of war.

After a late lunch of bread and cheese and a bruised apple, I dozed off under the shade of an umbrella pine, lulled by the rhythm of waves breaking on the shore. In my restless sleep I found myself walking down Victoria Street, across the main road, and over the rusty iron footbridge spanning the River Rhondda. The town was deserted, the only sound the clacking of my hob-nailed boots on the pavement. I continued on until I stood at the foot of the giant slagheap that rose high above the river.

I stared up its steep, gray-black slope and thought of climbing, but my feet felt heavy and, try as I might, I couldn't take the first step. I heard slag trams rumbling across the top, and then fresh slag came sliding down the slope, some chunks rolling against my ankles, covering my boots. I looked away and saw Dai Wilkins walking towards me leading a pit pony by its halter. Dai wore his army uniform except for the miner's helmet on his head. He stopped beside me and stared up at the slope. I glanced down and saw Dai holding his stomach, blood and entrails seeping out between his fingers. I followed his gaze to the top of the slagheap, but when I looked back down Dai had vanished, and just the pit pony was standing there looking forlorn.

A hand shaking my shoulder jolted me awake. "Better get into your uniform, mate," an Australian soldier said. "You'll be leaving before long."

§

Lieutenant Harry Graves, a congenial young Queenslander, accompanied me on the launch. He seemed pleased with his assignment, no doubt an agreeable diversion from the routine of war. "I'm to deliver you personally to your C.O.," he told me. "The captain wants to make sure his message is taken seriously."

I laughed. "My C.O. might think I wrote it myself, is that it?" Graves shrugged without replying.

The journey back to Suvla Bay was short but pleasant enough as the sea breeze took the edge off the hot August sun. But the lingering memory of my dream and images of Dai depressed me. Once ashore we were soon damp with sweat as we made our way across the bone-dry lakebed to the forward trenches.

Company commander Captain Guy Hollister read the letter as I stood at attention before him in the sandbagged command bunker. Graves stood to one side, hands behind his back, rocking up and down on the balls of his feet. Hollister's superior officer, Major Aubrey Wallace, sat at a map-covered wooden table nearby, watching us with an amused expression on his face.

"Hmm," Captain Hollister said a couple of times as he read the letter, twitching his blond moustache from side to side. "So you really got lost, Private. Don't see how that's possible, myself."

"I can vouch for what . . ." Lieutenant Graves began.

"It was uphill one way, downhill the other," Hollister interrupted. "How's it possible to end up with the Aussies?"

"Sir," I said, "there was so much smoke with all the brush on fire, we couldn't see where we were going. I'm sure I wasn't the only one to get lost. If you'd been there, Sir, I think you'd see what I mean."

Hollister's face flamed beet red at the implication behind my words. A lot of the men resented the fact that the C.O. stayed behind and left the advance in charge of his lieutenants. He looked me up and down, clearly angry. "You don't look much like you've been fighting."

"Private Morgan was a real mess when he arrived with Corporal Gammage," Lieutenant Graves said. "Our men cleaned and mended his uniform. It was the least we could do for saving one of our men."

Major Wallace pushed back his chair, stood up and sauntered over. "Let me see that," he said. He took the letter from Hollister and read its contents. "Seems clean cut to me, Guy," he said, raising his eyebrows. "Private Morgan here rescued an Aussie from a very sticky wicket. Not the action of someone who's running away, is it? Very commendable, Private," he said, turning towards me.

"Thank you, Sir," I replied.

"At ease, Private," the major said. He looked again at the letter and then back at me. "You wouldn't happen to be the Private Morgan who got a regimental citation at Cape Helles?"

"I got a citation there, yes, Sir."

The major turned to Captain Hollister. "I think maybe another citation is in order, Guy. Don't you agree?"

"Of course, Sir," Hollister said uncomfortably.

"Simplest thing would be to write up your recommendation and attach this letter from Captain Elliston. Let me look it over before you send it in to headquarters. I think perhaps with two regimental citations, a promotion to lance corporal would also be appropriate, don't you think?"

"Yes, Sir," Hollister said, his shoulders sagging.

"You may go, Private," the major said to me. "Put Lieutenant Graves on the right track back to his boat and return to your unit." He turned to Graves. "Thank you, Lieutenant. My compliments to Captain Elliston."

Graves and I both sprang to attention and saluted before exiting the tent.

"I'd say that went off pretty well," Graves said as I led him back to the lakebed.

"Can't complain, Sir. Your captain did all right by me."

"I'll be on my way, then," Graves said. "Good luck, Morgan."

"Thank you, Sir," I said, saluting. "Same to you."

Graves returned my salute and set off across the lakebed, wiping the back of his neck and forehead with a handkerchief.

§

Rhys Jones had always been a rather taciturn fellow, not usually given to displays of emotion. But when he saw me approaching, he practically bounced up and down and his eyes glistened with tears. Other soldiers shook my hand and slapped my back as I approached.

"Christ Almighty!" Rhys exclaimed, dropping his cigarette and throwing his arms around me. "Am I glad to see you! I thought for sure your luck had run out up there."

I extricated myself from his embrace and set my rifle down. I didn't feel much like talking, but at his insistence I gave Rhys and some other soldiers who had gathered around a quick account of what had happened. "The Aussies treated me really well," I said. "I'd forgotten how good fresh eggs tasted."

"What did it feel like to stick a bayonet in someone?" Rhys asked. "I'm not sure I could bring myself to do that."

"To tell the truth, I didn't even think about it. I didn't have time to reload, so I just ran at him before he had a chance to shoot me. Come to think of it, I didn't even scream at him like we're supposed to."

"Our drill sergeant at Brecon would give you a bawling out if he'd seen you," Rhys laughed. "Still, the idea of stabbing someone . . ."

"Better than the other way round," Bill Oliver, a fellow private said.

I suppose so," Rhys said. He sat down with his back against the trench wall. "You know, Evan, I think I must have a guardian angel sitting on my shoulder. All these battles and not even a knick from shrapnel. I get my injuries shaving."

"It's bad luck to say things like that," Oliver interjected.

"We lost over a third of our company yesterday," Rhys said, leaning his head back. "It's insane." He aimed his rifle butt at a large brown rat that ran between our feet, but it scampered off unscathed. "Insane," he repeated.

Perhaps someone at command headquarters considered it insane too because the pace of battle slowed considerably in the weeks following. Rather than full frontal attacks, we engaged in probing actions, seeking weaknesses in the Turkish lines, and trying to find fresh water.

Water had been a problem ever since we landed because the navy couldn't deliver enough to supply the thousands of men occupying the Suvla front. Attempts to dig wells had met with little success and the Turks, anticipating our need, had poisoned existing wells with rotting corpses. We had to fill our flasks from large canvas basins containing water piped in from the supply ships, or carried in on the backs of mules to the front lines. Foul tasting and brackish, the water did little to satisfy our raging thirst. Hundreds suffered from dysentery. Morale plummeted.

Summer ended abruptly, but the cooler days of autumn quickly gave way to biting cold winds and drenching downpours. We shivered under oilskin capes and our feet felt like blocks of ice. With fewer corpses to feed on, rats ran rampant through the trenches, invaded food supplies and climbed over hospital beds seeking scraps of food. In mid November I received my promotion and was placed in command of a squad of ten privates. And shortly thereafter the war ended for me.

§

It was a day of intermittent rain and sleet, a day of misery across the broad Suvla front where soldiers stamped their feet and swung their arms in a vain attempt to generate a little heat, or hunted for bits of wood for fires to warm their hands. At noon I was summoned to the company command bunker.

Here comes trouble, I thought. I'd tried to stay as far as possible from Captain Hollister since my previous encounter, but he didn't display any ill feeling towards me when I entered the bunker and saluted. Hollister had dark circles under his eyes, as though he hadn't been sleeping well.

"At ease, Lance Corporal," Hollister said, getting up from his chair by the map table. "I've got a job for you."

"Aye, Sir."

"Have you heard of General Gregory Heath?"

"No, Sir."

"General Heath's in the War Office in London. Lieutenant Heath is his son."

"Our Lieutenant Heath, Sir?"

"That's right, our Lieutenant Heath," Hollister said. "Yesterday evening Lieutenant Heath took a couple of men to scout out a village to our north, looking for clean wells. They never came back."

I didn't respond. I was pretty sure that Hollister wanted me to go look for him, not a job I relished. Lieutenant Heath had joined the company about three months ago. He was popular with the ranks. Twice wounded in combat, he had an easy-going manner that belied his bravery in battle. He never talked down to the men under his command; on the contrary, he took a personal interest, asking about their families, where they were from and what they did before the war. He was even known to join in impromptu rugby or cricket matches on the lakebed when there was a letup in the action. Not exactly what I'd have expected from a general's son.

"Obviously General Heath will want to know we did everything possible to rescue his son," Hollister continued. "That's where you come in." He took a pair of field glasses from a nail protruding from one of the bunker support posts. "Come outside. I'll show you the situation."

Hollister put the field glasses to his eyes, elbows resting on the sandbagged parapet in front of the bunker. "Take a look up there," he said, handing me the glasses. "There's a village called Kücük Anafarta, just a small place which we think is deserted. "That's where Lieutenant Heath went."

I peered through the glasses, adjusting the focus to sharpen my view. "Aye, Sir," I said. "I see the place." The village did indeed look deserted, with no sign of life apparent in the surrounding area.

"Now look to the left of the village," Hollister said. "There's a dirt road."

It took several seconds before I spotted the road, a narrow pale brown strip contrasting with the dull green vegetation. "Aye, Sir. I've got it. Looks like it takes a bend and disappears behind a small hill just short of the village."

"That's the one," Hollister said. "That's where we lost Lieutenant Heath and his men. We could follow them on the road, but when they went round the bend they disappeared and we never saw them again. There's a possibility they lost their way and decided to wait out the night. But then they didn't show up this morning."

"You want me to go look for him, is that it, Sir?"

"That's the idea," Hollister said, fiddling with his moustache. "Take a couple of good men with you. Go scout the area."

"I'll do what I can, Sir" I said, handing the captain his field glasses.

"Thank you, Lance Corporal," Hollister said. "This is an important assignment."

I'll bet it is, I thought. The last thing the Captain wants on his record is to lose a general's son. "I'll check out some extra ammo and field glasses and leave right away, Sir."

"Be careful. Don't go round that bend unless you're sure it's safe. We don't want to lose you too."

"I'll be careful, Sir." I saluted and turned away to return to the company trenches. I should have written to Gwyn, I thought. Because of this bloody weather, it had been over three weeks since I last wrote. I'll write as soon as I get back, I told myself, rain or shine.

The first two soldiers I encountered were Bill Oliver and Brian Greenwood huddled over a tiny fire made of dried scrub brush, trying to warm their hands. The two were a study in contrast, Bill tall with a shock of ginger hair, Brian short with receding black hair.

"Bill! Brian! I need a couple of good lads to help me out."

"Help you with what?" Bill said warily.

I explained the situation, telling them without conviction that we'd likely be back in time for supper.

"I'm sure you can find a couple of lads farther down," Brian said, turning his attention to the fire. "We're just getting warmed up."

With my new rank I could have ordered them to go, but I wasn't about to risk my friendship with any of the men by acting like the promotion went to my head. I still considered myself one of them, the only difference being a bit of extra pay at the end of the month and a stripe on my sleeve. "All right, lads, I'll ask someone else," I said.

"Wait," Bill said, getting up. "I'll go with you, Evan. Lieutenant Heath's a good man. I don't mind going after him."

"Bloody hell," Brian muttered, picking up his rifle and stamping out the fire. "All right, Evan. Lead the way."

§

Weighted down with extra ammunition clips on our belts and a pair of field glasses around my neck, we set out for Küçük Anafarta. Balaclavas under our helmets, gloves with holes cut for our trigger fingers, and cumbersome trenchcoats offered protection against the cold. An early winter sun did little to mitigate the biting wind.

Rather than taking a direct route, we stayed behind the nearer hills to avoid being seen by Turkish observers, and turned inland only when I judged us to be about level with the village. From there we moved forward cautiously,. Every few yards I peered through the glasses looking for signs of life ahead. It took some time before we reached the dirt road, which turned out to be little more than a narrow track worn down by sheep or cattle. Ruts in the road indicated frequent use by farm wagons. We moved at a crouch, trying to stay below the level of the shrubbery lining the road.

"No talking from here on unless it's absolutely necessary," I said softly.

The closer we got to the village the more misgivings I had. Three men don't just disappear or get lost in broad daylight. I didn't share my feelings with the others; they were smart enough to figure that out for themselves.

"Maybe we should just go back," Bill Oliver whispered.

I shook my head. "There's a bend up ahead. We'll at least go that far."

As we approached the bend I signaled to lie down. "I'll go first," I said. "Stay here until I wave you on."

I crawled forward cradling my rifle across my arms. As I rounded the bend, small isolated mud-brick huts came into view, some in a sorry state of repair. I inched forward and other more solidly built houses told me I had reached the village. I looked through the field glasses, panning from one building to the next and along brick walls and wooden fences that were probably paddocks for livestock. Nothing. No sign of life. I looked back and waved Bill and Brian forward.

"It looks deserted," I said, raising myself to a crouch. "Let's go a little farther, but stay out of the buildings for now in case they're booby trapped. We can check them later."

I stood and the others followed. We advanced slowly, our rifles pointed ahead, fingers on triggers. There wasn't much to this side of the village, just one street with overgrown fields behind the buildings, fields that were no doubt filled with vegetables in more peaceful times. The street ended in a small square dotted with olive trees. To one side sat a house with Arabic script above the door and a few weathered wooden tables and chairs set outside. I imagined villagers sitting there, drinking tea, socializing.

I looked across the square and was startled by a flash that could only have been caused by sun reflecting on metal or glass. Then I saw a rifle barrel protruding through a window. Other weapons appeared in windows of neighboring houses.

I lowered my rifle. "It's a trap," I said. "Back up slowly, and let's not do anything stupid."

To our right a Turkish soldier emerged from a doorway, his rifle at the shoulder aimed directly at us.

"Bloody hell!" Brian said, bringing up his rifle.

"No, Brian!" I screamed.

A deafening fusillade of rifle fire erupted and a sledgehammer blow to my left shoulder spun me around and sent me flying onto the dusty surface of the village square. Then silence. I lay on my back stunned and in a state of shock, feeling no pain.

I turned my head and saw alongside me the blood-soaked, motionless bodies of Bill and Brian. Several Turkish soldiers approached, one coming right at me, the point of his bayonet aimed directly at my belly. I closed my eyes, certain I was about to die. "Gwyn," I whispered.

I waited several seconds, but the expected thrust of cold steel, the agony of death, never came. I opened my eyes and saw a ring of soldiers staring down at me, their rifles shouldered. Some were lighting cigarettes. An officer clad in a fur hat and knee-length boots returned a revolver to its holster. One soldier bent over, removed the bloodstained field glasses from around my neck and wiped them on my uniform, while another picked up my rifle. The officer barked a command and two soldiers grabbed me under the arms and began dragging me across the square. Suddenly the pain was excruciating, and I moaned in agony.

From my ignominious position suspended between two Turks, I saw soldiers going through Bill's and Brian's pockets and gathering their rifles. Against my better judgment I'd gone around the bend in the road, and there was no going back.

Part III

The Bosphorus

The years pass and the scene changes, but at its core something eternal remains the same, as if this place had an immortal soul, as the Bosphorus continues to surge powerfully between the continents in its unending flow, streaming like time's river in the country of dreams.

John Freely, *The Bosphorus*

Chapter 11

I walked alone down Victoria Street holding an umbrella for protection against a steady rainfall, the patter of rain on the umbrella mingling with the click-clack of my hobnailed boots. The Old Lamb Inn, its slate roof wet and glistening, appeared deserted as I passed by and turned into Bodringallt Terrace, expecting to find Gwyn waiting for me. But she was nowhere in sight. At the steep, narrow steps leading up to the school playground, I stopped and looked up and down the terrace, desperate to find her. A stabbing pain in my shoulder caused me to drop my umbrella into a muddy puddle. Below the terrace a man sat on his backyard toilet, trousers draped around his ankles, the privy door ajar. He held an open newspaper across his knees as he stared up at me.

The steady drip of rain was overshadowed by a persistent thump-thump of machinery and the ground under my feet began to rock back and forth. A noise of shifting gravel brought chunks of slag against my feet and ankles. I turned and looked up toward the school, but instead of the steps that were there a moment before, a slagheap covered the hill. Lumps of fresh slag slid down its surface and clattered across the terrace. Above the pile rose the familiar stone facade of Bodringallt School. Perhaps Gwyn was up there, on the playground. I tried to climb, but the loose slag gave way under my weight and I kept sliding back. The thumping increased in intensity and the nightmare faded as my eyes opened. But the pain in my shoulder and the rocking persisted.

I lay on a canvas hammock in semidarkness immersed in an atmosphere of motor oil, urine and human sweat. My left arm, bound tightly in a sling across my chest, restricted movement. Inches above my head the contour of a human form shaped the canvas of another hammock. A new fear of the unknown replaced my panic at not finding Gwyn. I lay on my back frightened and claustrophobic as memories of mineshafts deep underground tormented me.

My mind cleared with the realization that I was in a boat, moving over choppy water, the thumping noise the pulse of the ship's engine. I turned my head and saw other hammocks suspended one above the other, each holding a human form. Occasional moans and snores competed with the engine noise. I closed my eyes and was soon deep in a morphine-induced sleep.

I don't know how long I slept. I was awakened to the agony of a hand shaking my shoulder.

"Drink!" a voice said. The hand cradled and raised my head and a cup was placed against my lips. Cool water trickled into my mouth and down my throat. I drank hungrily. The man's face, covered with stubble, was inches from mine and his breath reeked of garlic and decay. He removed the cup and turned his attention to the man above. A second man placed a husk of bread on my chest. I picked it up with my right hand and nibbled at the edges. The bread was stale and the crust leathery. I had no appetite; the thought of food nauseated me. I placed the bread in the hammock alongside my body.

I was a prisoner of the Turks. The recent past flooded back—the lifeless bodies of Bill Oliver and Brian Greenwood as I was dragged across the square, and the feeling of guilt at having led them into a trap; the excruciating pain in my shoulder when a rotund Turk with black hair and silver beard stanched the bleeding and bandaged me tightly. Around the coarse woolen sleeve of his uniform, the Turk wore a white armband bearing a red crescent. I must have been delirious because I recall thinking at the time that if he were to don a red hat, he would make a believable Father Christmas. "Morphine," he'd said as he stuck a syringe needle in my arm. When he was finished, two soldiers tossed me unceremoniously into the back of an ox-drawn cart. I quickly lost consciousness with the cart's motion over the rutted track. How I got on board the boat or how long I'd been at sea, I had no idea.

The hours passed slowly. Sometimes during periods of wakefulness I tried to get up, but the pain discouraged me. Once a day the same two Turks brought bread and water, and left with the slamming of bolts through what must have been the door to the ship's hold. Later the men returned to help the wounded from their hammocks and lead them, one by one, to the lavatory, which was nothing more than a hole in the metal floor with two raised steps in front. Those who couldn't walk were left in their own waste. At times I was quite lucid; at others I dwelt in a netherworld between sleep and a dazed consciousness.

I steeled myself for whatever fate the Turks had in store for me. Before we had landed at Gallipoli, high-ranking officers had drilled into us that our enemy was nothing more that a bunch of godless heathens with little or no respect for human life, cruel and depraved. But what of the Turk I'd met during the burial detail? He didn't seem much different from our own lads. And there was the Turk with the red crescent on his sleeve who'd bandaged my wound. Nothing cruel or depraved about that. Perhaps the future was not so dire, I told myself.

At last, after I'd lost all track of time, the ship's engine stopped and the boat bumped against a jetty. We lay in silence for a good two hours before the bolts were pulled back and several men who looked like peasants, talking loudly among themselves, entered the hold with stretchers. They began near the door, lifting onto stretchers those who couldn't walk, dragging those who could out of their hammocks and onto their feet. It took some time before it was my turn. One of the men pulled my legs over the edge of the hammock and grabbed my good right arm to lift me to my feet. I walked unsteadily between the now-empty hammocks to where bright sunlight streamed through the open door. Ahead of me a Turk supported a soldier who could barely walk and whose head was completely swathed in bandages with small gaps for his mouth and nose.

We climbed metal steps to the deck and waited our turn to be led down the gangway to the quay, a wretched-looking assortment of wounded men adorned with dirty bandages covering various parts of our anatomies, crowded together on the narrow deck of a rusty tramp steamer. But the bright sunshine warming my back felt comforting after the dark, fetid atmosphere of the hold.

Facing us loomed a stately yellow-stuccoed building, three storeys high, capped with a red-tiled roof. It must have measured close to a quarter of a mile in length. Five-storey towers, capped with what could have passed for church steeples, were located at the right end and at the center, which suggested that the left half of the building was most likely added at a later date. Behind us an expanse of water stretched to a far shore lined with wooden houses. The water's surface supported all manner of boats, some small and propelled by one or more oarsmen, others under sail, and larger vessels pouring black smoke from their funnels. On either side of the waterway, tree-covered banks rose steeply to a cloudless blue sky.

The man who had helped me from the hammock led me down the gangway and through massive wooden doors into the building. Spasms of pain radiated from my shoulder with every step. Several Turkish soldiers armed with rifles kept guard, though none of us looked in any condition to put up a fight. We climbed a flight of stone stairs to the second level and entered a long, high-ceilinged room lined on both sides with iron-frame beds, each bearing a thin mattress, a khaki-colored blanket and a pillow. Small wooden tables sat between the beds. Tall windows illuminated the room with winter sunshine, the rays defined by suspended dust particles. Apart from the windows, the yellow plastered walls were bare.

My guide led me about halfway down the cavernous interior to an empty bed and gestured for me to sit. The soldier with the bandaged head lay motionless on the bed next to mine. I sat on the edge of the bed feeling helpless and depressed, even lonely despite all the human activity going on around me. Turkish soldiers with rifles slung over their shoulders walked up and down the central aisle, some appearing indifferent, others glancing contemptuously at their captives. My shoulder ached and throbbed.

Thoughts of home brought little comfort. The only images my mind could conjure up were of gray skies, grimy terrace houses, noisy dust-filled collieries and slagheaps. I thought of my aunt and uncle living out their daily routine in the cramped kitchen of our home on Victoria Street, my aunt dismissing out of hand the pains in her stomach. I saw her chapped hands from endless days of laundering, ironing, and scrubbing floors, and hauling in buckets of coal to keep the stove burning even in the heat of summer so that we could wash in warm water and enjoy hot meals. But most of all I longed for Gwyn. My army tunic had been removed back at Kücük Anafarta when Father Christmas tended to my wound, so I no longer had her photograph to reassure me. Without it I had a hard time picturing her face.

Immersed in my thoughts I was startled when a voice said, "*Merhaba!*." I looked up and there, standing at the foot of my bed, was the man who had bandaged my wound back at the village. He was writing in a notebook, still dressed in the same ill-fitting woolen uniform with the red crescent on his sleeve and just as plump.

He looked up. *"Merhaba,"* he said again. "Say *Merhaba.*"

"Merhaba," I repeated.

"Very good! Since you are going to be our guest you should learn some Turkish. *Merhaba* means hello. What is your name?" His English was fluent.

"Evan Morgan."

"Do people call you Evan or Morgan?"

"Evan."

"Very well, you shall be Evan," he said, writing in his book. "Shoulder wound. Doctor Orhan will examine you shortly. Very good doctor, trained in Switzerland." He moved to the next prisoner.

I looked around and saw that not all the beds were occupied. Some of the men were clearly in much worse shape than I from the look of their bandages. A man across the aisle from me sat with a cheerless expression on his face. His right arm was missing except for a bandaged stump close to the shoulder. His dark, swarthy features suggested he might be Gurkha or Indian, for both contributed to the litany of empire that defined the British presence at Gallipoli. I stood and began walking over to him, but a Turkish soldier barked at me and pointed at my bed. I sat back down.

With difficulty I removed my boots and lay back, my free arm behind my head. The effort brought renewed torture to my shoulder. The pillow and mattress, lumpy and uncomfortable, were soiled and appeared to be filled with straw, but they were better than nothing. Behind me, when I craned my head back, I could see cobwebs around the edge of the window and bluebottle flies crawling up and down the dirty panes. I stared up to where paint peeled from the ceiling, then closed my eyes and dozed.

I was awakened by voices nearby. A man in a white coat, presumably Doctor Orhan, leaned over the soldier in the adjacent bed, moving his stethoscope over the man's chest. An orderly carrying a tray of medical instruments stood alongside. The doctor folded the stethoscope into his coat pocket. He spoke to the orderly who promptly placed his tray on the table and pulled the blanket from the foot of the bed over the soldier's head. I'd been lying next to a dead man.

The doctor lit a cigarette and turned his attention to me. "How do you feel?" he asked in fluent English.

"My shoulder hurts."

He nodded and began cutting away my bandages with a pair of scissors. His lips held the cigarette at an angle to keep the smoke from his eyes. I groaned as he probed my wound with a slim steel shaft. I wondered if smoking while treating patients was part of his medical training.

"You have a bullet that must come out," he said. "Your wound is infected."

He spoke in Turkish to the orderly. The doctor flicked ash from his cigarette behind my cot and stood aside while the orderly filled a syringe from a labeled bottle and injected the contents into my arm.

"This will be painful," the doctor said. "But the morphine will help. You are fortunate the Germans give us morphine." He inhaled deeply from his cigarette, dropped the stub on the floor and extinguished it under his foot.

The orderly stuck a short piece of wood between my teeth and put his weight on my chest while the doctor poked into the wound. The wood clenched between my teeth prevented me from screaming in agony. Within seconds he pulled out the bloody projectile and held it with forceps in front of my eyes.

"Not bad," he said. "The bullet is intact and seems to have missed the bone. You were very lucky."

The orderly removed his weight from me but left the piece of wood in place. He wiped blood from around the wound and sprinkled it with yellow powder from what looked like a salt shaker, while the doctor prepared a needle for stitching. I closed my eyes tightly and bit down as the needle pierced my flesh. When he was finished, he said, "Stay lying down until tomorrow." The orderly removed the wood from my mouth and handed me a thin stick with a piece of white cloth attached to one end. "When you need to use the lavatory," the doctor continued, "wave that and someone will help you."

The doctor walked across the aisle to the dark-skinned soldier while the orderly opened a fresh packet of bandages. The morphine dulled the pain and I drifted into semi-consciousness. I was barely aware when the bandaging was finished.

§

I awoke feeling ravenous. I'd eaten next to nothing since I'd left our trenches and had no idea how many days had passed since I was wounded. Sunlight no longer streamed through the windows, but it was still light. I looked around and saw that someone had left an open bottle of water on the table next to the bed. I reached over and drank about a third of the water before replacing the bottle. The bed next to mine was empty, the body having been removed while I slept. I wished for a piece of the stale bread from the boat.

I looked up at the sound of footsteps and saw Father Christmas walking down the aisle carrying his notebook. He stopped at the foot of my bed.

"*Merhaba,*" he said. He looked at me expectantly.

"*Merhaba,*" I replied.

"Very good. Did Doctor Orhan take care of you?"

I nodded. "I'm very hungry."

He moved between the beds and sat on the one previously occupied by the dead soldier. He laid the notebook on the blanket, seemingly in no hurry to move on with his duties.

"You will be given some sheep stew to eat in a short while, Evan *Bey*. That's a new word for you. Evan *Bey* means Mister Evan."

"What's your name?" I asked.

"I am Kerim *Bey*. But just call me Kerim." He pointed to the armband bearing the red crescent. "I'm a bloke."

"A bloke?"

"I look after wounded soldiers." He saw the quizzical look on my face. "Did I say the wrong word?"

"Is bloke a Turkish word?" I asked.

"I thought it was English. One of your soldiers touched me here,"—he patted the armband—"and said I was a good bloke."

I smiled at his misunderstanding. "Bloke is English, but that's not what it means. We say medical corpsman."

"Then what is bloke?"

"Well . . . I'm a bloke. You're a bloke." I pointed my thumb at the soldier across the aisle. "He's a bloke. We're all blokes."

Kerim laughed heartily. "So I, too, learn a new word today! Bloke. It means the same as chap, perhaps?"

"That's right, chap. Something like that."

"I prefer bloke to medical corpsman. Much easier to say."

"Were you on the boat with us?" I asked.

"I was. Soon I will be going home." He patted his belly. "My officer at Gelibolu, or Gallipoli as you call it, thinks I am too old and too fat to be in the war. That is why I came back on the boat."

The tantalizing aroma of cooked meat wafted into the room as two white-coated orderlies rolled in serving carts containing bowls and loaves of bread. Kerim stood and retrieved his notebook.

"How long was I on the boat?" I asked.

"Three days. We had to go slowly and stay close to the shore because of your submarines. Usually it only takes one day to cross the Sea of Marmara."

"Where are we now?"

"Kuleli. How do you like our hospital?

"It's very big," I said.

"Kuleli is a naval college. Only one part of the building is used as a hospital, and only since we joined the war. Florence Nightingale once had a hospital here."

"During the Crimean War?"

"Yes. She had a much larger one in the army barracks at Haydarpasha, but she ran out of room. Today I am your Florence Nightingale." He moved to the foot of the bed to make way for the orderly.

"Where is Kuleli?"

"Have you heard of the Bosphorus?"

"Of course," I said, remembering Miss Pinchen's geography class.

"Kuleli is on the Bosphorus, a few kilometers north of Constantinople. When you can stand you must look out the window. We are in Asia, and across the Bosphorus you see Europe. Isn't that marvelous? We are the only country to lie in two continents."

"What about Russia?"

Kerim thought about this. "I suppose so," he said. "But there is no Bosphorus separating Europe from Asia." He gestured with his notebook. "I must go, Bloke. Enjoy your supper." He paused and lifted a loaf of bread from the cart. *"Ekmek,"* he said, then replaced the loaf and left.

An orderly, who looked about my age, placed a bowl of stew, a spoon and a hunk of bread on the table next to me. He said something in Turkish and pointed to the spoon, then to himself, before moving off with the cart. I reached for the bread and bit off a piece. It was fresh and tasty. Once all the meals had been distributed, the carts were rolled back to the center of the room, and the man who had delivered my meal came back, sat on the edge of the bed and spooned stew into my mouth. It hardly measured up to my aunt's hearty mutton stew loaded with potatoes, carrots and leeks, with generous portions of meat. This concoction contained mostly lukewarm water with a few insipid vegetables and occasional pieces of stringy mutton, but after days of relative starvation it tasted delicious.

"Thank you," I said when the stew was gone. "I patted my stomach and said, "Very good." The man smiled and handed me the remaining bread. *"Ekmek,"* I said.

He smiled again and took the bowl and spoon back to the cart before assisting another of the wounded. I finished the bread, drank some water and lay back, my good arm cradling my head. My stomach gurgled as my gastric juices finally had something to work on. Despite the persistent ache in my shoulder, I felt reasonably content. But I was still a prisoner in a war that showed no signs of ending. I could be in captivity for years, and that didn't sit well with me.

My thoughts drifted to the broad channel separating two continents, just a short distance outside my window. I imagined myself stepping off the quay into the water and floating on my back, the current carrying me past Constantinople to freedom.

Chapter 12

After a night which I spent more in wakefulness than in sleep, the throbbing in my shoulder subsided and I was again feeling ravenous. I also felt dirty and craved a bath; and with several days' growth of beard, I was desperate for a shave.

Slowly, to minimize the pain, I eased my feet over the edge of the bed and raised myself to a sitting position. After several minutes I stood up and walked unsteadily to the window. A light drizzle had replaced yesterday's sunshine and the waters of the Bosphorus appeared gray and uninviting. Among a flotilla of fishing vessels an imposing gun-turreted warship bearing a German flag drifted slowly past against the current, the rumble of its engines barely audible through the glass. Seagulls swooped low over the water and perched on capstans along the quay. A short distance to the left of my window a trim white Turkish naval launch lay moored while a sailor, seemingly oblivious to the rain, ran a mop over its deck. Directly below where I was standing a half-dozen or so Turkish soldiers, their rifles slung barrel down over their shoulders, chatted among themselves on a broad cobblestone walkway as a man dressed in a business suit and red fez walked past. It occurred to me that the soldiers who had been very much in evidence yesterday were no longer patrolling our hospital room.

I turned away and made my way to the lavatory at the end of the room, but returned and slipped on my boots once I saw the state of the floor. The more I walked, the more steady I felt on my feet. I tested the door through which we had entered the day before, but it was locked.

How long will it be before I use a civilized toilet again? I thought, as I did my best with the hole in the floor. A tap protruding from the wall behind the hole provided water for flushing. At a rust-stained sink across from the toilet, I washed my face and functioning hand in cold water and dried them on a dirty rag hanging from a hook in the wall. I shouldn't complain, I told myself; conditions were no better in the trenches.

I stopped to chat with two soldiers who were sitting together on the edge of a bed. Albert Parker, a native of Blackpool and a sergeant with the 1st Battalion, Lancashire Fusiliers, had lost his left leg below the knee and hobbled around with the aid of a single wooden crutch. Cyril Montague, a New Zealander serving with the Wellington Battalion of the Anzac Army Corps, had received nasty shrapnel wounds to the head and chest. As we traded accounts of how we had become prisoners, white-jacketed orderlies arrived with a breakfast of bread, goat cheese and dates, and chipped cups of sweet warm tea.

I returned to my bed and made short work of the food. Afterwards I strolled over to the dark-skinned prisoner across the room from me. He was sitting on the edge of his bed sipping tea. His army tunic, lying on the bed next to him, bore sergeant's stripes. I sat across from him.

"Hello, Sergeant" I said. "I'm Evan Morgan, South Wales Borderers. How are you feeling?"

The man shrugged, but didn't say anything. He was slender and quite handsome, younger than one might expect for a soldier who had already earned the rank of sergeant.

"Are you Gurkha?" I persisted.

He looked up. When he saw I wasn't going anywhere, he said in a clipped Indian accent, "Sorry. Suresh Pandya, 66th Punjabis. I'm feeling a bit out of sorts."

"Can't say I blame you," I said, nodding toward what remained of his right arm. Miss Pinchen had drilled enough Indian geography into us at Tonypandy Secondary that I had a rough idea of Punjab's location in the north of India. "Where did you live before the war?"

"Amritsar."

"Does that make you Muslim?" I was determined to draw the young man out of his shell.

"No. I'm Hindu. But there are lots of Muslims and Sikhs in Punjab."

I nodded. "I'm sorry about the arm," I said. "Maybe there'll be a prisoner exchange and you'll be able to go home."

"What is there at home for me?" he said bitterly, placing his now empty cup on the table next to his bed. "I was a carpenter before the war and made a good living. Now I shall be a beggar. How will I support my wife and daughter?"

"Surely the army will give you a pension."

"The sahibs get pensions, not the men in the ranks. Not even a sergeant."

We were interrupted by an orderly who entered the room with a bundle of clothing. "Take off clothes!" he shouted several times as he walked through the room dropping off what looked like cotton pajamas at each occupied bed.

"Look," I said, standing up. "Anytime you feel like talking, just come on over. If you don't mind chatting with someone a couple of ranks below you."

Suresh smiled for the first time. "Maybe I'll just come over and give orders."

I laughed. "I'm not sure I'd have to obey, given the circumstances. I've always wanted to tell a sergeant where to get off." I started back to my bed. I paused. "Sergeant," I said, "if you need an extra hand for anything, just call me."

"Thanks, Evan," he replied. "I may do that. And please, don't call me Sergeant. The name's Suresh."

Using my good arm I peeled off my army vest and trousers and put on the sand-colored pajama bottoms. The top I draped over my shoulders. The cotton was threadbare and a bit short in the legs, but it was clean and felt comfortable against the skin. I wrapped the blanket around me because the room had taken on a decided chill now that sunshine no longer streamed through the windows. I was becoming resigned to pain in the shoulder every time I exerted myself.

I sat on the bed wishing for something to read. My poetry book sat in my kitbag at Gallipoli, and who knows what had become of the Fennimore Cooper book after Dai was killed. After reading and memorizing many of Riley's verses, I'd taken a shine to poetry and wished I had more. I'd even tried writing a bit myself, but I could never make the words come out right. I marveled at Gwyn's gift for writing poetry in both English and Welsh, verses that drew smiles of delight from Uncle Mervyn. I pictured my uncle sitting contentedly by the kitchen stove, puffing away at his pipe and sipping tea, his favorite book of Hedd Wyn's Welsh poems in his hand.

I anguished at how my aunt and uncle would react when they received the telegram saying I was missing in action, and how Gwyn would take it when they told her. I thought of her on the platform waving as I left for the last time, her figure shrinking into the distance. A fit of depression overcame me. I'd been away so long, perhaps Gwyn wouldn't even care any more. Maybe some other lad had caught her fancy. The thought was unbearable.

"Please pay attention!" Kerim's voice, shouted from the middle of the room, startled me from my foul mood. "You are to have baths. Please line up at this end." He pointed to the door at the opposite end from the lavatory. "You will be given a towel which you must keep. I will remove bandages and give you clean ones after you bathe."

I put aside the blanket and joined a queue of those who were able to walk at the shower room door. Kerim moved to the front of the line. "Four at a time," he said.

"Kerim *Bey*," I called.

"*Efendim,*" he said, looking at me.

"Any chance we can have a shave?"

"Don't you want to look like me?" Kerim said, running a hand over his bushy silver beard.

"I'd prefer that my face didn't itch."

"Perhaps I can get a razor," he said. "But I'm not sure we can trust all you bloodthirsty Tommies with a razor. We'll have to guard you while you shave." His smile told us that we should not take him too seriously.

Kerim pulled a small pair of scissors from his breast pocket and began cutting away bandages. Most of them, including mine, came away stained with dried blood and pus. "Do not use this arm when you bathe," he said to me. The stitched-up wound on my shoulder was ugly and inflamed.

As I waited my turn I noticed a small room adjacent to the shower room where clothing, probably belonging to the medical orderlies, hung on hooks along the walls. It must be where they changed for work, I assumed. On the left side of the broad hallway, a bored-looking Turkish soldier, his rifle cradled in his lap, sat on a wooden chair guarding a flight of stone steps that led to the ground floor and upper floors. Directly ahead, through an open door, a long corridor with doors on both sides stretched a good distance to another doorway.

I entered the shower room with the third group of four. The cement floor felt cold against my feet after the wooden floorboards of the hospital room. Pale green ceramic tiles covered the walls and ceiling, from which four shower nozzles extended. Single taps for each shower protruded from the wall above a waist-high shelf bearing large bars of gray-colored soap that smelled of carbolic. We stripped and draped our pajamas on chairs placed against one wall. A wooden table contained a stack of white cotton towels.

The icy water took my breath away, but once my skin adjusted to the temperature, I opened the tap fully and immersed myself while using my good arm to run the soap over the length of my body and through my hair. The pressure of water on my damaged shoulder was painful, but there was no way to avoid it. I rinsed away the soap, turned off the shower and picked up a towel. I dried myself awkwardly with one hand, dabbing gently around my wound. Still naked I returned to my bed, draped the damp towel over one corner of the table, and slipped into my pajama bottoms. After the cold shower, the room seemed a lot warmer.

I sat patiently while Kerim made his way from bed to bed applying fresh bandages. As he worked I studied his face. He looked to be in his forties, but I found it hard to put an age on a man with a beard. His eyes twinkled under bushy black eyebrows as he chatted with each of the men, while his hands manipulated bandages with skill and confidence. War, it seemed, had not made him cynical or embittered. We were the enemy, yet Kerim offered each of us friendship and compassion to lessen the burden of disfigurement and imprisonment. I don't think there was a mean bone in his body.

After he had taken care of Suresh, he came across and placed his tray containing bandages and dressings on the table next to my bed. "Evan *Bey*," he said.

"*Efendim*", I replied.

"Very good. You've learned a new word." Kerim pulled out a fresh dressing.

"I don't know what it means."

"*Efendim* is a very nice word. You should have such a word in your language." He sat next to me on the bed and peered at my wound. "Its meaning depends on how you say it. When you spoke my name by the shower and I said *Efendim,* it meant 'Yes, how may I help you?' or words like that. But if you said something that I didn't hear or didn't understand, I would say *Efendim?*" His voice rose at the last syllable. "Then it means 'What did you say?' or 'What do you mean?' Or, I might meet you on the street and say, *Merhaba, Efendim!* Then it is simply a polite way to greet you."

"Like sir?"

Kerim thought for a moment. "No," he said, taking a fresh dressing from the tray. "More friendly than sir. Not so formal." He sprinkled yellow powder on the dressing and applied it to my shoulder. "Hold, please."

I held the dressing in place while he wrapped a wide bandage around my shoulder and chest. I noticed his hands were rough and callused. Once the dressing was secure, I removed my hand. He finished rolling the bandage around my shoulder, then cut the end with his scissors into two strands which he tied around my arm.

"Kerim," I said, as he began wrapping my arm in a sling. "When I was taken prisoner I was looking for three of our men."

"Ah, yes, the officer and the two Tommies."

"You know what happened to them?"

"They were taken prisoner in the village, like you. But they were smarter. They surrendered as soon as we confronted them. No need for shooting."

A wave of guilt washed over me. Bill and Brian would probably still be alive if I hadn't gone round that bend. I should have told them to lay down their weapons and raise their hands as soon as I saw movement in the windows instead of telling them to back up. If only Brian hadn't brought up his rifle.

"All finished." Kerim brought me back to the present.

"How did you learn to speak English so well?" I asked.

"When I finish bandaging, I will tell you," he said as he retrieved his tray.

As Kerim moved off to treat Albert Parker's leg, I stood up and looked out the window. Only two soldiers patrolled the quay now, and the Turkish launch appeared deserted. A cluster of small fishing vessels sat a short distance off shore while seagulls swooped and squawked around them. A ferryboat belching black smoke from its single funnel crossed from one side of the Bosphorus to the other.

Suresh, who had been pacing up and down, joined me. "Beautiful," he said, looking out the window.

"Yes," I replied. "The war seems a long way away."

We made small talk while standing at the window. Suresh told me about his family, his wife Sangita and daughter Marisha, a lively five-year-old who before the war was already helping sweep up sawdust in his carpentry shop. The affection he displayed for his family reminded me of the Turkish soldier I'd met when we buried the dead.

"Are you married, Evan?" he asked.

"No. But I have a girlfriend back home I'd like to marry." I wished I had her photograph to show him. "Her name's Gwyn."

"She's your fiancée?"

"I haven't given her a ring, if that's what you mean, but she said she'd marry me when the war's over." I leaned on the windowsill and watched a new guard contingent march across the promenade. "To tell the truth, I'm not sure she'll want to marry me now. I'm not the same man I was when I left. I've done a lot of killing—even a Turkish lad who looked too young to be in the army."

"We've all done our share of killing, Evan. It's what we were trained for. She won't hold that against you."

"Our Bosphorus is beautiful, yes?" Kerim interrupted our conversation as he arrived with his tray of bandages. "You should see it in the springtime when the Judas trees are in blossom."

"What will happen to us when our wounds heal?" Suresh asked, turning towards him.

"You will be sent to a prison camp in Anatolia. A long way from here." Kerim placed his tray on the empty bed next to mine. "But I hope the war ends before you have to go because the camps are not nice places. Not much food and much disease. Many prisoners die there."

"The war isn't going to end for a long time," I said as we sat down, Suresh and I on my bed, Kerim next to his tray.

"Yes, Evan *Bey*, I think you are right. But I also think you should know what lies ahead so that you can prepare yourself."

"Prepare ourselves?" Suresh said bitterly. "How can we do that when we're prisoners?"

Kerim tapped his head. "I mean prepare for it up here. With the right frame of mind, soldiers survive better in the camps." He leaned over and patted Suresh on the knee. "Don't worry, my friend. The war will end, perhaps within a year, perhaps two. And then you will go home to Punjab." He turned towards me. "Where is your home, Bloke?"

I was amused at his idiosyncratic use of bloke. "Wales," I said.

"Ah, Wales. A beautiful country, I believe."

"Yes it is. Very green, with lots of mountains."

"And you were a coalminer in Wales?"

I looked at him in astonishment. "How on earth did you know that?"

"Because you have black lines." He took my good hand and pointed to a thin black line over the knuckles, and another at the end of my thumb. "You cut your hand and the coal dust gets in. And before you have a chance to wash, the cut closes. You have another such line on your forehead,"—he touched me above my left eye—"and I saw one on your cheek when I first treated your wound. Before it was covered with hair."

I was aware, of course, of those lines, but I'd lived with them so long that I took them for granted and never thought of them.

"I grew up in Zonguldak, on the Black Sea—or *Kara Deniz,* as we call it," Kerim continued. "People in Zonguldak fish or they work in the coalmines. Some do both. My father and my grandfather worked in the mines, and they, too, had black lines. They are the mark of the coalminer."

I studied my hands, tracing my fingers over the telltale lines. "Did you work in the mines?" I asked.

"No, my schoolmaster saw promise in me, and he arranged a scholarship for me to go to the American college."

"You went all the way to America?" Suresh said in surprise.

"No, no. I mean the American college here, on the other side of the Bosphorus," Kerim nodded towards the window.

"Why is there an American college here?" Suresh asked.

"It was started by an American missionary about fifty years ago."

"He wanted to turn you into Christians, is that it?" I said.

"Not exactly." Kerim folded his arms. "His only pupils in the beginning were already Christian—Armenians, Greeks, some Bulgarians. He taught them his religion, which was a very simple type of Protestant worship. He believed all those fancy churches, with their priests in fancy robes waving incense, were sinful in the eyes of God. His religion is much like mine, nothing fancy, everything simple. I was one of the first Turks to be educated at the college. Now there are many. But the teachers do not force their religion on us. They are very tolerant."

"Is that where you learned English?" I asked.

"Yes, everything is taught in English. I knew a little of the language from my school in Zonguldak, but at the college the pupils are taught to speak and write English for a whole year before they begin their regular studies."

"What did you study?" I asked.

"The usual subjects—history, science, mathematics, literature, classics. But we also learned to use tools. Mr. Hamlin—that was the missionary's name—he believed that his pupils should work with their hands as he did, so they could earn a living. After he died, the tradition continued. I learned to work with metal and, like you, with wood," he said, looking at Suresh. "But I think you are probably a much better carpenter."

I envied him his education. "What did you do when you finished college?" I asked.

"I went to Germany to study medicine. I wanted to be a doctor, like Doctor Orhan. But after two years I had no more money and had to return home. I almost starved in Germany. Now I am a farmer, but I also work at the college."

"Before the war," I said.

Kerim nodded. "I was called into the army because I had medical training and because I spoke German. We have German officers helping us at Gallipoli, and sometimes I translated for them."

"And soon you'll be going back to your farm."

"Yes, as soon as my authorization papers arrive. Maybe in a week or two. Things move very slowly in Turkey. Too many . . ." He paused, groping for the word. "I think you call them bureaucrats."

"Just like India," Suresh said.

"One of these days a bureaucrat will come here to get information from you that will be sent to the Red Cross. That way your families will know you are alive."

I looked at Suresh and smiled. "That's good news," I said. "They must be worried sick."

Kerim stood up and retrieved his tray. "I have work to do," he said.

"Is your farm far from here?" I asked.

"No, very close. Across the Bosphorus there is a very big castle. You can't see it from these windows, but it is just a short way north. Mehmet the Conqueror constructed the castle before he liberated Constantinople over four hundred years ago. We call it *Rumeli Hisarı,* the European Castle. My village is near the castle." He moved out from between the beds. "When the war is over, you must visit me. Just ask anyone you meet, *Kerim Bey nerede?* Where is Kerim? They will show you the way to my home."

He left carrying his tray, making pleasantries with the men as he made his way through the room.

"I'm going to miss that chap when he leaves," Suresh said.

"Yes," I agreed. I stood and walked to the window where several flies buzzed against the glass. "I don't want to go to any prison camp," I said, as I tried to gauge the width of the Bosphorus. "I wouldn't mind leaving when he leaves."

Suresh laughed. "Fat chance of that."

I shrugged and didn't reply.

"It's funny," Suresh said, joining me at the window. "I feel pain in my arm, but when I reach over to rub it, the arm isn't there. How can I feel pain in an arm I don't have?" He looked over at me and stared into my eyes. "Surely you're not serious, Evan? About leaving, I mean." I didn't reply. "We're under guard," Suresh persisted. "How could you possibly get away?"

I watched a dead tree branch floating quickly along with the current. "I have no idea," I said.

Chapter 13

We fell into a routine of two meals a day, showers once a week, and hours of boredom. The meals were too sparse to put much flesh on our bones, but enough to keep us healthy. Breakfast usually consisted of bread and fruit. The second meal, which arrived anywhere between noon and late afternoon, might be vegetable or mutton stew or simply bread and cheese with a few olives. Both meals were accompanied by lukewarm tea or water. We ate a lot of bread, which was fine by me because it was always fresh from the naval college bakery. Two or three times a day a Turkish soldier strolled through the room, rifle over his shoulder, to remind us that we were under guard.

Towards the end of the third week Kerim disappeared and returned three days later with a stack of English-language books, several decks of playing cards and a set each of dominoes and backgammon, the latter a game I'd never seen before. He had gone over to the American college, he told us, and spoken to some of the faculty members about the prison hospital at Kuleli, asking if they had any books to spare. They were more than generous. From the stack of books I picked up a well-used copy of Sir Walter Scott's *Ivanhoe* which I'd read as a school assignment back in Wales, but was happy to read again.

Kerim was diligent in taking care of our wounds, twice a week removing the bandages for Doctor Orhan's inspection. Some of the prisoners whose injuries had healed quickly were taken away, presumably to one of the dreaded prison camps, while fresh prisoners, some with ghastly wounds, took their place. My shoulder remained infected and painful, and at times I was feverish, a consequence of the infection, the doctor opined. I spent quite a bit of time walking up and down to keep my legs exercised, and in the process got to know most of the men. But of all the prisoners there, I was closest to Suresh.

Besides the proximity of our beds, Suresh and I hit it off very well. Some of the other men resented him, and more than once I heard them refer to him as a wog. I think they resented me as well because of my friendship with him. With their colonial mentality, they didn't like being outranked by someone with dark skin. Not that Suresh flaunted his rank;

we were all in the same boat, and stripes on a sleeve didn't mean much as far as most of us were concerned. The only prisoner to outrank Suresh was an Australian lieutenant, and he was in such bad shape he wasn't about to give orders to anybody.

One day, as we stood at the window watching the ever-changing myriad of Bosphorus water traffic, Suresh told me more about his home in Amritsar, and of his impoverished childhood in one of the crowded slums of the city. At an early age he had found a job in a carpentry shop, mostly cleaning up and running errands. In time, under the tutelage of the carpenter, he acquired the skills that allowed him to set out on his own in a shed behind his parents' house. When he turned twenty-one, his parents arranged his marriage to Sangita, a girl he had never met. He built an extension on his parents' small house for them to live in, and his wife took care of the accounts for his carpentry business.

"My father wasn't too happy when Marisha was born," he said. "In India it's very important to have sons, but I think that's nonsense. Marisha is the center of our universe, and now both my parents adore her."

"Wouldn't you want a son to help you with your work?" I asked.

"If God wills it, perhaps our next will be a son. That will make my father happy." Down below a group of soldiers stood at attention as another group accompanied by an officer marched in to relieve them. Beneath their feet the paving stones glistened from recent rain. Suresh turned his back on the window and leaned against the wall. "This Gwyn of yours," he said. "Have you known her a long time?"

"Ever since we were children in school."

A wistful expression crossed Suresh's face. "I was in love once with a girl I knew in school. We lived on the same street. It was very exciting. We would meet away from where her parents or mine could see us. But we both knew we would never marry. It just isn't done that way in India."

"Did her parents arrange her marriage?"

"Yes, to a shopkeeper twice her age. I was heartbroken."

I nodded to Albert Parker who hobbled past on his crutch, a pained expression on his face, cigarette dangling from his mouth. "But you love Sangita," I said.

"With all my heart. But not at first. We simply didn't know each other." He scratched at the bandaged stump of his arm. "But she was so sweet and considerate of my shyness that I soon felt a great affection for her, and in time that affection turned to love. I don't know which is better, your system or ours."

I pondered this for a moment. "I think I like ours better," I said. "If my marriage was arranged, I'd be scared to death I'd end up with someone I couldn't stand."

"I wonder if Sangita will still love me with one arm and no way to make a living," Suresh said as he turned again to look out the window.

"From what you've told me of her, it won't make a bit of difference." I changed the subject. "How did you end up in the army?"

"I was conscripted. When the war started the regiment needed carpenters to build new barracks. There were over a dozen of us called up at the same time. Once the barracks were finished, we were sent to the infantry."

"You must have impressed your officers to make sergeant so quickly.

Suresh shrugged. "All the carpenters were promoted to lance corporal when the work was finished, so we started out ahead of the others. Perhaps I was a good soldier, but I'd rather be a good carpenter." He looked down at the stump of his arm and shook his head. "You know, Evan, I miss my wife and daughter so much, but I don't think I can face them like this."

How could I, with just a few scars, but otherwise whole, understand the depth of his feeling, his sense of inadequacy? I moved away from the window and sat on my bed. "I think Gwyn would love me just as much if I lost an arm or a leg," I said at last. "I'm sure it will be the same with Sangita. She sounds like a wonderful wife. I'm sure she misses you just as much as you miss her."

He sat across from me. "I hope so. I really hope so."

"Look Suresh, when this war's over I'd like to keep in touch. I met an Aussie a while ago and he wanted us to be pen pals. I'd like to do the same with you, find out how things turn out for you at home. Maybe you could send me a photo of your family." I put my book on the table and took a piece of paper and a pencil from the drawer.

As I wrote my address, Suresh asked in a quiet voice, "Are you really thinking about trying to escape?"

I handed him the piece of paper. "I don't want to rot in a prison camp." I put the pencil back in the drawer. "What about you?"

"With one arm it's out of the question." He looked at my address. "Don't you want mine?"

"Not now. If I do get out of here, it wouldn't be a good idea to have your name and address on me. Not if I got caught"

He looked around to see if anyone was watching before removing his left boot and extracting several banknotes. "Here, take these," he said, pushing the notes into my hand. "I took them from a dead Turk."

I looked down at the notes. The likeness of an authoritative-looking man with a thick moustache and fez covered one end and an image of a mosque with several minarets the center; other than that they were covered mostly with indecipherable Arabic script. "I can't take these," I said.

"Take it," Suresh insisted, closing his hand over mine to obscure the notes. "The money is of no value to me. I was just saving it as a souvenir for my daughter. But it might come in handy if you really do get out of here."

My first inclination was to simply give the money back, but after hesitating for several seconds, I shoved the banknotes in the pocket of my pajamas. "I'll hold on to it for now," I said. "But if we get sent to a prison camp, I'll give it back to you. Thanks, Suresh."

It was foolish, perhaps, to even think of escaping; the obstacles seemed insurmountable. A sling still restricted my arm and the infection showed no sign of healing. I had no idea how to get out of the hospital unobserved. At night we were locked in, and soldiers patrolled the front and back of the building during the day. Even if I did get out, it was a long way back to Gallipoli. I figured the best plan would be to head west around the Sea of Marmara, traveling at night and hiding during the day, until I linked up with the French at the mouth of the Dardanelles. From there I could get a boat and cross over to Gallipoli. Whether I could get through the Turkish defensive positions to reach the French lines was beyond me at this point. Crossing the Bosphorus was another possibility, but that would be a tough swim, especially with a bad shoulder. And even if I made it, I'd still have to make my way through or around Constantinople.

Kerim might have been reading my mind. One day he sat next to me on the bed and explained the rules of backgammon. As we began playing a game, I asked him what it was like to swim in the Bosphorus.

He looked at me sharply. "Why would you want to know that, Bloke?"

"Just curious," I said, amused that I had become Bloke instead of Evan.

"You're not thinking of trying to swim across, are you?"

I laughed. "It's a bit cold for that."

"Sometimes, Bloke, you remind me of the animals in the Munich zoo. They all wanted to get out of their cages. I could see it in their eyes."

"It's your move," I said.

Kerim rolled the dice. As he moved his stones across the board, he said, "The Bosphorus current is very strong. One can swim in some of the bays, but only close to the shore." He handed me the dice. "But there are some idiots who try to swim across. I was one of them, several years ago."

"How far did you get?" I took my turn with the dice.

"You may not believe this," Kerim said patting his stomach, "but I made it all the way across. I was a student at the college then. Every year, in the spring, the students have a day where they do crazy things, and one of those things is to swim the Bosphorus. They still do, it's a tradition. They take a ferry across to a place a good distance up so that as they swim, the current carries them down to the shore below the college."

"Sounds dangerous," I said, handing him the dice.

"Like I said, we were idiots. But no one ever drowned, as far as I know. Boats always go with the swimmers to pull out those who get tired." He made his move and stood up. "I must get back to work. You'll have to find someone else to play with." He stood up and stretched, then looked at me pointedly. "Don't try anything crazy, Bloke." He patted me on the shoulder and left for the doorway.

§

Christmas came and went with little to show for it other than a half-hearted attempt at familiar carols. No special meal, no roast goose or Christmas pudding, just the usual insipid stew. I longed for the festive atmosphere of Christmas in Wales, and the holly-bedecked chapel where the rafters rang with joyous Christmas hymns, and Gwyn and I stood, shoulders touching, in the glow of mutual affection. Judging from the relative quiet in the hospital ward, I suspected I was not alone in such memories.

By the beginning of 1916 I was sporting a full beard. Kerim had provided a straight-edge razor for the ward, attached to the bathroom wall by a slender chain, along with shaving cream, brush and strop. But by the time he got around to it my face had stopped itching, and trimming my beard with scissors seemed a lot easier than waiting in line to shave. Besides, I had another motive. Most of the Turks I saw from the window, other than clean-shaven naval cadets, wore beards or moustaches. In the unlikely event I were to get away, I reasoned, a beard might make me less conspicuous.

Shortly after the year began, Kerim approached me with his tray of bandages as I lay back reading. The weather was ugly outside, and gale-force winds drove rain and sleet against the window behind me. He sat on the edge of the bed. His woolen uniform looked even more rumpled and it smelled as if he had been out in the weather. "I have news, Bloke."

I lay my book across my chest. "Your discharge papers arrived."

"Yes, two days ago," he said, picking up a pair of scissors from the tray. "I leave next week. But I have other news. First, I must look at your shoulder."

I sat up and put my book on the table. "I'll be sorry to see you go," I said. "You're a good bloke."

Kerim laughed. "Well, you're a good bloke too, Evan." He cut away at my sling and the bandages around my shoulder.

"Tell me your other news."

Kerim looked at my shoulder wound, still inflamed but healed since the stitches had been removed. He poked around with his finger. "How does it feel?" he asked.

"Still painful."

"The infection is better. I will put on a fresh bandage, but I think we no longer need the sling. You must move your arm and get some strength back into it." He placed a piece of gauze on the wound. "Hold, please."

I held the gauze as he took a fresh bandage roll and began winding it around my shoulder. "What is your news, Kerim?"

"My news, Bloke, is that the Gallipoli battle is over. The British and French armies have left."

I was dumbfounded. I tried to look casual, but his words hit like a blow to the stomach. "What do you mean, left?"

"Gone. Vanished." He snipped the end of the bandage and ripped it into two strands. "It was a magnificent retreat. They went out at night, several thousand at a time over several nights, and those left behind just made more noise so we would not suspect what was happening. They even took their mules and artillery. One day, the sun came up and . . ." He raised his hands in a gesture of finality. "Not a British soldier left on the peninsula. No live ones anyway. They fooled us completely."

I didn't know what to think. It seemed incredulous that after so much sacrifice, our army would simply give up the fight. So much for my plan to return to Gallipoli.

Again, he seemed to read my thoughts. "I thought you ought to know, Bloke, in case you were thinking of running back there."

I ignored his remark, just shook my head. "What a waste," I said.

He finished tying the bandage and picked up the old ones. "We couldn't lose. We had the best leader, Mustafa Kemal, better than all the British and German generals put together." His voice turned bitter. "How many dead are left behind? How many of your countrymen. And mine."

I thought of Dai Wilkins and Charlie Beresford and all the other friends I'd lost, and the scores of bodies I'd helped bury. The stench of death came back like a repellent fog. "You Turks put up one hell of a fight," I said. "We weren't expecting that."

"I think the soldiers on both sides acquitted themselves with honor. But it wasn't worth the slaughter." He stood up with his tray. "Something else, Bloke. I heard that this hospital is to be used for Turkish soldiers. You are all being sent to a prison camp."

"When?"

He shrugged. "Who knows?" Perhaps a week, perhaps two. But soon."

"What about the Red Cross? When are our names to be taken down?

"I don't know, Bloke. I keep asking, but I get no answer. Perhaps when you get to the camp. *Inşallah*—God willing."

A few days later Kerim came through with Doctor Orhan for a final look at our wounds. He shook hands with each of us and wished us luck. The next day Lieutenant Turan arrived, signaling his presence with two loud, prolonged blasts from a whistle.

Turan, a man who looked to be in his thirties, was the antithesis of Kerim, slender build, clean shaven, and the proper military bearing. Sunken cheeks, hooked nose, thin mouth, he stood in the center of the room holding a baton with his two hands behind his back, staring at us as if we were insects. White-coated Doctor Orhan and a soldier bearing a rifle stood with him. He spoke loudly and rapidly in Turkish, paused and nodded to Orhan.

The doctor translated. "I am Lieutenant Turan and I am in charge of this hospital."

Turan spoke again, and Orhan said, "You are leaving soon for a prison camp many kilometers from here. I will be taking you there." Again, more Turkish, moving his feet to address those behind him and at each end of the room. "Meanwhile, you are soldiers and will act like soldiers. You will stand at attention at the end of your beds."

No one moved. Turan shouted louder, his face reddening. He rapped his baton across the metal frame of the bed in front of him.

"The lieutenant insists that you stand by your beds," Orhan said, almost apologetically. "You had better do what he says." Slowly, those of us able to stand did as we were told. "He wants you to stand at attention," Orhan said. I brought my feet together, arms to my sides.

Turan began pacing up and down the room, slapping his baton against his knee-length boots. He stopped in front of Suresh and tapped the stump of his arm with the baton. He said something and the guard laughed. I could see Suresh was having a hard time containing himself.

Turan turned to me. He raised his baton and jabbed the end sharply against my bandaged shoulder, causing me to cry out in pain and fall to a sitting position on the bed. The soldier grabbed my arm and pulled me back to my feet.

"Stop it you bloody fool!" Suresh yelled.

The guard swung around and aimed the butt of his rifle towards Suresh's stomach when Orhan stepped between them. The doctor pushed the rifle down and began yelling at the guard and gesticulating wildly. Then he turned his attention to Turan. I didn't need to understand Turkish to know that the lieutenant was getting a tongue lashing from the normally mild-mannered doctor. The guard, nervous now, looked at Turan for guidance.

There was a moment of silence as the lieutenant and the doctor glared at each other; then Turan, his face redder than ever, turned and stalked out of the room followed by the guard, rifle dangling at his side. Orhan threw up his arms in disgust and followed them out. After that Turan stayed away from the ward, but I didn't doubt that he would make life miserable for us when we shipped out to the camp.

§

Deliverance came in the form of an explosion. It was three days after Turan had made his appearance. We were playing whist, Albert Parker and I against Suresh and Cyril Montague, sitting on beds with a table drawn between us. Suresh supported his cards upright between books so that he could play with his one hand. Cyril had just trumped a trick when a thunderous noise and concussion jolted us. Window glass cracked near where we sat, and further down the room glass from shattered panes tinkled against the floor.

We dropped our cards and rushed to look out. Through the cracked glass we saw a naval vessel partially submerged and engulfed in black smoke, about two thirds of the way across the water. Floating alongside a steamer burned furiously. From all directions boats of various types and sizes converged on the disaster, while below us the naval launch, swarming with sailors, pulled away from its mooring, engine rumbling. Naval cadets, soldiers and civilians crowded along the edge of the quay, staring at the drama unfolding before them.

"Bloody hell!" Albert swore. "I wonder if one of our subs did that?"

I stared down at the crowd. Several of our guards, rifles slung over their shoulders, stood along the quay watching the spectacle, paying no attention to the prison ward behind them. I stepped away and walked across to the rear-facing windows. The field where cadets spent so much time practicing their marching was deserted. Not a soul in sight, all the way back to where a few wooden houses and a small mosque with its single slender minaret beckoned me. I looked back at my bandaged comrades, still glued to the windows.

I walked over to my bed, picked up my boots, and made my way to the door leading to the shower room, keeping an eye out for broken glass and ignoring the wounded confined to their beds. No guard sat in the chair by the stairwell. Clothing belonging to the orderlies hung in their usual place. I picked out a pair of trousers and jacket about my size and returned to the hallway, looked up and down, and then took the stairs down to where an open door faced the parade field.

I pulled the trousers and jacket over my pajamas, put on my boots, tied the laces, and stepped through the door into cool sunshine. I looked right and left and, seeing no one, set out across the field. I walked quickly and never looked back.

Chapter 14

Fear held me in an iron grip with each step I took across the dusty parade ground, not knowing whether a bullet might find me before I reached the shelter of the village. I kept up a fast pace until, at last, I passed the red-bricked mosque and turned left onto a cobblestone street flanked by weathered wooden houses. An elderly woman dressed in black, carrying a bundle of slender branches on her shoulder, passed without looking up. Farther along another woman armed with a carpet beater, her head wrapped in a colorful scarf, pounded on a mattress draped out of an upper window. Acutely aware that I was now alone in enemy territory, I saw every individual I encountered a source of danger.

Cobblestones gave way to packed dirt where the houses ended. I followed a side road uphill past mud-brick cottages and wooden barns. Behind paddock walls bearded black goats eyed me with indifference. A boy dressed in ragged clothes approached propelling a large sow before him with a stick. He steered the pig to the side of the road away from me, but otherwise did not acknowledge my existence. About a quarter of a mile along, the buildings ended and the dirt road deteriorated to a rutted track. I paused and looked back. Off in the distance a pall of black smoke hung over the Bosphorus where the two ships still burned. Across a narrow stretch of water, directly across from where I stood, the massive European Castle of which Kerim had spoken faced a smaller fortress on the Asian shore. No sign of unusual activity was evident around the Kuleli naval college, still visible to the south.

This was no time to admire the splendid Bosphorus scenery. I continued uphill through leafless apple orchards into a forest of cypress and pine, turned north along a path that paralleled the Bosphorus and quickened my pace. As long as the sun shone overhead, I was warm enough despite a stiff breeze; but to the north billowing gray-black clouds threatened a change in the weather. I had no clear idea which way to go, other than that I had to get as far from Kuleli as possible while it was still light. My first priority was to avoid the hue and cry I was certain would follow once my absence was discovered.

With legs aching from the exertion, I continued on through the evergreen forest over an uneven track, with only an occasional squirrel and a variety of small birds darting among the trees for company. After about an hour I emerged from the trees into a shallow valley where the land sloped down to a narrow, twisting river, its banks lined with poplars and willows in the skeletal guise of winter. Overhead the clouds had won their battle with the sun, and I shivered as a brisk wind disturbed the trees' branches. Continuing along the path, flanking a field covered with the stubble of an earlier harvest, I reached the riverbank. Shallow crystal-clear water ran over the rocky streambed in its leisurely journey to the Bosphorus far below. A good distance upstream an arched bridge offered a way to the other side.

I knelt down and with cupped hands quenched my thirst with the stream's icy water. Back on my feet I followed the riverbank as far as the bridge, an ancient stone structure that looked as if it had served the local populace for centuries. As I stepped onto the bridge the first clinging wet particles of sleet settled on my shoulders and head. Across the river a rutted track led back uphill between cultivated fields. I continued on, getting wetter and colder by the minute, as wind and sleet assaulted my face. By the time I reached the top of the hill I was so cold I was beginning to regret that I'd escaped the shelter of Kuleli where, had I stayed, I might well be enjoying a warm meal and a blanket.

About a quarter of a mile farther the track forked, the right fork leading uphill away from the Bosphorus which was still partially visible in the dip of the river valley. The left fork ended at a cluster of farm buildings nestled among a stand of trees. Nearby a man with stooped shoulders, the first person I'd seen since leaving the village at Kuleli, herded a dozen or so scrawny cows towards a large wooden barn. I took the right fork away from the farmer, hoping to find more woodland to shelter me from the biting wind. But the open farmland and occasional scrub persisted for what seemed like several miles before the track dipped into another valley cut by a small river similar to the last, except that no bridge was visible in either direction.

As the sleet increased in intensity, soaking through my layers of clothing and coating me in a mantle of white, I followed the riverbank uphill. My injured shoulder began to throb and my feet, accustomed to the inactivity of hospital confinement, chafed with the uninterrupted slogging over increasingly rough terrain.

No bridge presented itself, but at last woodland reappeared and the river, where it emerged from the forest, took on the form of rocky cascades and picturesque pools trapped among granite boulders. The evergreen canopy afforded some relief from the wind and sleet, but I was deathly cold, at times shivering uncontrollably despite the physical exertion of a steady uphill hike. Daylight was beginning to fade and I needed shelter for the night.

Some distance into the forest, on the opposite side of the river, I spotted what appeared to offer a refuge. A good-sized pine had toppled away from the stream, its shallow roots exposed by erosion of the riverbank. The tree must have fallen recently because pine needles still clothed its branches. Its expansive root system, bedded in earth and rock, tilted at an angle in the form of a lean-to, which could provide some shelter. But first I had to get across the river.

A little farther uphill I reached a spot where several large stones protruded from the water in close enough proximity to serve as stepping stones. Keeping one foot firmly on the riverbank, I tested the first stone. It seemed solid enough. With no low branches to steady my progress, I decided the best course of action would be to move quickly, stone by stone, until momentum propelled me to the opposite bank no more than a few yards away. I picked out the most promising sequence of footings before pushing off. All went well at first, but just a couple of feet shy of the other side, a rock shifted under my weight and my right foot slipped off into water halfway up to my knee. I flung myself onto the bank to keep my other foot from suffering the same fate.

With daylight almost completely gone, I made my way back down to the overturned tree and crawled under its tilting root bed, cursing my stupidity for getting myself into such a predicament. I removed the waterlogged boot, peeled off the sock and rolled my trouser and pajama legs up to my knee, squeezing out as much of the water as I could.

Except for the penetrating cold, I don't remember much of that night. I dozed on and off, but most of the darkness was spent slapping my arms against my sides and massaging the exposed foot and leg, trying to keep the circulation going. Perhaps because I'd passed through so many apple orchards in my flight from Kuleli, I dreamt or hallucinated at one point that Rhys Jones and I were scrumpimg apples from Leonard's farm above Ystrad. I woke, hungry, and thought of those apples, more often than not green enough to punish us with stomach aches and diarrhea, not that that ever deterred us.

I wondered where Rhys was now. He and Dai Wilkins and I had joined the Borderers together in what seemed like an interminably long time ago in a place devoid of reality. Now Dai lay in an unmarked grave in some meadow. Was Rhys, too, buried in Turkish soil, or had he fled Gallipoli with what was left of the allied armies? After Dai's death I was Rhys's only link to home, our friendship forged in schoolboy adventures and misadventures, and in mineshafts deep underground. Would the day ever come when the two of us would once more enjoy a pint of bitter and a game of darts at the Old Lamb?

As the hours dragged on there were times when I thought I might not make it through the night. I remembered reading somewhere that lost Antarctic explorers fought to stay awake because they knew that if sleep were to overtake them, they would freeze to death. It was the most miserable night I can remember, worse even than those spent in trenches in the company of rats during the bitter cold of a Gallipoli winter. What wouldn't I have given for a piping hot cup of tea!

§

Once the first traces of dawn filtered through the pine branches, I pulled my still-wet sock and soggy boot over my foot. Stiff and cold, my left shoulder aching and tender, I crawled out from under the tree roots and made my way over uneven terrain away from the river. Hunger gnawed at my stomach; I'd eaten nothing since breakfast the morning before, and a meager breakfast at that. Was it only one day since I'd turned my back on Kuleli? It seemed like an eternity.

As I walked through the woods, wondering whether battalions of Turkish soldiers were scouring the countryside looking for me, rain began to fall, a steady cold drizzle that dripped from overhead branches onto my head and clothing, still damp from the previous day's soaking. Both feet were painful, and the more I walked the worse they became, so that by the time I smelled the first whiffs of smoke from a wood fire, I was limping badly. I moved forward cautiously as the forest gave way abruptly to an open area leading to a small farming village. Hidden among the trees, I looked for signs of life, but the rain and cold must have been keeping the inhabitants indoors.

The closest building to where I stood resembled a barn. Standing a short distance across a vegetable patch, the wood-sided structure bore a steeply sloping thatched roof unlike any I'd seen before in Turkey. On the end facing me, adjoining doors provided an entry large enough to accommodate a hay wagon. I walked across the vegetable patch using the building as cover and put my ear to the entryway. Gently I lifted the latch and inched one door open, and was greeted with a pungent aroma of hay and manure. Shuffling noises told me that animals occupied the barn. I pulled the door open a little more and slipped inside, pulling and latching the door behind me. Body heat from the animals imparted unexpected warmth, a pleasant relief from the cold outside.

My eyes took a few minutes to adjust to the gloom. I counted ten stalls holding cows, all dark brown in color. The closest one, chewing on a clump of hay that protruded from its mouth, eyed me with a mournful expression—or was it accusatory? Another gave forth a low moan to the accompaniment of much restless movement, as if the animals were telling me they knew I was an interloper. To the left of the entryway lay a pile of hay, and next to it a pitchfork leaning against the wall. Above my head a hayloft, reached by a wooden ladder, was piled high with a winter's supply of feed. Overcome with cold and fatigue I climbed the ladder and settled down into the hay. I lay for several minutes before pulling off my boots and socks. Both feet were raw and bloody.

I lay back and pulled clumps of soft hay over me like a blanket, relishing the shelter from the miserable weather outside, but in a quandary as to what to do next. I'd always thought of myself as a pretty self-reliant sort of chap, but self-reliance can only be taken so far. I was, I had to admit to myself, in a real pickle, alone in a hostile country where I couldn't speak the language, as cold as I'd ever been in my life, soaked to the skin, and weak with hunger. My feet hurt so much I could barely walk. And—with Gallipoli abandoned by the British and French armies—I had no clear idea of what to do or where to go. When confined to the hospital ward all I could think of was regaining my freedom, somehow making it back to friendly territory. Now, having given little thought to the practicalities of flight, my actions seemed nothing less than foolhardy. Of one thing I was certain, if I didn't get some food into my stomach, I'd be in no shape to do anything but give myself up, the consequences of which I didn't wish to contemplate.

I buried myself deeper under the hay and stared up at the ceiling. Staying on this side of the Bosphorus didn't seem at all practical. With the evacuation of Gallipoli, the nearest British forces outside of Europe were fighting in Palestine or Mesopotamia, but to reach them I'd have to cross the full extent of Asia Minor, hundreds of miles. The European part of Turkey lay on the other side of the Bosphorus, with Bulgaria to the north and Greece to the west. Since Bulgaria had allied itself with Germany, Greece presented the better option. There, perhaps, some military personnel might still remain from the Gallipoli evacuation who could put me on a ship back to Britain. Or if not military, British consular officials in one of the larger cities.

Greece—that's where I'd aim for, I decided. As soon as I rested up a bit, I'd head for the Bosphorus and try to get across under cover of darkness. If Kerim could swim across, why couldn't I?

The ceiling of the barn shifted out of focus. I closed my eyes and within seconds was sleeping soundly.

§

Something woke me. I had no idea how long I'd been asleep, but I wanted to prolong the luxury. I'd been lost in a most pleasant dream. I was a boy again, sliding with Hugh Griffith down the slagheap near my home on pieces of cardboard, seeing who could make it to the bottom first. I hadn't a care in the world, so exhilarated by the thrill of the race that I tried desperately to will myself back to sleep and resume my interrupted happiness.

Somebody moved below. A door creaked open, then footsteps and the sound of a wagon or barrow being wheeled in, followed by the scraping of a shovel. I lay still, almost invisible amongst the hay. I raised my head slowly until I could see part of the floor below. A man dressed in heavy clothing, a cap on his head, shoveled cow manure into a wheelbarrow. He hummed as he worked. I rested my head back in the hay as gently as possible to avoid any slight noise that might attract attention. The man finished his shoveling and wheeled the barrow out of the barn, but left the door open. Shortly afterwards he brought the barrow back and stored it somewhere below the loft. Still humming he went out again and was gone for several minutes before returning.

The man began talking. Someone was with him, I thought; but when I looked again I saw he was speaking to his cows and positioning himself on a stool for milking. Under his practiced fingers the milk streamed down into metal buckets with the same tinkling sound I remembered from the time Uncle Mervyn had taken me up to Leonard's farm. I must have been six or seven years old at the time. We had arrived during evening milking and Mr. Leonard's teenage daughter scooped cream from the top of her bucket with a tin cup and handed it to me to drink. Not only did the cream taste absolutely delicious, I developed an immediate crush on Elsie Leonard. My mouth watered at the thought of creamy fresh milk just a short distance from where I lay hidden.

It took the farmer a long time, perhaps an hour or more, to finish the job. I watched him place two large buckets of milk near the door, but then had to put my head down quickly as he turned and walked back under the hayloft. I looked again and saw him returning to the cows with a pitchfork full of hay. I lay back. Was there enough feed below, or would he climb the ladder for more? I had a nightmare vision of a pitchfork stabbing through the hay into my body like the bayonet of a Turkish soldier.

My fears were unfounded. After several trips back and forth he returned the pitchfork and left with his buckets of milk, closing and latching the door behind him. Relieved, I sat up. With activity around the farm, this didn't seem like the best time to leave my hiding place. Nor was I anxious to put my wet boots on again, given the state of my feet. My clothes had dried a little, but were still damp. I peeled off the outer garments I'd stolen from the hospital, then my pajamas, and spread them around well back from where they could be seen from below. Completely naked I lay down and covered myself with a thick blanket of hay. Soon I was back asleep, but my unconscious mind could not conjure up once again the innocent pleasures of childhood.

§

I awoke to darkness and silence. I had no idea of the time, but I knew I should be on my way before the farmer rose for his early morning labor. If Turkish farmers were anything like those in Wales—and I had no reason to doubt otherwise—they began their day well before dawn.

With the exception of the boots, my clothes had dried almost completely. I dusted off the hay and dressed quickly. The socks and boots I pulled on gently because my feet were still in bad shape. As quietly as possible, I descended the ladder. Perhaps the animals were used to having me as a guest because this time my movements elicited no reaction. In the gloom I saw the wheelbarrow where the farmer had left it with the shovel resting in its bed. Two other shovels leaned against the wall behind the barrow. I walked over and took one. A man walking with a shovel over his shoulder, I conjectured, would look less like an escaped prisoner. A shovel might even come in handy as a weapon, although it would be of little use against an armed soldier.

I walked to the door by which I had entered, lifted the latch silently and stepped outside. The sky had cleared and an almost-full moon bathed the countryside in light and illuminated my breath. It was still bitterly cold. For a fleeting moment I considered returning to the warmth of barn and hay, but I pushed temptation aside, closed and latched the door, and walked around the side of the building to a dirt road leading to the village. I placed the shovel over my undamaged shoulder and set out past the farm. I wondered how long it would take the farmer to discover he had one less shovel. I felt a twinge of guilt for taking it after having made use of his barn; but war, I told myself, allowed such liberties.

Light glimmered in an upstairs room of the farmhouse and in the windows of two other houses as I made my way through the village. I stayed to the edge of the road where the mud was not so deep and tried not to limp despite the pain in my feet. I continued through two more farming communities just coming to life, before the track ended at a dirt road. I turned left, presuming this would lead eventually to the Bosphorus.

After passing through farmland and orchards I arrived at the outskirts of a larger community with two-storey buildings and a sizeable mosque capped with a slender minaret. I paused and leaned on the shovel for several minutes to rest my feet and decide what to do next. My first inclination was to turn back, to avoid any town or village where the inhabitants might be on the alert for an escaped prisoner. But hunger was sapping my strength and I couldn't go on with nothing in my stomach. I decided to chance it. I returned the shovel to my shoulder and followed the road into the town.

A number of people moved along paved streets going about their morning business, among them an elderly woman walking towards me carrying two loaves of bread under her arm. As she approached I tried to recall some of the Turkish words I'd learned from Kerim.

"Ekmet nerede?" Where is bread? I hoped I'd said to her. My words seemed to have the right effect because she stopped and pointed down the street while saying something unintelligible. I smiled and nodded and continued on into the town. My presence on the street drew no reaction from the other pedestrians. No one, it seemed, was on the alert for an escaped prisoner of war.

I passed several shuttered shops before the tantalizing aroma of freshly baked bread led me a short distance up a side street. The bakery, its door open, was free of customers. It occurred to me then that I'd have to pay for the bread. The Turkish money Suresh had handed me was still in my pajama pocket. Trying to look as casual as possible, I reached inside my shirt and extracted a banknote. I had no idea if this was enough for a loaf of bread, or even whether it was still acceptable currency, but it was the only resource I possessed.

A blast of hot air greeted me at the bakery door and I stepped into what seemed like an inferno after the cold outside. A man clothed in a long apron and skullcap was removing loaves, two at a time, from a ceiling-high brick oven using a long-handled wooden pallet. He slid the loaves onto a counter that ran the length of the shop. Like a specter he was white with flour from head to foot.

I propped the shovel in the corner next to the open door, walked over to the counter and picked up a loaf still hot from the oven. I offered the baker the banknote. He lay down his pallet, eyed me with a curious expression and took the money. I turned to leave when he spoke. The man reached out and dropped several coins into my hand. I smiled and nodded which—lacking the words to express my sentiments—I had taken to be an acceptable way to express thanks.

I retrieved the shovel and left the shop, resisting the temptation to tear into the loaf. With a warm feeling toward Suresh for his generosity, I returned to the main street and followed the road back the way I had come until I was out of sight of the buildings. Some distance into a stand of trees I chanced upon a small rivulet pouring down a rocky outcropping.

I set the shovel down and bent my head to the stream to quench my thirst before finding a dry spot to sit and enjoy my first solid food since leaving Kuleli. I ate slowly, savoring each mouthful, ignoring the occasional remains of insects trapped among the bread's pores.

By the time I'd eaten half the loaf I felt much better. Even the bitter cold had dissipated as the sun arced higher in the morning sky. Rather than go back through the town I decided to head north through the countryside before resuming my trek down to the Bosphorus. I set out at a leisurely pace, shovel over my shoulder and the remains of the loaf tucked inside my shirt where the lingering warmth from the oven afforded a small measure of comfort. I was in no hurry because my aim was to cross the Bosphorus in the dead of night.

I wondered what the men in the ward were thinking about my disappearance. Cyril and Albert would be astonished; they had no idea I was contemplating such a move. And Suresh? He would understand, would wish he too could choose freedom over a prison camp. Just as I wished now that he was here with me. Suresh was a decent chap who'd been dealt a rotten hand. I missed his company and his clipped Indian way of speaking. I wondered if I would ever see him again.

Chapter 15

It was mid afternoon when I reached the Bosphorus, according to a clock in a shop window. I'd passed through miles of farmland and a half dozen villages, stopping and resting frequently to ease the pain in my feet. At my first view of the waterway upon reaching the crest of a hill, I was shocked at its width, much greater than at Kuleli and a far more formidable looking obstacle. A traveler new to the region might well think he had chanced upon a large lake. As I stood looking across to Europe in the distance, I was struck with the fact that I hadn't seen a single Turkish soldier since I'd walked away from the hospital. Why wasn't the countryside swarming with soldiers, hunting for me? Did the army consider a wounded man not worth the effort, or did they expect me to head south where I might lose myself in the confusion of Constantinople?

It was only when I turned onto a road that ran alongside the water that I saw soldiers for the first time. They were marching in formation towards me, rifles resting on right shoulders, left arms swinging in cadence. A noncommissioned officer strode with them to one side. In a moment of panic I almost turned back, but my fears were unfounded; the men marched past, no more than a foot away, without so much as a glance in my direction. They looked young and smelled of sweat as if returning from some rigorous training exercise. New recruits, perhaps. At least they no longer had to face the horrors of Gallipoli. But why weren't they looking for me?

Across the street fishing boats bobbed against the seawall and nets lay spread about the pavement. I crossed over and sat on a bench facing the water, resting the shovel against my leg. Impressive as the Bosphorus was from a distance, up close one could appreciate its true majesty, its aura of power and history. Wasn't this the same channel navigated by the Argonauts in their quest for the Golden Fleece? So Mr. Davies, our history teacher at Tonypandy, had taught us. In more recent times, just sixty years ago, British forces had passed through on their way to the Crimea. How many other warring armies had made passage over thousands of years of human conflict?

I rested for some time, nibbling on the remains of my loaf and watching fishermen offshore in about a dozen small boats pulling in their nets. A ferryboat belching black smoke—burning coal from Kerim's hometown of Zonguldak, perhaps—approached in a diagonal path toward a village farther up the Bosphorus.

The longer I sat, the more worried I became. Getting across to the European shore was a daunting enough challenge. But what would I do once I got there? I'd still be in Turkey. My few remaining banknotes would probably not be enough to keep me in food all the way to Greece. And this wasn't the time of year when I could pilfer from farmers' fields and orchards. Then I thought of Kerim, a man I considered a friend rather than adversary. He lived, he had told me, in a village near the European Castle. Kerim was such a decent sort, would he turn me away if I asked him for help? I dismissed the thought. Even if he were disposed to helping me, my actions might well bring trouble down on his head.

Under fading sunlight I picked up the shovel and began walking south, looking for a spot where the channel was not so wide. I didn't want to go too far because the current would carry me downstream, and I wanted to end up near the castle where the Bosphorus was much narrower. Besides the danger involved in getting across, landing near the castle posed other risks. People living in the vicinity, being not far from Kuleli, might well have heard that a prisoner had escaped.

Graceful wooden houses topped with red-tiled roofs lined the Bosphorus shore, their upper floors cantilevered over the water. Some had boathouses built below. Marble villas and fountains at periodic intervals alluded to a more opulent era. After passing through two villages, I came upon a large factory where horse-drawn carts laden with a variety of glassware moved in and out of its gates. I walked past the factory, then inland a short distance until, in a wooded area, I found a dead tree branch suitable for a float. Swimming in normal fashion was out of the question with my injured shoulder. I'd thought of stealing a boat, but all the unattended ones I'd seen were without oars.

The woods were deserted and isolated, the ground reasonably dry. I found a comfortable spot in a bed of leaves and lay down as darkness descended. I remained there several hours, dozing occasionally, until I was certain that the nearby villagers had bedded down for the night.

I leaned the shovel against a tree, picked up the dead branch, and walked back to the Bosphorus, stepping carefully because the moon provided little light in the forest. The village lay dark and quiet. I walked along the shore until I reached a paved area where a number of short, cylindrical stones had been set out for boat moorings, and stone steps led down to the water. Some distance offshore lights bobbed up and down, and the faint sound of oars splashing against water drifted through the darkness. I'd seen similar lights from the hospital window at Kuleli. They're night fisherman, Kerim had told me. The men use oil lanterns as a lure and beat the water with their oars to stun the fish so they can be easily lifted out with a net. "If you see a fisherman missing fingers or a hand," he'd said, "you know he uses dynamite."

A lone boat, drifting with the current, would attract attention; better to take my chances swimming. I looked around to make certain no one was in sight before descending the steps. The water felt cool to my touch, but not unbearably cold. I sat down, removed my boots, and tied the laces together. I draped the boots over the branch, said a silent prayer, and pushed off into the water. The shock of cold was unexpected, but not enough to make me turn back. To avoid attracting attention I moved my legs up and down beneath the surface until, a few yards out, I felt the current's grip, pulling me farther from the shore and moving me quickly downstream. I maintained a steady rhythm with my legs and kept my eyes open for water traffic. Periodically I looked back to check my progress. At first I was encouraged to see the shore receding steadily, but the next time I looked it seemed closer, as though the current were playing games with me. My legs began to tire.

Without warning, the water became turbulent, tossing me around like a cork, disorienting me, weakening my grip on the branch. As I fought to regain control I realized with horror that my boots had disappeared, thrown off by the buffeting and now on their way to the bottom. Cold sapped my strength. Desperately I continued kicking, no longer caring whether my legs remained under water. I tried to pull the branch under my body for support but couldn't force it below the surface. My kicking slowed to the point of being ineffectual and I put all my effort into just maintaining a grip on the branch. At last the surface water became calm again, but the Asian shore seemed even closer.

I knew then that I had seriously underestimated the difficulty of what I'd set out to do. Reaching Europe, or perhaps even making it back to Asia, seemed virtually impossible. Several minutes later a second batch of turbulence put the finishing touches on my foolhardiness. A wave washed over me, pulled me under, and I lost my grip on the tree limb. I flailed my arms and was able to get my head above water, but swallowed a good mouthful in the process. I rolled onto my back, coughed up water, and tried to float, no longer caring where the violent torrent might carry me. Numb with cold, I weakened, gulped more water, felt the life ebbing out of me. I knew then that I was drowning, even as I drifted between two continents. I had challenged the Bosphorus and it had shown me no mercy.

Barely conscious I felt a sudden grip on my collar and my head was out of the water. Strong hands grabbed me under the arms and lifted me, pulled me over something rigid against my stomach. My body lay half in and half out of the water. Then a hand pulled my legs over a gunwale and I found myself lying face up among a tangle of netting and dead fish while my rescuer, steadying his craft with the oars, his bearded face illuminated with a lantern, sat looking down at me as if he couldn't believe what he had caught.

We remained like that for several moments, staring at one another. Then the fisherman began speaking rapidly and gesturing with his hands. Slowly, and with much effort, I pulled myself into a sitting position. I shivered with cold and envied the man his woolen jacket and beret. I noticed then that I was barefoot; my socks had gone the way of my boots. When the man stopped talking I shook my head. "I speak English," I said. At that he rested his arms on the oars and stared at me, his brow furrowed. Did he know that his biggest catch was an escaped prisoner of war?

"*Rumeli Hisarı,*" European Castle, I said. The man nodded towards the far shore. I pointed at myself, then to Europe and repeated, *"Rumeli Hisarı."* He looked at me with a quizzical expression. I pointed to him, then to my chest, and again to Europe. *"Rumeli Hisarı,"* I said for the third time. The man laughed and raised his eyebrows while putting a cigarette in his mouth. I knew from dealing with Turks at Kuleli that raising eyebrows was a silent way of saying no. He offered me a cigarette and I shook my head. He struck a match and held it to his mouth, his hands cupped against the breeze, his eyes staring at me.

I reached inside my shirt and felt the pajama pocket. The money was still there. I retrieved a soggy banknote and held it out to him, pointed again to my chest, then to the European shore. He stared at the banknote for several seconds before raising his eyebrows again. I reached in and pulled out another note, adding it to the first. The fisherman sat silently for a while. He looked over towards Europe, then up at the sky, making up his mind. Finally he shrugged, nodded his head and took the money. Grasping the oars he turned the boat and began pulling strongly into the current.

I wrapped my arms around my chest, shivering with cold. The boat was not large, no more than ten feet in length and about four feet wide. Close to where one oar was anchored to the gunwale, a small wooden support for the lantern extended over the water. The boatman rowed tirelessly while using the current as an ally to propel his craft towards the European shore. Apart from a few distant fishing boats, their presence indicated by their flickering lanterns, we were alone on the water. To the east the first glimmer of dawn outlined the hills on the Asian shore. Where had the night gone? I asked myself.

The Bosphorus narrowed as the boatman brought us ever nearer to the European shore. Then I saw, silhouetted against the night sky, the crenellated walls and towers of the European Castle, massive and imposing. The boatman strained at the oars, but the current carried us well past the fortress before he was able to bring his boat to shore at a set of stone steps similar to those from which I'd embarked on my foolish quest. He pointed to a cluster of houses barely visible in the first light of day. "Bebek," he said.

"Bebek," I repeated, and he nodded. I lifted myself from my cramped sitting position and moved forward and out onto the bottom step. I reached into my pajama pocket and handed him all the coins from my bread purchase. The man had, after all, saved my life. He smiled in gratitude, tipped his beret and pushed off from the steps. I watched as he turned his boat and began pulling upstream, staying close to the shore where the current was more forgiving. He had a long, hard journey back.

I stood on the steps for several minutes contemplating my next move. Against the odds I had reached the European shore, but my clothes were thoroughly soaked, my feet bare, and I shivered with cold. Trying to reach Greece was out of the question. I decided then to seek out Kerim and throw myself on his mercy. But first I had to find him. I knew he lived somewhere near the castle and worked at an American college. And he had taught me the words I needed to find where he lived.

This village—presumably Bebek—seemed the logical place to start, as the castle was just a short distance beyond. I ascended the steps and hobbled toward what looked like the main street, a narrow cobblestone thoroughfare lined with shops and wooden houses. In the early morning light the village was just coming to life. A man approached, stooped over and carrying a remarkable number of boxes on his back. A leather strap circled his forehead and extended around his load, keeping it firmly secured to his body. He didn't look up as we passed. Farther along a woman, bent over a short-handled straw broom, swept the pavement in front of a house. I walked up to her and said, *"Kerim Bey nerede?"* She took one look at me and hurried into the house, slamming the door behind her. With my bare feet, wet clothes and unkempt hair I must have looked like a crazy person—and that may not have been far from the truth.

I shuffled on past shuttered shops and small cafés, my feet enduring the sharp pain of small stones. At a kiosk I turned left into a side street that led uphill. I tried my question on a turbaned man leading a donkey bearing large wicker baskets on both sides. The man gave me the negative signal of raised eyebrows while looking me up and down with a disbelieving expression. Two other men I approached reacted similarly.

At the top of the hill I turned north onto a dirt track that led through a gorse thicket of the type that covered the Gallipoli hills. Keeping the weight on the outside edges of my feet did little to ease the pain. I passed above a cluster of impressive multi-storeyed limestone buildings, some wearing the bare tendrils of ivy. Beyond lay the Bosphorus, shimmering in the light of the rising sun, and the hills of Asia. Was this the American college? I wondered. Certainly it had the appearance of how I imagined a university might look.

With the buildings behind me, I emerged onto a wide sloping field in the shape of an amphitheater. Below, the full extent of the castle dominated the landscape, stretching between lofty towers atop facing hills, its walls and smaller towers following the contour of the land into the hollow. Close by the castle walls a number of picturesque wooden houses marked the outskirts of another village. A stiff breeze stirred a stand of umbrella pines at the foot of the hill, blew dead leaves across the field and chilled my wet clothing. Weary from my ordeal, cold and hungry, I sat against the remnants of a stone wall above the pathway. What a mess I've made of things, I thought. I rested my head back and closed my eyes.

I don't know how long I'd been there, half asleep, when a voice startled me awake. A youth stood before me dressed in a gray blazer and baggy trousers. He carried two books bound together by a small strip of leather. His face, handsome and boyish, bore a look of concern. He spoke again, words I didn't understand. I just sat and looked at him, too tired to respond.

"Do you speak English?" the youth asked. His words jolted me to into attentiveness. I nodded. "Can I be of help?" he said in flawless, accented English. "You do not look well."

"I'm very tired," I replied.

The youth looked at my feet. "We have an infirmary on the campus. I can take you there, but I don't think the nurse will be there this early."

"The American college?" I asked.

"Yes." He shifted his books to his other hand. "I am a student there."

"I need to find Kerim Bey," I said.

"Kerim Bey at the college?" I nodded. "I know Kerim Bey. Everyone does. But he will not be there today. He does not work on Saturday."

"Do you know where he lives?"

"No. Somewhere in the village, I think."

I struggled to get up and he extended a hand to help me. "Wait," he said. "I will ask this boy."

I followed his gaze to a lad no more than ten years old approaching from the direction of the houses. The student spoke rapidly to the boy who pointed back towards the village. More words were exchanged and the youth turned to me. "He will show you where Kerim Bey lives." He looked again at my feet and wet clothing. "You are very wet. Are you sure you would not wish to see our nurse?"

"No, thank you. You've been very kind."

"You are most welcome," he said. "I hope Kerim Bey can help you." He spoke again to the boy, nodded to me and left in the direction of the college.

The young boy walked away from me and I followed, but my feet were so painful I had a hard time keeping pace. He paused now and again to allow me to catch up. We followed the field around behind the village for some distance until he stopped and pointed down the hill to a large two-storey wooden house and adjacent barn. He looked up at me, then turned and went back the way we had come without saying a word.

I watched the house for a while, but saw no sign of life, nor did anyone seem to be up or about in houses nearby. Slowly I made my way down the slope, my feet so painful now that I even considered getting down on my hands and knees. I crossed a cultivated field at the foot of the hill and approached the rear of the house, steadying myself on a stone wall enclosing a kitchen garden where several chickens and guinea fowl pecked away at scattered seed. A lone goat stood against the opposite wall rubbing its head against the stones. I hobbled around to the front of the house, to a weathered wooden door with iron hinges that gave access to the dirt street. An upper room extended over the street. I knocked on the door.

Several seconds passed before the door opened and a buxom, middle-aged woman wearing a white apron stood staring at me. "Kerim Bey," I said. She took in my bare feet and bedraggled appearance, then opened the door wider.

"*Buruyun,*" she said. I hesitated and she repeated, "*Buruyun,*" gesturing me to enter. She took my arm and propelled me inside, through a hallway and into a kitchen redolent with the aroma of cooking. A table covered with a variety of pots and cooking utensils occupied the center of the room. Against the far wall an iron stove reminded me of the one in our kitchen in Wales. A heavy saucepan sat on top, steam escaping from under its lid. One other person was there, a girl about seventeen or eighteen with delicate features and shoulder-length dark hair, sitting next to a window. She wore a white dress edged with an embroidered red and green floral design, and her hands held needle and thread and an item of clothing. She lowered her eyes the second I looked in her direction.

The woman spoke to me in Turkish, and when I didn't respond she pointed to a chair by the table and said in English, "Sit." I collapsed into the chair and leaned my arms on the table. The woman said something to the girl who put aside her sewing and left the room quickly through the door I had entered. The woman took a bowl and ladled out food from the pot on the stove. She placed the bowl in front of me along with a spoon. Tears clouded my eyes as the seductive aroma of beef stew embraced my senses. I ate slowly, savoring each mouthful—turnips, carrots, onions and tender chunks of meat, flavored with unfamiliar spices. My stomach gurgled. Never had food tasted so delicious.

She stood and watched as I ate. When I'd emptied the bowl I looked up and said, "Thank you. It's very good." She didn't respond. She came over and put her hand on my shoulder, feeling the wetness. She spoke again, but the words were meaningless to me. Then, in English, "Kerim come." Suddenly I was apprehensive of what Kerim would think of me, what his reaction would be when he found me in his kitchen. I didn't have to wait long.

The front door opened and footsteps approached. The familiar bulk of Kerim strode into the room, followed by the girl who immediately returned to her chair by the window. Kerim moved around to the stove, a puzzled look on his face, and stared at me for several seconds before recognition took hold. His jaw dropped, his eyes widened.

"Bloke! Where the hell did you come from?"

Chapter 16

"Get out!" Kerim's expression turned from astonishment to anger. "Get out! You have no right to be here. I will wait one hour and then I go to the police."

"I'm sorry, Kerim," I said, lifting myself from the chair. "I shouldn't have come. I was desperate."

The woman I assumed to be Kerim's wife came over and pushed me back down. She turned to Kerim and launched into a tirade, waving her arms and pointing to my bare feet. Kerim, stamping around the kitchen, responded with a harangue of his own. The girl by the window put down her sewing and watched but said nothing. The confrontation went on for several minutes before Kerim threw himself in the chair across from me, an exasperated look on his face. "My wife rules this house," he said. "She says you stay, then you stay. But only until tomorrow." To add emphasis to his proclamation he jabbed his finger up and down in my face.

I relaxed back into my chair. "I'll leave early in the morning," I said. The girl resumed her mending.

Kerim's expression changed to one of resignation. "How did you get here, Bloke?" he asked, resting his arms on the table.

"There was a big explosion on the Bosphorus. I just walked away in the confusion."

Kerim nodded. "The munitions ship. It collided with a large boat and blew up. A lot of men were killed." He looked down at my jacket. "Where did you get those clothes?"

I gave him an account of how I'd spent the last three days, from stealing the trousers and jacket to trying to swim across the Bosphorus and my rescue by the fisherman. Kerim listened intently, rubbing his hand through his beard. When I was finished he said, "You were stupid, Bloke. You should have stayed with your men."

"I didn't fancy being a prisoner."

Kerim shook his head. "I had a suspicion you were thinking like that. I tried to caution you, but you wouldn't listen."

The woman put a plate of goat cheese and olives in front of me. I looked up at her and smiled my gratitude. I didn't much like olives, but

I was still hungry and they went down well enough with a mouthful of cheese. "Your wife is very kind," I said as I extracted an olive pit from my mouth.

"My wife is very pig-headed. Never marry an Armenian, Bloke, they're nothing but trouble." He stole a glance at his wife and they exchanged smiles of affection. He looked back at me. "One thing I don't understand, Bloke. I haven't heard of any prisoner escaping. Why aren't the soldiers and police after you?"

"I wondered that myself. I didn't see any soldiers after I left Kuleli, none that were looking for me anyway."

Kerim pushed his chair back and stood. "You can't stay in the house, but I'll let you hide in the barn. Come."

The girl still sat in the window absorbed in her sewing, showing no interest in what must be a very disruptive episode in her day-to-day routine. Kerim led me through a back parlor to a door that opened to the outside. He looked out before motioning me to follow. We crossed the walled yard, skirting a small vegetable patch where a few cabbages still flourished. In one corner a rooster stood haughtily atop a chicken coop while his harem pecked away on the ground below. Beyond the coop a path led through a narrow gate to a barn of good size, but smaller than the one I'd stayed in two nights before. Inside, behind a wooden enclosure, two brown and white cows and a calf nestled against one another, and next to them two goats in a separate enclosure chewed on vegetable scraps. A stack of hay filled the other end of the building. "Hide here," Kerim said, pointing to the hay. "If anyone walks in and sees you, you tell them you stopped to rest, but never spoke to me or my wife. I'll tell you tomorrow when it's safe to leave." He went to the back wall and looked out a dusty window. "There is an outhouse there behind the barn. Make certain no one is around before you go there."

I pulled out my remaining two banknotes. "Please take this for the food."

Kerim looked at them and said, "Keep your money, you'll need it." He left and closed the door behind him. I settled down into the hay and rubbed my hand across the bottom of my feet to remove clinging dirt. The barn felt cold after the warmth of the kitchen, but it was better than a day and a night outdoors. I had no sooner lain back and begun dozing when Kerim returned with a blanket. "Give me your clothes," he said. "My wife will dry them."

"Kerim," I said. "What about the college student I spoke to? And the boy who showed me your house? What if they tell someone?"

Kerim scratched his head. "It could be a problem. *İnşallah,* nothing will come of it." He left with my wet clothes. I wrapped myself in the blanket and went to the back of the hay pile against wall. Desperately tired from my nocturnal misadventure, I lay down amongst the hay and within minutes was sleeping soundly.

§

I have no idea how long I'd slept when voices in the street woke me. Other sounds, village sounds, drifted into my hiding place—the clop of a horse's hooves and the rattle of cart wheels on uneven ground; children playing noisily; a dog barking its displeasure; the staccato tattoo of a woodpecker's beak against a dead tree that brought to mind the chatter of a far-off machine gun at Gallipoli. Then the familiar song of a nightingale transported me from the battlefield to the peaceful green hills of Wales.

Wales. What anguish have my aunt and uncle suffered since I was reported missing? And Gwyn—was she suffering too, or had I, after so long away and thought to be dead, been relegated to just a pleasant interlude from her past? A pang of longing gripped me and I pulled the blanket more tightly around my body as if to shield myself from an overpowering feeling of hopelessness. With no Red Cross report on my whereabouts, Gwyn and my family must assume I was dead. But I was just one missing soldier among tens of thousands, and I was luckier than most. At least I was alive.

I sat up and saw, a few feet away, a glass containing what looked like milk and a round copper container with a spoon resting on top. I sidled over and raised the lid. Inside chunks of mutton lay in a bed of yogurt and brown rice. I didn't feel particularly hungry, but I ate the meal, not wanting to appear ungrateful. I almost spit out the sour, acid-tasting liquid, but needing to assuage my thirst, I downed the rest in two quick gulps. I carried the empty containers to a spot near the door and left them on top of a wooden box. Through a dirt-covered window I saw the long-haired girl crossing the yard holding several eggs in the fold of her apron.

I returned to my hiding place and settled back amongst the hay. An inch-long black spider rested motionless on the wall a few feet above my head. I stared up at the heavy wooden beams supporting the barn's roof and wondered at my prospects of getting through Constantinople the next day on the first leg of my journey west. I had no idea how long it would take to reach the Greek border, but I guessed a week at least, possibly two. Perhaps longer if I couldn't find some shoes. I spent the rest of the day and a fitful night in the hay until the rooster woke me early the next morning. During the night I was awakened several times by a strange whistle, sometimes nearby, other times off in the distance.

Daylight had begun to filter into the barn when Kerim entered with my clothes, neatly folded, a pair of slippers resting on top. "My wife washed your clothes, Bloke. You can wear the slippers until we can get you a proper pair of shoes."

I stood up awkwardly, clasping the blanket around me. "Kerim, I have to go. I need to cover as much ground as possible today."

He pointed to my feet. "How far do you think you will get with feet like that? They must heal before you can think of traveling. And traveling is not possible without shoes."

"But . . ."

"Listen to me, Bloke. You stay here until you are well enough to go. How is the shoulder?"

"It still hurts."

"Let me look at it." I grimaced with pain as he probed around the wound. "I thought the infection was getting better. Either I was wrong, or you've done some damage inside—while you were on this stupid adventure of yours."

"In the British army we're told we have a duty to try to escape."

"Duty!" He spat the word out. "Why is it so important to you English to die doing your duty?"

"I'm not English, I'm Welsh."

"Ah, yes. I'd forgotten," Kerim's expression softened. "Well, Mr. Welsh coalminer, put on your clothes and come inside. My wife is cooking breakfast." He stood up. "After we eat I'll take out those stitches."

Kerim led the way back to the house and into the kitchen where his wife stood at the stove scrambling eggs in a large iron skillet, while the girl spread plates and cutlery around the table. We sat and Kerim's wife slid generous portions of eggs onto our plates. Kerim put his arm round his wife's waist as she served him. "My wife's name is Anoush," he said. "It means sweet-tempered, which she used to be before we were married." He laughed heartily as his wife playfully cuffed his head. The girl, who was now toasting bread at the stove, looked around and smiled, the first time I'd seen her show any emotion.

"Your wife speaks English," I said.

"Just a little. Anoush worked in the college dining hall and picked up some English from the students and teachers. That is where we met, at the college."

The girl put a large plate of buttered toast in the center of the table. I smiled at her and she quickly looked away. "Does your daughter speak English?" I asked Kerim. Anoush looked at me sharply.

"Siran is not my daughter, she is my niece. Our niece." He gestured towards his wife. "She understands English very well. She studied for two years at the American girls' school in Scutari."

"The Americans have been active around here," I said.

"He shrugged. "Missionaries. They think their religion is so much better than anyone else's. But I must admit they offer a very good education." He pointed to my plate. *"Yumurta.* Eggs." He pushed the toast towards me. "I know you English like marmalade on your toast, but we have only honey."

"I'm not . . ."

"I know, you're not English. So what do Welsh coalminers put on their toast?"

"Marmalade," I said, which brought forth another eruption of laughter. Kerim's anger at my intrusion into his world had dissipated, it seemed, under the weight of Anoush's sweet temper.

Anoush and Siran joined us at the table. We downed our eggs and toast and sipped hot sweet tea. I'd drunk a lot of Turkish tea since being taken prisoner, and I still found it a bit insipid after the strong brew that was such a mainstay of life at home, but this morning it couldn't have tasted better. During the meal Kerim and I carried on most of the conversation, with occasional exchanges in Turkish between Kerim and Anoush. Siran remained silent, barely raising her eyes from her plate.

The meal over, Kerim led me into the back room and told me to bare my shoulder. I took off my jacket and unbuttoned the pajama top while Kerim removed a black, stiff-sided leather bag from a cupboard near the kitchen door. Once he had opened it I could see that it was a typical medical bag, much like the one carried by Dr. Llewellyn in Ystrad, holding a variety of small bottles and instruments, each in its separate compartment, and a stethoscope folded in the center. From the German script on the side, I assumed Kerim had used the bag during his medical studies in Munich.

"Siran is very quiet," I said.

Kerim fumbled around in his bag and didn't look up. "Siran is quiet because she does not speak," he said.

"What do you mean?"

"What do you think I mean? She understands, but she does not speak. You may speak to her, but do not ask her any questions because she will not answer you."

"I'm sorry. I didn't realize."

Kerim sat me on a hassock and dabbed a cotton swab soaked in iodine solution around my wound. "Her name, Siran, means beautiful, which fits her well, I think. But she is not only beautiful on the outside." He touched his chest near his heart. "She is beautiful here too."

With a pair of tiny steel scissors and tweezers he snipped and pulled at my stitches. I clenched my teeth against the pain and let my eyes wander around the room. This was clearly the more formal room, much like our front room at home, where guests would be entertained. Comfortable chairs and a couch were set back against the walls and richly patterned oriental rugs covered the floor. Exquisite copper bowls and alabaster vases stood alongside brass oil lamps on highly polished wooden end tables. A multicolored covering, that I came to know as a kilim, hung along the back of the couch. Another of contrasting colors stretched across the opposite wall above a bookshelf packed with volumes in several languages.

"Now take off your slippers. Kerim knelt in front of me and gently bathed my blistered feet with cotton swabs soaked in alcohol. "Your feet are getting better. They will be painful for a few days, but the blisters are healing." He wiped off his tools and gathered up the swabs and remnants of my stitches. He nodded towards the bookcase. "If you wish to read, help yourself. Some are in English, the rest in German, Turkish or Armenian." I scanned the books and picked out a slim volume of Henry James's *Turn of the Screw.*

"*Kitap,*" Kerim said, pointing to the one I'd selected. "Book."

"*Kitap,*" I repeated. "It will help pass the time until I leave."

Kerim put his bag away and sat on the couch. "Look, Bloke," he said. "Something odd. While you were in the barn yesterday I went to the teahouse and asked my friends what news they had of Kuleli. I did not say anything about a prisoner escaping. I just wanted to see if anyone there had heard of such a thing. No one said anything. The only news they had was that your friends are about to leave and are to be replaced with wounded Turkish soldiers. I don't understand it. Someone must know you ran away."

"Perhaps the news hasn't reached this side of the Bosphorus yet," I surmised, sitting on the hassock.

"Perhaps, but unlikely. Tomorrow I think I will go to Kuleli and talk to my friends there."

"I can't stay here much longer," I said. "It's a long way to Greece."

"You're not well enough to travel," Kerim replied. He pointed to my feet. "Do the slippers fit?"

"They're a little big."

"I will find you some proper shoes. But trying to get into Greece is impossible. Greeks and Turks are enemies and the border is heavily fortified. Both sides will shoot at you."

"I can't go through Bulgaria. They're on the side of the Germans."

"You can't go anywhere until your feet and shoulder get better. You're crazy, Bloke. Perhaps you should try to swim across the Black Sea like you tried to swim across the Bosphorus." His voice was laced with sarcasm. "It's only a few hundred kilometers to Russia." He leaned back on the couch and folded his arms. When I didn't respond he said, "And what happens if by some miracle you get to England? Will you go back to being a soldier?"

"I'd probably have to." I thought of the man whose face had disappeared under the impact of my bullet and the boy impaled on my bayonet, and I felt the bile rise in my throat. "But do I want to? No. I've had enough of killing. I just want to go home."

Kerim nodded. "Home to the coalmines."

"Not if I can help it. I want a job where I can feel the sun on my back."

"In that case, Bloke, you should become a farmer." Kerim rose to his feet. "*Gel.* Come. I must send you back to the barn. We are expecting visitors today."

Kerim led the way outside where a late winter sun warmed the air and signaled the approach of spring. Two gray doves had joined the foraging chickens who seemed unperturbed by these strangers in their midst. Or perhaps they weren't strangers at all, just friendly visitors from the neighborhood. Once in the barn he shooed the cows and goats out a back door into a field enclosed by a railed fence.

"Don't forget to keep yourself hidden," Kerim said as he closed the door. "Especially if you hear people nearby."

"Thank you, Kerim," I said as he went to leave for the house. "You're very good to me. I wish there was some way I could repay you."

He paused for a moment before replying. "You can repay me by showing kindness to others."

§

I spent the rest of the day hiding in the hay and reading. At times I dozed, and was awakened once by men's voices in the yard behind the house, one I recognized as Kerim's. Much later, after daylight had faded, Kerim came to the barn and invited me in for an evening meal. By that time I'd finished the book and took the opportunity to exchange it for Mark Twain's *Adventures of Tom Sawyer.* When I entered the kitchen Anoush smiled and said, *"İyi akşamlar."*

"She's wishing you good evening," Kerim said.

"İyi akşamlar." I said in return.

"Very good!" Anoush proclaimed, and Siran, who was stoking the stove, smiled.

When I returned to the barn I felt restless, impatient to be on my way. I knew that my presence here was putting Kerim and his family at risk and I didn't want that on my conscience. At the same time I was well aware the condition of my feet would limit my movement. And even if they got better, where would I go? As dangerous as the border might be, Greece still seemed the best option. Perhaps further north, away from the sea, there might be some less populated areas where border defenses could be more easily penetrated. I settled in for the night, but my sleep was again interrupted by those peculiar whistles.

When Kerim arrived at the barn at daybreak, I asked him about them. "It's the *bekci*, the night watchman," he replied. "His whistle scares away thieves." Or lets the thieves know where the coast is clear, I thought.

At breakfast I asked Kerim if he knew of places along the border where it might be easier to cross. He shrugged. "I have no idea. Perhaps there are, but it would be dangerous wherever you go." He stirred sugar into his tea. "If you want my advice, Bloke, you should turn yourself in to the police. That way you're more likely to stay alive."

I spread honey on a crust of bread. "I don't want to be a prisoner again."

"Is freedom worth losing your life for? I could go with you to the police station. Tell them I found you wandering around, confused. That you had lost your memory and didn't know how you got here."

"I doubt they'd believe a story like that."

"Why not?" he said, pushing his plate away. "I've been around a lot of wounded soldiers, and such a condition is not unusual. I think you English call it shell shock." He put up his hands. "Sorry—Welsh. And besides, the police in the village are friends of mine." He pushed his chair back and stood up. "Go back to the barn, Bloke. I'm going to Kuleli and I must hurry to catch the ferry. Don't make any decision until I return."

Back in the barn I settled down in the hay and began reading. An hour or so later Siran entered with two pails. Without looking in my direction she went directly to the animals, drew up a stool and proceeded to milk them, first the cows and then the goats. When she finished she set the pails aside and propelled the animals out the back door. She glanced briefly towards me as she left for the house with the milk, kicking the door closed behind her. Kerim was right I thought. Siran was indeed beautiful.

§

It was well into the afternoon when Kerim entered the barn. He tossed a pair of shoes over to me. "Try these on," he said.

"Where did you get them?"

"In a shoe shop. Where else?"

I removed the slippers and pulled on the shoes. They were made of black leather, ankle high, with thin leather laces. "They're the right size," I said. I pulled out my banknotes. "I hope this covers the cost."

"Keep your money," Kerim said. "You can pay me back after the war. We'll get you some socks as well." He came over and sat in the hay next to me. "Now listen, Bloke. The news from Kuleli is that no prisoner escaped."

I looked at him with astonishment. "What do you mean?"

"What I said. When I got there the prisoners were just about to leave for the camp, some place south near Konya. Lorries were parked outside to take them to the railway station in Hayderpasha and lots of soldiers were there to guard them. But I had a chance to go in and say hello to your comrades and to wish them well. I spoke to your Indian friend."

"Suresh."

"Yes, Suresh. I asked him where you were. He said you had been taken away to the camp several days ago. I didn't tell him that I knew otherwise."

"How is he?"

"In good spirits. I do not think you need to worry about him. But I also had a long conversation with that young orderly, Mustafa. He told me an interesting story." Kerim lay back and put his arms behind his head. "Mustafa knew about the stolen clothes. They belonged to another orderly, Eytan, who was very angry about it. Eytan saw that you were gone and thought at first you had stolen them, but Dr. Orhan said that was impossible because you had been sent to the prison camp."

"Why would the doctor say that?"

Kerim shook his head. "That is a mystery. But my guess is that someone told him you had been sent away, and he had no reason to think otherwise. The new lieutenant, Turan, who took charge of the ward, may have told him. If word got out that Turan lost a prisoner, he would be in real trouble."

"Turan was a bastard," I said as I laced up my new shoes.

"So Mustafa told me. My theory, Bloke, is that Turan chose to ignore your absence to save his behind. The prisoners were leaving anyway, so the problem would go away with them, and he wouldn't lose face. Losing face is very important in this part of the world."

I stood up and walked a few paces to get the feel of the shoes. "If no one's looking for me," I said, "getting to the border will be a lot easier."

"Bloke, I did a lot of thinking on my way back from Kuleli. The war may be over soon. There is much talk of America declaring war on Germany. When a German submarine sank a British liner, a lot of American passengers died, some of them very rich and important. If the Americans come in on the side of the British, the war could end quickly." He sat up and pulled a strand of hay from his beard. "So why not forget about Greece. Stay here until the war ends, then go home."

"Stay here!" I sat back down in the hay. "I can't do that. It's too dangerous for you and your family. Someone is sure to find me eventually."

"I've thought of that too," he said. "Here's my proposition. I will tell the neighbors that you are an American student who came here to study Turkish culture, and you wish to live with a Turkish family. It makes sense because of the American college."

I pushed back and leaned against the wall. "I don't know, Kerim. It seems too risky. Besides, I can't just stay here and eat your food without paying anything."

"But you will pay," he said, slapping his knee. "You will pay me with work. Every spring I hire two laborers to work on the farm. Now it is almost spring, so instead of paying two men, you will do the work of two men. That will make up for this big headache you have caused me."

"I know nothing of farming."

"I will teach you. Then you can go home to Wales and be a farmer instead of working like a mole under the ground."

I sat silently for some time, trying to absorb what Kerim was proposing. "I'd like to think about it," I said.

"Of course."

After supper that evening I asked Kerim if he thought it safe for me to go for a walk. I was tired of being stuck in the barn and I needed some fresh air to clear my head. "No one is looking for you," he said. "Go and try out your new shoes. Follow the road downhill and you will find the Bosphorus."

I set off along the now-dark gravel lane and soon found myself on a narrow cobblestone street that led directly into the village. Weathered wooden houses lined both sides, their upper floors extending over the street. I passed a number of villagers, most of whom ignored me, but some extended greetings. A tantalizing aroma of fish, cooked meat and spices permeated the air, along with occasional whiffs of smoke from coal fires. As I approached the Bosphorus road I passed several small shops, most of them closed for the night, and a bustling teahouse where, I assumed, Kerim met his friends. I crossed over to where the Bosphorus current jostled fishing boats moored to capstans along the seawall. My mind racing, I strolled for some distance along the water until I came to the first tower of the European Castle, massive and foreboding in the evening darkness. My feet still hurt, but the pain was bearable. Across from the tower I sat on a bench facing the channel.

The moon had not yet risen, but the sky above fluoresced with a billion points of light in the clear night air, the same Milky Way that graced the skies of home. Night sounds spoke to me in ripples from the Bosphorus current and the chirping of crickets in a nearby thicket. Plane trees along the Bosphorus road whispered as a steady breeze ruffled their bare branches, the sound punctuated with the haunting cry of an owl. Even the distant whistle of a *bekci* making his rounds seemed a part of the evening solitude, like the defensive cry of some nocturnal animal.

I slid forward on the bench and rested my head back. Within seconds a shooting star careened across the sky with startling suddenness, appearing from some unknown place before vanishing into another. And then, unexpectedly, a full moon, majestically magnified by its low elevation, rose slowly above the Asian hills and painted a ribbon of silver across the water. For the first time in my life I felt totally isolated in a world of compelling loveliness that I wanted to last forever.

My reverie was interrupted by the clacking of a cane as an old man shuffled along the paving stones behind me. *"İyi akşamlar,"* the man said. I answered in kind. Reluctantly, I got up and began making my way back to the where the village road led up to Kerim's farm. Before turning up the hill I stopped and looked once more at the Bosphorus shimmering in the moonlight. This wasn't such a bad place to sit out the war, I thought.

And thus began my transformation from Lance Corporal Evan Morgan, Second Battalion, South Wales Borderers, to a farmer with the peculiar name of Bloke.

Chapter 17

I entered the farmhouse through the back door to find Kerim and Serin immersed in books in separate chairs in the parlor. Kerim was puffing on a Meerschaum pipe, the first time I'd seen him indulge in tobacco. Noises from the front of the house told me that Anoush was busy in the kitchen.

Kerim motioned for me to sit down. "Are the shoes comfortable?" he asked.

"Yes, they are," I said, sitting on the couch and leaning back. "My feet are getting better."

Kerim said something in Turkish to Serin and she departed with her book toward the kitchen. I felt an unexpected pang as she left the room. In the short time I'd been with Kerim's family, I'd become attracted to this girl whose eyes avoided mine. I hadn't been near a young woman since I'd said goodbye to Gwyn at the train station two years ago, and now I was in the same house with one of almost startling beauty. Had Kerim noticed how my eyes followed her?

He looked at me expectantly. "I've decided to become your farmhand," I said. "I promise you I'll work hard."

"If you don't, Bloke, I'll throw you out."

"Fair enough," I said. "But I'm worried about my family." The idea that everyone at home must think I was dead gnawed at me. "I need to let them know I'm alive. My girlfriend too."

Kerim placed his pipe in an ashtray and got to his feet. "Wait," he said. He left and came back a few minutes later with two bottles and two glasses. He handed me one of each. *"Bira,"* he said. "Turkish beer. We will drink to your joining the family." He sat down and poured beer into his glass, and I did the same with mine. He raised his glass in a silent toast. "Tomorrow I will show you the farm."

"About my family . . ."

"That could be a problem," he interrupted. "We are at war with your country. You can't just send a letter."

"But . . ."

"Forget about it for now, Bloke. When the war ends they will find out."

"I'm still worried about you and your family," I said. "If I'm caught, you could be in real trouble."

"Why should you be caught if no one is looking for you? Just make sure you don't change your story."

"I have no papers. No passport."

Kerim thought about that for a moment. "It could be a problem if the Americans enter the war. But there are ways to get papers. I'll see what I can do." He poured the remainder of his beer into his glass. "Always remember, Bloke, if anyone questions you, you must tell them you came to me seeking a place where you could learn about Turkey. My story will be that Americans often visit the college, so I had no reason to doubt you." He drained his glass.

"Very well," I said. Kerim could easily have handed me over to the authorities, but instead he had taken me into his family. I was determined to do my utmost to make certain he never regretted his kindness towards me.

I finished off the rest of my beer. "Turkish beer is very good."

"German beer is better," he replied.

§

A somewhat dilapidated but good-sized storage shed attached to the back of Kerim's house became my new home. I suspected there was ample room for a guest upstairs in the farmhouse, but perhaps Kerim and Anoush would rather not have a young man they hardly knew in close proximity to Serin. I was, however, allowed to use the bathtub adjacent to the parlor once every weekend; at other times I could wash at an artesian well near the barn.

I spent one more night in the company of the cows and goats. The following morning Kerim and I cleaned out the shed, removed most of the stored clutter to the barn, and repaired the roof where time and the elements had taken their toll. A coarse wooden table that had lain upended in the corner became the shed's centerpiece. From his attic Kerim retrieved a palliasse and blankets for sleeping, a rickety chair to go with the table, and a wicker armchair for comfortable sitting. From a neighbor he borrowed a small, rust-covered coal stove for use when the nights were cold, and he cut a hole in the wall of the shed to accommodate the stove's chimney pipe. My new accommodation was primitive, but adequate for a farmhand, and a step up from what I'd been used to since I'd left home to go to war.

We spent the afternoon touring the farm. There wasn't much to it—three fields on the slope behind the barn, each about ten acres, a pasture enclosing some two hundred sheep, an orchard with a good number of apple and pear trees, and a small olive grove.

"This year we will plant sunflowers," Kerim said as we stood on the hill overlooking his fields. "There is a man in the village who renders the seeds into oil. And soybeans. And over there, alfalfa."

"When will you plant?" I asked.

"As soon as you plough the fields for me." He touched my arm. "How is your shoulder?"

"Getting better."

"Good. Çikolata will help you."

"Çikolata?"

"Come. I will introduce you."

We walked through the sheep pasture toward a neighboring farm. "Before long they will drop their lambs," Kerim said, waving his hand towards his flock. "And after that they must be sheared. All hard work."

We entered the next farm through a broad wooden gate and followed a rutted track to a barn, outside which a brawny man split logs with a long-handled axe. His face had the ruddy, parchment-like appearance of one who spends too much time in the sun. He paused and wiped an arm across his forehead as we approached. Kerim shook hands with him and spoke at length, once pointing his thumb towards me. The only word I recognized was "Bloke."

The man turned towards me and extended his hand. *"Hoş geldiniz,"* he said.

That means welcome," Kerim said. "The proper response is *Hoş bulduk.*"

"Hoş bulduk," I repeated as I took the man's hand. He smiled and continued his conversation with Kerim for several minutes before retrieving his axe. Kerim and I entered the barn. "His name is Adnan," Kerim said. "He is a good man and a good friend. But I just lied to him by telling him you are Mr. Bloke, an American student." He pointed towards a dark-brown ox lying in a bed of hay and attached to a rail with a halter. "And this is Çikolata."

The animal was immense, at least a ton in weight. "Adnan and I share the services of Çikolata for ploughing," Kerim continued. He reached down and patted the animal on its rump. "His name means chocolate. Do you think you can handle him?"

"More like he can handle me."

Kerim laughed. "The two of you will soon become friends. He's much gentler than he looks."

And become friends we did. Under Kerim's guidance I learned how to attach moldboard to ploughshare, harness ox to plough, and coax the giant animal to do my bidding. My first clumsy attempts in the field created considerable amusement in the family as Kerim recounted how twice Çikolata had pulled me over and dragged me through the dirt. But I soon learned to coordinate my movement with the ox's, and in the space of two weeks, working from early morning until daylight faded, I had turned over the rich, dark soil of all three fields. My damaged shoulder ached with the effort, but I didn't complain; proving my worth was more important. Kerim, who spent most of his working days at the college, left me to work at my own pace.

As my familiarity with farm work developed, so too did my Turkish vocabulary as Anoush took it upon herself to teach me the language.

"*Lahana dolması,*" she said as she served cabbage leaves stuffed with rice and a mixture of vegetables and spices. She looked at me until I had repeated the words to her satisfaction. She did this with every meal she served, and with every kitchen implement she used. And I was expected to remember the words the next time the objects appeared before me. Sometimes my pronunciation brought laughter from Kerim and amused smiles from Serin, but as the weeks passed, I found myself less and less inhibited in attempting to express myself in Turkish.

There were other unfamiliar foods I came to enjoy in Anoush's kitchen. One day Kerim arrived home from the market with several purple-skinned vegetables, each the size of a pineapple. "*Patlıcan,*" he said when I expressed curiosity. He tossed one to me. "The Americans call it eggplant."

"It doesn't look much like an egg," I said.

He laughed. "Maybe in America chickens lay purple eggs."

Patlıcan quickly became one of my favorites, whether Arnoush served it stuffed, fried or roasted, but best of all when she brushed slices with olive oil and grilled them over charcoal.

And then there was the fruit, *kavun* that grew in Kerim's backyard garden, larger than any fruit I'd seen back home, with a hard, gray-white shell and sweet, succulent pulp on the inside.

Kerim expressed amazement. "You don't have *kavun*—melon—in Wales?"

"I've never seen it there."

He shook his head as if pitying me the shortcomings of my homeland.

§

By the beginning of May the hills overlooking the Bosphorus were awash in purple-pink Judas tree blossoms, and the water reflected the deep blue of clear skies. Oxeye daisies, bluebells and buttercups dotted meadows and fields, while village lanes and gardens were fragrant with wisteria, bougainvillea and cyclamen. Here there was no sound of war.

No corpse-infested battlefield. Working outdoors, surrounded by such exquisite beauty, led me to wonder how I had kept my sanity in the dank, grimy subterranean world of the coalmine.

And then there was the enigmatic beauty of Serin that I found so tantalizing and so distant, whether it was sitting next to me at the dining table in Anoush's kitchen or in the fields when she brought me my midday repast. She would leave the meal on the ground not far from where I worked at planting or hoeing, and would leave immediately the way she had come with barely a glance in my direction. I always took the opportunity to thank her or offer some pleasantry, while heeding Kerim's admonition to refrain from questions. I had no idea whether Serin's reserve toward me was at Kerim's or Anoush's bidding, or whether it was simply her nature; but I found it disquieting, and at the same time intriguing. How I wished she could stay and join me in conversation.

Most days she delivered my meal in a three-tier copper container, each rounded section containing something different. The top tier usually held rice and vegetables, and sometimes beef or mutton. Dates or olives and goat cheese occupied the second tier, and yogurt the bottom. Tin coated the inside of each section, and the copper exterior was engraved with Arabic script and floral designs. Latched copper bars on opposite sides held the three sections together and a swivel handle attached to the lid made it convenient for carrying. It was an elegant, ingenious device, far more handsome and more practical than the dented lunch tin I used to carry to the coalmine.

I quenched my thirst with water carried in a glass bottle from the farmhouse or filled at one of the many springs above the farm. A jug of *ayran*, the milky drink prepared by mixing yogurt with water that I had at first found so distasteful, sometimes accompanied my lunch. After having the liquid placed before me at most evening meals, my palate had adjusted and I now found the sour taste quite appealing.

Once the spring planting was behind us, we turned our attention to the sheep which, having produced their lambs, were overdue for shearing. Apart from watching Rhondda Valley sheepdog trials and seeing sheep grazing on Leonard's farm above Ystrad, I knew virtually nothing about the animals. Kerim's flock consisted of a breed called Türkgeldi, he told me, much prized in Turkey for their fine wool and excellent mutton. Welsh farmers favored a breed of sheepdog so intelligent it would herd sheep into the narrowest of spaces in response to its master's whistles. Kerim resorted to Adnan's scruffy mongrel to help chase his sheep into a paddock at one end of the pasture.

"Watch me, Bloke," Kerim said, as he waded into the flock, his right hand grasping a pair of wide-blade shears. With his left arm he seized one animal around its neck, wrestled it onto its side, and set to work removing the fleece with a practiced hand. Once one side was shorn, he flipped the animal over and sheared the other side. Adnan, who had joined us in the paddock, took the finished sheep and sent it out to join the lambs that had been separated from their parents and were bleating noisily behind the fence. A number of neighbors had assembled to see how a stranger from across the ocean handled Turkish sheep.

Kerim handed me the shears. "Your turn."

No harm in trying, I told myself. I reached for the nearest ewe, which quickly eluded my grasp and scurried away, losing itself in the rest of the flock. I went after another with the same result. I heard chortles of laughter from behind the paddock fence.

"You have to move quicker than that, Bloke," Kerim said. In a flash he captured another ewe and wrestled it to the ground. He motioned me over and nodded toward the shears. Awkwardly I began cutting into the fleece, but I couldn't do it at the pace Kerim had demonstrated.

The next time I succeeded in collaring a ewe and, with considerable effort, pulled it on its side. By the time I finished shearing the first side I was sweating profusely. I rested a moment before trying to turn the animal over, but it escaped my grasp and ran off, looking most peculiar with a thick coat of fleece on just one side. I looked over at my audience who were now clapping and laughing. I noticed then that Serin had joined them. She was leaning with her arms across the fence, smiling at my predicament. I nodded toward her and joined in the laughter.

Kerim and Adnan, satisfied with my baptism, came over and slapped me on the back, then joined in the shearing. By the time I had finished my tenth sheep I had more or less mastered the technique, but my arms ached with the effort and my hands chafed from the cutting. Two men from the village gathered up the shorn fleece and loaded it into a large wagon drawn by two horses for transport to a motorized barge moored at the foot of the hill. From there it would be carried to a processing plant in the city for washing and baling.

The three of us worked steadily until early afternoon when Anoush arrived with bread and cheese and a jug of *ayran*. By that time our audience had grown tired of the entertainment and had dispersed. After a short break we continued until daylight faded and the last sheep was shorn. Exhausted and filthy with wool grease and paddock dirt, I staggered back to the farmhouse.

"You did well, Bloke," Kerim said as he walked alongside me.

"I'm glad you only have a couple of hundred sheep, and not a couple of thousand," I said.

He laughed. "You've earned a rest. In two days we will go to Constantinople to settle accounts at the factory. It's time you saw our magnificent city."

Back at the shed I picked up my bar of soap, a towel and a change of clothes that I had purchased in the village with the small amount of money Kerim paid me each month. I dragged myself to the well near the barn where, hidden from the house, I stripped off my clothes and scrubbed myself thoroughly from head to toe. It was almost nine o'clock before I was invited in for a good-sized bowl of beef stew, but I was almost too tired to eat and had a hard time keeping my eyes open. Immediately after the meal I excused myself and returned to the shed where I collapsed on the palliasse. The next thing I knew the rooster was announcing the start of a new day.

§

On a sunny morning in early June, Kerim and I set out on the Bosphorus ferry for Constantinople. The boat followed a zig-zag route crossing from one shore to the other, picking up passengers, dropping off others, as we headed south for the ancient capital of the Byzantine Empire. As we sailed past the Kuleli naval college, I reflected on the peculiar chain of circumstances that began with the ambush at Kücük Anafarta, and the deaths of Brian Greenwood and Bill Oliver. Each link in the chain—my wounds treated by Kerim, escape from the prison hospital, rescue from the unforgiving waters of the Bosphorus—led to my present station in life as a farmer in a Turkish village, as unlikely a scenario as any I could have imagined when I first left Wales with my regiment.

I thought of Suresh and Albert Parker and Cyril Montague and the other prisoners I'd befriended, all now enduring the wretched conditions of a prison camp somewhere in the middle of Anatolia. Was I shirking my duty, I asked myself, for choosing a new identity that kept me isolated from the abomination of war? I dismissed the thought. I'd escaped captivity with good intentions, but Kerim was right, there was scant chance of making it to England while the war still raged.

As we neared the city I drank in an unfolding panorama of palaces, domed mosques and stately villas, set against blossom-painted hills. And as the ferry, trailing black smoke from its funnel, turned in towards the Golden Horn, I gazed in wonder at a remarkable vista of hills crowded with buildings and dotted with countless minarets. Compared with Cardiff, or even Alexandria, this was the most magnificent of cities.

Dodging a bewildering armada of caiques, barges, sailboats and steamers, the ferry arrived at a dock on the south shore of the Golden Horn, close by a bridge that blocked entrance to the channel.

"This is Stamboul, the oldest part of the city," Kerim said as we disembarked. "Over there"—he pointed across the bridge—"is Galata. That's where the modern shops are, and the hotels and foreign embassies."

Facing us from the ferry dock, a broad square teeming with people and pigeons led to an immense mosque with two minarets, each with three elaborately carved balconies. Cupolas and half-cupolas adorned the building's exterior. *"Yeni Camii,* the New Mosque," Kerim said as he followed my gaze.

"It doesn't look very new."

"It was built in the seventeenth century, which makes it newer than most mosques in Stamboul." Pigeons scattered before us as we made our way to the bridge. "Come, I'm hungry. We'll have lunch before we get down to business."

We set out across the bridge, a crowded, noisy thoroughfare where street vendors shouted to attract customers, horse-drawn wagons clattered over the potholed road surface, and motor cars sounded horns in a futile attempt to speed their passage. Upstream the Golden Horn was as busy with shipping as the Bosphorus, even with large transport vessels moored at loading docks along the banks.

"How do those boats get up there?" I asked. "The bridge is in the way."

"The middle span sits on pontoons," Kerim explained. "Late at night it floats aside to allow ships to pass. German engineers built the bridge before the war." He led the way down a staircase to the lower level of the bridge where restaurants and fish vendors competed for midday customers. As we entered a small restaurant, the proprietor greeted Kerim like an old friend.

"This is Hikmet's café," Kerim said. "Best fish in the city." To Hikmet he said in English, "You have *palamut?*"

"Of course," Hikmet replied.

"Palamut comes up the Bosphorus to spawn," Kerim told me. "It's the tastiest fish in these waters, and Hikmet knows how to prepare it."

We enjoyed a lunch of the meaty white fish, wrapped in bay leaves and grilled over charcoal. As we began our meal, Kerim took a piece of paper and a pencil from his pocket. "We need to give you a name." I looked at him blankly. "For your passport. We are going to see a man who arranges these things."

"My name's Evan Morgan."

"Yes, but everyone here knows you as Bloke. But you need another name. In Turkey most people go by a single name. In your country and in America, people have two names, sometimes three, or even more."

"How about Henry," I said. I was thinking of the American author, Henry James.

"Very well, you shall be Henry Bloke." He printed the name on the paper. "Where do you live in America?"

"Where do I live?" I knew little of American geography, but when Kerim asked the question I was reminded of a conversation Gwyn and I had with Mr. Leonard, the farmer. We'd been on a Sunday afternoon stroll by his farm and had chanced upon him repairing his henhouse. Gwyn had asked him about his chickens. "The white ones are leghorns and the brown are Rhode Island Reds," Leonard replied.

"Rhode Island Red? What a funny name," Gwyn had remarked.

"Aye," the farmer said. "They're named for a place in America."

"Rhode Island," I said to Kerim. "I came from Rhode Island."

Kerim printed the name. "You need a street address."

"Victoria Street. Number twenty-two." I saw no harm in giving my street address in Wales.

"And the town?"

"I've no idea."

Kerim looked at me, expecting more. Finally he said, "We shall say you lived in Winchester."

"Is that in Rhode Island?"

"I've no idea," he said."

"All right, Winchester," I agreed. Kerim printed the town name and returned the paper and pencil to his pocket.

We ended our meal with excellent Turkish coffee and continued across the bridge. On the hill above us, the imposing, centuries-old Tower of Galata guarded the confluence of the Bosphorus and the Golden Horn. A short distance from the bridge we traveled to the top of the hill via an underground funicular railway—built by the French forty years ago, Kerim told me. Not far from the railway exit, down a narrow alley, we entered a tiny shop selling prints and maps. A musty odor pervaded the interior, and the single window cast little light on storage shelves and framed prints lining the shop's walls.

A short, hunchbacked man wearing a beret stood behind the counter. Kerim spoke to him about my need for a *pasaport*. The hunchback glanced at me and nodded. He raised a hinged section of the counter and ushered us through a beaded curtain into a back room where a boy about fourteen years old was sweeping the floor. He said something to the boy, who immediately set his broom aside and left through the front of the shop. Kerim handed the man his piece of paper containing my fictional name and address. The man studied the words for a moment, holding the paper close to his eyes in the manner of one in need of spectacles. He said something to Kerim.

"How tall are you?" Kerim asked me.

"Five feet nine inches."

The man added my height to the paper. He looked into my eyes and said in English, "Eyes brown." After that there was much discussion, and my limited knowledge of Turkish told me the two men were haggling over a price. In the midst of the discussion, the boy arrived back with a tray containing three glasses of tea. We sipped tea until Kerim and the shopkeeper shook hands to seal their agreement. The man then motioned me to a chair situated in front of a large studio camera mounted on a tripod. He pulled curtains back from two windows to let in more light and told me in English to sit still. Standing behind the camera, he pulled a black cloth over his head, peered into the camera lens and took my photograph. The document, identical to an American passport, would be ready in a few days, he told us.

We returned by the underground railway to a dock on the upstream side of the bridge and traveled by ferry some distance up the Golden Horn, disembarking on the Stamboul shore. From the landing stage it was a short walk to the wool factory, where Kerim engaged in another price negotiation with the manager while the three of us drank tea. Tea, it seemed, was an essential ingredient in any bargaining ritual.

"Does Adnan share in the profit?" I asked Kerim as we left the factory.

"Adnan is rewarded with free mutton," Kerim replied. "And I help him with handiwork around the farm."

We took the ferry to a landing stage a short distance up from the bridge. From there Kerim led me up a hill dominated by a mosque so massive that the New Mosque seemed almost puny by comparison. Framed by four minarets and capped with a huge dome, the mosque was almost intimidating in its size, yet captivating in its beauty.

"This is *Süleymaniye Camii,* the Mosque of Sultan Süleyman, a great warrior," Kerim said as we stood in its courtyard, flanked by columns of white marble and pink granite. "It's the city's finest mosque, yet it was built by a Christian, an architect named Sinan. He designed many mosques for the sultans." We paid a brief visit to Süleyman's tomb in an adjacent cemetery before Kerim led the way through the expansive campus of the city's university into a narrow street resonating with a symphony of a hundred artisans hammering sheets of copper into elegant trays, plates, bowls and pitchers. The copper street led into the maze of the Grand Bazaar where we browsed among shops selling carpets, jewelry, alabaster, leather goods and a host of other products.

From the Bazaar we traveled by trolley to a small square where we descended steps into a dimly lit underground cistern, its roof supported by countless columns disappearing into the darkness. "Some people think the Romans built the cistern," Kerim said, his voice echoing in the cavernous interior. "Others say it was the Emperor Justinian." Kerim was clearly enjoying his role of tour guide, and he took pride in the bewildering collection of antiquities that met us at every corner.

He took me next to the exquisite Blue Mosque of Sultan Ahmet to admire its six slender minarets and colorful porcelain-tiled interior. We ended our tour at the massive Aya Sofia mosque, flanked by four thick minarets. "Constantine built this as a Christian basilica when people in your country were living in caves," Kerim said.

"But now it's a mosque."

"It was made a mosque on the day the Turks captured Constantinople in 1453."

On our walk back to the Galata Bridge, Kerim pointed out the Sirkeci railway station, the final destination of the fabled Orient Express. *"Inşallah, when the war ends, people will once again travel here from Paris,"* he said. We passed through the Egyptian Bazaar, the atmosphere redolent with the scent of hundreds of different spices, where Kerim stocked up for Anoush's kitchen. At last we boarded the ferry just in time for its departure.

Although my legs ached from so much walking and hill climbing, I stood at the ferry rail reveling in the beauties of the Bosphorus as we crossed back and forth between the two continents. But before we reached the sanctuary of Kerim's farm, I was to learn that even in Paradise, Hell lies not far beneath the surface.

Chapter 18

The ferry was leaving the landing at Ortaköy, a village on the European shore, when a startling change overcame Kerim. We were standing at the rail talking about the wool business when he stopped in mid-sentence and stared at a gaunt, elderly man propelling a fishing caique toward the shore. Kerim's expression changed to one of loathing, and his hands gripped the rail so tightly his knuckles turned white.

The man in the caique looked up and his eyes locked onto Kerim. He stood, almost capsizing his boat, waved his fist and let forth with a stream of invective. Kerim spit into the water and hurled back his own dose of venom. Passengers on the ferry and people on shore turned and stared. I looked at Kerim, dumbfounded. This wasn't the Kerim I knew, the cheerful, ever-optimistic and compassionate Kerim. He abruptly left the rail and shouldered his way along the crowded deck. I followed slowly and found him near the front of the boat, leaning on the rail, glowering at the approaching Asian shore.

"What was that all about?" I asked him.

Kerim didn't answer for some time. Then, without looking at me, he said, "I called him a dog and a son of a whore. And he said as much about me."

I'd been in Turkey long enough to know that calling someone a dog is about the worst possible insult. Son of a whore is about as bad. "Why was that man so angry?" I asked.

Kerim seemed to be grappling with his thoughts. Still staring ahead, he said in a low voice, "Because I killed his son."

I stood staring at him, stunned by his words. Kerim killing another human being? The very idea was preposterous. I gripped his arm. "I don't understand . . ."

His face red with anger, Kerim wheeled away from me and sat on a bench outside the passenger cabin. I sat next to him, but didn't speak; I'd been shocked into silence.

We sat in silence for several minutes as the ferry buffeted its way through whitecaps whipped up by a stiff afternoon wind. Finally Kerim turned to me and said in a controlled voice, "Did you ever wonder why Serin lives with us?"

"Yes, but I didn't think it was any of my business. I was raised by my aunt and uncle."

"Then you . . ." He stopped as a middle-aged couple carrying a number of shopping bags pushed through the cabin door and sat next to him on the bench, spreading their bags around their feet. Kerim said nothing more until we had passed the European Castle and gone ashore. On the voyage back, as the ferry crossed from one side of the Bosphorus to the other, Kerim's stinging confession had hung over me like a shroud, blotting out all other thoughts and casting a chill over my pleasant, uncomplicated life on the shores of the Bosphorus. I tried to make eye contact, but he either stared straight ahead with a sullen expression, or down at the deck.

After we disembarked, Kerim walked slowly toward the teahouse, his shoulders sagging, barely acknowledging my existence. He sat at a table outside, placing his bag of spices on the ground next to his chair. This was unusual for Kerim; his habit was to go inside and greet his friends. I sat across from him. "Tell me about Serin," I said.

Kerim looked up as the owner of the teahouse arrived promptly with two glasses of tea, sugar cubes and spoons resting in the saucers. The two men shook hands and spoke briefly to one another before the owner returned to his other customers.

"What do you know of Armenians?" Kerim asked me.

"Not much," I said. "There seems to be a lot of them in the village. It's not something I've thought much about."

"Armenians live all over Turkey. Most are in the east because that is their traditional homeland. And they don't get on well with the Turks."

This was a surprise; life in the village seemed a model of harmony. I turned and looked inside the teahouse where Turks and Armenians sat together chatting, puffing on narghiles, playing backgammon, enjoying one another's company. The teahouse represented the social and political center of the village. It was here where village elders discussed weighty issues, and resolved disputes. It was not a place for women. Not long after I settled on Kerim's farm, I'd walked into the village late one Saturday afternoon. I saw women carrying water from the communal well, hanging laundry on backyard clotheslines, sweeping front steps, shopping for vegetables and meat, even whitewashing a fence. Not a man was in sight—until I reached the teahouse which was crowded with them. I seldom saw any signs of discontent. Apart from some minor differences in dress—Armenian women tended to more colorful dresses, the men less inclined to wear the fez—Turks and Armenians didn't look much different from one another.

"They seem to get along well enough around here," I said.

"Most do. But there are hotheads who make life difficult for the rest of us." He stirred a sugar cube into his tea. "The government guarantees religious freedom for everyone," he continued. "But everyone must also accept that Islam is the predominant religion. All others are subservient to Islam. Not all Armenians accept that arrangement. And they want independence, their own country."

"I can understand that," I said, wondering where Kerim was leading me. "No one likes being subservient."

"Turkey's government is dominated by three men, a triumvirate," he went on. "When war broke out in Europe, these men foolishly aligned the country with Germany instead of having the good sense to remain neutral. To make matters worse, the Minister of War, Enver Paşa, decided we should attack Russia." He paused to sip his tea. "The campaign in the Caucasus was a disaster. We lost tens of thousands of men and the Russians took over much of our land in the east."

He stopped as Adnan and Bedros, an Armenian neighbor, approached our table. They shook our hands and made small talk before going into the teahouse. Kerim watched as the two men relaxed at a long table with a group of other men, a mix of Turks and Armenians.

"What does the war with Russia have to do with Serin?" I asked.

"I'm getting to that." He nodded toward the door of the teahouse. "Here everyone gets along. No one gives a damn what a man's religion is. We judge one another by whether we are good neighbors, how hard we work, how honest. These are the important measures of a man, not his religion."

"That's how it should be everywhere," I said. "And you married an Armenian."

"I did, and she has made me a happy man. Serin is also Armenian."

"But what . . ."

"Let me finish, Bloke," he interrupted. "In the campaign against Russia, Armenians took the side of the Russians. Some took up arms against the Turks, and some even fought with the Russian army. And that has led to a backlash, much ill feeling toward the Armenians."

I was beginning to sense where the conversation was heading. "And this caused problems for you and Anoush?"

"No." He shook his head impatiently. "Not here in the village. This is a peaceful community. But in the east, the situation is very bad." He pushed his now-empty glass and saucer away. "Last year Enver Paşa proclaimed there is an Armenian conspiracy against the Turks, and he ordered that Armenians in the east be deported because they pose a threat to the empire. I don't know the details of the deportations, but I've heard rumors that there is much killing. I overheard a man visiting the college from a missionary school in the east. He said he witnessed women and children being driven from a village. The men had been slaughtered. Defenseless people. Anoush is very upset. She has family in the east."

"But there hasn't been anything like that around here, has there?"

"Nothing like that. But there have been isolated incidents of violence." He paused and looked at me with eyes moist with tears. "Serin's parents were killed by Turks in Ortaköy."

I felt a chill spread through my body. "And the man in the boat was involved?"

"Not him. His sons." He paused again as a man left the teahouse and stopped at our table to tell us one of his cows was ill. I waited for Kerim to continue.

"Two years ago," he said, "before I joined the army, Serin and her parents went to Ortaköy to order new furniture for their home. They stopped for an evening meal before taking the ferry back. It was dark when they left the restaurant. A Turkish mob—young men, all drunk—was on a rampage, looking for Armenians to beat up and rob. They smashed windows in shops owned by Armenians. Serin and her parents were set upon by three men. Her father, Anoush's brother, resisted and was beaten to death. They poured petrol on his wife and set her on fire."

Horrified by Kerim's words, I felt a deep anger rising from the pit of my stomach. "Serin witnessed the killings?"

"It was worse than that," he said, his voice almost a whisper. "They dragged Serin down some alley and . . ." He was having difficulty talking. "They did unspeakable things to her," he said, his voice conveying both hatred and sadness. "The furniture maker, a good man and a Turk, found her bloodied and naked. He wrapped her in blankets and brought her to us in his delivery cart."

I shook with fury that men could perpetrate such savagery. Even the abomination of war paled in comparison. At least on the battlefield we fought for our nation's honor, and we respected our adversaries. Serin could not have been older than fifteen when the attack occurred. How does one recover from such an experience? By what miracle was she able to bring an occasional smile to her lips? It's no wonder she barely looks at me, I thought bitterly.

"The furniture maker told me what had happened," Kerim continued. "He knew the men who had done it, two brothers and their cousin. Serin stopped speaking that night, and no matter how hard we try to console her, she will not speak."

"I didn't realize," I said. "I just thought she'd been born that way."

"We give her love and protection. She is our daughter now. But she will never marry, never bear children."

"What do you mean? In time, surely, she'll get over what happened to her. Then she'll marry."

"No one will marry Serin, not after what happened to her."

"That's ridiculous! It's not her fault."

"But that's the way it is in this part of the world. Is it so different where you come from? Even in Europe rape carries a stigma."

"I suppose you're right," I said, fuming at the injustice, the stupidity of human prejudices. "What about the police? Didn't they do anything?"

"I went to them, of course. But the father is an important man, a rich man. He has the police in his pay. There was nothing they could do, they told me. They said the men I named were playing cards at a friend's house that night. They had an alibi."

"So you took matters into your own hands."

Kerim reached out and gripped my arm. "Promise me, Bloke, you will not repeat anything I tell you today to my wife or Serin. It is better that they think you know nothing."

I nodded. "You have my word."

He released my arm. "Serin likes you, I think. Perhaps you can draw her out of her shell."

"Likes me?" I laughed. "She ignores me."

"Even so." He took a handkerchief from his pocket and wiped his eyes.

"Tell me about what happened. When you killed the man."

"I killed two of the men, the cousin and one of the brothers," he said in a low voice. "Your army saved me the trouble with the third. He was killed at Gallipoli—and good riddance. The father knows I killed his son and his nephew. Some day he will come to kill me."

"No one saw you kill them?"

"No, I was very careful. A few days after what happened, when the streets were quiet again, I walked to Ortaköy at night, across the hills so no one would see me. I took a knife from the kitchen, a sharp knife we used for cutting meat. I went to a tavern where, the furniture maker told me, the nephew spent his nights drinking *rakı* or cognac."

"How did you recognize him?"

"I was told what he looked like—short, with a thin moustache and goatee, and always wearing a blue fez with gold markings. And I knew his name was Tariq. I waited nearby, where I could see the door. When he walked out, I followed him. I could tell by the way he walked that he was drunk.

"When we entered a dark street I caught up with him and called his name, 'Tarik!' He turned and said, '*Efendim?*' I told him I had a gift from my niece. Then I stuck the knife in his belly, twisted it, pulled it out and stabbed him again and again. Blood ran from his mouth." Kerim's eyes had taken on a steely intensity. "When he fell to the ground, I slit his throat and left him in the gutter. Afterwards I threw the knife in the Bosphorus and walked home the way I had come."

I stared at him, my tea still untouched. "I never thought of you killing a man," I said quietly.

"Nor I, before all this happened. I have no regret for what I did."

I sipped the tea I'd been neglecting. "And the other man?"

"I waited a few weeks for the brothers. I followed them around, learned their habits. One of them, Oktay, fished from his boat every Thursday night. I caught up with him one Thursday when it was foggy, a good night for killing because no one would see me. I followed his boat from the shore, keeping my eye on his lantern in the fog. When I was certain there were no other boats nearby, I came alongside him. He didn't even know I was there. Before he could turn around I hit him on the head with a hammer, one I'd taken from the shed where you now live. He fell into the water and went under. When I saw the bubbles of air come up from his lungs, I threw the hammer in after him. His body was found floating in the Sea of Marmara by fishermen several days later."

He tossed some coins onto the table. "Come, we must be getting back or Anoush will be wondering what became of us."

"I'm glad you didn't have to kill the third man," I said, as we walked up the hill. "You're lucky no one saw you."

"But Oktay's father knows. He knows Serin lives with us. Who else would kill his son?" As we approached the farmhouse, Kerim said, "Remember, Bloke, you must tell no one what I've told you."

We walked around the side of the house to the back door. Serin was in the yard petting one of the goats. She glanced up at us for one brief second, lovely, vulnerable—but she didn't smile. I looked at Kerim and his eyes met mine. He shook his head and turned to enter the house.

§

The months passed, the crops reached maturity and were harvested, and my skin took on the bronze color of one who spends his days in the sun, accentuating the scars of bullet and shrapnel wounds. The daily labor broadened my chest and thickened my muscles to the point that when I looked at myself in a mirror, I hardly recognized the thin, pale-skinned youth who had left the coalmine to go to war.

In the autumn, when the pace of farm work slackened, I was invited along on family excursions. We picnicked in the nearby Belgrade Forest alongside ancient reservoirs that provided Constantinople with water, or lazed on sparkling Black Sea beaches. On one occasion we crossed the Bosphorus to Paşabahçe, from where I'd embarked on my foolish attempt to swim across. From a spot near the glass factory, we traveled inland to a village that looked as though it had been transported from Europe, with thatched houses and barns, similar to the barn in which I'd spent the night after fleeing Kuleli. There was even a Catholic church instead of the usual mosque. "This is Polonezköy, the Polish Village," Kerim told me, settled by Polish soldiers who fought with the Ottoman army during the Crimean War. "We buy pork here," he said. "It's the only place we can get pork because Moslems are not supposed to eat it."

"But you eat it," I said.

"I'm not the only Moslem who does," he replied, patting his belly. "We are not supposed to drink beer either. I think God has more important things on his mind than to be concerned with what I eat or drink."

§

As cold winds from the north heralded the arrival of winter, the war in Europe raged on; and to the east the British and Turkish armies were in a death struggle for control of Mesopotamia and Palestine. Despite the disturbing news of deportations in Anatolia, the Turkish and Armenian communities along the Bosphorus remained peaceful. But Kerim's revelations about Serin and his bloody revenge cast a pall over everything I did. I had at one time entertained the thought of living out my days here on the Bosphorus. Now I had a premonition that not all would be well in the months ahead.

As for Serin, I made no headway with her. She remained as distant as ever. By year's end she had become so enmeshed in my thoughts that I began to fantasize—sitting with Serin in the hills above the farm, her head resting on my shoulder; or Serin entering my shed at night and lying next to me on the palliasse, her dark hair caressing my cheek. Sitting alone at night in the dark, I saw her slender fingers, sad eyes and delicate features, her complexion as fine as Anoush's alabaster vases. I relived those quick glances with which she sometimes favored me, and how she would immediately avert her gaze when our eyes met. I longed to put my arms around her and hold her close, to try in some way to convince her she had nothing to fear, and that in time she would once again enjoy life as she had before. When I realized, guiltily, that Serin had become an obsession, I tried to bring Gwyn's face into focus; but it eluded me—all I saw was Serin.

Then, at last, I realized that I was in love with her. I would have loved her even if Gwyn were here with me, for it wasn't that type of love at all, but more as if I'd become infatuated with an exquisite painting of a woman, distant and untouchable.

Chapter 19

April of the next year, 1917, America finally entered the war. Kerim told of optimism in the American college community that the conflict might now reach a quick conclusion. At the same time there was considerable anxiety, for they had now become enemy aliens. Would they be deported? Interned? Remarkably, the Turkish authorities ignored them, and the college continued to function as it always had in times of crisis. As a precaution, however, I carried my false American passport with me whenever I ventured away from the farm.

It was not long after we received the news of America's involvement that I sensed the first crack in Serin's façade. Anoush had dispatched me to the village one morning to buy *palamut,* as the fish had begun their annual migration up the Bosphorus. As I approached the waterfront in search of a fisherman, a ghostly vision unfolded. Warm, moist air from the Mediterranean had conspired with the cold Bosphorus current to form a low blanket of fog over the water, muffling sound and obscuring the vision of those who ventured away from the shore. Some distance out a three-masted schooner glided silently past in the direction of Constantinople. Only the top part of the vessel was visible, floating along atop the mist like an apparition.

On the paved surface near the water's edge, Serin stood holding a basket of groceries with both hands in front of her. Her eyes were fixed on the dreamlike image that had attracted several other spectators. I crossed the street and stood next to her. "A ghost ship," I said.

She turned her head and rewarded me with a smile. Her eyes held mine for two or three seconds before she turned back toward the mist. In all the months I'd been a guest in her home, this was the first time she hadn't immediately averted her eyes. I continued to look at her in wonder, but if she was aware of my attention she showed no hint of it.

We stood, shoulder to shoulder, for a short while before Serin hoisted the basket into the crook of her arm, smiled at me once again, and turned to cross the street. I was tempted to follow, to accompany her back to the farm, even offer to carry her basket; but I still had fish to buy.

§

"I didn't think you'd be here this long," Kerim said one Saturday as we worked together repairing the stone wall bordering his uppermost field. We were now in the busy season at the farm, shearing sheep, ploughing fields, planting crops. "You're a good worker, Bloke, and you can stay as long as you like, but I can't blame you if you try to go to Greece. I know you worry about your family."

I leaned back against the wall, removed the cap I'd bought in a village shop, and wiped sweat from my eyes. Below, the blue water of the Bosphorus appeared deceptively calm, and the Asian hills stood in sharp contrast in the clear morning air. "I just wish there was some way to let them know I'm alive," I said. "But I'm in no hurry to leave."

Kerim hoisted another heavy stone and positioned it into the wall. "Perhaps by year's end the war will be finished," he said.

Quite apart from my feelings toward Serin, I'd developed a real affection for Kerim and his wife. Anoush had an endearing way of mothering me; perhaps she saw in me the son she never had. Kerim was such a gentle man, so filled with good humor and compassion, I still could not envision him killing another human being. Then I would look at Serin and ask myself, how could he not?

I never broached the subject of Serin with Kerim and Anoush. Did they suspect that I had more than a passing interest in her? Kerim had once expressed the hope that I might be able to break through Serin's silence, but I was no more successful than they were. I saw Serin's mental state as too precarious for expressing any feelings toward her. Better to wait until she came to me. Was her lingering smile as we stood by the Bosphorus her opening move?

Later that year when I worked in the fields, Serin resumed her habit of bringing me lunch in the three-tiered copper pail; but instead of returning immediately to the farmhouse, she now sat a short distance away until I'd finished eating. Then I would take my lunch pail to her so she could return with it. I wrestled with the idea of sitting next to her while I ate, but I was still fearful of any action that might upset her. Then one day, as I harvested alfalfa, she sat closer to where she had left the pail, as if inviting company. I lay down my scythe, picked up the pail and went to her.

"Do you mind if I sit with you?" I said. She looked up at me and shook her head. I sat near her, but not so close as to be intrusive. She was wearing her white dress with the floral design, the one she had worn the first time I'd seen her, and which I thought complemented her beauty as much as anything in her limited wardrobe. The cotton fabric accentuated the olive smoothness of her bare arms. I wanted to reach out and touch her, feel my skin against hers, but knew that was a line I couldn't cross.

"I think we're in for some rain," I said. Storm clouds had assembled in a darkening sky above the Asian hills, even as we sat in bright sunshine. I made small talk about the farm work as I ate, which elicited occasional glances in my direction, but not the words I longed to hear. Even so, the very fact that she had accepted my company, I considered a victory.

When I'd finished my lunch, she took the pail, stood and dusted off her dress. "Serin," I said, as she began walking away. She stopped and looked back. "Back in my home country I lived with my aunt and uncle. I had no mother or father."

She stared at me for several seconds, nodded slightly, and continued on her way. I followed her with my eyes until she disappeared among the cypress and umbrella pines at the foot of the hill.

In no hurry to return to work, I sat for a while watching the storm clouds intensify, illuminated intermittently with flashes of lightning. I lay back in the grass, pulled the brim of the cap over my eyes, and within seconds had dozed off. Perhaps it was words about Wales that caused me to dream of Bodringallt School, for I awoke suddenly from the image of Mr. Andrews, the music teacher, coaxing melodious sounds from young throats. My favorite, that I'd loved as long as I could remember, was the Welsh lullaby, *All Through the Night,* a feature at every concert sung by the school choir.

I returned to my scythe and resumed cutting alfalfa while the melody ran through my mind. I sang softly.

> *Sleep my child, and peace attend thee*
> *All through the night.*
> *Guardian angels . . .*

What were the words? There was a time when I could sing all the verses without having to think twice about it. When I was a very young lad, my uncle would sometimes sit me on his lap by the kitchen stove and sing the lullaby in Welsh in that sweet baritone of his.

> *Holl amrantau'r sêr ddywedant*
> *Ar hyd y nos.*
> *Dyma'r ffordd I fro gogoniant,*
> *Ar hyd y nos.*

Funny how the English words escape me, but now the Welsh comes back like a welcome visit from an old friend. I began to sing more strongly, moving the scythe in rhythm with the melody.

Golau arall yw tywyllwch,
I arddangos gwir brydferthwch
Teulu'r nefoedd mewn tawelwch,
Ar hyd y nos.

I continued through the second verse, tears in my eyes, almost overwhelmed by an emotional kinship I felt for my native land. As beautiful as my Bosphorus surroundings were, as enjoyable as my daily labor in the fields might be, I could never disentangle myself from family and the green valley of my birth. By the time I reached the final line—*Ar hyd y nos*—I felt the full chorus of Bodringallt boys and girls singing with me.

My reverie was interrupted by the sound of clapping. I swung around to see a young girl standing on the dirt path behind the wall, smiling at me as she applauded.

"What strange words you're singing," she said. "But you have a very nice voice."

She looked no older than sixteen, with large blue eyes and fair hair that cascaded about her shoulders. Her wholesome, attractive face was framed by a straw bonnet held by a yellow ribbon like a halo behind her head.

"Are you Mr. Bloke, the American who lives with Kerim Bey?" She spoke flawless English with an unfamiliar accent.

Startled by the unexpected appearance of my audience of one, I wasn't sure at first how to respond. I rested the scythe on my shoulder and nodded. "Aye," I said.

"Aye? Does that mean yes?"

A mental lapse. So taken was I with my Welsh singing, I'd inadvertently fallen into the idiom of my homeland. I nodded.

"I'm American too," she said in an earnest, lilting voice. She rested her forearms atop the stone wall. "Except I've never been in America. I was born here in Turkey. I'm Charlotte Summers."

"Pleased to meet you," I said, tipping my cap. I'd made a point of avoiding the college campus because I was afraid any American I might meet would immediately see through my subterfuge. But now I found the conversation refreshing, for apart from Kerim, no one I'd met in the village knew more that a few words of English.

"Bloke is a funny name," the girl persisted. "Is it Polish? Was that Polish you were singing? Or Slavic?"

"Actually it's Welsh," I said. "My mother was born in Wales."

"How interesting," she said. "But you were born in America." It was more a statement than a question.

"Aye. I mean yes. Rhode Island." I had a feeling this winsome girl would accept at face value anything I told her.

"Really! My parents are from Connecticut, right next door."

I didn't respond, not wanting to advertise my ignorance of American geography.

"My father teaches engineering," she went on. "Have you met him?"

"No. I don't know anyone at the college."

"What a shame," she said, pushing herself away from the wall. A middle-aged woman, shaded from the sun by a cream-colored parasol, approached her along the path.

"Charlotte," the woman said. "You really should keep your hat on when you're in the sun." She was a handsome woman, with hair and facial features that bore a strong resemblance to those of the girl.

"Oh, Mother!" Charlotte said in feigned exasperation. "Look who I've just met. This is Mr. Bloke, the man who works for Kerim Bey."

The girl's mother stopped and stared at me, an amused expression on her face. She twirled her parasol. "So you're the elusive Mr. Bloke. We never see you on the campus."

I laughed. "I don't mean to be elusive. The farm keeps me busy."

"Do you have a first name, Mr. Bloke?"

"Henry." I brought the scythe down and rested on the handle.

"He's from Rhode Island," Charlotte said.

"Really?" her mother said. "Where in Rhode Island, Henry? You don't mind if I call you Henry?"

"Winchester."

"Winchester—is that near Providence?"

"Not too far," I said, having no idea that such a place as Providence existed.

"Of course, nothing is far from Providence in Rhode Island," she said. "And what does your family do in Winchester, Henry?"

"They raise chickens."

"Chickens?"

"Rhode Island Reds."

"Oh." She looked a little perplexed.

"Henry must come to tea, Mother. Mustn't he?" Charlotte looked expectantly at her mother.

Mrs. Summers turned to her daughter as if to admonish her forwardness. She looked back at me. "Yes, of course he must. Shall we say four o'clock tomorrow?"

"I don't . . ."

"Oh, Henry, you must come!" Charlotte said. "You have to see my insect collection."

I wasn't sure how to respond. Perhaps a short visit would do no harm. Even though I was now reasonably comfortable speaking Turkish, it would be a welcome change to have a conversation with people fluent in English.

"Well, I . . ."

"I won't take no for an answer," Mrs. Summers said. "Charlotte will meet you here a little before four and show you the way. And don't dress up, we're very informal."

§

That evening I asked Kerim what he thought about my having tea with Mrs. Summers and her daughter.

"She's a very nice lady, Mrs. Summers," Kerim said between puffs on his pipe. "It's about time you met some of the Americans."

"But I don't speak like an American."

He shrugged. "There are all sorts of people at the college, people with different accents. I wouldn't be concerned. I don't think British and Americans sound much different."

"I'm not so sure."

The storm that had moved in from Asia blew rain against the windows and lit the night sky with vivid flashes of lightning. Thunder reverberated back and forth between the hills of Asia and Europe.

"I told some Americans that you were a university student before you came here," Kerim said. "In case they ask you, you should be prepared to tell them which university."

"I don't know of any American universities."

Kerim chewed on his pipe and frowned. "There must be lots of universities in America." He took the pipe from his mouth and thought for a moment. "When I was studying in Munich, two Americans came to give lectures on anatomy. They were from a university called Harvard." He placed his pipe in an ashtray and went to the bookshelf. "Perhaps my encyclopedia . . ." He leafed through a thick Turkish book, running his finger down the pages.

"Here it is. Harvard University in Cambridge, Massachusetts, United States of America. Founded in 1636. That's very old for America."

"Cambridge like in England?"

"There are many towns in America named for towns in England," Kerim said. "Maybe even Wales. If they ask, tell them you were a student at Harvard."

There were other reasons I wanted to accept the invitation. I'd been living with Kerim for well over a year now, and I'd read all the English-language fiction from his bookshelf, some of them more than once. At the moment I was struggling through the third volume of Thomas Carlyle's

The French Revolution, having already learned more about the subject than I cared to know. Perhaps by meeting some Americans, I could gain access to the college library, maybe even some Dickens.

And there was my family at home. With the Americans I saw a possible way to get a message to my aunt and uncle. A note inserted in one of their letters to America—if they were agreeable—might be forwarded to Wales. It was worth considering.

§

Charlotte Summers flashed a dazzling smile as I approached her at our appointed meeting spot. She wore a light, flowery dress with short sleeves that complemented the clear, breezy sunshine that had been ushered in by the previous night's storm, a pleasant contrast to the usual midsummer heat and dust. Her figure, hidden the day before behind the wall, was slender and well proportioned. In my plain brown shirt and baggy corduroy trousers, the only wardrobe I owned outside my work clothes, I felt distinctly underdressed.

Charlotte linked her arm in mine as she led the way to her home, a gesture that took me by surprise, but which I found most pleasant. She emanated a faint trace of perfume.

"Is that your girlfriend?" she asked.

I looked at her. "Girlfriend?"

"I've seen a girl with you when you're working. I'm sorry, Henry. I'm being very nosy, aren't I?"

"She's Kerim's niece. She brings me lunch."

"Oh," she said, then, "She's mute, isn't she? My mother said something happened to her that made her stop speaking, but she won't tell me what it was. Do you know, Henry?"

"No," I lied.

She was quiet the rest of the way. We walked up a narrow lane fragrant with wisteria and trumpet lilies, past a number of stone houses set back against colorful flower gardens. She led the way up a short flight of steps to a gate that opened through a privet hedge into a spacious garden, beyond which sat the Summers' home, a two-storey brick house with red trim around the windows.

"What a beautiful place," I said.

"Yes. We have a lovely view of the Bosphorus. And Mother is a very good gardener, although she pays a Turk to do most of the work. Come on, let's go inside."

Mrs. Summers greeted me cordially and led me through the house, richly furnished with Turkish rugs and kilims, to a small brick patio in the back. In the center of the patio four rattan armchairs surrounded a large copper tray supported on a wooden stand inlaid with mother-of-pearl. Cups, saucers and plates were stacked on the tray, together with a nosegay in an alabaster vase. Beyond the patio a small expanse of closely cropped lawn stretched to a terraced hillside where a variety of vegetables grew in well-maintained plots. A greenhouse occupied one end of the lawn.

"Charlotte, why don't you show Henry your collection while I make tea," Mrs. Summers said. "Or would you prefer lemonade, Henry?"

"Tea is fine, Mrs. Summers."

I followed Charlotte into the house, through the living room into a spacious, wood-paneled study lined with bookshelves. She took my arm and led me to a long table where several glass-topped cabinets displayed an astonishing variety of insects, from tiny houseflies to exotically-colored butterflies and dragonflies, all mounted with pins on a green felt backing.

"This is magnificent," I said. It was a collection worthy of a natural history museum.

"Do you like it, Henry?" she said, obviously pleased. "Professor Ziegler in the Biology Department helps me. He's German. He knows absolutely *everything* about insects." She pressed provocatively against me as I leaned over the cabinets. "My favorites are the Lepidoptera."

"What are Lepidoptera?"

"Butterflies and moths. Look, this one's a white admiral. And next to it is a swallowtail. And that one's a painted lady. Isn't that a funny name, painted lady?"

"Do you catch them yourself?" I moved away from her to the next cabinet.

"Mostly. But some of them Professor Ziegler gave me." She moved down next to me. "Henry, what happened to your forehead? There, I'm being nosy again."

"Just a farming accident."

"In Rhode Island? It looks like a bad accident."

"Nothing serious. I have a hard head."

She smiled, then reached out and touched the scar, just as her mother called to say tea was ready. "I suppose we'd better go," she said, disappointment clouding her face.

We sat on the patio in the shadow of the house, entertained by songbirds and the hum of bees homing in on beds of nasturtium and marigold. While Charlotte poured tea into tulip-shaped glasses, Mrs. Summers nudged slices of baklava onto plates.

"The pistachio crop has just been harvested," she said, licking her finger after handing me a plate. "Baklava is so much better with fresh pistachios."

"Delicious," I said as I bit into the flaky, honey-drenched pastry.

"So tell me, Henry, what brought you to Turkey?"

"I studied Ottoman history and decided I'd like to see the country first-hand. Learn some of the language. Meet some people." It was a question I'd anticipated.

"So you were a history major in college?" She waved a wasp away from the baklava.

"My major area of study was literature."

"Who's your favorite author, Henry?" Charlotte fixed her eyes on mine.

"Dickens."

"I like Dickens too, but my favorite is Jane Austen."

"Charlotte is an unrepentant romantic," her mother said.

I laughed. "Sorry, Charlotte, I've not read any of her books. One thing I miss here is not having access to a library."

"Why not use the college library?" Charlotte asked.

"I'm not a student at the college."

"Can't Henry get a library card, Mother? I have one, and I'm not a student."

"I'll talk to Marjorie Huntington, the librarian," Mrs. Summers said to me. "I'm sure she'll issue you a card." Just the outcome I'd been hoping for!

"Don't you think Henry has a funny accent, Mother?"

"Yes, you don't sound much like a New Englander," her mother agreed.

"Probably my mother's influence," I said. "She was born in Wales."

"And where in the States did you study?" Mrs. Summers asked.

"Harvard University."

"You must be very smart to get into Harvard," Charlotte said as she leaned forward to refill my glass.

"I was able to get a scholarship . . ."

"Oh, that must be Carleton, my husband," Mrs. Summers broke in at the sound of a door slamming. "He'll want to meet you. He did his postgraduate work at Harvard."

A moment of panic; this was an unexpected turn. My brain raced trying to anticipate questions I might be asked.

After sounds of movement in the house accompanied by cheerful whistling, Carleton Summers emerged onto the patio. He stood about six feet tall, slightly built, with unkempt reddish hair flecked with gray. Wire-rimmed spectacles and a thick moustache that drooped at the corners of his mouth defined his face. He wore a loose-fitting white shirt, sleeves rolled part way to his elbows, and a tie loosened at the neck.

"Carleton, come meet Henry Bloke." Mrs. Summers greeted her husband. "He went to Harvard."

Professor Summers reached across the table and shook my hand. "Nice to meet you, Henry. Call me Carl—only my wife calls me Carleton." He leaned over and kissed his wife on the cheek. He smiled at his daughter. "How about some tea for your weary father."

"And some baklava," his wife said.

"No, tea is fine." He slumped into the chair next to mine.

"You look tired, darling," his wife said.

"Too many committee meetings. And I still have a stack of exams to correct tonight. No peace for the wicked, eh, Henry?" he said, turning towards me.

I sipped my tea and smiled, but didn't respond.

"So Henry, you've been with Kerim for quite some time. You must enjoy it here."

"Yes, Sir," I said, adopting the formal mode of address I felt appropriate for a middle-aged professor. "He's a bit like a father to me."

"He's a good man," Carleton said. "Really keeps the campus shipshape. I don't know what we'd do without him." He reached into his shirt pocket and pulled out a briarwood pipe. "I bet you didn't bank on becoming an enemy alien, eh, Henry?"

"No, sir. I've been a bit out of touch with what's been happening in the war."

"The Turks have been more than reasonable with us." He pulled a pouch of tobacco from his trouser pocket. "But we've had some anxious moments. There was some talk of closing the college and using the campus for a typhus clinic, but that all seems to have blown over."

"Henry studied literature at Harvard," Charlotte said.

"Really?" her father said. "My field's civil engineering. Helen probably told you. Which dorm did you live in?"

"I didn't, Sir. I stayed in a rooming house."

He nodded, tamped tobacco into the bowl of his pipe with his finger. "Cheaper that way I suppose." He stared at me as he put a match to his pipe.

"How did you end up in Turkey?" I asked him.

Summers flicked the match into a nearby flowerbed. "I taught at Yale after getting my doctorate. There are historical connections between Yale and the college here. So when I heard they were looking for an engineering professor, I jumped at the chance. We were young then, looking for adventure."

I thought of asking where Yale was, but decided against it. Perhaps it was a place a Harvard student should know about.

"You've been here a long time?" I asked.

"Almost twenty years. And I've no desire to go anywhere else. We really love it here, don't we Helen?"

"It's so beautiful," his wife said.

"Tell me, Henry," Carleton said. "If you studied literature, you must have taken Everett Blackwell's English lit course."

Dangerous ground again. "No, I never had the pleasure."

"What a pity. You've heard of him, of course."

"Yes, Sir, he's a legend at Harvard. He was on some kind of leave when I was there."

Carleton Summers did indeed look tired. He relaxed back in his chair, alternately sipping tea and puffing on his pipe. Helen Summers and I and her daughter talked about the farm work I was doing for Kerim, and how I found life in a Turkish village.

"I should be going," I said, after a convenient break in the conversation.

At that Carleton sat up. "Helen, why don't you and Charlotte take care of the dishes? Come on, Henry, I want to show you our greenhouse."

We strolled across the lawn together and entered the almost overbearingly hot structure. There was little to see there. Early spring seedlings had long since made their way to the Summers' garden, and planting trays lay scattered about in a state of neglect. Only a few hanging baskets holding strawberry plants, no longer bearing fruit, still needed attention.

"Henry," Carleton said as he led the way to the far end of the greenhouse. "One of my passions, besides engineering, is mountain climbing. I've climbed often in Wales." He gave me a penetrating look. "If I were to hesitate a guess, I'd say your accent is pure Welsh. You're not really American, are you?"

I felt a sudden chill despite the heat of the greenhouse. "My mother was born in Wales. I got my accent from her."

"We get our accents from the culture in which we live, not our mothers." He took the pipe from his mouth and tapped out the spent ashes on the workbench. "What game are you playing, Henry? There's no Professor Blackwell at Harvard. I made the name up."

Perhaps it was the suffocating heat that all at once made me feel so weary. More likely it was the realization that Carleton Summers had seen through my flimsy curtain of false identity. I leaned against the bench and folded my arms. After years of deception, the truth had to come out.

"I'd rather you didn't voice your suspicions about me to anyone else," I said. "My life could be in danger."

Carleton put the pipe in his shirt pocket. "Are you a British spy, Henry? Keeping records of Bosphorus shipping, perhaps?"

"I'm a British soldier. An escaped prisoner of war." His expression changed from contempt to surprise. "I escaped from the Kuleli prison hospital. When the ship blew up on the Bosphorus, I got away in the confusion."

Carleton grabbed his pipe again and stuck it back in his mouth. Beads of sweat glistened on his forehead. He chewed on the stem, staring at me, grappling with my admission. "Let's get out of this heat," he said at last. When we stood outside, he spoke in a low voice. "I suppose Kerim is complicit in your escape."

"No. He thinks I'm an American student." Given the tension of the moment, I barely noticed the change in temperature.

"Kerim was stationed at Kuleli. How can he not know?"

"He knows nothing!" I'd given Kerim my word and was not about to betray his trust.

Carleton Summers stared at me for some time before replying. "Very well, I'll accept what you say." His eyes betrayed his skepticism. "You put my family at risk by coming here. Did that ever occur to you?"

"To tell the truth, it didn't. I suppose I've been here so long, I've become complacent. And I had an ulterior motive."

"Which was?"

"My family has no idea I'm alive. I was hoping that if you wrote letters to America, you could enclose a note from me that could be forwarded."

"Not possible, not now we're in the war. We won't be writing to anyone until this business ends. We have to tread very lightly."

I couldn't hide my disappointment. "I suppose I should have realized that."

"Henry, I won't tell anyone what you've told me, not even Helen. And definitely not Charlotte. But for God's sake, be careful."

"I will, Sir. I'm very grateful. Now I'd better say goodbye to Mrs. Summers."

He reached out to shake my hand. "Good luck, Henry. I hope you get home safely. It is Wales, isn't it?"

"Aye, Sir. The Rhondda Valley."

"I never got to that part of the country. Did all my climbing in the north."

As we walked back across the lawn, Carleton Summers said, "One other thing, Henry, Watch out for my daughter. She's a bit of a flirt."

Chapter 20

Three days after my encounter with the Summers family, Charlotte found me in the sheep pasture checking on the flock. "Henry! You must come with me. We have a library card for you!"

I released the lamb I'd been petting. "That's good news," I said. "Does your mother have it?"

"It's being held at the circulation desk. Come on, I'll show you the way."

We followed the pathway through the wooded area below the farm, past the rear wall and towers of the European Castle, and then up a short hill where we emerged onto the college campus. Stately ivy-covered sandstone buildings surrounded a dirt quadrangle where a small group of youths kicked a football back and forth.

"The campus is usually much busier," Charlotte said. "Most students are away for the summer." She led me in front of one building to a landscaped terrace overlooking the Bosphorus.

"What a wonderful spot for a college," I said as we stood by the stone wall marking the edge of the terrace. "I can't think of any place more beautiful."

The view encompassed one of the massive towers of the castle on one side, and the full expanse of the Bosphorus in the direction of Constantinople on the other. Across the water the tree-covered Asian hills formed a scenic backdrop for marble kiosks, fountains and porticoed villas. Directly below the terrace, a cemetery crowded with cylindrical gravestones sloped down to the narrowest part of the channel where smoke-belching ferryboats dodged the ubiquitous fishing caiques and water taxis. Many of the gravestones were tilted haphazardly at oblique angles; others lay amid dense undergrowth and wildflowers where a handful of goats grazed under the watchful eyes of a young goatherd.

"That cemetery is sacred ground for the Turks," Charlotte said. "Soldiers who fell in the battle for Constantinople are buried there."

"That makes it as old as the castle," I said, nodding towards the crenellated tower.

"Aye," she said teasingly, her eyes twinkling.

I laughed. "Aye yourself. Next you'll have me teaching you Welsh."

She turned her back to the Bosphorus and leaned against the stone wall. "My father said I shouldn't be seeing you, Henry. He said we don't know enough about you."

"Sound advice," I said. "Now, where's the library."

"I don't care what he says. I think you're a very nice, honest person. And you go to Harvard."

And what would you think of me, dear Charlotte, if you were to learn that I was far from honest, and nothing more than a simple coalminer in my former life?

We crossed the quadrangle to a smaller building set into the side of a hill that led down to the Bosphorus road. Much of the structure lay below the level of the main entrance where the circulation desk was located. Charlotte introduced me to Mrs. Hutchinson, the elderly, white-haired librarian, who handed me the precious piece of cardboard that was my passport to the library stacks.

"Come on, Henry, I'll show you the fiction level." Charlotte led the way down two flights of stairs to a room crowded with well-stocked wooden bookshelves, poorly illuminated by mullioned windows at the ends of the aisles. The room's characteristic musty atmosphere reminded me of the town library in Tonypandy.

I followed Charlotte down a narrow aisle where she looked up and down the shelves until she found what she was looking for. "Here we are, Charles Dickens, your favorite author." She stood back to allow me access. There were only a few titles on the shelf, but a welcome sight indeed for one starved for good reading. I pulled out a dusty copy of *Martin Chuzzlewit*, held it lovingly as I looked inside at the title page.

"Is that the only one you're taking?" Charlotte whispered.

"For the time being. I've read it before, but I'm ready for another go at it."

"Then I'm going to find you one by Jane Austin. You have to try her."

I followed her to the next aisle. "It's down there," she said, "near the wall." I walked to the end of the aisle, Charlotte close behind. She reached up and pulled a book from the top shelf. *"Sense and Sensibility,"* she said. "My favorite."

She placed the volume on a section of empty shelf and turned to face me, trapping me against the wall. She placed her hands on my shoulders. "Wouldn't you like to kiss me, Henry?" The scent of her perfume teased my nostrils.

I swallowed. "I don't think that's a good idea. You know what your father said."

"My father is too protective."

"Charlotte . . ."

She pouted. "You don't really like me, do you, Henry?"

I placed my volume next to hers and pulled her towards me, kissing her lightly on the lips. Given her father's admonition, I prolonged the moment longer than was wise—but it was my first kiss since I'd said goodbye to Gwyn an eternity ago.

"Of course I like you," I said. "I think you're charming and beautiful. And if I were five years younger, I'd probably fall madly in love with you."

"I'm not a child, Henry! I'm sixteen years old!" I put a finger to my lips as her whisper increased in volume. "You're not that much older than I am."

"True," I said, "but enough older. And I have a girlfriend back home."

Her shoulders sagged. "I should have known." She was unable to hide her disappointment. "But we can still be friends, can't we?"

"Of course we can."

"My parents want me to go to Wellesley next year. Maybe we can see each other when you go back to Harvard."

"Where's Wellesley?"

"Oh, Henry, don't be so thick! You *know* that's where Harvard boys go to meet girls."

That could make Wellesley either a college or a brothel, I thought, although the latter seemed most unlikely. "Of course," I said. "I'd forgotten."

§

I saw little of Charlotte after that, which was just as well. I hated telling lies, even when necessary for survival. That her father knew the truth came as a relief, and I took him at his word that my secret was safe with him.

As for the treasured library card, my gratitude to Charlotte and her mother knew no bounds. I read both books, devoting one evening to one, the next to the other, two or three chapters a night. The upper-crust romanticism of Austen I found a pleasing counterpoint to the gritty, street-wise world of Dickens. On one of our few chance encounters, Charlotte was delighted to learn that I had now added her favorite author to those I admired. From that time forward, whenever I read or reread an Austen novel, I would taste that kiss in the library stacks.

When I finished reading *Sense and Sensibility*, I gave it to Serin who was fluent in English, even if she wouldn't speak a word of it. She read avidly, finishing well before I had to return the book. I checked out others for her, ones I hoped she'd find uplifting or humorous, and she rewarded me with a smile of gratitude with each volume I handed her. Sometimes we sat outside in the yard reading together, which elicited smiles of approval from Anoush.

We always sat together now, Serin and I, when she brought my lunch to the fields. Sometimes I shared her silence, just savoring her closeness. Other times I spoke about farm work or other trivialities, hoping my words would elicit some verbal response. I told her of my aunt and uncle and the house in which I grew up, the schools I attended and what life was like in the Rhondda Valley. I couldn't bring myself to lie to her about being an American student. In fact, I suspected that she and Anoush already knew.

The months passed quickly, but even with American forces now fighting in Europe alongside the British and French, there seemed little likelihood of the war ending before the year was out. One fine December Sunday, when Serin sat by the window mending some item of clothing, I asked her if she would like to go for a walk. She looked up at her aunt, busy at the stove, who nodded her assent. Serin put aside her mending and we set out, skirting Kerim's fields, until we reached the highest point overlooking the Bosphorus. We rested at the edge of a small stand of poplars, enjoying the unseasonable warmth. Scattered billowy white clouds drifted above under an azure sky. Swallows swooped low over the meadow below where we sat, before soaring up and arcing over for their next pass.

Serin leaned forward with her arms clasped about her knees, her eyes fixed on the meadow. In a few short weeks oxeye daisies and buttercups would burst from the soil and spring breezes would bend the poplars. When we were children, Gwyn had once held a buttercup under my chin. "Your skin's turned yellow," she'd said. "That means you like butter." I smiled at the memory. Butter was such a rare commodity in the Morgan household, appearing on the table only on special occasions; usually we lubricated our bread with lard or dripping. I wanted to hold a buttercup under Serin's chin.

I rested on one elbow, my legs stretched out. Captivated by her delicate, olive-skinned beauty, I stared at Serin's profile for some time, wondering if she was aware of my attention. She leaned forward and rested her head on her knees. Tentatively I reached out and placed the back of my fingers gently against her cheek. She tensed, but didn't recoil from my touch.

"*Çok güzelsiniz,*" I said. You are very beautiful.

An intake of breath. She reached up with her hand and pressed mine against her face. A faint smile played about her lips as she turned towards me.

"Speak to me, Serin."

Her mouth opened, tongue moistening her lips. I held my breath as her eyes, still locked on mine, welled with tears.

"Please, Serin," I pleaded. "Let me hear your voice."

A tear ran down her cheek, which she wiped away with an impatient gesture, shaking away my hand as she did so. She began crying softly, perhaps reliving the dreadful events that had shocked her into silence. I reached across and pulled her toward me, held her head against my shoulder until her crying subsided. After several minutes she pulled away, shook her hair away from her face, and rose to her feet. She dusted off her dress and began walking back down the hill. I quickly caught up with her. As we walked back to the farmhouse, Serin linked her arm in mine. Almost, I thought. Almost.

After that we took many walks together. I'd broken through her reserve, but not her silence. She smiled a lot more now and showed modest displays of affection toward me, which clearly met with the approval of Kerim and Anoush.

"Serin seems much happier," Kerim said one day as we returned from a visit to Adnan on the neighboring farm. "She's very much taken with you, I think."

"She still won't speak to me," I said.

"Give her time. I heard her humming a tune while she milked the cows yesterday."

"I'm taken with her, too."

"I know that, Bloke. You have been for a long time."

§

There were evenings when Serin and I remained outside with our books even after it became too dark to read. We'd sit next to each other until the stars, wondrously close, cast a silver glow over our universe. I'd reach out and take her slender hand in mine, and we'd sit in silence enjoying the symphony of crickets and owls. Anoush and Kerim left us alone until they were ready to retire, then would slam doors or make other noises to let us know Serin was expected in the house.

Ironically, the closer I became to Serin, the more my thoughts gravitated to Gwyn, back home in the Rhondda in the shadow of those grimy coalmines. Three years had passed since I'd said goodbye to her at the railway station, and two of those years I'd been listed as missing in action. The last Gwyn would have heard from me was a letter written late in 1915, three weeks before I'd been ordered out to look for the general's missing son. Before I'd become a prisoner of war. With no Red

Cross report on my whereabouts, Gwyn and my aunt and uncle had to assume I was dead. I was happy here in Turkey, more so, I think, than at any time in my life, but I couldn't go on living a lie; I owed it to Gwyn and my family to set the record straight.

And where did that leave me with Gwyn and Serin? At times I felt as if I were living in parallel universes. They were so different from one another, the one outspoken and buoyant, the other silent and enigmatic. When I eventually made it back to Wales, as I knew I must, would I want to resume the old life there, pick up where I'd left off, so to speak? Gwyn and I had been together since we were schoolchildren, yet there was little doubt in my mind that by now she would have gone on with her life, perhaps be married and have children. As distressing as the notion was, I could hardly expect her to sit around waiting to see if by some miracle I returned from the dead.

I tried to picture myself back in the Rhondda, going to work day after day and returning in the evening to my aunt and uncle's tiny house on Victoria Street. Meeting Hugh for beer and darts at the Old Lamb and trying to be a proper godfather to his son; getting together with old school pals for rugby matches on the weekend. One thing was certain; I wouldn't go back to the mine no matter what they paid me. Or would I, if no other work was to be had?

And what if I were to find myself desperately unhappy back in my old haunts? Where could I go? Would I be able to return to Turkey and spend the rest of my life farming the land by the Bosphorus? I wouldn't think the Turkish authorities would look kindly on having one of their former enemy in their midst, although I was sure Kerim and Anoush would welcome my return. Perhaps even Serin . . .

As it turned out, the choice was taken out of my hands.

§

It was well into the new year when rioting began in the outskirts of the city. Like a forest fire it spread quickly to the Asian shore, destroying homes and lives in its path, while police and soldiers looked on with indifference. Peaceful villagers, who had spent their entire lives along the pleasant shores of the Bosphorus, were, because of their religion, deported to desolate areas to the east—or simply killed.

Kerim tried to be reassuring. "I spoke to my friends at the police station," he said, his fingers fidgeting with his beard. "They tell me not to be concerned. They won't allow such things to happen here."

For a few weeks the madness was brought under control, only to erupt again in isolated villages like a deadly infection. I was in Kerim's upper field late one afternoon, stacking the first harvest of hay into piles for later gathering, when I heard the unmistakable sound of rifle fire echoing off the thick walls of the castle. Black smoke rose above the thicket of trees that hid my view of the village.

With a growing sense of dread, I gripped the pitchfork and ran downhill as more shots rang out. As I neared the edge of the village, screams punctured the air. My first glimpse of Kerim's farmhouse revealed smoke curling from upper windows, and flames taking hold on the roof of his barn. I ran faster. Tortured bellowing of farm animals led me to the barn's back door. Choking on thick smoke, I felt my way inside and released the panicked cows and goats from their stalls, almost getting trampled as they careened through the open door. I followed them out, coughing, eyes burning, and rounded the barn toward the house. The back door was wide open.

Trembling uncontrollably, I gripped the pitchfork with both hands and walked inside. As I entered the parlor, where I had spent so many happy hours, a sight so horrifying confronted me that it would haunt me the rest of my days. For atop the sideboard where Anoush kept her best dishes lay the severed head of Kerim, eyes closed, mouth curved upward in a hideous grin, his thick beard matted with blood. Paralyzed, I stood staring at the grisly sight, oblivious to the thickening smoke diffusing in from the kitchen.

A movement in the doorway leading to the kitchen—a man stood staring at me, shotgun in one hand and a long, blood-stained knife in the other. I recognized immediately the gaunt boatman from Ortaköy, on whose son and nephew Kerim had exacted his revenge. *Some day he will come to kill me,* Kerim had said.

The man stepped into the parlor, smiling. He tossed the knife onto the sofa. Slowly he raised the shotgun toward me, his finger curling around the trigger. I swung the pitchfork and knocked the weapon aside at the moment he fired. With a deafening explosion in the confines of the room, the blast splintered a cherry-wood table and reduced an alabaster vase to fragments.

Desperately the man reached in his pocket for a fresh shell, but I was already in motion, a wave of blind fury propelling me forward, screaming. I drove the pitchfork into his stomach with such force that the tines penetrated the wall behind him, pinning him upright. Blood drained from the man's face as the shotgun clattered to the floor. He gripped the handle of the pitchfork in a futile effort to dislodge it. Blood trickled from the corner of his mouth. I picked up the shotgun and rammed the butt end of the barrel into his face, flattening his nose, dislodging teeth.

Serin and Anoush! Where were they? My ears ringing, and eyes stinging from the smoke, I dropped the shotgun and stepped into the kitchen. The room was in shambles, table overturned, dishes smashed, but no sign of the two women. I picked a doily up from the wreckage on the floor and held it over my mouth and nose. From the kitchen I entered the front hallway and started up the smoke-filled stairs.

"Anoush!" I shouted.

Halfway up the stairs I was met with intense flames that made further progress impossible. "Anoush!" I shouted again.

I backed down. If Anoush and Serin were up there, there was little chance they would be alive. I returned through the kitchen to the parlor, arriving at the very moment the pitchfork came loose under the weight of the gaunt man's body. He pitched forward and rolled on his side, the bloody tines protruding from his back, his head resting against the sideboard. Blood from Kerim's severed head dripped down on the man's face. He was still alive, but barely.

Voices sounded from the back yard, men talking. I retrieved the shotgun and felt in the man's pocket for a shell. Inserting the shell in the chamber, I moved to the back door. Two bearded men stood in what was left of the vegetable garden, trampling tomato and pepper plants under their boots. One held a flaming torch that gave off the odor of burning pitch, the other carried a rifle and had a bandoleer slung across his shoulder. One man said something that caused both of them to laugh. Near the back wall, chickens scurried and jumped about, chattering, clearly agitated.

The man with the rifle looked up at the sky, then turned toward the house. He stopped, startled to see me standing in the doorway. Quickly he raised his rifle at the same instant I discharged the shotgun. The blast caught the man in the chest and threw him back into the dirt. I walked forward with deliberate calmness, set down the shotgun and picked up the rifle. The other man had dropped the torch and was holding his face where stray pellets had drawn blood. He backed away, turned and began running. I raised the rifle to my shoulder and shot him in the back. He fell against the gate leading to the barn and dropped to the ground, his body twitching before going still.

The lessons in killing, learned first at Brecon Barracks and refined on the battlefields of Gallipoli, had not been forgotten.

I reached down, pulled the bandoleer from the dead rifleman's shoulder and draped it over my own. For several minutes I just stood there, looking at the two bodies in the yard. Timbers crashed behind me as the flames rose higher in their relentless destruction of Kerim's home. I hung the rifle by its strap over my shoulder and went back into the parlor in the vain hope of finding Serin and Anoush. The gaunt man's eyes were open. He reached out a hand as if beseeching me. It was futile to look further; the dense smoke and heat drove me outside, my eyes and throat burning. If Anoush and Serin had not died in the farmhouse, they might have fled somewhere. I had to find them.

Without looking back I left the yard through the gate leading to the barn and walked up towards the sheep pasture. The sun beat down on the farm where I'd never work again. Crops still needed to be harvested and the hay taken in for the winter. As I neared the pasture, I placed a round from the bandoleer into the chamber of the rifle. It was an old, single-shot, bolt-action weapon with rust along the barrel, a hunting rifle perhaps.

I thought I'd escaped the war, but war of a different kind had caught up with me. With one sudden, deadly clap of thunder, my life as Bloke the farmer had ended, and once again I was Lance Corporal Evan Morgan, Second Battalion, South Wales Borderers, with a rifle in my hands and a mindset for killing.

Chapter 21

My eyes flickered open. Blurry images danced in front of me, sun streaming through curtained windows, a human form, first upright, then tilting sideways, then upright again as my vision cleared. Charlotte Summers, hand to her mouth, her eyes wide, stood at the foot of the bed on which I lay.

Pain in my side, dull ache in the stomach. Sore legs. I moved my hands over my body. I was naked, with a sheet covering enough of me to preserve modesty. A thick bandage, held in place with adhesive plaster, covered my right waist.

"All those scars," Charlotte said in a loud whisper.

"Yes, you do look like you've been in the wars, Henry." It was Charlotte's mother, appearing at the side of my bed. "How do you feel? You've been out a long time."

How do I feel? Sick and dizzy, and in no frame of mind for chatting with anyone. I closed my eyes.

"Let him sleep," Helen Summers said. "Come downstairs, Charlotte."

How did I get here? The last I remembered . . . Think!

Images of the burning farmhouse drifted back into my consciousness. Kerim . . . I shuddered. A shroud of evil had descended over my world. *Tüfek*—the rifle, shooting.

And then I remembered—I'd gone searching for Serin and Anoush . . .

* * *

When I reached the pasture I found sheep and lambs grazing in scattered groups, unperturbed by the violence nearby. I rubbed my hand over a ewe's back, ruffling her fresh growth of fleece. She nuzzled her head against my leg as if greeting a trusted friend. It was little comfort, for hatred, like a thick veil, had clouded my vision, blotting out all but the grim events that had transpired at the farmhouse.

From the pasture I continued on to Adnan's farm. I found him sitting on a tree stump next to the barn, elbows on his knees, supporting his head with his hands. Adnan had been one of Kerim's closest friends, and he'd become my friend too.

He looked up on hearing my boots scrape the gravel. Hunched over, his eyes red and sunken, Adnan looked defeated. "Madness," he muttered. He looked at the rifle in my hands. "One gun isn't going to stop them."

"Kerim is dead," I said.

Adnan covered his face with his hands. He sobbed silently, shoulders shaking. I rested my hand on his shoulder. "I killed the man who did it," I said, hoping my words might offer a measure of comfort. "But I can't find Anoush or Serin."

Adnan looked up, his face wet. "The same men who took Bedros and his wife must have taken them. Bedros was here with me when they came—a mob, men with guns." He pointed aimlessly, as if the gesture would help me understand. "Thugs, that's what they are, men from the city."

"The man who killed Kerim was from Ortaköy."

Adnan nodded. "They come from the villages too. They're taking the Armenians, deporting them to the east or to Syria. They loot and burn their homes." He nodded toward the barn. "Look at what the bastards did."

Expecting the worst, I entered the barn. Çikolata, my faithful partner in the ploughing, lay lifeless in its stall, a gaping hole in its side. Carrion flies had already descended on the wound. I felt a wave of revulsion.

"They killed my ox because Bedros was my friend," Adnan said when I rejoined him. "What kind of people do things like that?" He shook his head in disgust. "Bedros and I have been friends since we were children. We never cared about each other's religion."

"Perhaps he'll be back soon," I said.

"They never come back."

"Can't someone stop them? Where are the soldiers and police?"

"Where do you think they are?" he said bitterly. "They are behind what's going on, just like they always are."

A sense of hopelessness took hold of me. "I'm leaving, Adnan," I said. "Kerim's sheep are yours now."

Adnan rose to his feet and took my hand in both of his, his ruddy face inches from mine. "You were very good with the sheep, Bloke. The shearing." He looked into my eyes, his expression softening. "You know, Bloke, Kerim and I thought that you and Serin . . ." He looked away again, his eyes glistening with tears.

"I have to go," I said.

Adnan grasped my arms and kissed me on both cheeks, his whiskers rough against my face. "You will always be welcome in my home, Bloke."

I detached myself from him and took hold of the rifle. "I'll remember our friendship, Adnan."

The street leading to the village was eerily quiet, not the usual weekday bustle. As I approached Bedros's house I saw a man wearing a red fez standing outside holding a flaming torch away from his body. He stood next to a handcart containing a stack of furniture. I hid in the shadow of a beech tree and watched. A second man, bareheaded, emerged from the front door holding several carpets, which he added to the cart. The two exchanged a few words before the one man reentered the house. Two guns, rifles or shotguns—it was hard to tell from where I stood—rested against the side of the cart.

I dropped to one knee and aimed the rifle, sighting on the right leg of the torchbearer. Slowly I squeezed the trigger. The rifle jerked against my shoulder as the man dropped to the ground, screaming. The torch lay across his body, igniting his clothing. The other man appeared in the doorway, his arms cradling a blanket piled with copperware and porcelain plates. He stared in disbelief at his companion. Quickly and deliberately I inserted a fresh round in the chamber, aimed and shot him in the lower abdomen. He collapsed back into the house as his spoils fell to the ground with a clatter that drowned out the other man's screams.

I pulled back on the bolt, but it didn't retract smoothly and I had to extract the spent cartridge with my fingers. I inserted another round in the chamber and walked across to where the man lay in the street, groaning in agony. The awful stench of burning flesh evoked flashbacks of Gallipoli. He had pushed the torch away, but was badly burnt about his body and face, and blood ran from the wound in his thigh. He looked up at me in fear, expecting another bullet.

I pointed the rifle at his head. "Where have they taken them?"

He stared at me wide-eyed, then gestured down the street. "To the boat," he whimpered. I kept my eyes on his for several seconds before turning the rifle away. His partner lay motionless in the doorway surrounded by copper bowls and broken Kütahya plates.

A few men milled about on the main street leading into the village and women peered from upper floor windows. One group of men stood aside to let me pass. I ignored them all as I made my way quickly—half walking, half running—toward the Bosphorus. Several houses showed evidence of looting, broken doors, smashed windows, but no burning.

"*Dur!*" Halt! The shout came from behind me. I whirled around. Two soldiers, rifles in hand, motioned me to stop. As I began backing away, one of the soldiers brought his rifle to his shoulder. The shot echoed down the street and wood splintered from the house inches from where I stood. I steadied myself against a doorjamb and fired back. The impact of my bullet spun the man around and he fell to a sitting position, clutching his arm. The second soldier fired, and what felt like a hot poker burned into my right side. Grimacing with pain, I tried to eject the spent cartridge, but the bolt had frozen.

I dodged into an alleyway as a bullet shattered a window near my head. A labyrinth of unpaved alleys separating wooden houses and animal enclosures offered refuge, but how long could I evade my pursuers? I ran, holding my side, for several minutes. When the soldiers were no longer in view I paused and attempted to reload the rifle, but the bolt wouldn't yield no matter how hard I pulled on it. My hand, the one I'd held to my side, left the rifle stock sticky with blood. Behind a paddock fence a scrawny dog barked angrily.

Ignoring the pain in my side, I dropped the weapon and bandoleer and ran downhill, in one alley, out another, until, unexpectedly, I found myself back at the main village street, close by the now-deserted teahouse. Cautiously I looked up and down the street, but no soldiers were in sight. Shops usually busy this time of the day were closed and shuttered. Some twenty or thirty men, many I knew from the teahouse, stood near the water watching as a ferryboat, its funnel belching black smoke, pulled away from the shore and began moving north against the current. The ferry's deck was crowded with men and women. I ran forward through the onlookers and along the water's edge, keeping pace with the boat. Almost immediately I spotted Serin and Anoush on the upper deck, jammed against the rail.

"Serin!" I shouted.

Her head turned and her eyes, wide with fear, fixed on mine. She reached out towards me and her scream rang across the water. "BLOKE!"

"Bloke!" she cried again, her voice fading into a paroxysm of sobbing. Anoush wrapped a protective arm about her niece's shoulder and pulled her head against her own. I stopped running and stood clutching my side, now soaked with blood, as the distance between the ferry and the shore lengthened. Never had I felt so helpless.

Strong hands gripped my arms as two soldiers ran up behind me. They shouted angrily and began dragging me back towards the teahouse, but I resisted, trying to keep my eyes on the ferry. A third soldier approached and rammed his rifle barrel into my stomach. I groaned and collapsed to my knees, unable to breathe. The soldiers pulled me upright and pain, excruciating, shot through my midsection.

The grip on my arms suddenly slackened. The villagers gathered at the shore had turned and confronted us, blocking the way. Disconcerted, the soldiers released my arms completely. They looked at one another, not sure what to do. Slowly they raised their rifles, but the villagers held their ground, none speaking. Fearful of what might happen next, I stepped backwards, turned and ran towards the water. Before the soldiers realized what had happened, I dove across a caique that was moored at the seawall, my shins banging painfully against the gunwale as I entered the water. I pulled myself under and away from the shore until the strong Bosphorus current took hold of me and propelled me downstream. I held my breath as long as I could before pushing up, gulping in air, and submerging again.

The next time I surfaced I was a good distance away from where I'd entered the water, and the ferryboat was barely visible on the horizon. Dizzy and lightheaded, I lay on my back, arms stretched out for buoyancy, as the current carried me past the walls of the European Castle. The temptation was strong to just float, to let the current determine my destination; but when I began drifting closer to the shore, I willed myself to roll over and swim toward the seawall. With much effort, I was able to maneuver onto a flight of stone steps that led out of the water, close to where several fishing caiques were roped to capstans.

On hands and knees, exhausted, I struggled up the steps and emerged onto the Bosphorus road near the sacred burial ground. Alongside the caiques, fishing nets lay spread out on the paving stones, drying in the sun. Across from the seawall steps a gravel track led uphill, flanking the cemetery on one side and a stone wall buttressing the steep hillside on the other. At the top of the hill the college buildings loomed large, like giant sentinels guarding the Bosphorus narrows.

Unsteadily I crossed over to where the gravel track met the Bosphorus road, earning curious looks from two men passing by in a horse-drawn wagon. I was wounded, bleeding badly, and I needed help. And there was only one place I could think of that would likely offer it.

Slowly, steadying myself with my left hand against the buttress wall, I started up the path. The dizziness was worse now, the tombstones to my right appearing as surreal, distorted images. After what seemed like an eternity of dragging one foot in front of the other, I reached the terrace fronting the college buildings. No one was around to help; the college seemed deserted. I shuffled on, trying to keep the buildings in focus. With inexorable slowness I made my way through the campus to the cobbled street leading to the faculty residences. Trees and hedgerows floated in crazy patterns before me—then darkness . . .

* * *

Creaking floorboards brought my eyes open. Helen Summers had entered the room carrying several items of folded clothing.

"Hello, Henry," she called out in a cheerful voice. "How are you feeling?" She placed the clothing on a dresser near the bed.

"Actually, not too bad," I replied. I took in my surroundings—flowered wallpaper, pale blue curtains, a vase containing bright orange marigolds on a table near the window. "I'm very grateful to you for taking care of me."

"Think nothing of it," she smiled.

"Have I been here long?"

"Two days. The gardener found you outside our gate. He thought you were dead. Care to tell me what happened?"

"There was looting and burning in the village. I made the mistake of trying to stop them and was rewarded with a bullet." Images of Serin on the ferry and the ghastly scene in the farmhouse came back into vivid focus. I shuddered at the memory.

"I heard about the looting—and the deportations. You lost a lot of blood. It's lucky Mahmut found you when he did."

A whiff of tobacco smoke preceded Carleton Summers into the room, his pipe stuck in the corner of his mouth. "So, the patient is awake," he said.

"Yes, and feeling better," his wife said. "We must get him something to eat. You must be starving, Henry."

"Some of that stew you made?" the professor said.

"I'll warm it up and have Charlotte bring him a bowl. I told Henry that with all those scars, it looks like he's been in the wars."

"He has," her husband said. "Those are shrapnel wounds, aren't they, Henry?"

"Aye, and a bullet wound in the shoulder."

Mrs. Summers stared at her husband. "I don't understand . . ."

"Henry's a British soldier, Helen, not an American. Tell her, Henry."

Helen Summers looked confused. I gave her a brief account of what had transpired at Gallipoli and Kuleli. "I'm sorry about deceiving you," I said. "I needed to keep my identity secret."

"But . . . But what's going to happen now?" She looked nervously at her husband.

Carleton pulled a chair up to the bed, it's back facing towards me. He sat astride the chair, arms resting on the back. "I don't know," he said. "Any ideas, Henry?"

"I think I'll try to make it to Greece," I said. "That was my original plan after Kuleli, before Kerim took me in." A feeling of emptiness took hold of me at the loss of my Turkish family. "I suppose you heard that Kerim was killed."

"Yes." Carleton lowered his eyes. "And about his wife and niece. Kerim was one of the best. He always called me *Hojam*—my teacher. I found it very touching."

"I'd better take care of the stew," Helen Summers said, shaking her head. She left and I heard her footsteps as she descended the stairs.

"My wife and daughter are leaving for America in a few days," Summers said. "They're sailing in an Argentine freighter with a bunch of other Americans, at least as far as Alexandria. Special permission from the Turkish authorities. Too bad you can't go with them."

"I have an American passport."

His eyes widened. "How did you manage that?"

"Kerim."

"So he did know."

"Yes. We got to know each other at Kuleli. I promised him I wouldn't tell anyone that he knew who I really was."

Summers nodded. "Still, he's a Turk. Or was. I'm surprised he helped you like that."

"Kerim was incapable of meanness." Except to seek retribution for Serin, I thought. But there was no need to raise that issue. "I think his wife had a lot to do with it."

Summers looked into the bowl of his pipe. He lit a match and tried unsuccessfully to relight the remnants of tobacco. "Where's the passport? It wasn't with your clothing."

"At Kerim's house." I remembered the burning and my spirits sank. "I don't know if it survived the fire. I kept it in a shed behind the house."

Summers looked thoughtful. "If we can find it, and it's a good facsimile, I may be able to get you on the sailing list. No harm in trying." He gestured with his pipe toward the clothing. "Charlotte altered some of my old rags to fit you. Yours weren't in the best of shape."

"I don't deserve so much kindness," I said. "I cause nothing but trouble."

He shrugged dismissively. "Helping people in trouble is our Christian duty, Henry."

"Moslem, too," I said, "considering what Kerim did."

Summers smiled and nodded. "Moslem, too," he conceded.

"Who took care of my wound?"

"Helen stopped the bleeding. She's a trained nurse. Then we summoned Doctor Ysuf, the college doctor. He stitched you up. It seems the bullet went right through you at the waist, in at the front, out at the back. You don't have to worry about Ysuf telling anyone, he's very discreet." He took the pipe from his mouth and stuck it in his shirt pocket. "One more scar to add to the rest, eh, Henry?"

"One of these days my luck's going to run out."

"Perish the thought." He pushed himself off the chair and stood up. "Here comes Charlotte with some food. When you're feeling better, let's see if we can find that passport. We don't have a lot of time."

Charlotte came into the room with a tray holding a large bowl of vegetable stew and several slices of thick-crusted bread smeared with butter. "Hello, Henry," she said cheerfully. "Time to eat."

Her father turned the chair around for Charlotte to sit on. "You may as well tell Charlotte who you really are," he said as he left the room.

Charlotte looked at the open door. She placed the tray on the dresser and turned toward me, a quizzical look on her face. "What did my father mean by that?"

"Your father told me you altered some clothes to fit me. You're a young woman of many talents."

"*Henry!* What did my father mean?"

"Confession time, Charlotte." I pulled myself to a sitting position. "I've never set foot in America, let alone Harvard." I gave her a quick account of my life—my home in Wales, the battle for Gallipoli, the escape from Kuleli. She listened without interrupting, her face betraying a mix of disbelief and disappointment. "I'm sorry, Charlotte. I hate lying to people, but it was my only recourse."

"I wouldn't have told anyone," she said at last.

"No, I'm sure you wouldn't have. But for your sake, and your parents', it was better you didn't know. Your father saw through me immediately."

She stared at me for several seconds. "And to think, I was hoping all Harvard boys would be like you."

I smiled. "Perhaps it would be better if they weren't. I hear you're leaving here soon. You and your mother."

She nodded. "I'll be starting at Wellesley in the fall. My mother's going along to get me settled. Quite a few Americans are leaving, not just from the college." She picked up the tray. "Is Bloke a Welsh name?"

"No, just a name Kerim gave me."

"So what's your real name?"

"Evan Morgan. But until I get out of Turkey I'm Henry Bloke. So keep calling me Henry."

"Evan's a nice name," she said as she placed the tray on my lap. She sat on the chair facing me, then reached up and touched the scar on my forehead, as she had the time she'd shown me her insect collection. She brought her finger down and traced the scar on my shoulder. "I think war's horrible," she said.

§

The following morning I dragged myself out of bed and donned Carleton's clothes. Charlotte had actually altered two sets of trousers and shirts, even a blazer. Sets of underwear and socks completed the ensemble. I left the unused clothes on the dresser and went downstairs. Walking was painful; besides the bullet wound, my shins, where they had hit the boat's gunwale, were badly bruised and my stomach ached from the rifle blow.

After eating a light breakfast served in the Summers' spacious kitchen, I left with Carleton Summers for the wreckage of Kerim's farmhouse. We picked our way carefully, making sure no police or soldiers were patrolling the neighborhood. The bodies in the yard behind the house had been removed and Kerim's hens and rooster were nowhere in sight. Perhaps Adnan has them, I thought hopefully.

The house lay in ruins, with only the stone walls still standing, but the shed that had been my refuge for the past two years was in better shape than I'd anticipated. The roof had collapsed, but the rest of it was intact. I made my way inside, kicking aside charred roof timbers, and reached under the palliasse where I'd dug a small hole in the dirt to hide my few valuables. I removed the flat piece of board that served as a cover and reached down. The passport was still there, along with several banknotes and coins.

I put the money in my trouser pocket and looked around to see if there was anything else worth salvaging. From my small bookshelf I removed the last book I'd been reading, a singed compilation of poems and short stories by Edgar Allan Poe. I left the shed, blew off the passport and handed it to Carleton.

"Looks authentic," he said. "I'll go into the city today and see if it will get you on the ship."

I turned and looked up at the stone walls of the farmhouse, reliving scenes of spirited conversations with Kerim over bottles of *bira*, good-natured jostling between Kerim and Anoush, silent glances from Serin as she served me food.

"One moment," I said. "I'd like a last look."

I entered the ruins of the farmhouse through the front door, afraid of what might still be left in the back parlor. With difficulty I made it into the kitchen, but so much debris covered the floor that it was impossible to go farther. Then, on the floor among the scattered remains of Anoush's cooking pots, I saw the three-tiered lunch pail, blackened by fire. I picked up the pail and took it outside.

"Souvenir," I said.

§

Three days later the Summers family and I, along with about a dozen others, gathered in the village of Bebek to board the *otobüs* that was to take us to the city docks. With remarkable ease and a little baksheesh, Carleton Summers had had my name added to the list of those approved for departure. I spent the remaining time enjoying the hospitality of the Summers family, who firmly rejected any attempt on my part to give them my Turkish currency in payment. I worked a little in the garden, but mostly I sat reading while my bruises and bullet wound healed.

The weather was perfect, sunny and breezy, neither too hot nor too humid; and as the time came for our departure, the thought that I'd probably never see Turkey again—never see Serin—filled me with melancholy. In the last two years I'd grown to love this beautiful land despite the violence I'd been a party to. But there was no future for me here. I valued the friendships I'd made, Turk and Armenian, but I'd lost the ones I loved the most. Charlotte, with her cheerful disposition and playful good humor, rescued me whenever I sank too far into the doldrums.

The day before we left, Helen Summers removed the stitches from my waist. She even produced a small leather suitcase for my extra clothes and meager belongings. To be shown such kindness after my world had been shattered by acts of unspeakable cruelty did much to dispel the bitterness that had taken hold of me. I handed her the Poe book so that she could return it to the library, but she told me to keep it. They wouldn't want it in that condition, she said; she would explain to Mrs. Hutchinson what happened.

That night winds and rain battered the windows as a summer storm erupted over the Bosphorus, cleaving the sky with vivid lightning and deafening claps of thunder. We'd had a storm like that in the Rhondda just after the war began.

"It's the wrath of God," my aunt had said.

Part IV

Home From The Dead

*It's a colour you can't buy, lad,
No matter what you pay.
But that's the colour that we want:
They call it Rhondda Grey.*
                    Max Boyce, *Rhondda Grey*

Chapter 22

With suitcases piled on the roof, the rickety wood-sided bus left Bebek along the Bosphorus road. The seats were hard and uncomfortable and the vehicle's suspension did little to soften the constant jarring caused by the uneven road surface. I sat next to Carleton Summers, his wife and daughter behind us. As we passed through the neighboring village of Arnavutköy, the Kuleli naval college stood bathed in sunshine on the opposite shore.

I suppose that place holds a few memories for you," Carleton shouted over the growl of the engine.

I nodded. "I got to know some good men there. I was wondering what became of them."

The engine noise discouraged further conversation. It wasn't just the thought of Suresh Pandya, Cyril Montague, Albert Parker and the others, wondering whether they were still languishing in some Anatolian prison camp; my life had changed so much because of Kuleli.

The villages grew larger as we neared the city, the streets more crowded. As we passed through Ortaköy I tried to imagine the gentle Kerim, so filled with rage that he had ended the lives of two men, one somewhere in the narrow streets of the town, the other in the cold waters of the Bosphorus. And I thought of Serin, suffering so terribly here at the hands of those he'd killed. Poor Serin, she had found her voice at last, only to call out to me in anguish. The virtual certainty that I would never see her again filled me with such an unbearable sense of loss that tears filled my eyes.

My thoughts were interrupted by our arrival at the city port. A guard bearing a rifle waved the bus through an iron gate onto the dock where the Argentine freighter *Rio Puelo* sat at its mooring. Dock workers scurried about loading goods, preparing the vessel for departure. It wasn't a particularly large merchant ship, and judging from the abundance of rust, not well maintained. But whatever its shortcomings, the *Rio Puelo* represented my passage out of Turkey.

We stepped off the bus and *hamals* unloaded suitcases and carried them up the gangplank while a gendarme scrutinized the boarding list and our passports. Finally it was time to go aboard. Carleton Summers kissed his wife goodbye and hugged his daughter.

"Good luck, Henry," he said, shaking my hand. "Keep an eye on them for me."

"I will, Sir," I said. "Thank you for everything you've done for me."

He turned away and waved to his family who had reached the top of the gangplank. I followed them up.

The *Rio Puelo* was not equipped to carry passengers. Crew members had given up their quarters to accommodate the women, and the rest of us had been provided with mattresses for sleeping on deck. There was some grumbling about the sleeping arrangements, but for only three nights at sea, I wasn't about to complain. Late that afternoon the ship's galley produced an ample meal of stewed beef and vegetables, and shortly thereafter tugs pulled the freighter away from the dock. As we left the Bosphorus behind and entered the tranquil waters of the Sea of Marmara, I stood at the ship's rail for my last look at Constantinople, its hills, domes, minarets and palaces no longer some exotic panorama to be found in a school geography text. The city was as familiar to me now as Cardiff was in Wales.

Early the next morning I awoke from a fitful sleep and walked to the front of the ship. The land on either side had begun converging, and I realized then that we were entering the narrow channel of the Dardanelles. I stared, fascinated, at the hills of the Gallipoli Peninsula, just as lovely in the early morning mist as when I'd first set my eyes on them so long ago. It was difficult to think of the place now as a burial ground for tens of thousands of Turkish and British soldiers, among them my old friend Dai Wilkins, and Charlie Beresford who had rescued me, shell-shocked and bloody, from the chaos of battle. So much killing—and for what?

Charlotte appeared at my side and immediately my spirits rose. "How did you sleep?" I asked.

She shrugged. "Not very well." She stared at the passing landscape. "That's Gallipoli, isn't it?"

"Yes, it is."

"Was it really awful, Evan? I can call you Evan now, can't I?"

"Yes. And yes, it was awful. But it's all behind me now. Soon I expect I'll be going home."

"Home to your girlfriend."

"By now she's probably married with a couple of babies chasing after her."

Charlotte smiled. "I hope she'll still be there for you."

"What about you, Charlotte? Looking forward to America?"

"Yes and no. I've never been there. It's a bit scary thinking about it. I expect I'll be horribly homesick and lonely after Mother goes home."

"The Harvard boys will be falling over themselves chasing you," I said.

She laughed and nudged me with her elbow. "Let's see if they have breakfast for us."

"You go ahead. I'll be along shortly."

I couldn't tear my eyes from that landscape of such terrible beauty. I remained at the ship's rail until the Gallipoli hills disappeared below the horizon. A chapter of my life had ended.

§

The voyage to Alexandria passed uneventfully. Charlotte, her mother and I spent the days reading or playing cards, and by the time the Egyptian coastline came into view, Charlotte and I had become such good friends that I regretted our imminent separation. "I'll write to you, I promise," she said as I gave her my address in Wales.

We assembled on deck with our luggage as the ship's gangplank was lowered. At a neighboring dock a British light cruiser lay moored under the hot sun, its guns reminding us that the war had not yet run its course. A portly, white-suited man carrying a briefcase, his head protected with a straw hat, hurried up the gangplank. He stopped in front of us, puffing, wiping his forehead with a handkerchief.

"Welcome to Alexandria," he called out, his accent distinctly American. "I'm Curtis Bradford from the United States Consulate." He reached into his briefcase and pulled out a sheet of paper. "When I call your name, please show me your American passport." His pronouncement caused some commotion and delay because several of the passengers had, without thinking ahead, secured their passports in their luggage. My name was last on the list.

When each passenger had been identified, Bradford said, "You will be staying at the Regency Hotel in nice accommodations until the American passenger liner *Cleveland Star* arrives, two or three days from now. You will then sail on the *Cleveland Star* to Gibralter where you will be meeting up with a naval convoy before crossing the Atlantic." He put the list back in his briefcase. "If you would follow me, please. I have taxis waiting to take you to the hotel."

Once we descended to the dock, I went up to Bradford. "I'm not American," I said. "My passport is a forgery."

The consular official glowered at me. "What the hell are you talking about?"

"I'm a British soldier. The passport was a subterfuge to get me out of Turkey. I need to find the nearest Bristish army garrison."

Bradford looked apoplectic. "This is highly irregular," he spluttered. "No one said anything to me about this."

Helen Summers stepped forward and touched Bradford's arm. "I can vouch for Mr. Bloke," she said. "He's telling the truth. He was badly wounded at Gallipoli."

Bradford looked me up and down as if viewing a just-convicted felon. "In that case give me the passport," he snapped.

"For the time being, I'd like to hold on to it. I may need it when I explain myself to the British authorities."

"That would be very sensible," Helen Summers interjected. "Don't you agree, Mr. Bradford?" She smiled sweetly.

Bradford was disarmed. "Well, it's most irregular. Just make sure you get that passport to me immediately after you've checked in. I'll be in touch with the British Consulate."

"Thank you," I said.

Bradford led us to the end of the dock where a line of taxis waited. "It's all paid for, including the gratuity," he announced in a loud voice.

I went up to Helen Summers. "How can I ever thank you? You and your husband."

"No need for thanks," she said. "Good luck"—she paused—"Henry Bloke." She kissed me on the cheek. "Come back to Turkey for a visit, when we are at peace again."

"I'd like that," I said, knowing full well the improbability of it happening.

I turned to Charlotte. "I'm going to miss you. You've really kept my spirits up."

"I'm glad," she replied, her eyes glistening. She put her arms around me. "Best of luck, Evan. Do you think we'll ever see each other again?"

"I hope so." I kissed her lightly. "Good luck in America." I turned and followed Bradford to the taxi at the head of the line. "Don't forget to write!" I called back.

§

"Do you expect me to believe a poppycock story like that?" snorted Colonel Neville McFarland, the garrison commander, in an accent that bespoke the north of England. Balding, sunburned face accentuating his thin sandy moustache, sleeves rolled up above the elbows, McFarland sat behind his desk glaring at me as I stood at attention before him. A faded portrait of the king and queen hung on the wall behind him. Off to the side stood the young lieutenant who had been summoned when I arrived at the garrison gate.

McFarland drummed his fingers on the desk. "Sounds to me like desertion. Is that it?"

Perhaps that's not far from the truth, I thought. Enjoying the hospitality of one of the "enemy" and working at a job I found infinitely more satisfying than standing in a rat-infested trench doing my best to kill someone I had no quarrel with.

"Not at all, Sir." I did my best to convey an air of calm and resolve. "I was hiding out, looking for an opportunity to get out of Turkey. The Argentine ship served my purpose." When the colonel didn't immediately respond, I continued: "I'd be happy to show you where I was wounded, before being taken prisoner. If you contact the South Wales Borderers, they can confirm who I am."

McFarland picked up a pencil and tapped it up and down on the desk. "I'll do better than that . . . What's your name again?"

"Morgan, Sir. Lance Corporal Evan Morgan."

"Morgan. I'm going to telegraph the War Office in London. See what's to be done with you. What was the name of that lieutenant you were supposed to be looking for?"

"Geoffrey Heath, Sir. General Gregory Heath's son."

The colonel wrote the name on a sheet of paper. He looked at my escort. "Lieutenant." The young officer sprang to attention. "Have this man examined by the medical officer and get his report in my hands as quickly as possible." He returned his eyes to me. "Morgan, you'll be confined to quarters until we sort this out. Dismissed."

I saluted and left the room accompanied by the lieutenant. It had been so long since I'd been a part of saluting and other military protocols that I found the interview mildly absurd. Better get used to it, I told myself.

A sympathetic medical officer gave me a thorough going over and pronounced me healthy. "With all those battle scars, you deserve a trip home and a good rest," he said as he returned his stethoscope to the top drawer of his desk.

"Actually I had a bit of a rest in Turkey."

"Don't tell that to the colonel or he'll have you digging ditches. Do you feel fit?"

"Fit enough, Sir. Still a bit sore where this last bullet went through me."

"Don't overdo things until it's completely healed. Now get out of here so I can write my report."

For the next two weeks I bided my time, sleeping at night on an army-issue metal cot in a small, bare room separate from the other men; working during the day at whatever odd job the duty officer saw fit to hand out. The first two days I scraped brittle paint from wooden buildings that had deteriorated under the relentless Egyptian sun. The next three I peeled potatoes and washed dishes in the garrison kitchen. On weekends I sat reading in the base library and took walks along the gravel streets of the garrison under the shade of date palms and banyan trees. Every day I thought of Serin, her voice so sweet to my ears even in despair, her lovely face buried in Anoush's shoulder as the ferry carried her away to an uncertain future. Away from me.

And every day I wondered if the War Office had sent word to Wales that I was alive.

When I was summoned back to the colonel's office, I found him in a much better mood. He actually smiled at me and said, "At ease, Sergeant."

"Thank you, Sir. But it's lance corporal."

"No it's not, by Jove!" He picked up a sheet of paper from his desk and waved it at me. "According to this communiqué I received from the War Office, you've been promoted. Skipped a rank, in fact."

This didn't make sense. How could I be promoted when I'd been away from the war for more than two years? McFarland saw my confusion. "This says you're an exemplary soldier, Morgan. And you showed great fortitude and ingenuity in escaping from the Turks and evading capture."

Escaping from the Turks? This was getting to be farcical. I'd been living with them! Hiding from the war!

"Colonel Aubrey Wallace, South Wales Borderers, made the recommendation," McFarland continued. "Was he your C.O.?"

"He was one of the battalion officers, Sir. He was a major last time I saw him."

"Well, he's at the War Office now. Seems to think very highly of you. He's put you in for the Military Medal as well."

"This is all a bit . . ."

"It's for bravery and devotion under fire," McFarland interrupted. "A new medal authorized by His Majesty King George for enlisted ranks. Same as the Military Cross for officers."

I shook my head. "Sorry, Sir, but I'm a bit overwhelmed. It's not what I expected."

The colonel stood up. "Congratulations, Sergeant." He reached across the desk and shook my hand. "I suppose you're anxious to get back to the front."

I had to restrain myself from laughing. "What I'd like, Sir," I said in as calm a voice as I could muster, "is to get home to see my family."

"Well, yes, of course. A few days at home will do you good. But first you're to report to the War Office in London." He scrutinized the communiqué. "Present yourself to a Colonel Edwin Raxworthy."

"Why, Sir? Why the War Office?"

"Ours not to reason why, Sergeant. We just do as we're told."

"Has the War Office notified my family that I'm alive, Sir?"

McFarland sat back down, frowning. "The Red Cross would've done that. Standard procedure for POWs."

"I escaped before the Red Cross took any names."

"Well, in that case the War Office would certainly have informed them," he said testily. McFarland was showing signs of impatience. He placed the paper on the desk in front of him. "Now," he continued, "we have to get you back to Blighty. There's a naval flotilla making its way through the canal, due in Port Said in a couple of days. After that they'll be making a stop here. You'll be going with them to Portsmouth, and from there to London."

"Couldn't I go home first, Sir?"

"Damn it, Sergeant! I've told you what your orders are. The War Office will tell you when you can go home." McFarlane's face had turned even redder.

"Yes, Sir."

"Right. Now get yourself to the quartermaster and get fitted up with some uniforms." He tapped his sleeve. "Including those sergeant's stripes. I'll have a copy of this communiqué typed up and delivered to you."

"Thank you, Sir." I saluted and walked out of the office, marveling at the absurdity of life.

§

A week later the flotilla arrived, a small force consisting of a destroyer, minesweeper, two frigates and a troopship bringing soldiers home from Arabia and Transjordan. The light cruiser I'd seen at the Alexandria dock joined the flotilla for the voyage back to England. For some inexplicable reason I was assigned to the frigate *Lancelot,* isolated from the combat veterans who might have provided good company. As the only soldier on board, I was generally ignored by the crew, which made the journey interminably long. Only a small ship's library afforded some relief from the boredom. I still had my counterfeit American passport; McFarland never asked to see it, and I saw no necessity for delivering it to Curtis Bradford. I'd considered writing to Gwyn and my aunt and uncle during my stay at the Alexandria garrison, but decided against doing so, reasoning that I would probably arrive in Wales before the letter.

The voyage to England was much as it was on the way out, calm waters in the Mediterranean, heavy swells in the Bay of Biscay. Seven days after we left Alexandria, the flotilla rounded the coast of Brittany and turned into the English Channel. As the cliffs and green fields of Dorset and the Isle of Wight hove into view, I thought back to that day some three and a half years before when I and my comrades in arms had set out with such bravado from Pembroke Dock, the cheers of civilians still ringing in our ears. So much had happened, so many improbable events. I'd flirted with death too often and had the scars to show for it. And I'd lost good friends, dear friends, along the way. To be about to set foot on English soil seemed almost unreal. Was I the same Evan Morgan, ready to blend back into the rhythm of life in the Rhondda Valley, so that in a few days it would seem as though I'd never left?

"Sergeant." A seaman had approached, interrupting my musing. "The captain said you're to get your things together. We'll be docking shortly and there'll be someone waiting for you."

It wasn't long before a naval tug nudged the *Lancelot* into its berth at the Portsmouth naval base. I picked up my new kitbag and descended the gangplank. An army corporal, who stood out among the bustle of navy personnel on the dock, approached as I stepped ashore.

"Sergeant Morgan?" I nodded. "Welcome to England, Sergeant. Corporal Ferguson." He shook my hand. "Let's get away from this confusion." I saw that he walked with a limp, much the way Hugh Griffith walked after the cave-in at the mine.

Ferguson, a tall, affable young man with black hair and handsome features, led the way past several warehouses into the main part of the base, stopping at a covered enclosure where several white-uniformed sailors milled around, chatting and smoking cigarettes.

"The bus stops here," Ferguson said. "Originally we were going to put you up for the night here in Portsmouth, but you arrived early enough that we can take the four o'clock train to London. I'm to deliver you to the War Office."

"I don't know why they want me in London when my home and my regiment are in Wales."

"I gave up trying to figure out the army a long time ago," he replied. He looked up at the scar on my forehead. "I hear you chaps had a rough go at Gallipoli."

"No worse, I should think, than France or Belgium." I nodded towards his leg. "War wound?"

"Verdun. The Huns got a piece of my thigh. Could be a lot worse. I was one of the lucky ones—I'm still alive." He turned as a noisy passenger coach approached the bus stop. "This will get us to the station," he said. "We'll have time for a cup of tea before the train leaves."

"Corporal, do you have a first name?" I asked.

"Norman, Sergeant."

"Right. Suppose I call you Norman and you call me Evan. I'd just as soon we dispense with rank for the time being."

Ferguson smiled. "Suits me fine."

We climbed aboard the bus and I deposited the kitbag in the luggage rack. Once we were settled in our seats, Ferguson said, "When we get to London, you'll spend the night at the Liversey Hotel on Sutton Gardens, around the corner from Hyde Park. There's a room reserved for you. It's a small place, but it has a nice pub." He reached into his pocket and handed me an envelope. "Here's a few pounds to tide you over until you get paid. But don't use it on the hotel, that's already taken care of. You're supposed to get back pay once you report to the Borderers' HQ in Brecon. Should be a tidy sum, I imagine."

I pocketed the envelope. "I'm not used to the army treating me so well."

He laughed. "Your combat record and escaping from the Turks had something to do with it. Once you get back to your regiment it'll be life as usual, take my word for it."

After we had boarded the train and found our third class seats, Ferguson said, "What's Turkey like, Evan? I mean, besides the fighting and all."

I thought of the Gallipoli hills and meadows, carpeted with yellow-flowering gorse and scarlet-red poppies, before they were despoiled by war; and the blue waters of the Bosphorus sparkling under a summer sun. "Beautiful," I said. "Just beautiful."

"I hear the Turks are pretty fierce."

"They're just like you and me, Norman."

I put my head back against the seat and closed my eyes. Within minutes I had dozed off, lulled by the hypnotic clicking of train wheels over rails.

Chapter 23

From Victoria Station we traveled by Underground to Sutton Gardens where Norman saw me into the Liversey Hotel, promising to meet me in the lobby at nine o'clock the next morning. My second-storey room was spare but comfortable, and had a window looking out over a small garden in the back. I left my bag and walked to a corner shop to pick up some fish and chips. In the tiny pub set in a room behind the hotel reception desk, I ate my meal and washed it down with my first pint of bitter since leaving Wales more than three years ago.

True to his word, Norman arrived on time as I was reading a newspaper in the lobby.

"My bag's still in my room," I said. "Should I bring it with me?"

"No, leave it there. Hold on a sec." He walked over to the pretty girl behind the desk and engaged her in conversation, at one point nodding in my direction. "I've made sure you have the room for another night," he said when he rejoined me. "You could be at the War Office most of the day. Colonel Raxworthy's expecting you at ten."

We took a bus from the end of Sutton Gardens to Westminster, and walked from there to Whitehall. At almost every turn, statues of luminaries greeted us, men who had framed the nation's dominion over large swaths of Africa and Asia, some on horseback, others on foot. Surrounded by imposing monuments and stately buildings, I was awestruck—just as I'd been when Kerim first took me to Constantinople.

"One of these days I'm coming back here and really take in the sights," I said as we walked passed Horse Guards Parade.

The War Office occupied a three-storey building just off Whitehall, its entrance guarded by two rifle-bearing grenadiers. We entered into a spacious foyer where numerous uniformed officers chatted in small groups or moved up or down two facing curved staircases that converged on an upper level. Norman led the way up the right staircase and down a wide hallway decorated with paintings of battle scenes and portraits of generals from wars long past. At a few minutes before ten we arrived outside a door bearing Colonel Edwin Raxworthy's nameplate.

"This is where I leave you, Evan. Same bus back to Sutton Gardens. Trains to Wales leave from Paddington, just around the corner from your hotel. I can be reached care of the War Office, next time you're in London." He knocked on the door.

"Enter," a voice called. We walked together to the colonel's desk and saluted.

"Thank you, Corporal," Raxworthy said. "You may go. Please tell Miss Shaw to come in."

"Yes, Sir." Norman saluted again, turned, winked at me, and walked briskly from the office.

"At ease, Sergeant. Let's sit over here by the window." He motioned towards two padded armchairs on either side of a low wooden table bearing an ashtray. I still wasn't used to being addressed by my new rank.

His red-braided uniform neat and devoid of wrinkles, Raxworthy had the look of a professional soldier. A receding hairline accentuated his wide forehead, and his face tapered down to a narrow, angular chin. He was clean-shaven and had piercing blue eyes.

"I'd like to hear your story, Sergeant, top to bottom," he said as we settled into the chairs. "You're the only soldier we know of who escaped from a Turkish prison."

"It was actually a prison hospital, Sir."

"Even so, when we got the word, it created quite a stir around here." He pulled out a pack of Players cigarettes and offered me one.

"I don't smoke, Sir."

He nodded and inserted his cigarette into an ivory holder. There was a knock on the door and a young brown-haired woman entered with pencil and notepad in hand. She pulled a chair over near us and sat down, poised to take shorthand.

"I suppose you were treated pretty roughly by the Turks," Raxworthy said.

"Quite humanely, in fact, Sir. A Turkish doctor removed a bullet from my shoulder. I can't complain about the care I received."

"Is that so? Well, give me all the details from the beginning—when you were wounded."

As the colonel struck a match and lit his cigarette, I began my story and took him up to where I walked away from the Kuleli hospital and almost drowned in the Bosphorus. He interrupted at various points, probing for details.

"Why didn't you try to make it back to the Gallipoli front?" he asked.

"I'd been told our forces had withdrawn, Sir."

"Yes, of course, they would have been." Raxworthy was especially attentive when I talked of Kerim and his family and my passing myself off as an American. I detected a certain skepticism in his voice that a Turk would be sympathetic to a British soldier. "It took you long enough to get out of Turkey," he said.

"Getting out was something I thought about all the time," I lied. "I thought my chances of getting into Greece were pretty slim, and Bulgaria was enemy territory." When he didn't respond, I continued. "To tell the truth, Sir, I didn't expect the war to last as long as it has."

Raxworthy sat quietly for several seconds, his chin resting on his fingers. Finally he turned toward Miss Shaw and dismissed her with a nod. She returned her chair to its original position and left the room. The colonel leaned back and folded his arms. "I think we're finished here, Sergeant. Do you have any questions for me?"

"I just want to be sure my family knows I'm alive."

"The Red Cross would have seen to that." That same aggravating answer.

"I'm not so sure, Sir. I escaped before we were interviewed."

"In that case, I'm sure the Borderers would have notified them. They've been apprised of your escape."

"I just want to be sure, Sir."

"Tell you what, I'll have Miss Shaw telephone Brecon, just to make certain. And I'll have her contact the Red Cross first to make sure they have a record of you." He extinguished his third cigarette in the ashtray and returned the holder to his pocket. "One other thing," he said, leaning back in his chair. "I expect you're looking forward to a few days' leave. You have a week off before you're to report to the Borderers in Brecon. They're expecting you on the morning of Tuesday, October first, no later than ten o'clock."

"Very well, Sir. What happens then? Will I be going to France or Belgium?"

Raxworthy shook his head. "I doubt it. The war's winding down. We've broken through the Hindenburg Line and the German chancellor has resigned. The Bulgarians have already signed an armistice. I expect it'll be over in a week or two, thank God." He stood up and I followed suit. "It's almost twelve-thirty," he said, looking at his watch. "I want you to look sharp, Sergeant. You're about to see General Heath."

I was startled. "General Heath!"

"That's right. He knows all about your attempt to find his son. He wants to meet you."

Some attempt, I thought. Walking into a trap, two men dead, and a bullet in the shoulder.

"Come on, Sergeant. Doesn't do to be late."

We left the office and walked together along the hallway and back down the staircase to the foyer. As we descended the stairs, he said, "Look, Sergeant, when this lot's over, we're still going to need some good men. Why don't you consider staying in after the war? Show the new recruits the proper way of doing things. With your record you'll have no trouble getting a commission."

"I'll have to think about it, Sir." I'd had more than enough of war and soldiering, but this wasn't the place to voice my feelings.

Raxworthy led the way down a side corridor to an open door leading into a spacious wood-paneled office. He knocked and entered. General Heath sat behind his desk, a man I guessed to be in his sixties with graying hair and neat moustache. He looked almost grandfatherly, with twinkling eyes and a gentle expression, unlike the battle-hardened field officers I was used to.

Raxworthy gave a perfunctory salute. "Sergeant Evan Morgan to see you, Sir." I sprang to attention and saluted.

"And right on time, too," the general said, looking me up and down. "At ease, Sergeant." He turned his attention to Colonel Raxworthy. "Edwin, I'm taking this young man to lunch at my club. Care to join us?"

"Thank you, Sir," Raxworthy responded, "but I have a senior staff meeting at one."

"All right, Edwin, off you go." General Heath pushed back his chair. "Come on, Sergeant, I'm famished." He gestured towards the door. "I was hoping Colonel Wallace could join us, but he's off doing something in Brecon. He spoke very highly of you. Said you were a credit to the South Wales Borderers."

Was I? Because I'd earned myself a couple of citations and a medal? For the last two years I'd been hiding out from the war. If that made me a credit to the Borderers, so be it.

"It's good of him to say that, Sir."

We left the War Office and walked a short distance to the general's club on a side street near the Thames Embankment. I wondered what Dai and Rhys would have thought if they could see me, sergeant's stripes on my sleeves, strolling through London with a general on our way to lunch and chatting as if rank didn't matter. I could hardly believe it myself.

As we walked the general said, "When the cable arrived from Alexandria, mentioning that you'd been taken prisoner while looking for my son, I made it known I'd like to meet you. And, of course, we needed to debrief you." He gave me a wry look. "Probably you'd have preferred to be sent straight home."

"I was a bit surprised when I was told to report to London. But it's a privilege to meet you, Sir."

"Your C.O. had no right sending you after Geoffrey. I regret the consequences. Just because his father's a general shouldn't have given him special treatment." His tone turned bitter. "And now two unfortunate fellows are dead because of it."

"They were good men, Sir. They went willingly," I said, stretching the truth a bit. "Lieutenant Heath is a fine officer, very well liked by the men."

His expression softened. "I'm glad to hear you say that. I've always been proud of him."

I saw the same qualities in the old man that had made his son so popular with the ranks. "Have you had news of him, Sir?"

"Oh, yes. He's in Palestine. Was sent there after a prisoner exchange. He wrote that the prison camp was no picnic, but the men made the best of it."

"Colonel Raxworthy said the war's just about over."

"It looks that way. And none too soon. Then it'll be retirement for me. Time to put my feet up in the country."

We entered the general's club into a spacious lounge furnished with comfortable armchairs and low tables holding ashtrays and the day's newspapers. High-ranking officers, sipping drinks, smoking, reading the papers, or chatting with colleagues, occupied many of the chairs. A tall thin man, older than the general by a few years and with practically no hair on his head, approached deferentially.

"Good afternoon, Hawkins," the general said. "Just the two of us for lunch. What's on your menu today?"

Hawkins, unaccustomed to seeing soldiers from the ranks in this sanctuary of class and privilege, looked at me as if he had just spotted a cockroach. "We have a nice bit of brisket, Sir." His eyes returned to the general.

"Then we'll sit here while you get a table set up for us. Care for a sherry, Sergeant?"

"I'd prefer beer, Sir." Hawkins rolled his eyes.

"Capital idea," the general said. "Two pints of your best bitter, Hawkins."

Over lunch I gave the general a full account of my ill-fated mission to find his son. He seemed genuinely moved when I spoke of the deaths of Bill Oliver and Brian Greenwood, and astonished at my sojourn on Kerim's farm. "Remarkable story," he said as the waiter arrived with a pot of tea.

As we got up from the table, the general said, "No need for you to return to the War Office. Get yourself on home. I'm sure your family's looking forward to seeing you after all these years."

"I'm not sure they know I'm alive, Sir."

"I wouldn't worry about that, Sergeant. The Red Cross would've told them."

§

Rather than taking a bus back to the hotel, I decided to stretch my legs. Armed with a street map I'd picked up at the hotel, I followed the Embankment as far as Cleopatra's Needle, then up Northumberland Avenue to Trafalgar Square and along Haymarket to Piccadilly. Westminster Abbey, Saint Paul's, the Tower, and all the other marvels of London, would have to wait for a more extended visit—perhaps with Gwyn, I thought wistfully.

I wandered at a leisurely pace through Mayfair until I came upon the greenery of Hyde Park. Following the riparian curve of the Serpentine, I arrived at Bayswater Road, just a short walk from Sutton Gardens. Before returning to my hotel, I stopped at Paddington and purchased a third-class ticket for the next morning's eight-thirty express to Cardiff.

§

As the Great Western express gathered speed, London's suburbs gave way to farmland, pastoral villages, and houses and churches built of flint. Strange, I thought, I'd been all the way to Constantinople, but until I'd landed at Portsmouth, I'd never seen the country that bordered my native Wales. How lovely England looked in the crisp autumn sunshine. How much the sheep and cows grazing in green fields reminded me of Kerim's farm. God, how I loved working the land! The splendor of orchards in their springtime finery, the miracle of fresh seedlings springing from the soil, the fragrance of freshly cut hay, communion with simple, loyal farm animals. How could I ever work again in dark tunnels far below the earth's surface without the feel of sun on my back?

The train stopped briefly in Swindon, and then a change in scenery to steeper hills and thicker woodland signaled our approach to the Welsh border. I felt a tightness in my stomach. I'd been looking forward so much to getting home, but the closer I got, the greater was my anxiety about Gwyn. Had the long separation changed us so much that we would no longer see each other as we had before? Would Gwyn even be there? She was a lovely young woman, not one I'd expect to stay single if she'd accepted my death.

A little after noon the train glided into the cavernous interior of Cardiff station. I took hold of my bag and stepped down to the platform, my feet once again planted on my native land. There was a forty-five-minute wait for the next local up the Rhondda Valley, enough time to grab a sandwich and a cup of tea in the station cafeteria.

The knot in my stomach tightened as the train began its slow trajectory from Cardiff into the valley I knew so well. The journey seemed interminably long, with stops at Whitchurch, Pontypridd, Trehafod and Porth. Iron-gray overcast had obscured the sun, and pitheads and slagheaps intruded on farmland. Everything appeared gray—streets, houses and shops, the slagheaps. Alongside the railway track the River Rhondda flowed as black as it always had. Suddenly I was seized with nostalgia for the clear skies and blue waters of the Bosphorus, golden wheat fields, purple-blossomed Judas trees, and village streets painted red with bougainvillea. Yet even that land of dreams had lost its color to unspeakable cruelty.

As the train chugged slowly through Trehafod I spotted a group of coal-black miners chatting on a street corner—and I saw myself. Was it real, my going away to war? Had Serin, Kerim and Anoush actually existed, or was I just waking from a long dream? I touched the scar on my forehead for reassurance.

And then we were pulling into Tonypandy and memories of schooldays at Tonypandy Secondary danced before my eyes. Would Gwyn be at her bank still? *Here's something to take with you when you go. A couple of American books . . .* Her words, spoken when she'd handed me the James Fenimore Cooper novel and the book of Riley poetry, came back as if spoken yesterday. *I know poetry isn't your cup of tea, Evan.* And yet on the voyage out to Gallipoli and in the trenches, I'd read and reread those poems. Even memorized most of the ones written in plain English, and not that hillbilly jargon Riley was enamored with. And in one of those ironic twists of fate, I'd even assumed an American identity to escape the insanity of war.

The train began moving again, following the river into Ystrad, and I sat mesmerized, my eyes glued to the unfolding scene. Nothing had changed. Bodringallt School still loomed over my home on Victoria Street. Passing under the footbridge that spanned river and railway, I recognized the back of our Welsh Nonconformist chapel and just beyond, Gwyn's house with its tiny fenced-in garden. Though too far to see inside, I stared at the windows, picturing Gwyn and her mother sipping tea by the stove or Gwyn in her room composing poetry. Silently I mouthed lines from one of those Riley poems,

> *A thousand ways*
> *I fashion, to myself, the tenderness*
> *Of my glad welcome: I shall tremble, yes;*
> *And touch her now, as when first in the old days*

I touched her girlish hand, nor dared upraise
Mine eyes, such was my faint heart's sweet distress,
Then silence, and the perfume of her dress.

Would there be a glad welcome? I turned away and reached for my bag as the train decelerated into the station.

§

Rumbling from Upper Pentre colliery accompanied me along the main road, kitbag over my shoulder. The sweetshop where as children we spent our pennies on aniseed balls and toffees, the newspaper shop and ironmonger—all still there. With trepidation I arrived at Gwyn's house, lowered my bag and knocked on the door.

There was movement inside and the door opened a little. Gwyn's mother, looking cantankerous as always, peered out at me.

"Yes?" she said.

"Hello, Mrs. Williams."

"What do you want?"

I smiled. "It's Evan Morgan, Mrs. Williams."

Her jaw dropped as recognition took hold. She stared at me, open-mouthed, for several seconds. "It can't be. You're dead!"

"Not yet," I said.

She opened the door wider, staring at me as if her eyes were deceiving her. "Evan Morgan! Well I'll be . . ." She stepped back. "Come inside then. I don't . . . I don't believe it." Her eyes registered astonishment. "You look so different, I didn't recognize you. We all thought you were dead."

I stepped into the familiar room. She'd been knitting a pullover by the look of it. Wool and needles sat on a table next to her armchair, alongside an ashtray filled with cigarette butts, a packet of Woodbines and a box of matches.

"You never used to smoke," I remarked.

"Well I do now," she said grumpily. "And don't you give me any grief about it. I get enough of it from my daughter. And I don't smoke in public." Her voice softened. "Would you like a cup of tea, Evan?"

"No thank you, Mrs. Williams, I have to get home. When will Gwyn be home?"

"I've no idea. She's off in London."

"London! I just came from there."

"It's something to do with the bank. She has a lot of responsibility now. I think she said she'd be training new people at the head office. Won't be back 'til the end of the week."

"Is she still single?" I asked pointedly.

"If you mean, is she married, then the answer's no. But she's taken up with a chap at the bank. One of the managers, her young man is, and well off, too. He's up there with her. Expects to have a branch of his own before he's much older," she said smugly. "Not like some coalminer."

I picked up my bag. The disappointment I felt at her words came like a blow to the body and stopped me from responding to her slight. So another man had caught Gwyn's fancy. The last thing I wanted now was to get into an argument with her mother.

"Well, I wouldn't have expected her to wait for me forever," I said. "But I would like to see her. You'll tell her I was here?"

"Aye, I'll do that, soon as she gets home." She moved over to the sideboard and pulled open a drawer. "Before you go, I've got a present for you," she said, handing me a small book. "Gwyn's just had this published."

The cover read *Rhondda Verses by Gwynneth Williams,* and bore the imprint of a publishing house in Swansea. I thumbed through the pages and saw poems in both English and Welsh. "That's wonderful," I said. "Thank you, Mrs. Williams. I'm very happy for your daughter." I slipped the book into my bag.

She pulled her muffler closer about her throat. "I'm glad you made it back, Evan. Gwyn was in an awful state when they said you were missing."

§

In a black mood I left Gwyn's mother, walked past the chapel and turned up Victoria Street. The skies had darkened and a light drizzle added to my foul frame of mind. At least I'd be seeing my family again. I didn't expect my uncle to be home this time of day, assuming he was still working at his railway junction box, but my aunt should be there. I looked forward with anticipation to our reunion.

As I walked up the hill a boy on a bicycle entered the street from Bodringallt Terrace. He was dressed in the blue uniform of the telegraph office. Was he about to deliver one of those dreaded telegrams telling of the death of yet another young Welshman? I watched as he rode ahead of me scanning the house numbers. Then he stopped. Could it be? He was outside our house! I quickened my pace, watching him knock on the door. He knocked again, but no one answered.

"I live here," I said. "I'll take that."

The boy eyed my uniform suspiciously. "What's your name?"

"Morgan."

He scrutinized the envelope. Satisfied, he handed it to me and rode off on his bicycle.

I tore open the telegram. It was from the Red Cross: *Pleased to inform you Sergeant Evan Morgan alive and well. Returning home shortly.*

So it wasn't just Gwyn's mother; no one knew I was alive!

I picked up my bag and entered the narrow alley leading to the back of the house. Perhaps my aunt was off shopping or visiting a neighbor. I turned the handle of the back door. It was unlocked, as it always was. No one around here ever locked their back doors.

"Auntie!" I called, as I pushed the door open. No answer.

"Auntie, it's Evan!"

I stepped inside and the familiar smells of furniture polish and freshly ironed linen hanging on the pulley above the stove took hold of my senses. The kitchen looked exactly as I remembered it, pots and pans neatly in place, coal scuttle half full, the worn armchairs by the stove awaiting my uncle's return from work. I was truly home.

Why, then, did I feel like a stranger?

At the foot of the staircase I called again. The stairs creaked as I climbed to the upper landing, just as they always had. In my aunt and uncle's room the double bed was neatly made, the chamber pot visible underneath. The book of poems by Hedd Wyn, my uncle's favorite Welsh poet, sat on the stand next to the bed.

My room looked as though I'd never left, the only unfamiliar item being a cardboard box on top of the chest of drawers. I pulled open the flaps and stared, fascinated, at its contents. The shaving kit I'd used throughout my time in the army and my extra pairs of boots and puttees lay on a stack of neatly folded clothing—spare uniform, undergarments, socks. I'd forgotten that personal effects were always gathered up and sent to next of kin. Was I the only one who'd come back from the dead to reclaim his belongings?

Then I noticed the book, pushed down one side of the box. I pulled it out and stared at the cover: *Poems Here At Home by James Whitcomb Riley,* the book I thought I'd never see again. The cover still showed the dirt of the trenches and the bloodstain from the time I'd cut my finger on barbed wire. Thumbing through pages creased and soiled from constant use, I held the small volume lovingly, felt Gwyn's presence.

I placed the book on my bed and returned to the kitchen feeling restless and unfulfilled. Through the still-open door I saw that the rain had stopped. Leaving my kitbag in prominent view and the telegram open on the table, I stepped outside and began walking—down Victoria Street, across the main road, and by footbridge over the river. The atmosphere tasted of coal dust. Directly ahead, the slagheap I'd dreamed about when far from home beckoned me, challenged me. I began to climb . . .

* * *

And this brings me back to the beginning; standing on an ugly pile of pit waste, reflecting on all that had happened in my life since my aunt first brought me into her home, for all intents and purposes, an orphan.

Chapter 24

Stepping sideways to avoid losing my footing on the wet surface, I made my way down the slagheap. I needed a change of clothes; I'd been up there daydreaming too long and my uniform had begun to soak through. As I walked back up Victoria Street, I was startled to see a number of people in the middle of the road staring at me. And then Uncle Mervyn, waving and grinning broadly, emerged from the crowd and ran down to meet me.

"Evan! By God, it's really you!" He threw his arms around me. I was taken aback because my uncle had never been one to show such outward displays of affection. "I couldn't believe it when I saw your kitbag," he said excitedly. "And the telegram! I'd about given up hope of ever seeing you alive."

He stepped back. "My, but you've changed, lad. You're taller—and all tanned." He pointed to my forehead. "What happened there? It looks nasty."

"Shrapnel wound, Uncle," I said, at last able to get a word in. My uncle hadn't changed much; a few more lines on his face, perhaps, and a bit less hair on his head. "You look well, Uncle. Looks like you have a welcoming committee for me."

"Well, I had to tell the neighbors, didn't I?"

"How's Auntie? I can't wait to see her."

His expression changed abruptly and his shoulders sagged. "Didn't they tell you, son?" He looked stricken. "Your auntie passed away, almost two years ago."

My legs turned to rubber at the impact of his words. "Oh, no, not Auntie," I said, searching his face for some hint that I'd misheard him.

My uncle put his hand on my arm. "I'm sorry, lad. I thought you knew. I wrote to the Borderers and the Red Cross, asking them to tell you in case you were still alive."

I shook my head. "No one told me, Uncle." I looked up the street. "Let's go home," I said, my voice choking. "I don't think I can face anyone now."

For the rest of the way I walked in a haze, my eyes wet with tears, only vaguely aware of familiar faces greeting me. "Welcome home, lad,"

Roger Surtees said in his wheezing voice. He shook my hand. Forcing a smile, I nodded in recognition before turning into the alleyway leading to our back door.

"Doctor Llewellyn said it was cancer," my uncle said as he settled into his favorite chair by the kitchen stove. "You remember how she used to get those pains?" She always said it was just an upset stomach."

I walked into the front room and returned with my aunt's photograph. "Did she suffer much?" I asked, as I sat in the facing chair.

"At the end she did, but only for a short time. She went downhill really fast after you were reported missing. She took it very hard when the telegram came." He got up and picked up the kettle. "Let's have a cup of tea, shall we?"

"I'd prefer something stronger, Uncle. Is the Old Lamb open?"

"Not for a while yet. But I have a spot of whiskey." He went to the sideboard and brought out a bottle and two glasses. "Here, son, he said, handing me a generous portion. It struck me then that I had no recollection of my uncle ever calling me son when I was growing up. I felt a warmth of affection for the man who had been such a good provider for his family. He was stern with me when I was a boy, but always kind. I sipped the whiskey and found the taste harsh but comforting.

I stared at my aunt's photograph. She'd been as much a mother to me as any boy could possibly wish for. I thought of the sacrifices she'd made, of all the times she'd scrubbed me clean after I came home black from the mine, and how she would always send me off on my daily rounds with words of encouragement. That I'd never see her again was almost too much to bear.

"You know, son," my uncle said as he took his pipe and tobacco pouch from his pocket, "your Gwyn was a real angel when your auntie was so ill. I don't know what I'd have done without her, looking after her and all while I was off at work."

"She's not my Gwyn any more, Uncle. I saw her mother. She told me Gwyn has a new boyfriend. She's up in London with him."

He nodded. "Aye, her mum told me about the boyfriend last time I saw her." He pushed a plug of tobacco into the bowl of his pipe. "I'm hoping that when she sees you, she'll change her mind."

"I have to report to Brecon Tuesday," I said. "I hope it won't be for long, now the war's about over."

"But you'll see Gwyn before you go?"

"I hope so. She'll be back from London by week's end." I looked up at the linen suspended above the stove. "Doing your own wash now, Uncle?"

"No, lad. I've got a woman who comes in once a week." He lit a match and puffed his pipe into life. "What will you be doing, Evan, once you're demobbed?"

"I don't know. Not the mine, that's for sure."

"Why don't we go talk to Ned Byford tomorrow. See about that railway job he promised you when you joined up."

"Alright, Uncle." I took another sip of whiskey. "I'd like to see Mr. Edwards, my old headmaster, as well. He told me he might be able to help me get a scholarship to Aberystwyth University."

"University! I never heard of anyone of our class going to university."

"An officer I met at Gallipoli said he thought the war would change things. I think he meant there'll be more opportunities for chaps like me."

"Well, that would be grand," he said, puffing contentedly on his pipe.

"Did you know Gwyn has a book of poetry, Uncle?" I reached into my kitbag and handed it to him.

My uncle's brow furrowed as he turned the pages, staring intently at the verses. "Her mum said Gwyn might have some poems published. She has a real gift, that girl, a real gift." He closed the book and stared at the floor. "Did you know Hedd Wyn was killed?" We knew the family, Uncle Mervyn had once remarked about his favorite poet.

"No, I didn't," I said.

"Passchendaele, in Flanders. Just before he died he wrote a poem that won first prize at the National Eisteddfod. They awarded his chair posthumously." I saw his eyes glistening with tears. "So many Welsh lads killed. So many here in the valley . . ." His voice trailed off and his shoulders slumped.

I reached over and put my hand on his shoulder. He looked up and placed his hand over mine. "Well, at least you're here, Evan. We can thank the Lord for that."

And a Turk who'd fished me from the Bosphorus, I thought.

§

"Tell me about what happened to you," my uncle said as he heated some leftover rabbit stew for supper.

"It's a long story, Uncle." As we ate I told him of the Gallipoli fighting and the events that led me to Kerim's farm. "I just wish I could have sent word I was alive," I said.

He nodded. "Aye, it would have been good for your auntie if she'd known."

The news of my homecoming was spreading, for later that evening, as we cleared our supper dishes, Hugh and Mary Griffith and their two boys came knocking at the door. It should have been a joyful reunion with my closest boyhood friend, but with my aunt's death still hanging like a cloud, I wasn't in the mood for socializing. Even so, it was good to see them all, and their visit gave me more a sense of belonging.

"I don't think young Dylan remembers me," I said as I shook my six-year-old godson's hand. "He's a strapping lad, just like you, Hugh."

"Aye, and this one's Bevan," Hugh said of Dylan's younger brother.

"He's named for my dad," Mary said.

As Hugh limped out of the door on his way home, I was struck with the thought that if he hadn't been so badly injured in the cave-in at the mine, Mary might well be a widow now.

§

Instead of riding his bicycle to work the next morning, Uncle Mervyn rode with me on the bus to Cwmparc, where we found Ned Byford in his cramped office in the engine shed. At my uncle's insistence, I wore my uniform, dried out and ironed. "It might help you get hired," he'd said.

"Glad to see you back, Evan," Byford greeted me from behind his desk.

"It's about that job you had for me back when the war started," I said. "I was wondering if there's anything for me now. I'll be out of the army before long."

Byford shook his head. "Not at the moment, lad. Things are a bit slack around here these days. Not as many coal trains as in the past." He turned to my uncle. "I'll let you know, Mervyn, the minute something comes up." Disappointed, my uncle repaired to his signal box and I rode the bus back through Ystrad and into Tonypandy.

In the familiar surroundings of Tonypandy Secondary, I sought out the school secretary, a middle-aged woman who sat behind a desk flanked by steel filing cabinets. "The previous headmaster, Mr. Aled Edwards, told me to look him up when I came home," I said. "He said you'd have his address."

A look of sympathy crossed her face. "I'm afraid Mr. Edwards died over a year ago," she replied. "He had a heart attack just a year after he retired." Her eyes were fixed on the scar on my forehead. "The school was such a part of his life. It often happens when people retire, doesn't it?"

So another link to my past had been severed. The man who had instilled in me a love of books was gone, and along with him my chance for a scholarship to Aberystwyth.

§

That night my uncle sprang his second surprise on me. As I sat by the stove with my after-supper cup of tea, he came in from the front room with an envelope and a bankbook. He handed me the envelope. Australian stamps and a New South Wales postmark occupied the upper right corner.

"That letter arrived about two weeks ago."

As I stared at the envelope, I was back in Gallipoli, carrying the wounded Australian soldier over my shoulder. "I met an Aussie in the war," I said. "He wanted us to be pen pals."

"Well don't open it just yet," he said. "I have something to tell you first." He sat across from me and patted his knee with the bankbook. "When you first started working at the mine, you gave your auntie most of what you earned. Well, we put the money in an account in your name." He waved the bankbook at me. "We didn't spend a farthing of it, just saved it for when you got married. It would have made a nice nest egg for you."

"That was very generous of you and Auntie. I just thought I should be paying for my keep."

"I've another bit of news. I didn't tell you last night because you were so upset about your auntie."

"Tell me what?"

He sat back and fixed me with a stare. "I had a visit from your father about six months ago."

"My father!" I hadn't given him a thought for years. Uncle Mervyn was my father for all practical purposes. I hadn't even known my real father was still alive.

"Aye, lad, your father. Arrived out of the blue, he did. You could have knocked me over with a feather."

"What was he doing here?" I said.

"He came to see you. And he brought you some money."

"Why would he do that?"

"He told me that after he left, he often thought of you, but couldn't bring himself to come back because you'd have been a constant reminder of your mother, the woman he loved very dearly." Uncle Mervyn shifted in his chair. "He said he regretted that over time, but by then we'd adopted you, and his coming back would have made a mess of things."

"I don't need his money," I said.

"Look, son, your dad's a very clever man. Always was. He's done well in England. Has his own company in Coventry, making drilling machines, he told me." He handed me the bankbook.

My name appeared on the cover. I opened it and tried to make sense of the columns of figures. Then I saw the bottom line with the word *Balance*. I could hardly believe my eyes. "There's over a thousand quid in here!"

"Aye, son. And most of it's from your father. He handed me the cash and said it was for you. When I told him you were missing in action, he said, 'If my boy comes home, give it to him. If he doesn't, you keep it as a token of my thanks for being the father I should have been.' Those were his exact words."

"I don't know what to say, Uncle." I looked again at the balance. "Some of this is rightfully yours."

"No, son. I've no need for more money. What would I do with it?" He got up and poured himself a cup of tea. "When I retire, I'll have my pension." He sat down and balanced his cup and saucer on the arm of his chair.

"What if I hadn't come back?" I said.

"I thought of that, son. Gwyn did so much for your auntie, I thought of giving the money to her. There'd be no better way to repay her." He put his hand over his eyes and began to cry softly. "Oh, son, I miss your auntie so much."

I sat sharing his grief. But why didn't the tears come to my eyes too? Was it because I'd seen so much death that it lessened the blow of my aunt's passing? At last I said, "Why don't you pour us some more of that whiskey, Uncle, while I read this letter. I can't get my mind on that kind of money right now."

While my uncle put his tea aside and went for the whiskey, I tore open the envelope.

> *Canterbury Station*
> *Mulltown, NSW, Australia*
> *August 15, 1918*
>
> Dear Evan,
>
> Remember me, Jack Gammage from Anzac Cove? Well, I made it home all right, but they took off most of my leg on Imbros. It's not too bad. I have a wooden leg and I get around just fine with the aid of a cane, and I can still ride a horse. Betty, my wife, took it all in stride. She likes to joke to our friends that now I only kick her half as much when we're in bed!
>
> How about yourself? Did you make it home in one piece? (In case Evan didn't make it home, whoever reads this should know I wouldn't be writing if it weren't for him. He saved my life at Gallipoli, and killed a couple of Turks doing it. I'll never forget what he did for me.)

> *Evan, the main reason I'm writing is that I saw an article in the Sydney newspaper about Welsh coalmines, and it made me think of you. It said the mines would be falling on hard times once the war is over because the French will be getting coal from Germany. So I was wondering if you'd like to come out to Australia for a spell, to help me out with the sheep station. My dad is getting on in years, and I don't get around as well as I used to. I could use a chap with a bit of gumption*
>
> *Look Evan, I'm not just offering you a job. I owe you a lot more than that. I'm thinking of a partnership, the two of us running the business together. I've already spoken to my dad about it and he thinks it's a capital idea. He said he'd pay for your passage out, and if you don't find sheep farming or Australia to your liking, he'd buy you a return ticket. He said it was the least he could do for saving his son's life. If you like it here, once you've learned the business, we can carve out a slice of the station so you could have your own spread.*
>
> *Evan I don't expect you to make up your mind right away, but think about it. As a coalminer, you won't know much about sheep, but my dad and I can teach you the business. And if you don't like it, that's fine. You could stay with Betty and me as long as you like.*
>
> *I don't know anything about coalmining, but I don't think I'd want to spend my working days underground. Just digging that tunnel under the Turkish trenches was enough for me. If nothing comes of it, you can still have a free holiday here in Australia. My dad and Betty would love to meet you.*
>
> *With best wishes to you and yours,*
>
> *Jack*

If only Jack knew, I thought, how much I'd learned about sheep on Kerim's farm. A sheep is a sheep, Turkish or Australian.

As my uncle poured us each a measure of whiskey, I relived that awful day when I'd shot one Turk and bayoneted another, before spending the night with the gravely wounded Gammage under soaking wet thorn bushes. I could understand why he felt grateful toward me, but there was nothing heroic in what I did. I just happened to arrive at the opportune time. He'd have done the same for me, and so would Dai and Rhys under similar circumstances. But these days everyone wants to make you out to be a bloody hero for doing things like that, when you were simply doing the job you were trained for. The heroes in my book were the ones who tried to stop wars from starting in the first place. Now Kerim, he was a real hero, treating his prisoners as friends and giving a wounded, disillusioned enemy soldier sanctuary from the war.

My uncle handed me a glass. "So what did your Aussie pal have to say?"

"He wants me to go to Australia and help him out with his sheep farm." I raised my glass. "Bottoms up, Uncle."

We sipped whiskey silently for a few minutes, then my uncle said, "You aren't thinking of going out there, are you?"

I shook my head. "No, that's too far away for my liking. But I wouldn't mind finding a farm job when the war's over. I took a real shine to it when I lived in that Turkish village."

"Why don't you go up to Leonard's farm and speak to Mr. Leonard? Maybe he can put you on to something."

"Good idea, Uncle."

§

I spent the next two days doing odd jobs around the house and taking long walks, impatient to see Gwyn and to put my remaining army time behind me. By Saturday morning, when I'd still not heard from Gwyn, I set out for Leonard's farm. I wore my old civilian clothes, which now barely fit.

It was a beautiful November day, cool and sunny, with billowy white clouds scudding across the sky. On the other side of the valley a line of coal trams moved slowly down from the pithead to add more pit waste to the slagheap. I stopped to watch its progress until the faint whiff of manure drew me back toward the farm. As I walked between the hedgerows separating Leonard's fields, and approached the barn and paddocks, a comforting feeling swept over me.

I found Harry Leonard feeding slop to his pigs. After we exchanged pleasantries, I explained to him the purpose of my visit.

"I wish I could help you, lad, but my daughter and her husband are all I need around here. This farm's too small to take on extra help."

"If you hear of anyone looking to hire farm workers, I'd appreciate your letting me know when you deliver our milk."

"I'll do that, lad. And when the farmers market starts up in the spring, I'll ask around for you."

"Thanks, Mr. Leonard."

I walked back the way I'd come, but took a side track into the woods leading to the chestnut tree that I'd loved to climb as a boy, sometimes with Hugh and later with Gwyn. I gazed toward the mostly leafless upper branches. Why not? I thought, and hoisted myself up. Once at the top I was again swept up in the exhilaration of conquest and the touch of cool breezes ruffling my hair.

It was then that I saw a distant figure moving up the mountain. I knew immediately it was Gwyn.

Chapter 25

It was Gwyn's walk, unmistakable. Even after my long absence I'd have recognized it anywhere. She was hurrying, her long plaid dress swirling about her ankles, her hand shading her eyes as she peered up in my direction. I clambered down and dropped to the leaf-covered ground as she crested a nearby hillock along a pathway through the dense bracken.

She stopped when she saw me, then began forward at a more deliberate pace, her eyes fixed on mine. I didn't go to meet her; I wanted her first encounter with my ghost to be here beneath this splendid tree that symbolized the beginning of childhood love.

A few paces from me, she stopped and spoke softly. "It really is you."

She hadn't changed—still the wholesome beauty that had captivated me when I was a schoolboy. I held out my arms and she stepped into my embrace, her arms tight around my waist. *The perfume of her dress.*

We clung to each other for several minutes before she pulled back. "Your uncle said you were up here. I thought my mother was playing some cruel joke when she told me you were home. I was so sure you were never coming back." Her brown eyes glistened with tears.

"There were times when I didn't think I would."

She moved her hand over my shirt. "When you were working in the mine, I used to hate the way you looked, all black with coal dust. After you left I'd have given everything I owned just to see you that way again."

"You won't see me that way again, Gwyn. I'm done with coalmining." I stared into her eyes, trying to fathom whether any of her old feeling for me persisted.

"You've aged, Evan. I don't mean you just look older. There are lines in your face that weren't there before. And your eyes . . . I don't know, they look harder, not the twinkle in them that I remember." She reached up and touched my forehead, running her finger over the ugly scar. "And you brought home a souvenir."

"I've a few more down here," I said, patting my chest.

With both hands she began unbuttoning my shirt, a sensual gesture, to reveal the bullet wound on my shoulder and the shrapnel puncture marks below. She pressed her cheek against my bare chest and I felt the wetness of her tears. I held her against me and stroked her hair. A few gray strands intruded among the brown. As if sensing my observation, she said, "See how you're turning my hair gray?"

I kissed the top of her head. "Give me the chance, Gwyn, and I'll turn the rest of your hair gray. We could grow gray together."

When she didn't respond, I pulled her away from me, but kept my hands on her arms. "Your mother told me you have a boyfriend. Someone at the bank."

She bit her lip and stepped away from my grasp. "Percy Dutton," she said.

"Are you serious about him?"

She leaned against the trunk of the tree and looked away. "He's not like you, Evan. He looks down his nose at anyone who gets his hands dirty."

"Then surely you can't have any respect . . ."

"It's more complicated than that," she interrupted, looking off into the distance. "I never expected to see you again." She looked back at me. "What about you, Evan? All those years you were away, you never took a fancy to any other girl?"

"I never stopped loving you, Gwyn."

"You didn't answer my question," she said, pushing strands of hair away from her eyes. "I know you too well, Evan. You met someone, I can see it in your eyes."

"I met a girl in a Turkish village," I admitted. "She was Armenian. A mute."

"What became of her?"

"I don't know. She was deported. All the Armenians were."

Gwyn stared at me for several seconds, her eyes probing mine. Above us the wind stirred the branches and a few more leaves settled to the ground. "There's a sadness in your eyes, Evan."

"I'm not the same man I was before the war, Gwyn. I've done some terrible things. There was so much killing."

"It was war, Evan."

I wanted to change the subject. "Uncle Mervyn told me what you did for my Aunt Beryl. He said you were an angel."

"I miss her, Evan. I'm so sorry for your loss."

Unsettled by the way the conversation was going, I turned away and buttoned my shirt. Percy Dutton was a silent presence between us.

Gwyn broke the silence. "Evan, do you remember the first time I kissed you under this tree?"

I turned back and smiled at the memory. "How could I forget? I'd never been kissed by a girl before. That's quite a shock for a young lad."

"Kiss me now, Evan." She leaned her head back against the trunk, her hands at her sides.

I went to her, placed my hands against the tree, and kissed her slowly and deliberately on the mouth, a long intimate kiss that rekindled all the passion I'd felt in the prewar years.

She cradled my head in her hands. "Oh, God, Evan, life is so bloody complicated."

I didn't reply. Her fingers explored the scar on my forehead. "Rhys Jones told me what it was like at Gallipoli," she said.

I stepped back. "Rhys? Rhys is here?"

"Aye, Evan, but . . ."

"That's wonderful news. I have to go see him."

"Evan, Rhys was wounded very badly at Passchendaele."

Not Rhys, I thought, as a cold chill permeated my bones. In my mind I saw him in the trench when I'd returned with my shrapnel wounds all bandaged up. "Rhys told me once that he had a guardian angel because he only got wounded when shaving. How bad is he?"

"He's getting along all right. He married Mavis Wooley. You remember Mavis, daughter of Mr. Wooley, the ironmonger." I did remember Mavis. She was a year or two younger than Gwyn, a thin, plain girl who sometimes helped out in her father's shop. "Rhys is working at the shop now," she said. "He'll be fine."

"My uncle told me Hedd Wyn was killed at Passchendaele."

"I know, he told me too. He was very upset about it."

"I have to go see Rhys."

Gwyn nodded. "That letter you wrote about Dai Wilkins, I took it to his parents. They took the news of Dai's death very badly, but I think your letter made them feel a lot better. It was good of you to write."

"I'll have to go see them. Pay my respects."

The image of Dai, one hand reaching out to me, the other clasping the terrible wound in his stomach, came back with vivid clarity. Screams of wounded men emerged from the recesses of my mind, and once again I was in the nightmare of trench warfare. I turned away from Gwyn and looked towards the colliery, but tears obscured my vision. The screams were louder now, mingled with the chatter of machine guns and explosions of mortar shells. Tears ran down my cheeks and my shoulders shook as I tried without success to dispel the ghosts of Gallipoli. Embarrassed to lose control in front of Gwyn, I buried my face in my hands.

Gwyn's arms circled my waist, her face pressed against my back. "Let it all out, Evan. Get it out of your system."

Her words, spoken softly, silenced the cacophony of war, and I knew in that instant I loved Gwyn as much as I ever had, as much as I would ever love anyone. I turned and held her close to my chest.

"God, you must think I'm a sissy, crying like that," I said.

"You're no sissy, Evan. Rhys told me about your citations for bravery."

We stood that way for some time, holding on to one another, until I said, "Let's go and see Rhys now. We were very close in the war."

§

Arms around each other's backs, we walked down the mountain and on to Wooley's ironmongery. Mavis Wooley was arranging shelves behind the counter when we entered. Her father stood with a customer by a display of garden tools.

"Well, hello stranger," Mavis said to Gwyn. "Where have you been hiding yourself?" She looked at me. "Who's your boyfriend then?" She stared at me for a few seconds and her eyes widened. "Rhys!" she screamed. "Rhys! Get out here!" Mavis's father and the customer turned and stared.

A door at the back of the shop opened and a man I didn't recognize stepped out, supporting himself on a cane. A black patch covered his left eye, and below the patch his cheek and jaw bore terrible scars, as if exposed to fire. His mouth was distorted in a perpetual grimace.

"It's Evan Morgan!" Mavis shouted.

Rhys Jones hobbled forward, his one eye staring intently at me. "Evan! By God, you made it home! We all thought you were dead. Man, it's good to see you." His voice rasped; it wasn't the voice I was used to hearing.

I put my arms around him and held him for a brief moment before pulling back. "Good to see you, too, Rhys. Looks like you got banged up a bit."

"Aye, not much good for my dad's coal business now." He shifted his cane from one hand to the other and coughed hoarsely. "When you didn't come back from that patrol, I feared the worst. And I'm not the only one. Do you know your name's on the Roll of Honor for war dead in the chapel?"

I laughed. "Mr. Lewis won't be too happy when he has to cross my name off."

Rhys turned to his wife who had come from behind the counter. "We'll have to have Evan and Gwyn over for supper, eh, Mavis?" I noticed Mavis's stomach displayed a distinct bulge, and Gwyn couldn't seem to take her eyes from it.

"Looks like you're going to be a mum, Mavis," she said.

"Aye, but not for a few months." Mavis linked her arm with Rhys's.

"I've got to get home, Evan," Gwyn said. "My mum's expecting me." She smiled at Rhys. "You two get caught up with each other."

"I'll stop by your house on my way home," I said as Gwyn turned for the door.

"I thought you'd have taken me with you on that patrol, Evan," Rhys said.

"We'd already lost Dai. I didn't want to lose you too. Bill and Brian were both killed."

Rhys slapped my arm. "Well at least you made it out. And in a lot better shape than I did."

"But you're here, Rhys, that's the important thing. And you're going to be a father!"

§

There was no answer when I knocked at Gwyn's door, nor was anyone home when I returned later that evening. The next day I went to chapel with my uncle, but neither Gwyn nor her mother was in attendance. My concern grew. Why hadn't she told me she'd be going somewhere?

During his sermon, Mr. Lewis welcomed me back to the flock, remarking on the sacrifices the young men of Wales had made in the service of their nation. After the service he told me that there was a story in the Cardiff newspaper telling of my escape from the Turks.

"The Borderers must have put it in," I said. "I could do without the publicity. I just want to get on with my life."

"And you will," he replied. "But as you know from the Bible, resurrection affords a man a certain amount of fame." His attempt at humor was lost on me.

The next morning I found Gwyn and her mother at home. Gwyn offered no explanation for her absence. Her face looked puffy, as if she had been crying.

"Gwyn," I said, as her mother handed me a cup of tea, "I have to report back to Brecon tomorrow. I don't know how long I'll be in the army, but once the war ends I expect to be demobbed." I sat across from Gwyn at the kitchen table. Mrs. Williams returned the teapot to the stovetop and sat next to her knitting, looking up at me. I wished she would leave the room.

"Before the war, I asked you to marry me," I continued. "I love you, Gwyn, and I still want to marry you. This Percy Dutton isn't right for you."

Gwyn put her hands over her face for several seconds, before drawing them down to her chin. Her eyes, red and swollen, met mine. "I can't marry you, Evan."

Her words cut into me like a thrust from a bayonet.

"Why not?" Gwyn's mother said in a loud voice. I turned to stare at her; it was the last thing I'd have expected from her lips. "Marry him!" Mrs. Williams admonished her daughter. Then in a softer tone, "You've been in love with Evan since you were a silly schoolgirl. If you let him get away from you now, you'll never be happy."

"I can't, Mum . . ."

"Don't be stupid, girl, of course you can. You don't have to worry about me and my arthritis. Your Aunt Gladys has been after me to move in with her. Help her out with the rent. Besides, Evan's uncle will keep an eye on me. We've become friendly, if you know what I mean."

I looked in astonishment at Gwyn's mother. Urging her daughter to marry me seemed completely out of character. I turned to Gwyn who had again covered her face with her hands.

"Gwyn . . ."

"I can't marry you, Evan!" she cried in an anguished voice. "I'm pregnant!"

Stunned into silence, Gwyn's mother and I stared at Gwyn as her shoulders shook with sobs. I felt cold, as if a blast of arctic air had entered the room.

"You stupid, stupid girl," Gwyn's mother said at last, her voice laced with anger. "Is this what I raised you for?"

I stared at Gwyn. "How could you . . ."

"You were dead, Evan! I was heartbroken! What did you expect me to do, give up on life because you were no longer available? Enter a nunnery, for God's sake?" She pushed back her chair. "Go, Evan! Just go and leave me alone!" She ran up the staircase, leaving her mother and me staring after her. I slammed my fist on the table and stalked out of the house.

§

I finished out my army time performing mostly useless tasks and generally making myself unpopular with my black moods. My homecoming had turned out to be anything but the joyful occasion I'd anticipated.

I thought a lot of Gwyn in the days after I reported to the Borderers. Once my initial anger and bitterness subsided, I knew I was still in love with her. As soon as I can get home, I decided, I'll ask her again to marry me, Percy Dutton be damned. If he didn't want his child, then Gwyn and I would raise the infant as our own.

Armistice Day arrived at last and the nightmare of the Great War ended. We were given a few days' leave, and I returned to an Ystrad festooned with flags and bunting. I hurried from the station to Gwyn's house and pounded on the door. No one answered.

"I don't care if Gwyn's pregnant," I said to my uncle after I got home. "This Percy Dutton isn't meant for her. I'm going to persuade her to marry me."

"You're too late," he said softly. "Gwyn married him two days ago in Chester, where his family lives."

Utterly demoralized, I slumped into a chair at the kitchen table. "But why, Uncle? She couldn't love a snob like Dutton. And she's not the type who'd marry for money."

"She married him because she's bearing his child," he said. "In normal times, she'd never take up with someone like that. But you were gone. We all thought you were dead. And then she's thrown together with him at work and on business trips at a time when she's vulnerable." He put his hand on my shoulder. "Look, son, I had my heart set on you two being married. The way I see it, Gwyn's a casualty of the war, just as you are."

I climbed the stairs to my room, sat on the edge of the bed and held my head in my hands, unable to stop the tears running down my face. I didn't want my uncle to see me crying like that.

§

The more I thought of what my uncle said, the more I realized he was right. Had I not foolhardily walked away from the Kuleli hospital, word would probably have reached Wales that I was alive. I knew with certainty that Gwyn would never have given up on me if she'd known there was a chance I'd be coming home. That she was now someone else's wife depressed me beyond measure. Sitting alone in my bedroom or walking in the hills, I couldn't shake off the bitterness or sense of hopelessness. In the years ahead I would look back on Gwyn as the great love of my life. She'd been a part of me for so long, I doubted I could ever love anyone as much as I loved her.

When I was given a weekend pass later that month, I had no desire to return to Ystrad. Instead I went to the Cardiff city library to look up the address of my father in the Coventry city directory. There was only one Cecil Evans listed. I traveled by train to Coventry and took a taxi to the address, a rather nondescript house on a tree-lined street a fair distance from the center of the city. I knocked and had to wait some time before my father answered the door.

The man who had walked away on the day I was born was tall with dark hair like mine, but I saw little resemblance to the face that I stared at in the mirror each morning. When I introduced myself he appeared startled, unsure how to respond. "So you came home from the war after all," he said, not moving from the door.

"Uncle Mervyn told me of your visit," I said. "I thought it was time we met."

"I'm sorry," he replied. "I'm being rude." He stepped aside and motioned me to come inside. For a man who owned his own company, I expected more lavish accommodations. This house was of modest proportions, with furnishings that looked a bit on the seedy side, the wallpaper faded. He led me through the kitchen where dirty dishes filled the sink, into a paneled living room with French doors leading to a well-maintained garden. "Can I get you a drink?" he said.

"A cup of tea would be nice."

"Of course." He disappeared into the kitchen and I looked over the bookshelves that occupied two walls of the room. There were lots of technical books and a biography of the great British engineer, Isambard Kingdom Brunel. But there was also a fine collection of literary classics, including a complete set of Dickens. Perhaps part of my love of Dickens was inherited, I mused.

"I see you have all of Dickens," I said when he returned with a tray. "He's my favorite author."

"Mine too," he smiled. "He gestured for me to sit in a leather armchair near the fireplace. He set out cups and saucers and added sugar and milk to the cups. "Your uncle didn't think you'd be coming back from the war. It makes me very happy that you did." He stared at me, perhaps looking for something of himself. His accent was still that of a Welshman, but with occasional intonations of the Midlands.

"It was very generous of you to give me the money," I said. "But it wasn't necessary." I felt awkward. I was talking to a stranger, even if he was my father. There was a lapse in the conversation while he removed the tea cozy and filled the cups.

"Your aunt and uncle did a fine job raising you, Evan," he said as he handed me my tea. "I know your uncle is very proud of you." I didn't respond.

"If you want to know the truth, I've lived with a lot of guilt for deserting you the way I did," he continued, while staring at the ashes in the fireplace. He looked back at me. "When your mother died, I didn't want to go on living. She was such a fine woman, Evan. I loved her more than life itself. It took me a long time before I got back on my feet. By then it was too late to be your proper father."

"You've done well," I said. "Uncle Mervyn said you started your own company."

"Well enough. I've got around seventy men working for me. We do a lot of business with the motor industry—cars, buses, lorries. And, of course, with munitions companies since the war started." He reached up to the mantelpiece and brought down a pack of Players. "Cigarette?" he said, offering me one.

"No thank you."

He lit his cigarette and tossed the match into the fireplace. "I never remarried," he said. "There was no one who could replace your mother."

"Aren't you lonely, living here all by yourself?"

He shrugged. "Funny isn't it, you're the only family I have and I don't even know you. There'll be a lot more money coming to you eventually."

"As I said, I don't need . . ."

He put up a hand to quiet me. "Who else would I give it to?"

We sat there for about an hour, each of us trying our best to establish some kind of family relationship that went beyond a birth certificate; but when it came time to catch my train, I was relieved to be on my way, and I think he was just as glad to see me go. He offered to drive me to Wales, but I settled for a ride to the station.

"I'll write," I said as we shook hands in parting.

§

In mid December I returned to Ystrad from Brecon as a civilian. After a couple of days being at loose ends, I sat in the kitchen as my uncle fixed supper and reread Jack Gammage's letter. *You were very good with the sheep,* Adnan had said to me on that last terrible day in the village.

"Uncle," I said, "I'm thinking of going out to see this Gammage chap in Australia."

My uncle didn't answer at once. As he put a plate of sardines on toast in front of me, he said, "So we get you back home, and now we're going to lose you again."

"It may not be for long," I said. "Jobs are scarce here in the valley, and with Gwyn out of the picture . . . Well, I feel I need a change of scenery for a while. And I've money in the bank now, so I can afford to travel a bit."

He sat across from me and picked up his knife and fork. "I can't say I blame you, son," he said in a sad voice. "Even the miners are being laid off. But I hate to think of you being that far away."

"I may be back before you know it. But if I really like it there, you could come down too, Uncle."

He shook his head. "I don't think so, son. My life is here. My friends. And then I wouldn't be able to visit your auntie's grave."

§

That night, as I lay in bed, I opened Gwyn's *Rhondda Verses*. I'd thumbed through it a couple of times before, but hadn't read more than two or three of the poems. I hadn't even congratulated Gwyn on having the book published. As I turned the title page, I stared, mesmerized. At the top of the next page were the words *For Evan*; and in the center of the page, a single short verse:

> *Neath bracken hills and slagheaps gray*
> *I met a Rhondda lad one day.*
> *He went to war—And now I cry*
> *That one so young should have to die.*

I closed the book, extinguished the oil lamp, and lay awake much of the night. The next morning I went to Cardiff and booked passage to Sydney.

Part V

Rhondda Station

But, lo, I am with you, side by side,
As we have walked when the summer sun
Made the smiles of our faces one,
And touched our lips with the same warm kiss.
       James Whitcomb Riley,
        What a Dead Man Said

Chapter 26

This is my favorite place. It's where I come to regain my equilibrium. Clear the cobwebs from my brain. On a bench I'd fashioned from fieldstone and scrap timber, I sit above Dinkle's Cove listening to the thunder of Pacific surf. Here the ocean is a thing of power and beauty, unlike the placid waters of the Bristol Channel at Porthcawl or the lake-like temper of the Black Sea near Constantinople. Here there's drama in the relentless assault of sea on land, sensuality in the way an ocean swell engulfs a projecting boulder like arms about a lover, only to recede and curl back into a towering breaker that unleashes its fury on the rocky shore, throwing up a triumphant tapestry of spray that shimmers in reflecting sunlight. I can sit here for hours, captivated by nature's symphony, reading, thinking.

The familiar hand touches my shoulder. "It's getting late, Evan. You should be getting back."

I place my hand over hers. "Aye, love. I'll be there shortly. I just want to sit a while longer."

"I'll be making up a salad then. Don't be long."

Yes, the company will be arriving soon, but I'm in no hurry. How much I love this place. Perhaps I spend too much time here, but it's the perfect spot to reflect on life's journey. So many seasons have passed since I first stepped down that gangplank to set foot on Australian soil. Since Jack Gammage came back into my life . . .

* * *

I might not have recognized Jack had he not been waving his walking stick. There was quite a crowd waiting on the Sydney dock, and Jack was in the middle of it, grinning broadly, a short, fair-haired young woman at his side. When I finally reached him, he grasped my hand and shook it vigorously.

"Welcome to Australia, Evan. I'm glad you decided to come." He put his arm about his wife. "Betty, meet the bloke who saved my life."

I shook hands with her. "Don't believe a word of it," I said.

Apart from the wooden leg, Jack looked about the same as I remembered him, ruddy complexioned, deeply tanned, but without the agonizing pain that creased his face when our paths first crossed at Gallipoli. Betty was short and pretty, with blue eyes and a cheerful, self-assured caste to her features.

"So you're the Welshman Jack's told me about a million times," she said.

"You must be bored hearing about it."

She smiled. "Never. I'm just happy to meet the man who brought my husband home."

I turned to Jack. "Should I be carrying you out of here, Jack?"

He laughed. "Why don't we wait 'til we've had a few beers, then you can give Betty a demonstration. Right now we have to see you through the entry formalities and get your luggage."

"This is it," I said, indicating my solitary suitcase.

"You travel light," he said.

"I don't own much."

In the Gammage's dusty Vauxhall sedan, we drove south, Betty at the wheel and Jack next to her, looking back and chatting with me in the back seat. We traveled through pleasant, rolling farmland dotted with eucalyptus, oaks and pines, with fine views of the ocean. Sheep and cattle grazed in open grassland between small farming communities. Along the way I gave them a brief account of my adventures and misadventures before finally returning to what Jack liked to call Old South Wales. After about two hours, we passed through Mulltown and turned into a dirt road lined with pine trees leading to a two-storey stone house fronted with a wide wooden porch.

"Welcome to Canterbury Station," Jack said.

Jack and Betty lived much better than I was used to in the Rhondda. This was a prosperous farm, with fenced-in fields that stretched to the distant horizon, a number of paddocks and barns, and one very large shed devoted to sheep shearing. Four cottages stood a short distance from the house, one of which, Jack said, had been fixed up for me. The others housed permanent and seasonal farm workers. The Gammage home was spacious, with pine paneling and built-in bookshelves in most rooms, and a huge stone fireplace and a grand piano in the family room. There were even the luxuries of indoor plumbing and electric lighting. An informal elegance about the place suggested money was not a problem, but there was no flaunting the fact.

Once inside, Jack introduced me to their two boys, ten-year-old Ian and seven-year-old Harry, and Jack's father, Sydney Gammage. "Call me Syd," he said, shaking my hand.

Syd Gammage stood about six feet tall, with graying, sandy hair and a trim moustache, and not an ounce of fat on him. His face had the texture of parchment from a lifetime of working outdoors. Outwardly he seemed a stern man, but I soon learned that he had a warm and kindly disposition. He was a widower, his wife having succumbed to diphtheria around the turn of the century. Not a man to waste words, Syd possessed a keen intellect and liked to spend his evenings in a comfortable leather armchair reading from their extensive family library.

Jack and Betty were a congenial couple. Unlike his father's country gentleman demeanor, Jack was gregarious and outwardly affectionate with his wife and sons. Betty was the perfect complement, one of those farming wives equally at home cooking a sumptuous meal or helping a ewe deliver a lamb. She was a little on the plump side, but very pretty, and seldom without a smile on her face.

"Look Jack, let's get one thing straight," I said as we relaxed after supper that first evening, full from Betty's lamb roast. "You don't owe me anything. What I did—well, you'd have done the same for me. I'm here because things didn't work out for me when I got home. Jobs were hard to come by, and my girlfriend got pregnant and married some rich bloke. So I decided to come down and see what Australia has to offer. How long I'll stay, right now I have no idea, but I'm a hard worker and I've learned a bit about farming."

"Fair enough, Evan. But if you hadn't had the presence of mind to put a tourniquet on my leg, I wouldn't have lasted the night, besides killing two Turks and lugging me God knows how far back to our lines. If you ask Betty or my father, they'll tell you they owe you a debt, whether you like it or not. You're welcome to stay here as long as you like." He took a long draft of beer. "First thing tomorrow my dad and I will give you a tour of the place."

Canterbury Station encompassed over five thousand acres of grazing land seeded with grass and clover, fields planted with wheat and alfalfa, and perimeter firebreaks sown with rapeseed. Fences kept rabbits away from the cereal crops. Livestock consisted of three horses for patrolling the boundaries, a small herd of Jersey and Guernsey dairy cows, and an equal number of Angus and Hereford beef cattle. And, of course, there were the sheep, around fifteen hundred merino and Corriedale, and sheepdogs for herding. Most of the station's revenue derived from sales of wool and mutton. Transient workers, some of them Aborigine, worked the region's sheep stations during shearing season. Canterbury Station had six belt-driven Wolseley shearing machines in the wool shed, which made shearing such a large flock practical.

"When I first started here, I had only a few sheep, like in England," Syd told me. "Once the Wolseley was invented, we could expand the flock. And it's getting bigger all the time. Same with all the other sheep stations."

I loved the sense of space. Unlike the Rhondda Valley, where gray row houses crowded upon one another, mile after mile, New South Wales was lightly populated, the hills green and devoid of ugly slagheaps, the cornfields golden, and rape fields bright yellow. Even the sky seemed a deeper shade of blue, the sunsets more vivid. And on the eastern edge of the sheep station, the Tasman Sea displayed shades of blue that fluctuated with the time of day and the weather. When I'd first met Jack at Gallipoli, he'd said this was God's country; he was not far off the mark.

My knowledge of sheep farming came as a pleasant surprise to Jack. I caught on quickly to the routine of life on the station, and found the work equally as satisfying as that on Kerim's farm. In short order I even took to riding a horse, my only previous experience being a pony ride on the beach at Porthcawl when I was five years old. I threw myself into the work to get my mind off the unhappy events of my homecoming, and the Gammage family paid me handsomely. When I suggested to Jack that they were, perhaps, overly generous, he reminded me that I was considered a partner in the enterprise, not merely an employee, and my pay represented a percentage of the profits.

At times I felt nostalgia for the familiarity of the Rhondda Valley, and I regretted being away from my uncle; but then I told myself that life was decidedly better here. No more walking home from work black from head to toe, kneepads and helmet still in place. Besides, with Gwyn out of the picture I saw no point in going back. There were even times when I craved the sight of a domed mosque with slender minaret, an architecture I'd grown to love during my years in Turkey, but a Moslem in this bastion of Anglican Christianity was as unlikely as an African Hottentot.

As much as I tried to keep Gwyn out of my thoughts, she still rose to the surface, sometimes in conversation.

"That Welsh girlfriend of yours," Jack said one evening as we sat drinking beer on the front porch of his house. "Were the two of you really serious?"

"We were to be married after the war."

"And she just went and got herself pregnant while you were in the trenches? Sounds like you're better off without her."

"No one had heard from me for over two years after I was reported missing. She—and everyone else—assumed I was dead." I took a long swig of my beer. "I can't blame her, Jack, for what she did."

"Well, there are lots of fine Australian lasses, Evan."

A more unexpected reminder of Gwyn came in a package forwarded by my uncle after I'd been in Australia about six months. I tore off the outer wrapping to reveal a set of colorful Indian stamps adorning a sturdy cardboard box. It was from Suresh Pandya, the Hindu sergeant I'd befriended in the Kuleli hospital. I'd forgotten that he had my home address.

Inside the box, a folded piece of paper sat atop a pile of coarse wood shavings. When I picked up the paper, two photographs fell out. I recognized Suresh immediately. In one he stood alongside his wife, Sangita, dark skinned and exotically beautiful, dressed in one of those saris that make every Indian woman look like a princess. Their daughter Marisha, a pretty child, stood in front, Sangita's hand resting on her shoulder. Suresh wore his uniform, a medal on his breast, his right sleeve pinned up to the shoulder. They all looked very formal.

The other photo showed Suresh standing alongside another man, turbaned and heavily mustached and bearded in the manner of Sikh soldiers I'd seen at Gallipoli. Both men smiled broadly, behind them a shop bearing the sign *Pandya and Singh, Carpenters*. Suresh held a saw and the other man a hammer. In this photo an artificial arm filled Suresh's sleeve, with a hook protruding from the end. A letter written in an uneven scrawl filled the sheet of paper.

> *Dear Evan,*
>
> *As you can see, I made it home safely. I've often wondered what became of you after you escaped from the hospital. I expect the Turks captured you, but you seemed to me to be a survivor, so I'm writing in the hopeful expectation that you, too, made it home and that you are in good health.*

Yes, Suresh, I did survive, in no small measure because of the Turkish money you'd thrust into my hand before I walked away from the hospital, money that kept me from starving. He'd been saving the money as a souvenir for his daughter. What a godsend those banknotes and coins had proved to be. Somewhere I still had some Turkish currency I'd taken with me when I left Turkey; I must find it and send it to Suresh.

> *We covered up your escape. When Dr. Orhan came to check you, I told him you had been sent to the prison camp. He never questioned me, just accepted it as fact. I was expecting more trouble from Turan, but he never questioned your absence either, which was a surprise. We were sent to the prison camp shortly after that, but we weren't there very*

long before there was an exchange of wounded prisoners, and I was sent straight back to India.

How ironic; had I not escaped from the hospital, I would probably have been home a lot sooner. Then again I might well have been sent to France or Belgium once my shoulder wound healed, and ended up like Rhys—or worse. And I'd never have known Serin, nor learned the joys of farm life.

> *Please excuse my handwriting. I'm still not very good with my left hand, but I'm getting better. As you can see from the photo, I'm still a carpenter. I teamed up with Ranjit Singh, a chap I met when we were building those barracks at the beginning of the war. We have our own workshop, with enough orders to keep us busy. The army fitted me with an artificial arm. A lot of jobs I can't handle yet, but Ranjit is very skillful and he helps me. We are a good team.*
>
> *Evan, when you and I first met in the hospital, I was sure I'd end up a beggar. Your friendship gave me new hope. As a token of our friendship I'm sending you this gift, something I made before the war when I had two hands. Consider it a wedding present for when you get married. I remember you telling me your fiancée's name was Gwyn.*
>
> *Sangita and I send our best wishes to you both for much happiness.*
>
> *Your friend,
Suresh Pandya*
>
> *P.S. In the unfortunate event Evan did not return from the war, perhaps the reader of this letter will see that Gwyn receives the gift. Tell her it's a present from a friend of Evan.*

Ironic, too, that Gwyn was no longer a part of my life. Then again, she would always be a part of my life. And so would Serin.

Buried among the wood chips I found a carving of a boatman propelling his craft with a long pole. The boat measured about eleven or twelve inches from prow to stern, and from the hard, yellow-brown appearance of the wood, I took it to be made of teak. The boatman knelt on the flat deck, and the boat's prow, facing back toward the boatman, resembled the head of a fierce-looking mythical sea creature, its mouth open to reveal sharp teeth. Each side of the boat had been carved with floral designs. It was an exquisite piece of workmanship.

It was gratifying to learn that Suresh had fared well despite the loss of his arm. It didn't take me long to find the Turkish money in the back of my desk. I wrote a letter thanking Suresh for his gift, and recounting all that had happened following my escape. Would he, I wondered, feel the same sadness I felt when he reads of Kerim's death? Knowing Suresh, I had little doubt he would.

I climbed on the bicycle I'd purchased for transportation, and rode to the Mulltown post office where I mailed a package containing the letter and money. Suresh would be paid back with interest.

Not long after that package from Suresh, another reminder of Gwyn arrived in a letter from my uncle. She had given birth to a daughter and was living now in Chester.

§

On the voyage out to Australia I'd had lots of time to think about Gwyn, feeling sorry for myself on the one hand for losing her, and angry at myself on the other for not getting word back to Wales that I was alive. Gwyn had every reason to assume I was dead. How devastated I would have been had I received word that she had died.

I reflected too on the months I'd spent on the farm by the Bosphorus. Had I truly been in love with Serin, or was it infatuation with her beauty, a result of our close proximity at a time when I was starved of female companionship? Did my feelings for her derive from pity because of the atrocity that had driven her to silence? Was it possible to love a person who had never spoken to me?

That I'd always been in love with Gwyn was without question. We'd been together since childhood, inseparable, one almost an extension of the other. Gwyn dwelt in the real world of the Rhondda Valley, a world where I lived as Evan Morgan, a coalminer. Serin lived in the surreal world of the Bosphorus, where I was a farmer named Bloke. Two parallel worlds with an almost insurmountable gulf between them. Only through an improbable and calamitous series of events was I able to bridge the gulf and move from one world to the other. Perhaps, like a sailor with two wives in ports an ocean apart, it was possible to love two different women at the same time, but only in separate existences. Now it hardly mattered; in the end, I'd lost them both.

Jack and Betty did their best to get me married, and they weren't too subtle about it. I had a standing invitation to their Sunday dinners, and more often than not some young, single woman would be seated across the table from me. On other occasions they arranged for a date to accompany me on an evening out in Mulltown.

Mulltown was a pleasant community of about fifteen thousand inhabitants, almost half of whom were immigrants from Britain. The

Welsh socialized at the Society of Saint David, where they could speak in their native tongue, if they so desired, without feeling inhibited about it, and where they could pin leeks to their lapels on Saint David's Day. The English and Scottish had their own societies devoted to their patron saints, Saint George and Saint Andrew. A friendly rivalry existed among the three, played out in informal rugby and cricket matches, or lawn bowling on the town green. There was a cinema, four pubs, Methodist, Anglican and Catholic churches, a clinic, and a variety of shops.

The first settler to the region was a Scottish sheep farmer named Angus Dinkle, from the Hebrides island of Mull. According to the local historian, Angus fled Scotland after running afoul of the law over some dubious dealings involving wool trading. He built a cabin at what was now called Dinkle's Cove, and tried without much success to raise sheep on the surrounding land. Giving up on that, he moved inland a couple of miles and established a trading post to accommodate the increasing number of settlers, naming the establishment Mull Provisions after his former home. Over time a community grew around the trading post, eventually becoming incorporated as Mulltown. A night out for the Gammages usually involved a film at the Royal Cinema, followed by drinks and a game of darts at one of the town's pubs.

Try as they might, Jack and Betty made little headway with me. None of the young women, nice as they were, appealed to me in a way that made me want to develop any kind of serious relationship, and they probably saw me in the same light. Jack commented that I'd developed a reputation as one of the community's eligible bachelors, but also one who shunned long-term commitments. The closest I came to a serious relationship was when I met Peggy McKendrick.

When the farm work allowed, I often took the bus into Sydney on weekends. I enjoyed the vitality of the city, its fine restaurants and theaters, and excellent library. It was in the library that I met Peggy. James Whitcomb Riley's poetry had become so fixed in my mind over the years since Gwyn had given me the book, that I'd decided to try some other American poets. On a warm November morning I approached the circulation desk armed with books of poetry by Longfellow and Lydia Sigourney.

"One doesn't often find sheep farmers reading poetry," the girl behind the desk said as she took my library card.

She had brown hair, about the color of Gwyn's, bound up in a severe bun at the back of her head, and wore spectacles that magnified her green-brown eyes.

"How did you know I'm a sheep farmer?" I asked.

"The address on your card is a dead giveaway." She looked up and smiled. "Then there's that lingering smell that follows every sheep man after the shearing season."

"It's that bad, is it?"

She laughed. "No, you're bearable." She handed me the books. "Have you always liked poetry?"

"No, an old girlfriend got me hooked."

"And what became of her?" She was getting personal.

"She married someone with a lot more money than I have." I looked down and saw no rings on her fingers. "I'm about to have some lunch," I said. "Care to join me?"

She pulled a paper bag from under the counter. "I brought mine with me."

"I was thinking of fish and chips down at the harbor."

"Hmm. That sounds better than a cheese sandwich," she said. "Can you wait half an hour until my lunch break?"

Peggy McKendrick had that quick intelligence and love of literature characteristic of librarians. More important, she was very good company. Matching me in height, she had long, shapely legs and a slim waist, and once she let her hair down and removed her glasses, she was positively attractive. We began spending a lot of time together, both in Sydney and at the sheep station where she occasionally came to visit. Jack and Betty were only too happy to put her up in their house, Betty being a stickler for propriety.

Whenever I spent the night in Sydney, I usually stayed at the YMCA, a rather seedy establishment that didn't charge much. I could afford a nice hotel, but I preferred the companionship of the Y, meeting chaps from various walks of life. One night, after Peggy had fixed us a late supper at her flat, she said, "You're welcome to stay here if you'd rather not go to the Y. I hear it's a bit of a dump."

"If you really don't mind," I said.

"You can either sleep on the sofa or in the bed. Do you have a preference?"

"The bed."

"The bed's not very wide," she said. "If you sleep there, we'll have to cuddle up."

Peggy and I never spoke of marriage. I told her I expected to return to Wales in the not too distant future, not that I was thinking along those lines; it was an excuse, I suppose, to avoid becoming too entangled. Whether Peggy entertained thoughts of marriage, I had no idea. Then one day, out of the blue, a letter arrived that put a damper on our relationship.

Peggy had bought tickets to Oscar Wilde's *The Importance of Being Earnest* at the Odeon Theater in Sydney, and I was running late. By now I'd learned to drive and had purchased a secondhand Austin two-seater, so to get to Sydney on time I elected to go by car rather than take the bus. As I left the cottage, I saw a letter from my uncle that someone had placed under a stone on the porch table. I put the letter in my pocket and hurried on my way.

Later that evening, as I lay in bed and Peggy fussed about in the bathroom, I opened the letter. A second envelope bearing Turkish stamps was inside. The return address on the envelope told me it was from Charlotte Summers, the first I'd heard from her since we'd said goodbye on the Alexandria dock. The news it contained left me trembling with excitement.

> *Dear Evan,*
>
> *Surprise! I bet you never expected to hear from me! Well, here I am, back in Turkey and teaching science at the American girls school in their new campus in Arnavutköy, and living with my parents. And yes, I still collect bugs! I graduated from Wellesley with a degree in biology. I had a boyfriend (Harvard student!!!) who wanted to marry me, but he didn't fancy going to Turkey and I didn't fancy living in America. So if you're not married . . . Oh, well, I'm being silly. Same old Charlotte!*
>
> *The main reason I'm writing is I have news of Kerim's niece!! My father was invited to give some engineering lectures at the Syrian Protestant College in Beirut, or American University as they call it now. At his first lecture, there was this one girl sitting among all the boys in the audience. You guessed it, it was Serin! She's a student at the university and she'd seen a poster about my father's lectures. After the lecture, she went up and spoke to him.*
>
> *Anyway, Serin is fine, and if you want to contact her, you can send a letter to Miss Serin Sevadjian, Department of Nursing, American University of Beirut, Beirut, Lebanon. I'm sure she'd love to hear from you.*
>
> *Everyone here is fine. My mother and father send their best wishes. (And I send my love!) Turkey is as beautiful as always, but there's all sorts of trouble with the Greeks. But I can't think of living anywhere else.*
>
> *I do hope you'll come visit us some day. I think of you often.*
>
> *Much love,*
> *Charlotte*

So it was Serin Sevadjian. I was so used to Turks going by one name that all the time I'd known the Armenian Serin, I never knew of her family name. How gratifying to learn that she was speaking! And not only speaking, but a university student. From the time when she had been taken away in the ferry, I was certain I'd never see her again. But now, was it possible?

It was good of Charlotte to write. Charlotte—beautiful, flirty, filled with life. Charlotte of the long, fair hair and provocative eyes, who could make me laugh even when I was in the depths of despair. She had graduated already? How fast the years had passed.

Peggy emerged from the bathroom brushing her hair. "Who's the letter from?"

"A girl I used to know."

"Your poetic girlfriend?" She slipped out of her nightgown and climbed into bed.

"No, just a friend. Someone I met in Turkey." I handed her the letter.

She read it quickly and gave it back to me. "What about Serin?" she said. "Was she someone special?"

"Yes."

"She meant a lot to you?"

I nodded. Peggy, leaning on her elbow, studied my eyes for several seconds. "Then you must write to her," she said.

"I think so, yes."

§

After that evening, our relationship changed. We remained friends and we still did things together, but Peggy became more distant. I think the letter reinforced what she already suspected, that it was unlikely I'd ever look upon her as really special. Eventually I went back to staying at the Y. A few weeks later when I stopped at the library to see Peggy, the lady behind the counter told me she had eloped with a lecturer from the University of Sydney.

Chapter 27

It was raining hard, had been all day, and the brook that emptied into Dinkle's Cove ran furiously, lapping over its banks. Under skies as gray as the slate roofs of the Rhondda Valley, I'd been out all afternoon repairing fences, not the most pleasant task when wrapped in a heavy poncho and with water running off the brim of my leather hat. But it was work that had to be done if we wanted to keep the livestock in and the rabbits and wallabies out.

As I arrived back at the cottage after stabling the horse, I spotted a letter in the usual place under a stone on the porch table. My breath quickened when I saw that the envelope bore two stamps imprinted with the word *Liban*. Weeks had passed since I'd written to Serin, and I'd about decided my letter was lost, or Serin had decided not to reply. I threw off my poncho, dried my hands on my shirt, and took the letter inside. Damp air had turned the envelope and its contents limp. I sat on the couch by the window, took a deep breath, and carefully extracted the letter.

Serin must have been taught well at the American girls school in Scutari, for her English was flawless, the handwriting neat with perfectly formed slanting letters.

> *Dear Bloke,*
>
> *I hope you don't mind my calling you that. Professor Summers told me your name is really Evan, but to me you will always be Bloke. It was so good of you to write, and to hear that you are well and happy.*
>
> *I don't know what Miss Summers told you about me, but you should know that I am well and happy too. My aunt and I suffered a great deal after we were deported. They took us on the ferry to Tarabya, and from there by ship to Samsun. We walked all the way across Anatolia and almost starved to death. Many did. The men, including Bedros, were separated from us and we never saw them again. Sometimes kind people took pity on us and gave us food, or took us for short distances in wagons. Without them, we might not have survived.*
>
> *After many weeks we crossed into Syria and made our way to Aleppo, where relatives of my aunt took us in. The city was crowded with refugees*

like us. My aunt wanted me to continue my schooling, but I was told I was too advanced. Instead, an Armenian charity arranged for me to go to the American University in Beirut on a scholarship. It's like the college where Professor Summers teaches, only larger, with classes in English. I'm studying to be a nurse. I miss Uncle Kerim terribly, and, of course, my mother and father.

And yes, Bloke, I am talking, probably more than I should! It was so silly of me, not speaking all those years. Think of the conversations we missed because of my silliness. We could have talked about the books we read together, and all sorts of things. I thought of you every day during that awful journey to Syria, and afterwards.

So now you know what became of me. I'm very happy here, with lots of good friends, Armenians and Arabs. I even have an Armenian boyfriend, a medical student at the university. He knows all about what happened to me in Turkey, but he doesn't care. You would like him. He is much like you, very clever and very kind. As soon as he finishes his medical studies here, he is going to America where he has a residency arranged at a university hospital in Baltimore. I will be going with him as his wife.

Now it's time to say goodbye. I've buried the past, all the bad things, but I'll hold onto the good things. I'll never forget you, Bloke. A part of me will always love you.

Your dear friend,
Serin

So she had found her voice, and happiness, at last. The important thing, the only thing that mattered, was that Serin had escaped the traumatic events of her youth, and could look forward to a life of normalcy, family and children. Why then were my eyes moist, and why did my throat ache with longing? I folded the letter back into its envelope.

Images from the past flashed before me—Serin looking up from her sewing, smiling; walking hand in hand with me under blue skies in the hills above the Bosphorus; sitting next to me under a nighttime sky ablaze with stars; crying out in anguish from the ferryboat that carried her away. She had endured so much, even before I'd known her. And then with Kerim's murder and a cruel exile, it was a miracle she had retained her sanity.

Rain pounded a drumbeat on the corrugated tin roof of the cottage, and wind disturbed the curtains by the open window. *Now it's time to say goodbye.*

§

It was time to go home. I'd been away almost four years, and my uncle, according to his last letter, was feeling his age. His words disquieted me, made me want to see him again. I wouldn't stay away too long; Jack and Syd had come to rely on me more and more, but we were entering the winter months—summer in Wales—and the reduced workload afforded a chap some time off. And I had more money in the bank than I knew what to do with.

A retired English couple I knew in Mulltown went back to England for a visit every year, usually sailing from Fremantle, over on the west coast. Their route took them across the Indian Ocean and through the Red Sea and Suez Canal to the Mediterranean. Well, Charlotte had written that she'd like me to visit, and by going that way I could stop off and see her. I had mixed feelings about setting foot in Turkey again after all that had happened there; my scars were a constant reminder. There was even the chance that I might be arrested for what I'd done after Kerim's murder. But it would be good to see Charlotte and her parents again; they had, after all, saved my life, just as I'd saved Jack's.

A travel agent in Sydney arranged all the details, cross-country train to Perth, passage from Fremantle on the ocean liner *Stirling Castle* to Alexandria, Italian steamer to Constantinople, then by train through the Balkans and on to Paris. I recalled Kerim saying that he hoped the Orient Express would return to Constantinople once the war was over. The travel agent assured me that service had, indeed, resumed, if I didn't mind the cost. I told him to book me a first class ticket to Paris.

§

Armed with enough books to occupy me during the long voyage, I set out for Fremantle early on a June morning. Three weeks later I stood at the ship's rail as the Italian steamer entered the Dardanelles, and once again I was staring at the beautiful landscape of Gallipoli, but in an oddly detached way as though the nightmare of trench warfare had happened on a different plane. Time, it seemed, had helped heal the psychological wounds, as well as the physical. Then it was across the Sea of Marmara, a far more pleasant journey than the time I'd been confined to a stinking ship's hold with a Turkish bullet in my shoulder.

At last, beautiful, fabled Constantinople, its domes and minarets and crowded water traffic just as captivating as when I'd made Turkey my home. It was no wonder Charlotte wanted to live out her life here.

There she was on the dock, wearing an ankle-length lime-green skirt and matching blouse, looking more serious than I remembered, more mature certainly, with her hair bound back with a filigree clip.

"Evan! You came back! I could hardly believe it when your telegram arrived." She embraced me, then stood back. "You look very handsome. Australia's been good to you."

"And you look just as ravishing as when I said goodbye to you in Alexandria."

"Oh, Evan, don't be silly." She linked her arm in mine. "We must hurry. I have a taxi waiting."

Charlotte talked animatedly on the drive along the Bosphorus road; her work—Professor Ziegler had listed her as coauthor on one of his entomology papers; the fighting with the Greeks; college years in America. I responded perfunctorily as memories crowded back with the unfolding scene outside the taxi window. Dolmabahche, its Ottoman palace, and mosque graced with two exquisitely slender minarets; Ortaköy, where Kerim had exacted his revenge against those who had violated Serin; and then, across the water, the stately naval college of Kuleli, from where I'd escaped into a new, unanticipated world. I drew my eyes back to the road as we rounded the curve that led into the village of Bebek where I'd come ashore, half drowned, in search of Kerim.

"Almost there," Charlotte said as the taxi turned up the college road.

Charlotte's mother kissed me on the cheek. "Welcome back—Henry Bloke," she smiled.

"It's good to see you all again," I said as I shook her husband's hand. "I never thought I would."

"Nor I," Carleton Summers said. "You look a lot healthier than the last time you were here."

"Aye, I am a lot healthier, thanks to you and Mrs. Summers."

"He's a lot richer, too," Charlotte said. "Evan told me he's leaving here on the Orient Express. Isn't that exciting?"

§

I'd allowed myself three days in Turkey, not wishing to push my luck with the authorities. My first order of business, after socializing with the Summers family, was to find Adnan. Accompanied by Charlotte, I walked along the upper pathway flanking the fields where I'd once worked myself to exhaustion, and where I'd taken on a passion for farming. Where Serin used to bring me lunch and sit with me. What had been Kerim's farm was well maintained, with wheat and alfalfa ready to harvest. At the lower end, near the grove of pine and cypress, a young man hammered at a gate that led through a stone wall, the sound echoing off the bulk of the European Castle. Beyond the castle's crenellated towers, the Bosphorus reflected the vivid blue of the sky; and across the water, picturesque wooden houses and mansions built of marble sat against a backdrop of the gently sloping hills of Asia. Everything was just as beautiful as I remembered; but the mayhem of that final day in the village still haunted me.

Kerim's farmhouse had been rebuilt and looked much as it did before. We continued through the sheep pasture to the neighboring farm where we found Adnan pitchforking hay into his barn. He looked up as we approached.

"*Merhaba, Adnan Bey.*" I called.

Adnan, squinting in the bright sunlight, set down his pitchfork and wiped sweat from his forehead. He looked about the same, a little heavier perhaps, but still the rugged farmer with unkempt hair I'd known in past years. It took a few seconds before he recognized me.

"Bloke! You came back!"

"Only for a short time."

"I hardly recognized you." He grasped my arms and kissed me on both cheeks, his whiskers rough against my face. "You look well, Bloke. I never thought I'd see you again." He turned to Charlotte and greeted her deferentially, asking after the health of her parents. "Come, we must go to the teahouse and see old friends." Charlotte hesitated, for the teahouse was a man's world, but Adnan insisted she come.

My Turkish came back quickly and I understood most of what Adnan told me. After Kerim's death, he paid a fee, more likely baksheesh, for title to the land, as there were no survivors other than Anoush and Serin. "If they return, *inşallah*, the land is theirs," he said, but he saw little likelihood of it happening. Adnan's son, Hasan, had been working Kerim's farm since his discharge from the army, and he and his wife, Seyhan, had a newly born son.

"A grandson, Bloke! Isn't it wonderful!"

When I told him I was now a sheep farmer, he roared his approval.

It was a Saturday and the teahouse was crowded, all the outside tables occupied. A trio of musicians sat off to one side smoking cigarettes, their instruments on the ground beside them. While I greeted villagers I'd known from my months in Kerim's home, Adnan went inside and soon emerged with the proprietor, three chairs between them. No one seemed to mind Charlotte's presence; on the contrary, she was treated as an honored guest.

The musicians retrieved their instruments and walked out onto the dusty street before the teahouse. One placed his nagara, a small drum, under one arm and began beating on it with both hands. Almost immediately the others joined in, one blowing into a cone-shaped zurna, the other drawing a bow across the strings of a violin-like baglama, filling the square with a lively, toe-tapping pagan rhythm that soon had men, Adnan among them, leaving their chairs and forming a line of dancers, arms about one another's shoulders, dancing the intricate steps of a *horon*. After several minutes, Adnan, sweat forming on his brow, dragged me into the line, but my feeble attempts to synchronize my feet with the others brought gales of laughter and clapping from the audience. This was the Turkey I used to love, the ambience and good-natured fellowship of the village.

There was one thing missing—there were no longer any Armenians.

§

On my last day, Charlotte took me to what she called her favorite spot in all of Turkey, the ruined Genoese castle that sat above the village of Anadolukavağı, last ferry stop on the Asian shore of the Bosphorus. After lunch at a fish restaurant on the water, we climbed to the ruins to enjoy panoramic views stretching away to the Black Sea. It was a lazy day, the air warmed by the summer sun, with just the faintest of breezes. We sat for some time on the grassy slope, our backs against one of the castle towers, enjoying the scenery and each other's company.

"Turkey is so beautiful," Charlotte said. "Is Australia anything like this?"

"No, but beautiful in its own way." I reached over and fingered her hair clip. "You always wore your hair down when I was here before. You look like a schoolteacher with it up."

"I am a schoolteacher." I snapped open the clip and teased it out of her hair. "Evan Morgan, give that back!'" she laughed. She shook out her hair and wrestled playfully for the clip until, in a brief moment of passion, our lips met.

She pulled away. "Don't try to take advantage of me, Evan."

I sat up and leaned against the wall. "I seem to remember you taking advantage of me once," I said. "In the library."

She smiled. "Yes, I did, didn't I. It was very naughty of me." She rested her head on my shoulder, her hair soft against my cheek. "Back then, when you were Henry Bloke, I was a giddy schoolgirl, protected from what my mother said was the corrupting influence of boys. Maybe that's why I had a crush on you." She looked up at me, then turned her head away. "After Alexandria, after I went to America, I recognized it for what it was, just a schoolgirl crush."

"I expected you to be married by now," I said. "No boyfriends waiting in the wings?"

"Actually there is, a music teacher at my school. He's very sweet on me. Dmitri's a superb violinist, plays for a symphony orchestra in the city." She sat back against the wall. "He's a White Russian. Lots of White Russians came here after the Bolshevik revolution."

"Are you sweet on him?"

She didn't answer at once. "I think I am, very much so. My parents adore him." She brought her knees up and folded her arms about them. "Henry—I mean Evan—have you thought of staying here in Turkey? If it isn't too obvious, I'm rather sweet on you as well. No more schoolgirl crush." She stared straight ahead, waiting for me to respond.

I shook my head. "Charlotte, I think you're wonderful. But there are too many demons here. I killed some men after Kerim's murder, and it would only be a matter of time before the past caught up with me. Australia is home now. It's where my work is."

"I thought you'd say something like that." She rested her chin on her knees. "What became of that girlfriend you had back home in Wales?"

"She married someone else."

"I'm sorry."

The next morning Charlotte was at the station as I boarded the Orient Express. She cried when I kissed her goodbye. "Dmitri is a lucky man," I said.

§

The train journey to Paris was a bit too luxurious for my taste; I didn't do well around fawning, obsequious waiters and porters, or aristocratic passengers flaunting their wealth. I had two weeks to spend in Wales before my return sailing from Southampton, enough time to visit old friends and take long walks in the hills above the valley. Apart from a single day of intermittent showers, the skies remained clear and the bright sun softened the gray tones of row houses, collieries and slagheaps. Uncle Mervyn looked well, even took time off work to spend a day with me at the seaside in Aberavon.

Each time I walked past Bodringallt School or her old home near the chapel, I felt Gwyn's presence. In the window of a bookstore in Tonypandy, I saw that she had published a second book of poetry, *Rhondda Memories*. I bought copies for my uncle and myself. Gwyn wasn't that far away in Chester, but she might as well have been on a different planet. God, how I missed her, even now after so many years apart. Especially now when surrounded by reminders of the blissful times we'd spent together.

Near the end of my stay I traveled to Coventry to see my father. This time the visit was more successful, for the ice had already been broken. We had dinner together at a posh restaurant and drank beer at his local pub. He took me around his factory, explaining the intricacies of machine drilling and the economics of running a sound business. I talked to him of sheep farming. We came together more as equals than father and son which, given the circumstances, was not unexpected.

I set sail for Australia, happy that I'd returned to my native soil, but anxious to get back to what was now home. Before we parted, I made my uncle promise that he'd come down to see me in the not-too-distant future. I left him more than enough money for the passage.

§

Back at Canterbury Station I settled into my usual work routine. In my spare time I raised flowers and vegetables in a garden behind my cottage, played rugby with a group of young men from Mulltown against teams from nearby communities, and began singing with the Saint David's Society men's choir. Jack and Betty had despaired of seeing me married, and I'd about convinced myself that I was destined for a life of bachelorhood. I went out with a number of young women, but when with them I invariably found myself thinking of Gwyn.

Did having Gwyn in my thoughts so often send some kind of telepathic signal to prompt her to put pen to paper? I liked to think so, for almost five years to the day since I'd first set foot in Australia, her letter arrived on my doorstep.

It was a fresh autumn morning, the air still fragrant with the scent of wildflowers. The black-and-white tomcat that had arrived unannounced at my door one day and never left, sat on the porch table next to the letter, purring contentedly. The handwriting was immediately familiar—delicately shaped lettering that had sustained me during the cruelest months of the Gallipoli fighting. I removed the envelope from under the stone and held it for some time, trying to anticipate what might be written inside. I carried the letter to Dinkle's Cove, sat on the bench, and with trembling hands tore open the envelope.

> *Dear Evan,*
>
> *I hope you don't mind my writing. You have every reason to hate me for what I did, and I can hardly blame you if you were to tear up this letter. But I hope that time might have soothed your anger, and that you will come to think of me as someone who was a special part of your life, and not a hateful part.*
>
> *I've left Percy. I never loved him, and he knew that. Our darling daughter Anne, the joy of my life, died from scarlet fever six months ago. I loved her so much, I'm still trying to cope with the loss. Percy and I separated soon after. In the end, he was kind and understanding,*

although his parents were just the opposite. He agreed to a divorce despite the scandal.

I'm staying temporarily with your uncle while I try to sort out my life. My mother is living with my Aunt Gladys, and there is no room for me there. Both your uncle and my mother have been urging me to write to you. I resisted for a long time, but I do want to try, at least, to settle the past with you.

My old bank has offered me a job at a very good salary, running a new branch in London. The job will be starting in two or three months when renovations to the building are complete. I can't stay with your uncle much longer, it's not fair to him, so I'll be moving to London as soon as I find a flat near the bank.

Evan, I'd like very much to see you the next time you come home. Or I could come out to Australia for a quick visit while I'm waiting for my job to start. I have more than enough money to buy a return passage. The bank has told me that if I go to Australia, they will hold the position until I get back. If you would prefer that I don't visit you, I will understand completely. I just didn't want to go through the rest of my life without trying to make peace with you.

Please let me know one way or the other if you wouldn't mind seeing me, if only for a short time, so that we may part as friends.

As always,
Gwyn

I stared at the letter, oblivious to the waves crashing ashore.

> *Let me come in where you sit weeping,—aye,*
> *Let me, who have not any child to die,*
> *Weep with you for the little one whose love*
> *I have known nothing of.*

How often had those poems that rose so spontaneously to my lips served as a silken thread to bind the two of us together. How many years had passed since she had given me the Riley book as I left for the war. *I know poetry isn't your cup of tea, Evan.* Her words even now, resonate in my ears.

My mind racing, I retraced my steps to the cottage, left the letter on the kitchen table, and rode my bicycle to the Mulltown telegraph office. I printed out a telegram: BOOK PASSAGE SOON AS POSSIBLE. CABLE ARRIVAL DATE. EVAN.

As I was about to hand the paper to the clerk, I paused, went back to the writing table, and inserted the words ONE WAY before passage, and LOVE before Evan.

§

In a mackintosh belted at the waist and a scarf about her head to protect against a wintry chill, Gwyn walked down the gangplank at the Sydney dock, her eyes searching for me in the crowd. She was as beautiful as always, but suffering had eroded the carefree veneer of youth. I took her into my arms and held her for a long time, unwilling to let go.

"Of all the people in the world," I whispered in her ear, "how could I possibly hate you."

Chapter 28

Gwyn didn't say much on the drive to Mulltown. She rolled down the car window, placed her elbow on the sill and rested her head on her hand. I stole a glance leftward and took in the faded freckles and upturned nose that had captivated me so many years ago. She was a mature woman now, an accomplished poet and businesswoman.

She spoke, as if in response to my attention. "God, Evan, I've made such a bloody mess of my life."

"Don't punish yourself, Gwyn."

"It's just that life was so full of certainties before that stupid war. I was going to marry you and that was that. It was all I ever wanted." She turned her head toward me. "Then you were missing in action, and you weren't on the POW lists. Everyone knew that meant you must be dead."

"I read the dedication in your book," I said. "I was touched."

She smiled. "I cried when I wrote it."

"I cried when I read it."

When she didn't respond, I said, "I'm sorry about your daughter. I was reminded of Riley's poem about the loss of a child."

"*Bereaved*," she said. "So you really did memorize his poems. I remember that first letter you wrote. You said you would, but I never really believed you."

"I memorized a good many of them. And I still have the book."

"She was such a lovely child, Evan, filled with happiness and love. I fell apart when she died." She removed a handkerchief from her sleeve and dabbed at her eyes.

After staring ahead silently for several minutes, Gwyn put out her hand and touched my shoulder. "Evan, it's wonderful to see you again. I was so sure you wouldn't want anything to do with me."

"Don't be daft, Gwyn. I told you to get a one-way ticket."

"I have a return reservation," she said. "This new job will be a chance to get my life back in order. I'm fed up with uncertainties."

"So am I."

She stared out at the passing countryside. "It's really lovely here," she said. "Your uncle told me you'd become a farmer when you were in Turkey. I'm so glad you gave up coalmining."

"Aye, I love farming. Spending my days outdoors, feeling the sun on my back. It's a great way to make a living." We approached the outskirts of Mulltown. "You'll like the Gammages, Gwyn. Betty has fixed up a room for you in their home."

"Where do you live?"

"In a cottage near the house. It's small, but comfortable."

"Too small to have me stay there?"

I bit my lip. "Gwyn, there's nothing I'd like better, but let's go one step at a time."

She was silent the rest of the way as I pointed out landmarks around the town. When we pulled up in front of the Gammage home, Betty came out to greet us with a warm smile and a wave of the hand. "Welcome to Australia," she said, kissing Gwyn on the cheek. Then to me, "Why, Evan Morgan, you never let on what a beauty she is." Gwyn, I noticed, had not lost her capacity for blushing.

§

I kept Gwyn busy during the next two weeks, intent on rekindling the love we shared in the prewar years. We took long walks across the cliffs overlooking the ocean, browsed the shops in Mulltown and Sydney, rode ferries around Sydney harbor and rambled in the Blue Mountains west of the city. We toured the sheep station, explored the surrounding countryside in my car, and enjoyed picnic lunches on a small, secluded beach close by Dinkle's Cove.

After one of our picnics, I lay back on the sand, a towel under my head, and dozed off while Gwyn sat next to me, reading. When I awoke, still hazy from sleep, she was looking down at me, a slight smile about her lips.

"Ne hoş gözleriniz var," I said.

She reached out and brushed sand from my cheek. "I expect you say that to all your lady friends."

I laughed. "I must have been dreaming about Turkey. I said you have lovely eyes."

"Flattery will get you nowhere."

"We'll see about that," I said, and pulled her down on top of me. Playful wrestling quickly led to a passionate embrace, and for the first time in all the years we had known each other, passion soared into intimacy—glorious, mind-bursting intimacy.

After our lovemaking we lay back on the sand, our hands clasped. "God, I love you so much," I said.

She pulled herself against me and laid her head on my chest. "I can't for the life of me understand why."

Gazing up at high cumulus clouds drifting lazily across the blue sky, I ran my fingers through her hair. After a few minutes she spoke. "Evan, I never stopped loving you." She lifted her head and stared into my eyes. "I came here because I had to find out if you felt the same way about me."

The next morning I drove Gwyn into Mulltown where she canceled her return ticket to England and sent a telegram telling her boss in London she wouldn't be going home. One month later, in the small stone Methodist church that could have been plucked from any English village, Gwyn and I were married before a crowd of well-wishers from Mulltown and surrounding farms. Jack and Betty stood with us as best man and maid of honor; and Jack's father, dignified as always, escorted Gwyn down the aisle.

It was the happiest day of my life.

§

For a wedding gift the Gammage family allotted us six hundred acres of land adjoining Canterbury Station, green pasture that extended down to Dinkle's Cove and the cliffs and dunes that opened up to the Tasman Sea. Along with the land came a promise of two hundred merino sheep, to be delivered once our property was secured with fencing and paddocks. We agreed that the two sheep stations would form a loose partnership rather than compete with one another.

Together Gwyn and I designed our new home atop the sea cliffs, a sturdy stone house with broad windows facing seaward, a short walk from the cove. Months later, when the house was finished and paddocks and a shearing shed awaited the arrival of our flock, we christened our farm *Rhondda Station*.

* * *

I hear Gwyn's footsteps over the sounds of the ocean. Is she is about to admonish me for still sitting here and not getting the barbecue started? Today we've prepared Turkish fare—lamb kebabs with yogurt, grape leaves stuffed with spiced vegetables and crushed almonds, and eggplant pilaf. Most of the meal is ready to set out; I just need to toss the kebabs on the fire. We can enjoy a nice bottle of wine while they're cooking.

She sits on the bench, her body nestled against mine, and I put my arm around her shoulder. There's more silver in her hair now and her features are beginning to show the passage of years, but she will always be beautiful no matter how long she lives.

"I've made the salad," she says. "But there's no rush. Hugh called to say they'd be a bit late."

Hugh. It had taken some persuasion to wrench Hugh Griffith out of the Rhondda. Not so with Mary. Her parents had been taken in the influenza epidemic that followed the 1918 armistice, and she was fed up with Hugh moping around the house during his endless months on the dole.

I first approached our old friends about coming to Australia when Gwyn and I took a delayed honeymoon trip back to Wales. We'd finished the house and farm buildings, but not yet taken possession of the sheep, so it was a good time to travel. We didn't go directly to Wales; first came a detour to Bombay and a train to Amritsar, with sightseeing stops at Agra and Delhi. Suresh Pandya and I had corresponded on and off after he'd sent the wood carving, and I was keen to see him again, and to have Gwyn meet him.

Suresh and Ranjit Singh have done well since the war. They run a profitable enterprise employing a team of Hindu, Moslem and Sikh carpenters. Suresh and Sangita now have two sons in addition to their daughter, Marisha, who is soon to be married. Suresh had reserved a room for us at a small, pleasant hotel near the exquisite Golden Temple, the holiest shrine of the Sikhs, and every bit as beautiful as the Taj Mahal.

It was a joyful reunion. We laughed now at our time spent in the prison hospital, which could have been a lot worse without Kerim's compassion for his wounded prisoners. The Anatolian prison camp wasn't as bad as he'd expected, Suresh told me. Perhaps he'd taken Kerim's advice to heart and prepared himself mentally. While Suresh and I reminisced about the war, Gwyn played badminton with Sangita and the Pandya boys. I noted with satisfaction that Gwyn displayed none of the colonial mannerisms that so often built barriers between the British and their dark skinned subjects. For her to do otherwise would have been completely out of character.

Once we got to Wales I teased Hugh and Mary with photographs of Canterbury Station and New South Wales scenery, using the same argument that Jack had used with me—I'd pay their way out, and for Hugh's widowed mother; and if they didn't like it there, I'd pay their way back. A free holiday in Australia was better than sitting around feeling sorry for yourself, I told him. Hugh finally gave in, but only when I agreed that he would pay me back once he started earning some money. I also took the opportunity to make my uncle's life more comfortable by having workmen add an enclosed bathroom to the back of the house with one of those new-fangled coal gas heaters for hot water. No more tin tub in front of the kitchen stove. We offered to do the same for Gwyn's mother and aunt, but they said they were perfectly happy the way things were, thank you.

Much to Hugh's surprise, he liked Australia from the beginning. He'd developed something of a green thumb in Wales, growing vegetables in a small plot behind his in-laws' house, and this placed him in good stead when the owner of a Mulltown horticultural center was looking to hire someone. Before long Hugh had worked his way up to manager, and when the owner retired, he bought the business. The family lives now in a pleasant bungalow in town, and their two boys are firm friends with the Gammage lads. I never expected, nor wanted, Hugh to pay me back for their passage out, but he was a proud man and he lived up to his promise.

"Dinner may be a bit exotic for Hugh's tastes," Gwyn says. "Do you think he'll like it?"

"He's daft if he doesn't. I'm trying to teach him there's more to life than leeks and turnips."

She laughs. "Evan, when I was making the salad I was thinking, we really have a good life here, so much better than my parents ever had."

"Or my aunt and uncle." I pull her closer to me. "But it wouldn't be much good if you weren't here." She squeezes my hand. "We were meant for each other, Gwyn, ever since we were nippers at Bodringallt."

We sit silently for a while listening to waves breaking over the rocks below and watching seagulls circling and skimming the foam-capped surf. It's a fine afternoon, just enough of a breeze off the ocean to keep the air fresh.

She's right, life has been good to us. Who would have thought that a poor Welsh coalminer would end up a well-to-do sheep farmer? The two abutting sheep stations work well together, and Jack and I are as close as brothers. Jack is fully in charge of Canterbury Station now, Syd being very frail and for the most part housebound. I've given up trying to express gratitude to the Gammages for all they've done for me. They simply remind me of what I did in the hills above Anzac Cove.

Rhondda Station has prospered, even now with the depression and the decline in wool prices. We're double the size when we started, and we have a fine Aborigine family living in one of our cottages. Tommy—his real name in Moonga, but he prefers Tommy—is a terrific worker, handles sheep better than any man I know. And his wife Polly is just about as good. Australians don't treat their native people well at all, but we pay Tommy and Molly good wages, and we've established a tradition of having Sunday brunch with them, the two families enjoying an informal meal together.

Their two delightful little girls are well on their way to becoming scholars under Gwyn's tutelage.

And there are our children. Alan, now ten, and a whiz at science; and Enid, eight, who says she wants to be a teacher. Two wonderful children. Well, I never got to university, but I intend to see that they have the opportunity.

"Come on, Gwyn, let's be getting back. I'll get the fire going."

I feel a surge of contentment as we stroll back along the gravel path, arms around each other. Molly is out slaughtering a chicken, and we exchange waves. We have lots of chickens, mostly Rhode Island Reds. I'd told Gwyn about how I lied to the Summers family about raising chickens in Rhode Island. She'd laughed and said that meant we must raise them here—to make an honest man of me, as she put it. They're beautiful birds, ranging from fawn-red to mahogany, their feathers iridescent in the sunlight. Along with a few leghorns, they keep us and Tommy and Molly supplied with eggs and, on occasion, meat for the stewpot or barbecue.

Molly's children and our two are playing some kind of board game at a table outside their cottage, our border collie Gertie resting at their feet. The children play together so often that Alan and Enid are just about fluent in the tribal language.

Gwyn leans back in her chaise lounge, sips wine and jots something in her notebook, perhaps the nucleus of a new poem. She has five books in print now and her publisher in Sydney is after her for more. Or she may be making a list of things to do before her mother and my uncle arrive a couple of weeks from now. Every two years or so they spend a month with us, widow and widower assuaging their loneliness in shared companionship. They're getting on in years and we aren't sure how much longer they'll feel like traveling. My father has yet to visit, but in his last letter he said he was selling the company and retiring, and perhaps coming down to see us. I hope he does; we've become close over the years.

My wine glows ruby red in the late afternoon sunlight, and the coals radiate heat. In the distance the whine of a motor signals the imminent arrival of the Griffith family. I think back to the years Hugh and I spent deep underground, digging out anthracite with heavy pickaxes, breathing in coal dust, and killing cockroaches. And of the day Hugh told me Mary was pregnant and they had to get married; we were just eighteen at the time. In my innocence, how shocked I was. And then I returned from the war to learn that Gwyn was pregnant. Their marriage survived Hugh's mining injury, the uncertainties of employment, and their different social status. Hugh and Mary are devoted to one another, just as Gwyn and I are. So things turned out all right in the end.

Does Gwyn sense my eyes upon her, lovingly? She looks up and smiles. We have no secrets from one another. She knows all that happened in Turkey, including my infatuation with Serin. Some day I'll take her there so she can see where Byron swam the Hellespont. In Constantinople—or Istanbul as they call it now—we shall walk the narrow, twisting streets and broad, tram-clattering boulevards together, breathe in the atmosphere of crowded bazaars and gaze in wonder at its magnificent mosques. And best of all, she must travel with me by boat from the city to the Black Sea, to feel the drama and poetry of the Bosphorus, surging like a mighty river between Europe and Asia.

I don't dwell on my years in Turkey. But the subconscious mind never lets go of the past. Like the ebb and flow of the tides that wash against Rhondda Station, the past returns, recedes, returns . . .

There are times, in the depths of sleep, when nightmare visions emerge from the shadows. A boyhood friend reaching out to me while trying desperately to keep his entrails from spilling onto the ravaged soil of Gallipoli. The terrified look on the face of a Turkish boy soldier as he anticipates the deadly thrust of my bayonet. Rotting corpses and the stench of death. Sometimes I cry out in the darkness, or bolt up involuntarily to a sitting position, shaking. Then Gwyn reaches out, and the touch of her hand exorcises the ghosts of war.

It may be something inconsequential that jars my senses. Sunlight reflecting off the polished surface of the three-tier copper lunch pail that sits on a shelf in the kitchen. An ocean breeze that draws the scent of salt and seaweed into my nostrils, or the tang of the day's catch at Sydney fish market. The fragrance of freshly cut hay. Then I'm carried back in memory to the Bosphorus, its banks awash in pink-purple Judas blossoms, to be once again in the company of the silent, olive-skinned girl with the complexion of fine Turkish alabaster—who had loved me once as I had loved her, and whose only words I heard from her lips were cries of despair. And try as I might, I can't seem to keep the tears from my eyes.

Although I rejoice in Serin's newfound happiness, I can never think of her without some sense of sadness and loss. But one glance at Gwyn draws me back to the present—and the certainty that she has fulfilled the promise of our childhood among the slagheaps of The Rhondda by making me the happiest of men.